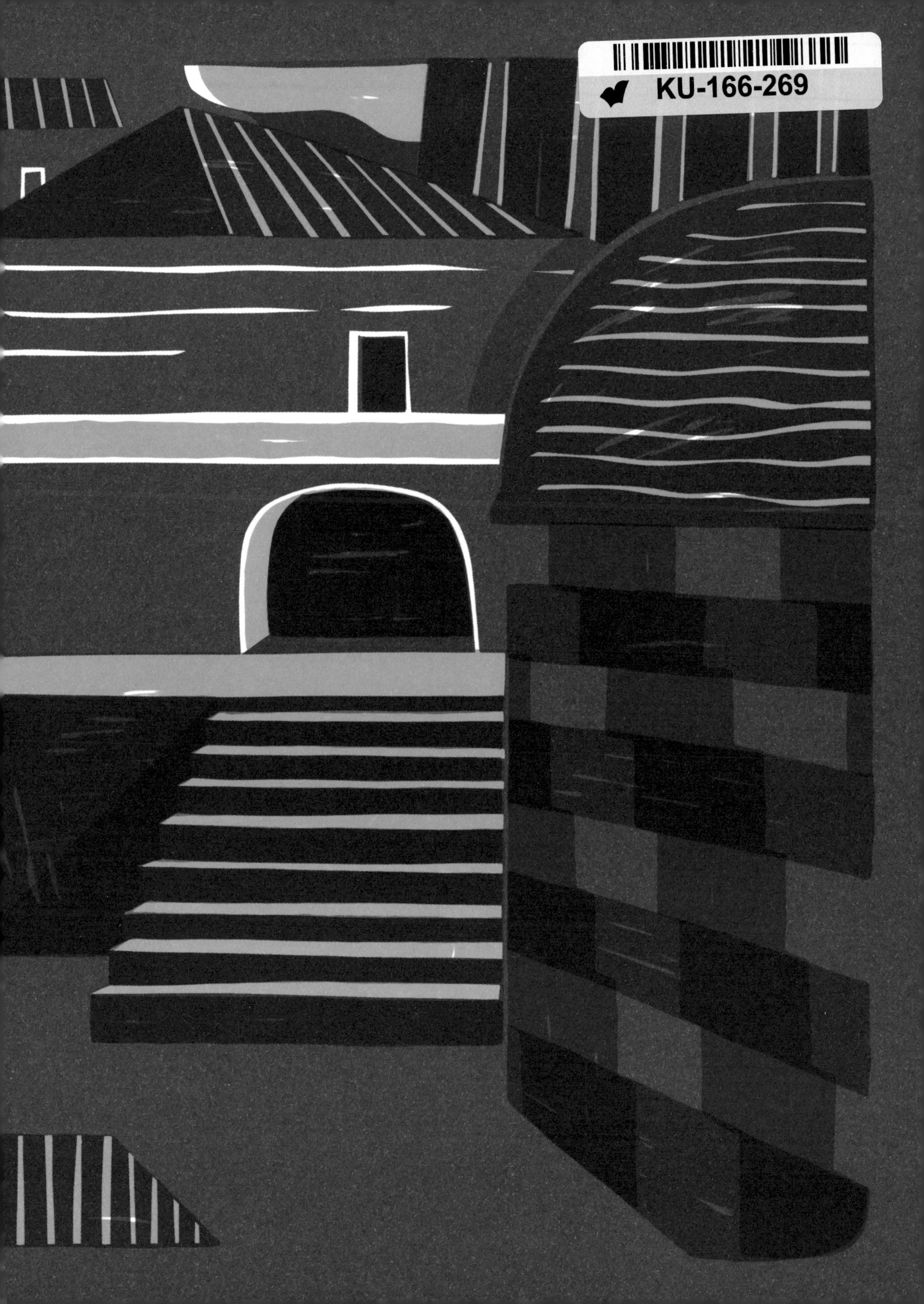

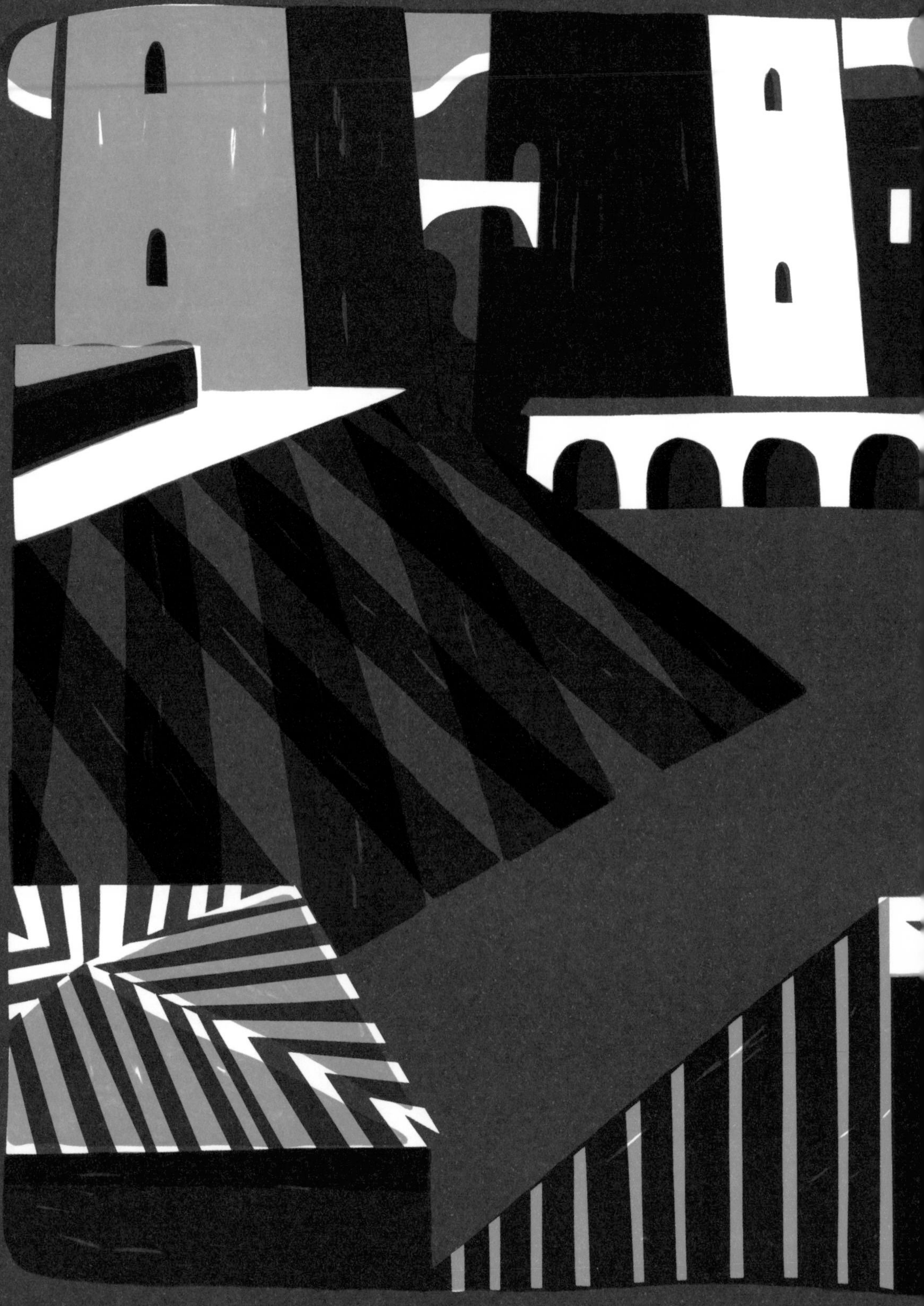

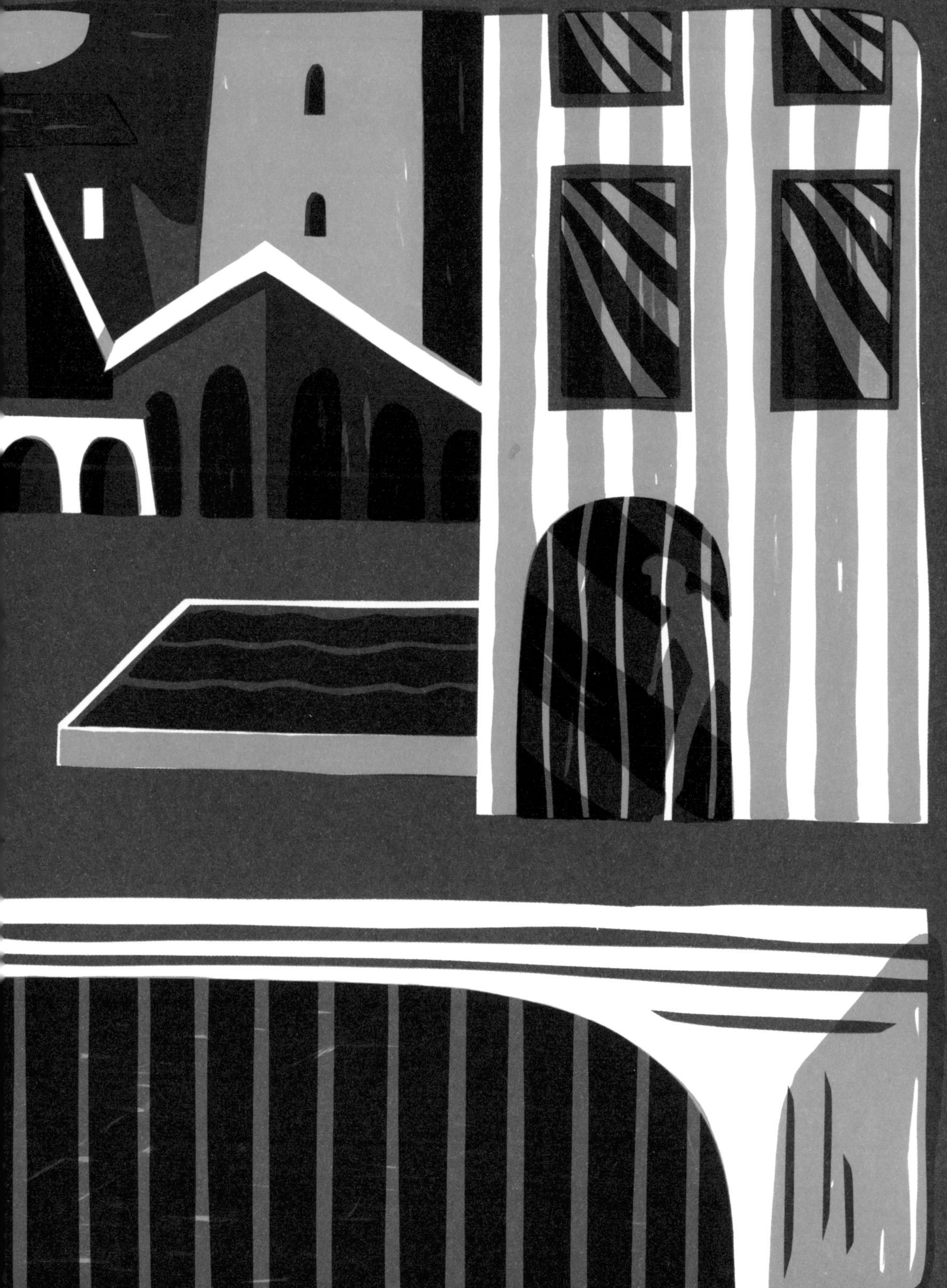

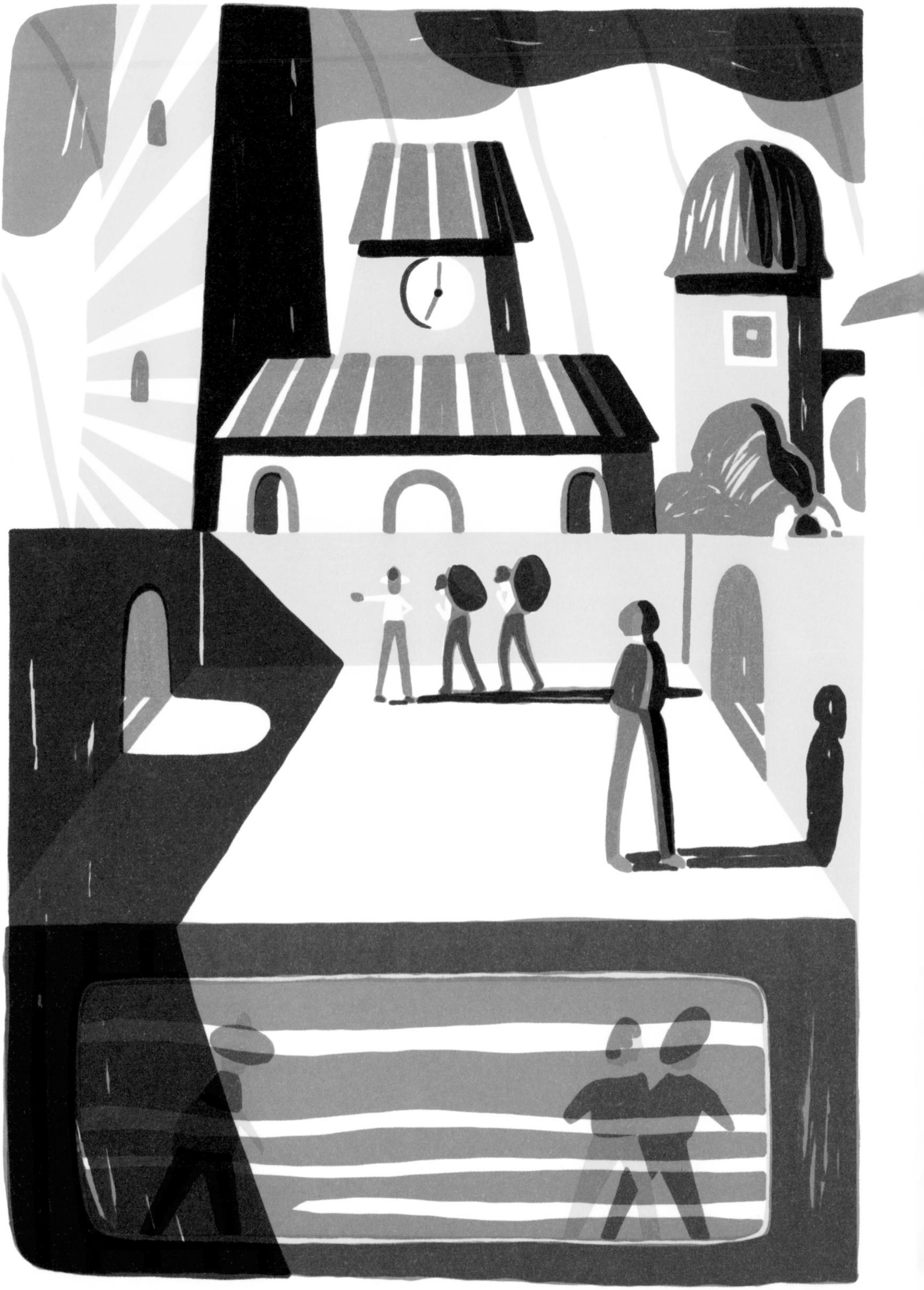

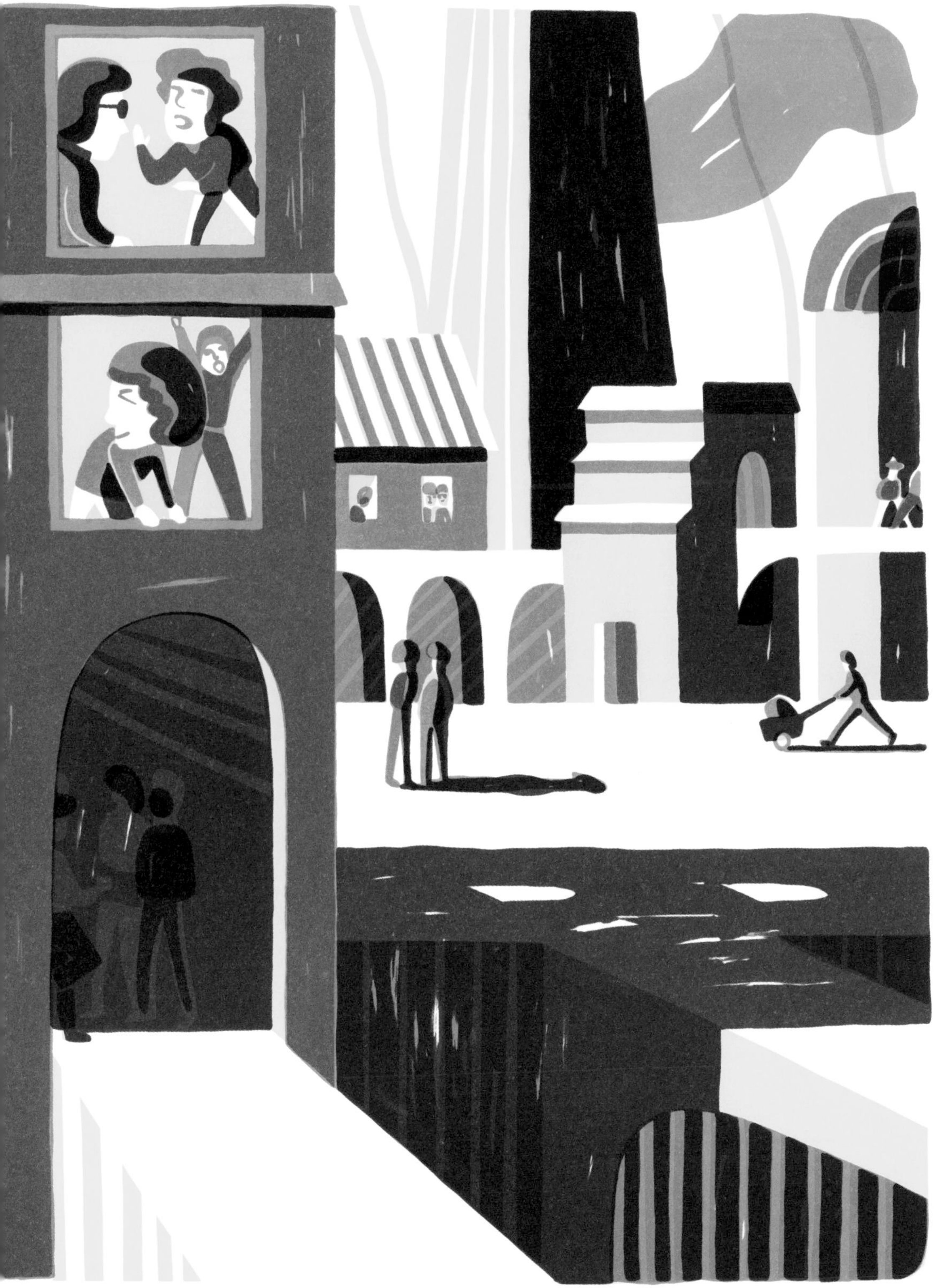

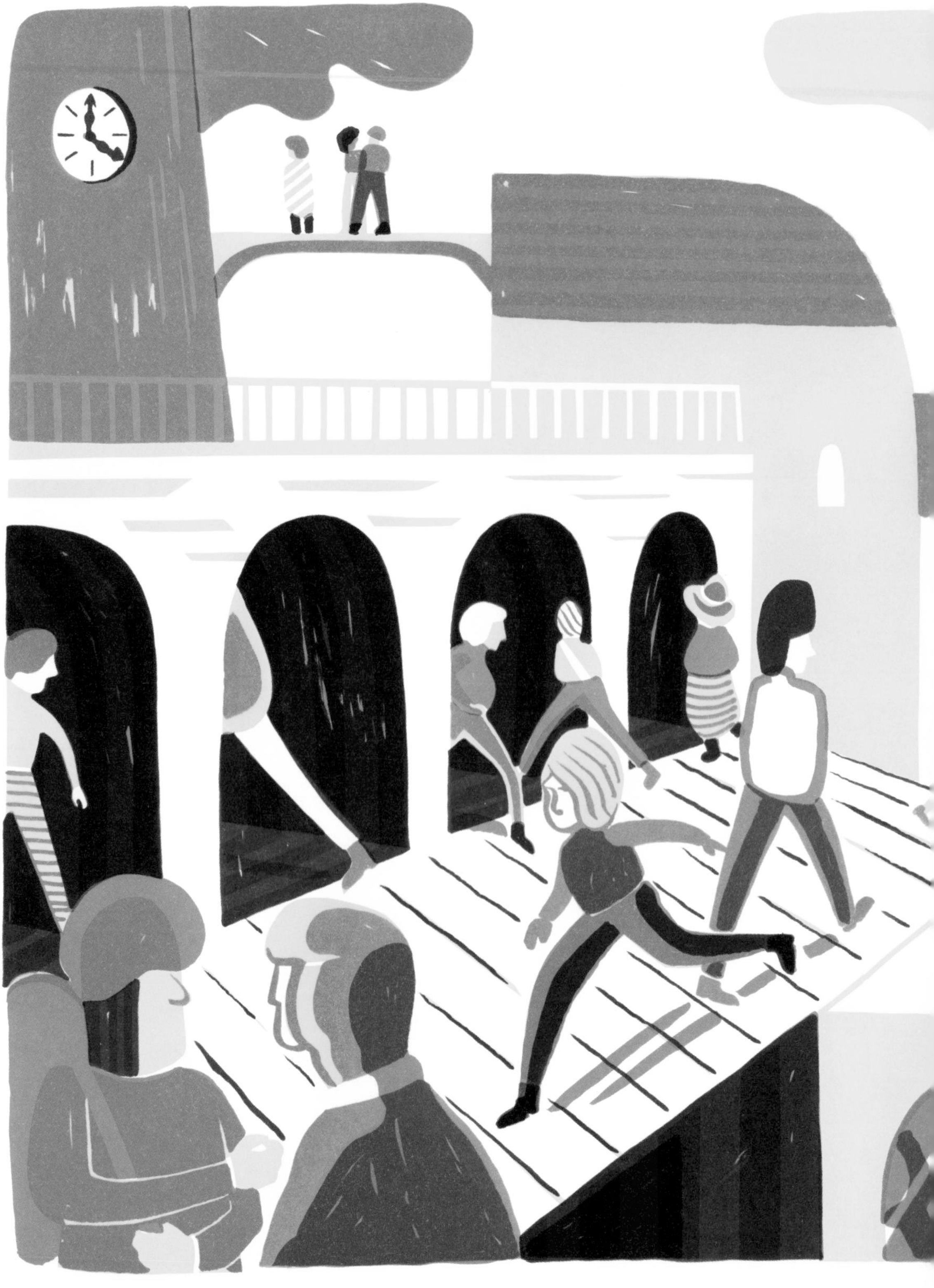

The Night Watchman

A book by Jérémie Fischer
and Jean-Baptiste
Labrune

Translated by
David Henry Wilson

LITTLe
GeSTaLTeN

First Night

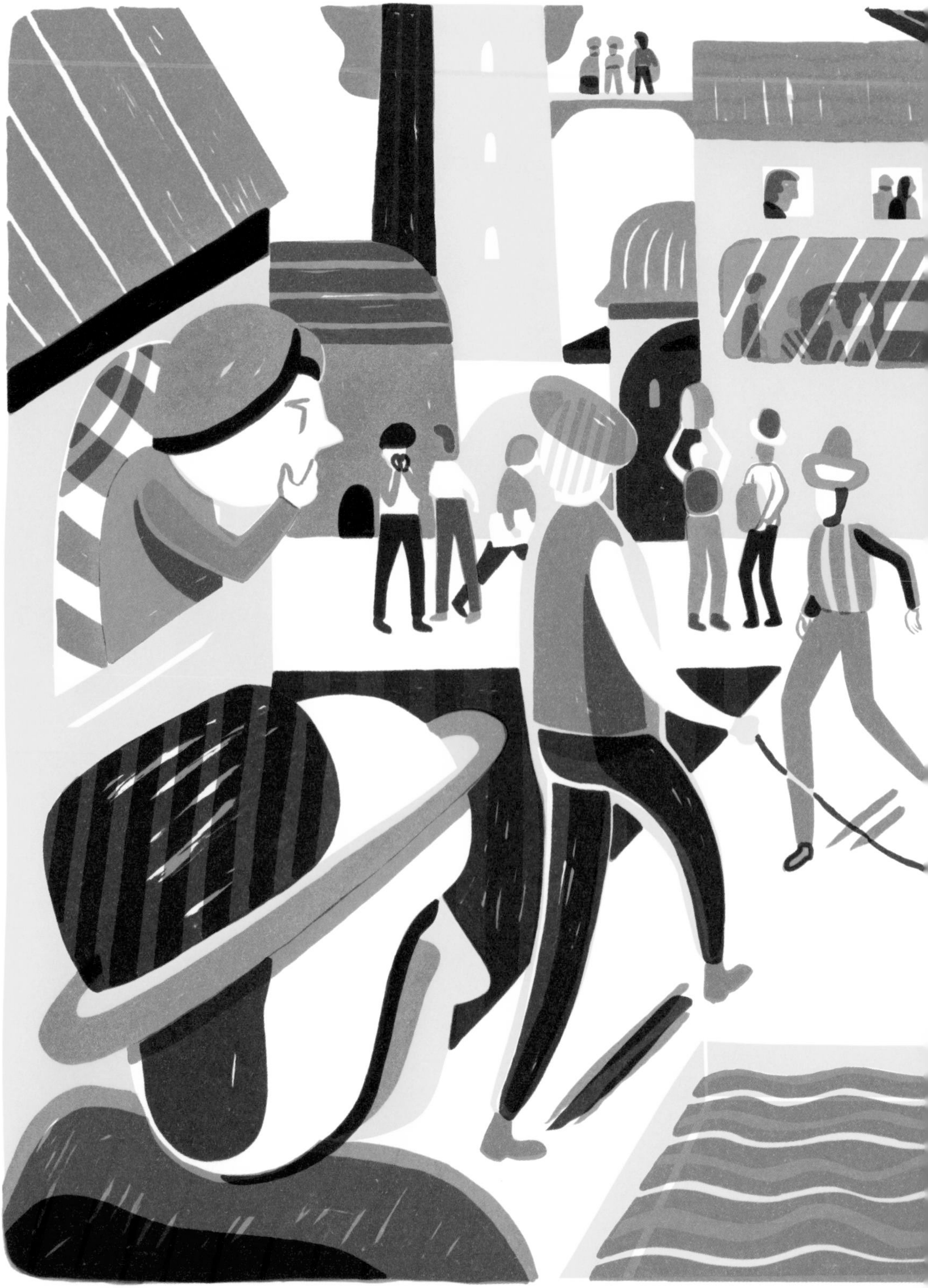

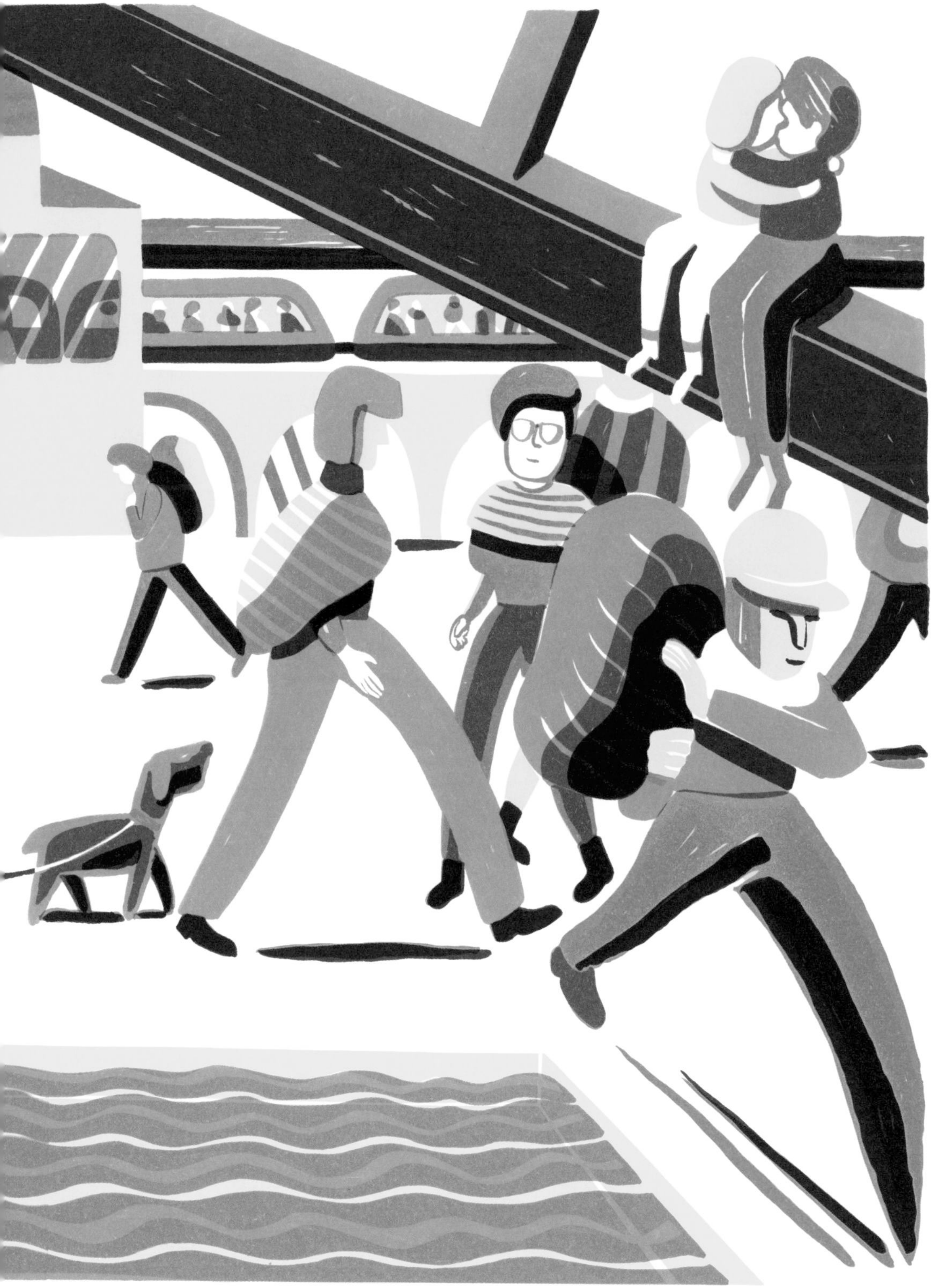

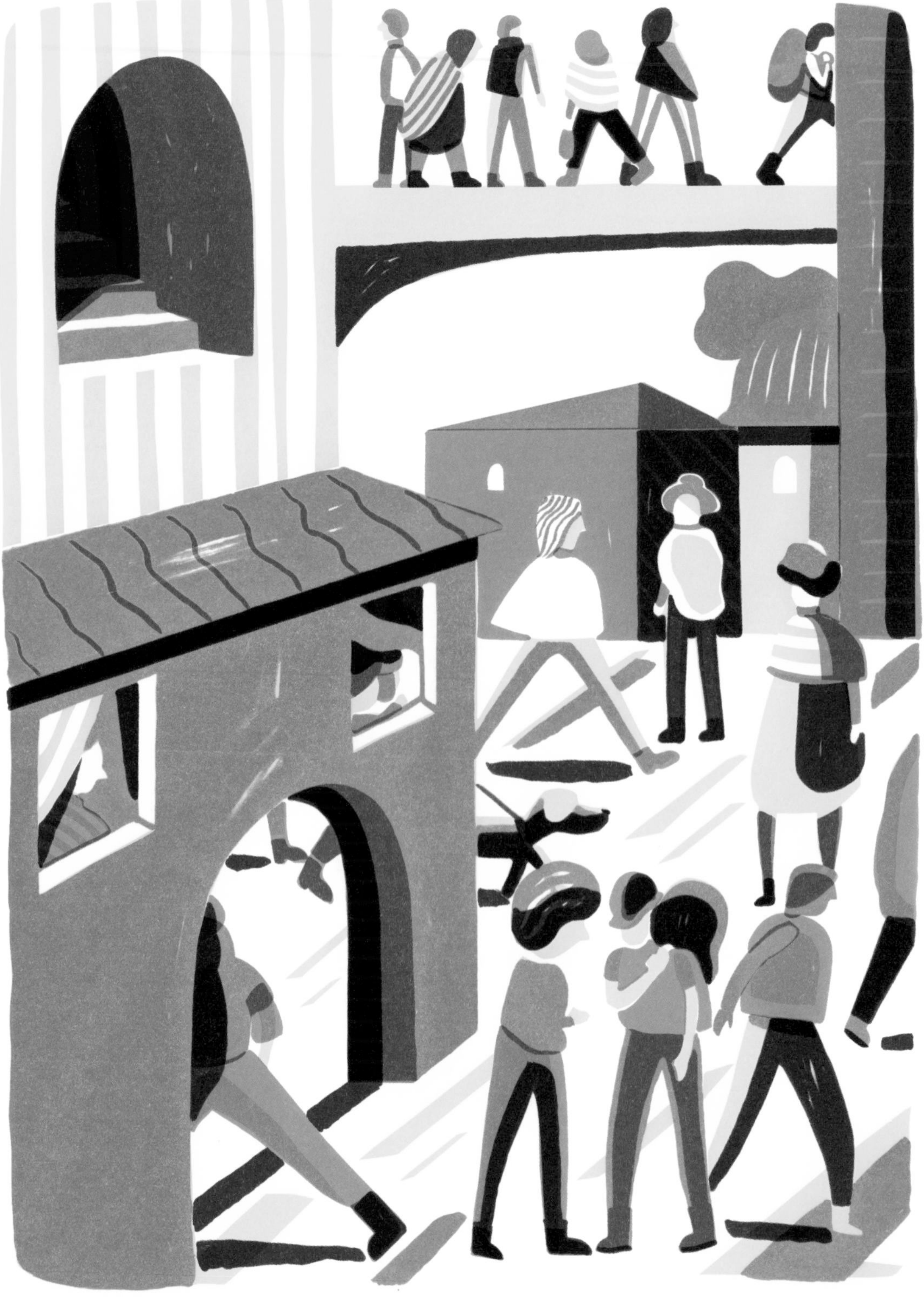

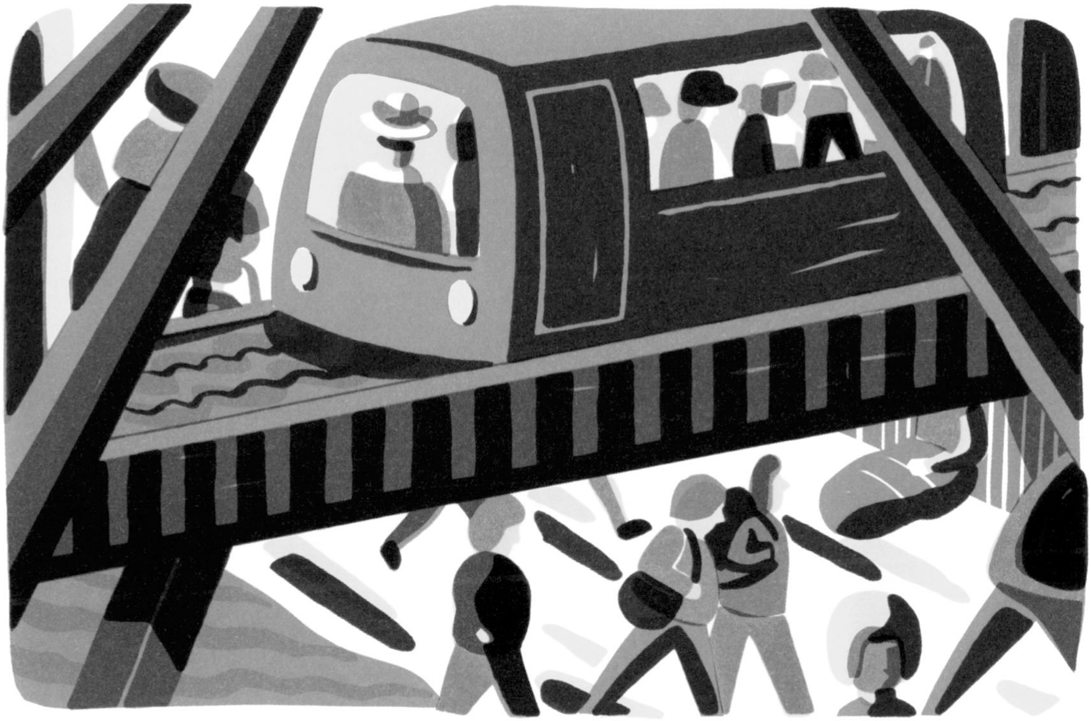

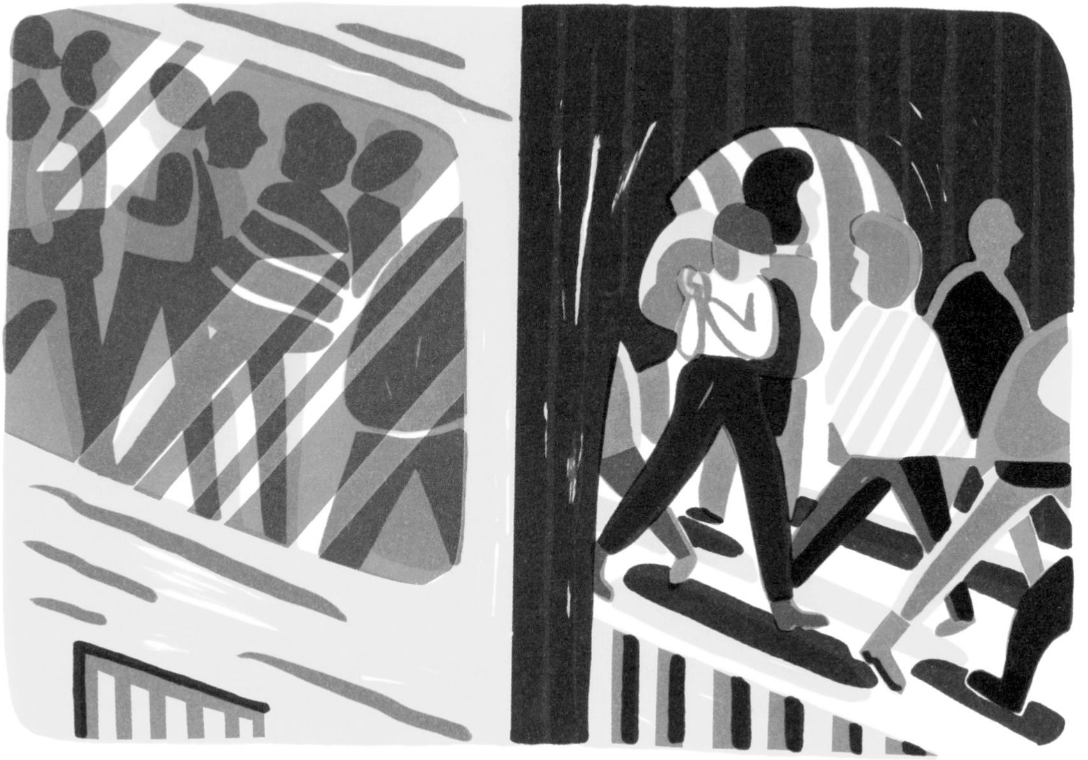

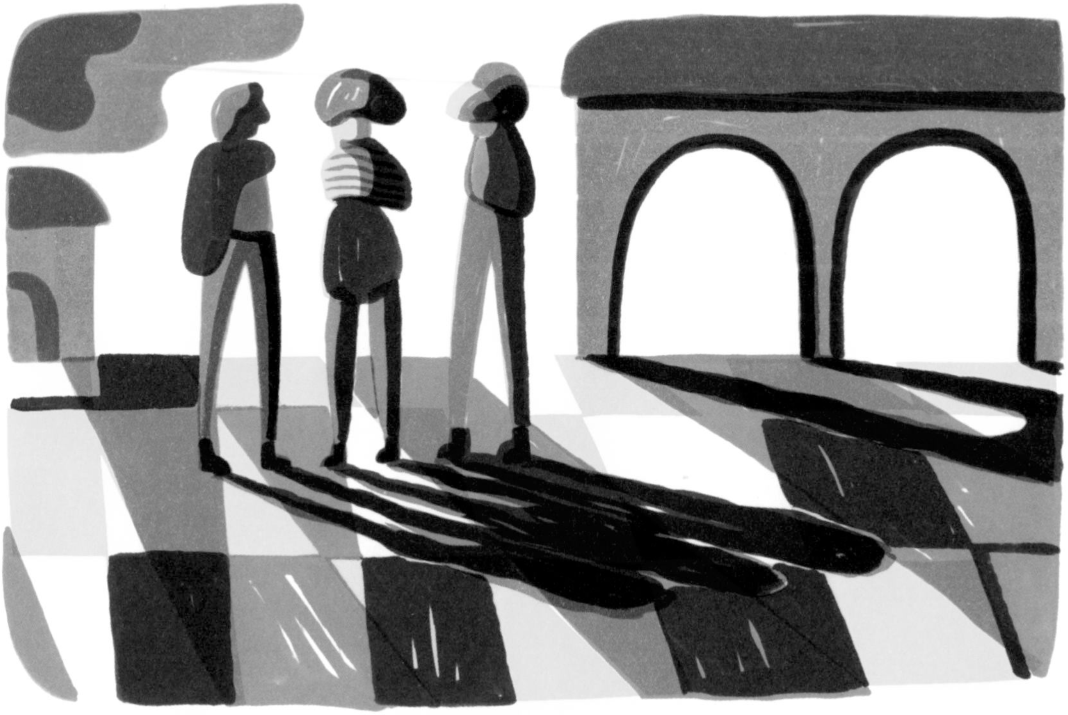

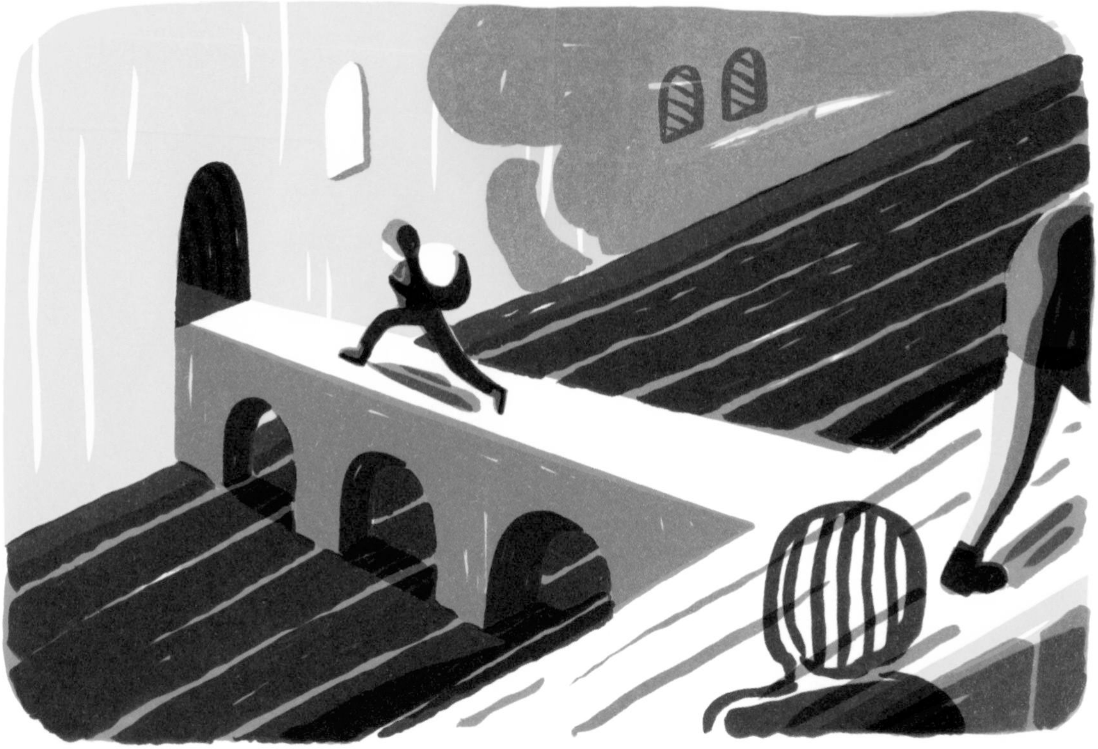

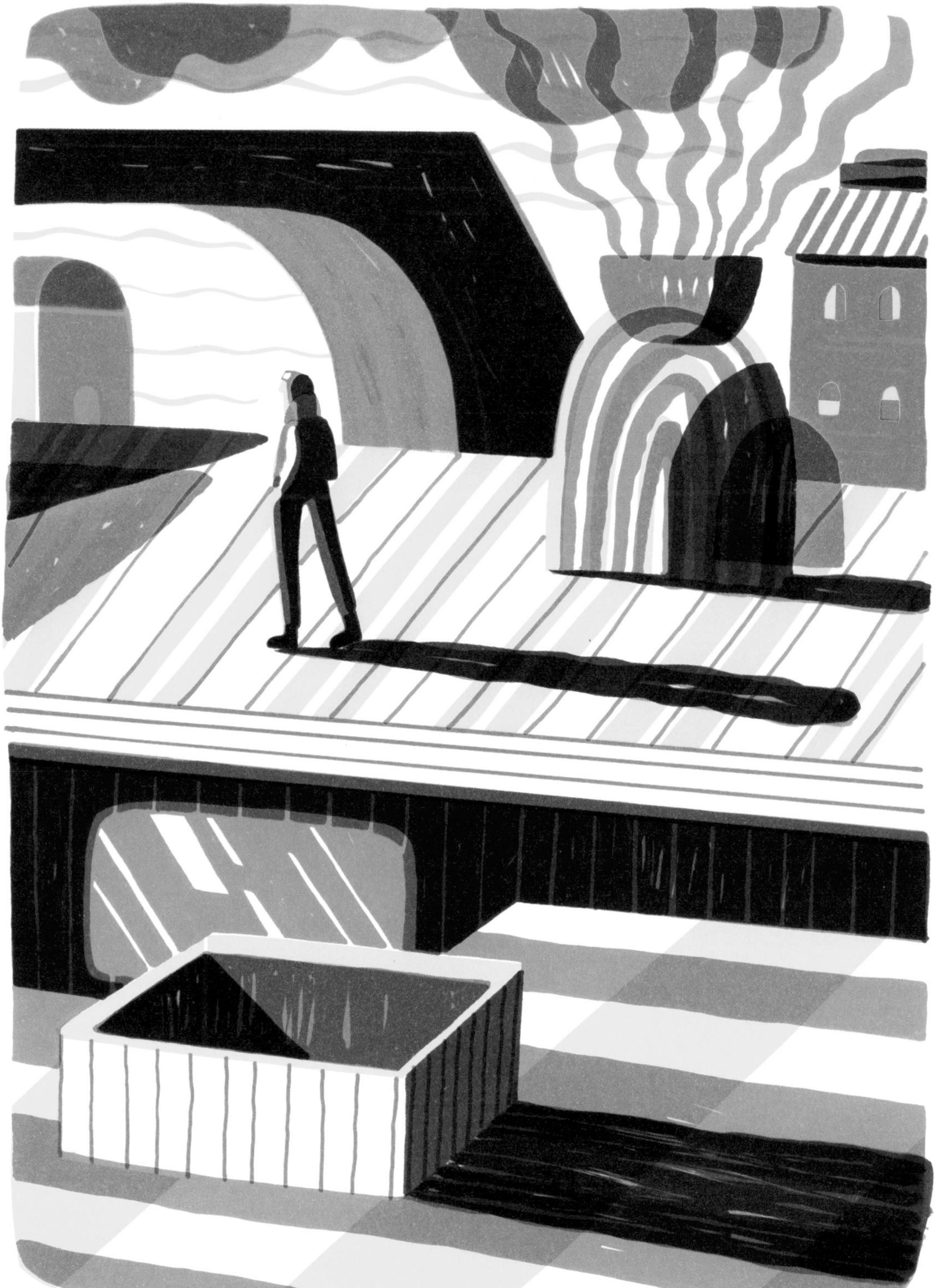

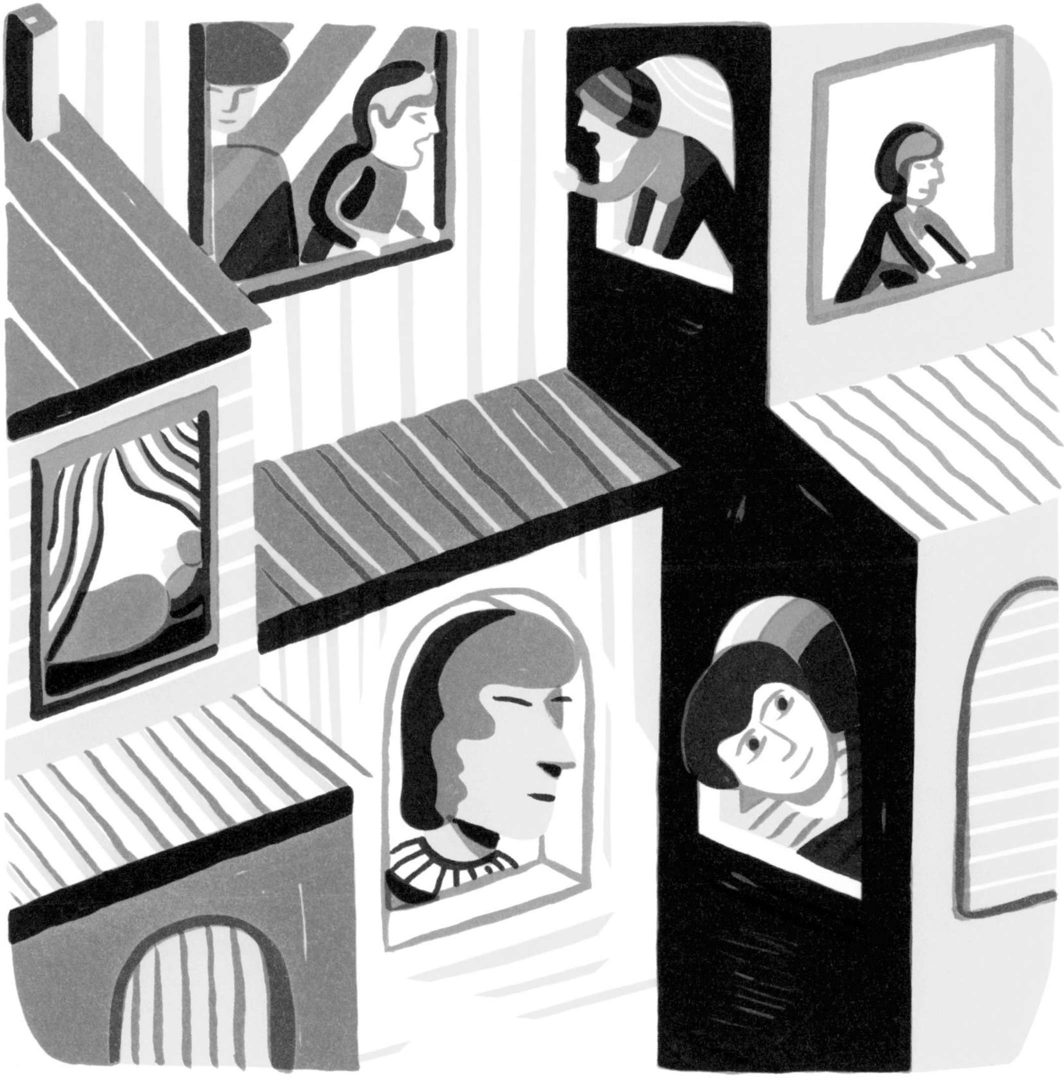

This is my time.

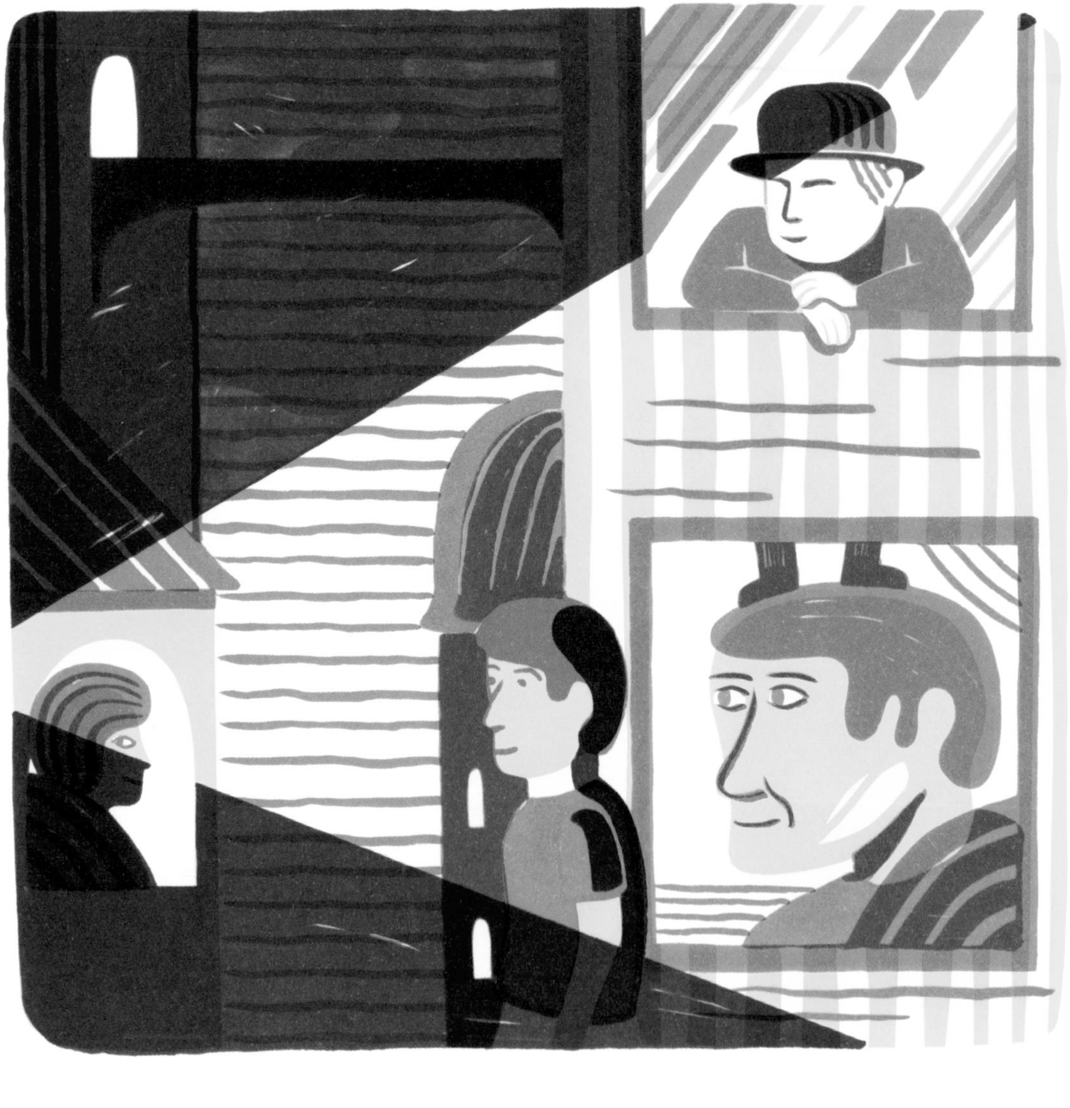

I see the laborers of the day going
to their beds until tomorrow. People greet me.
They know they can sleep in peace
so long as I am here.

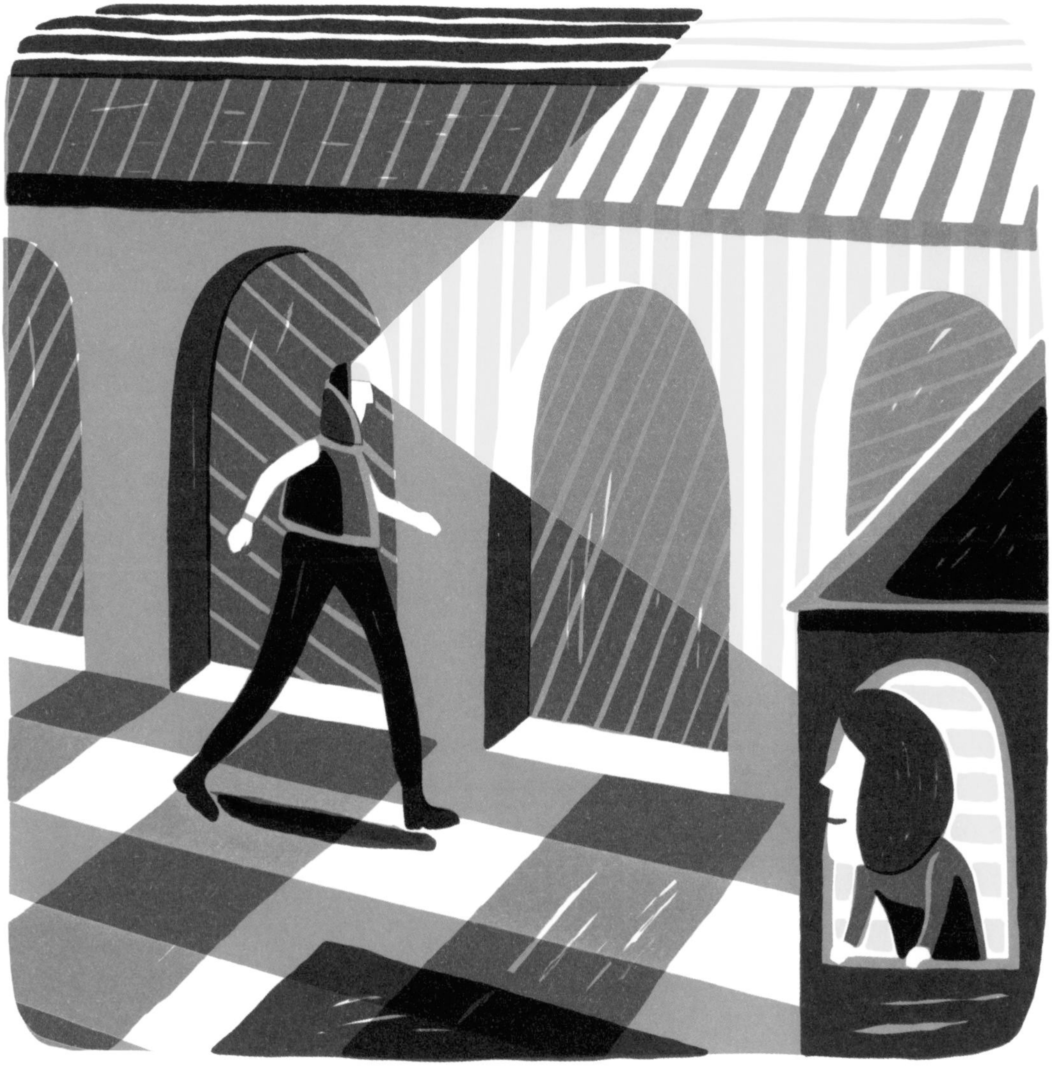

I close all the doors of the city and cry:
*"Ten o'clock and all's well!"*

Then the lights go out, and I patrol the ramparts.
The city has become a sea of shadows, from which
there emerge in splendid isolation, like three
monumental masts, the Three Clock Towers. In unison
they mark the coming and going of the days,
relentless metronomes ticking the rhythm
of the city's life.

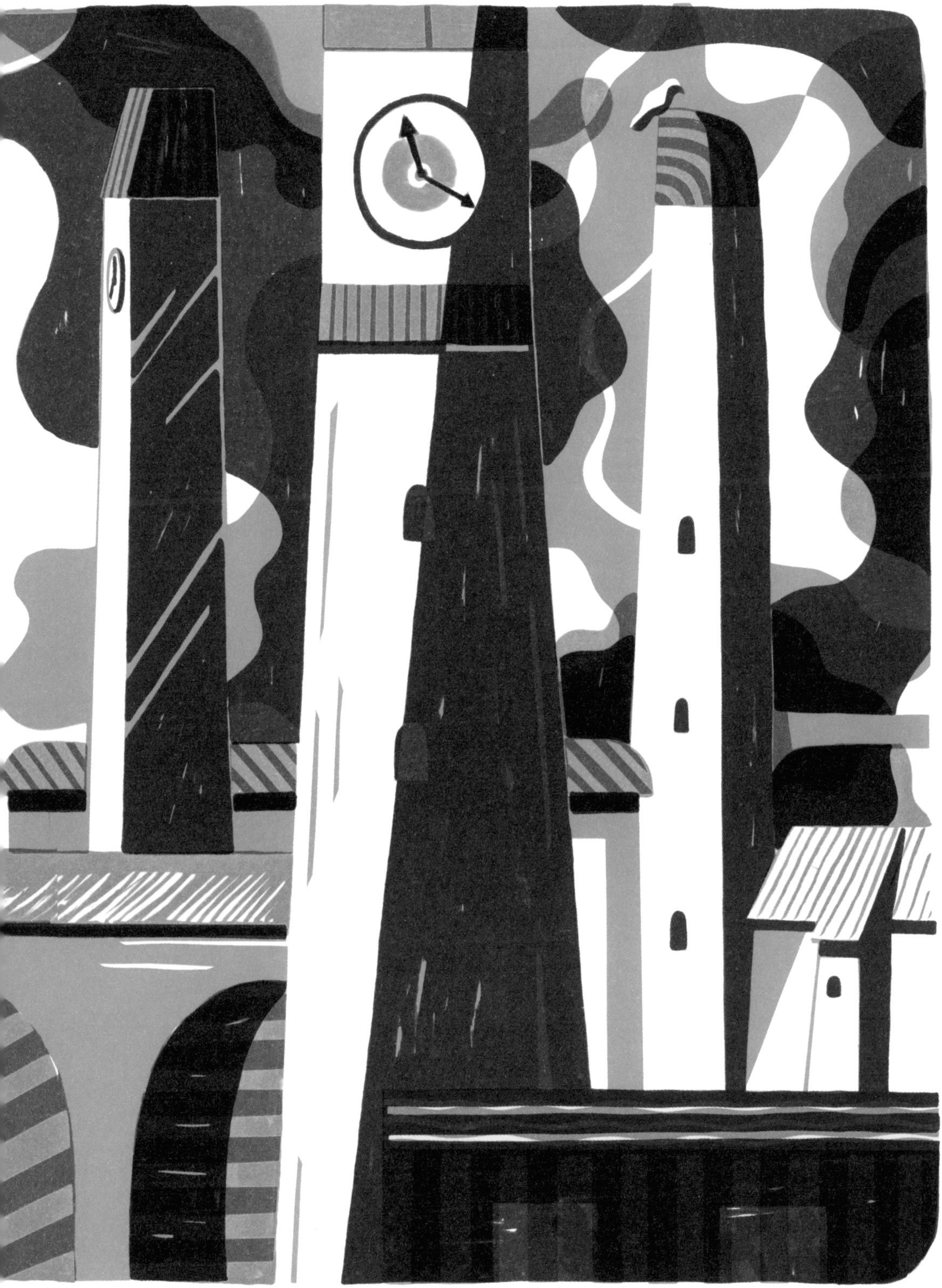

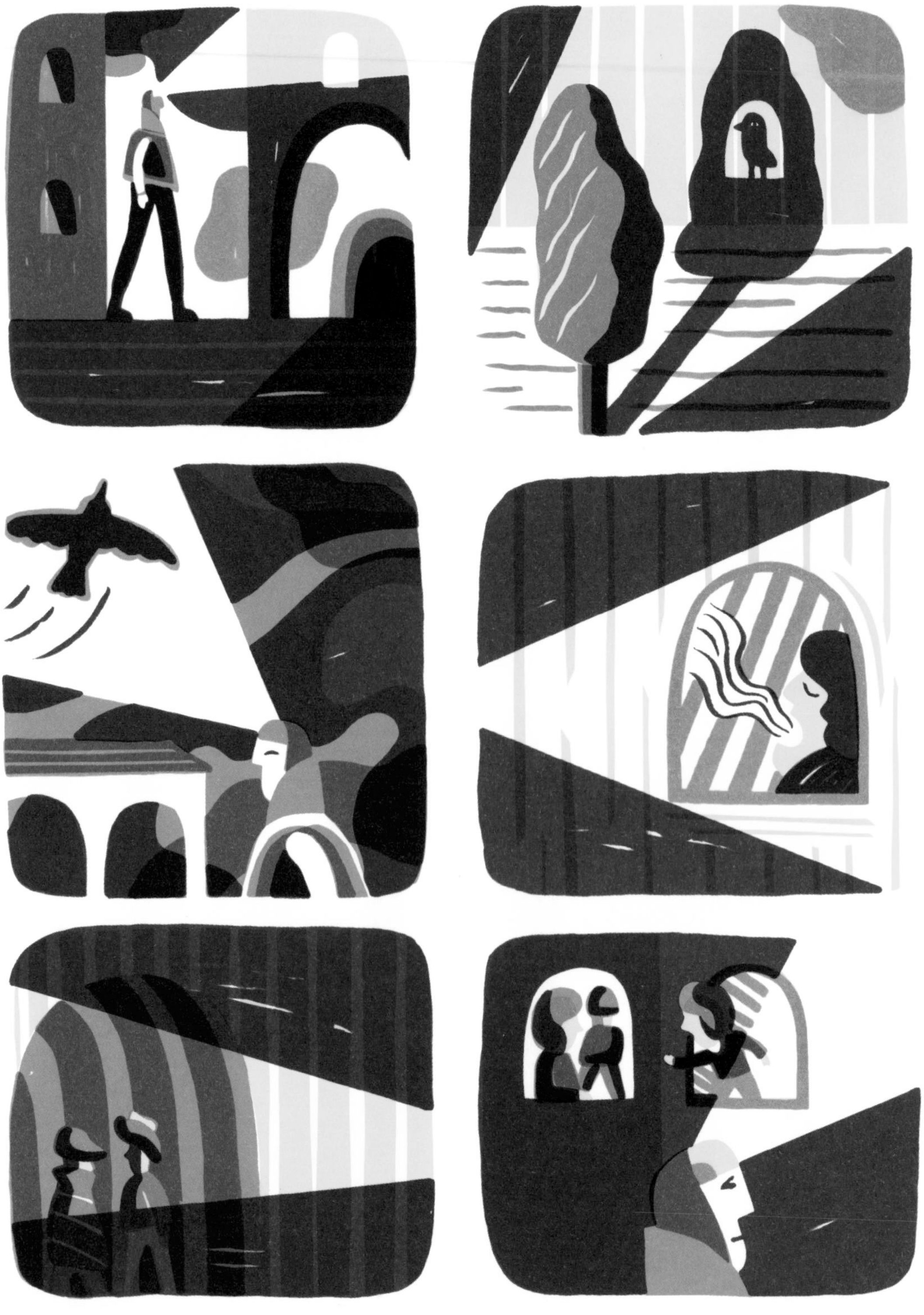

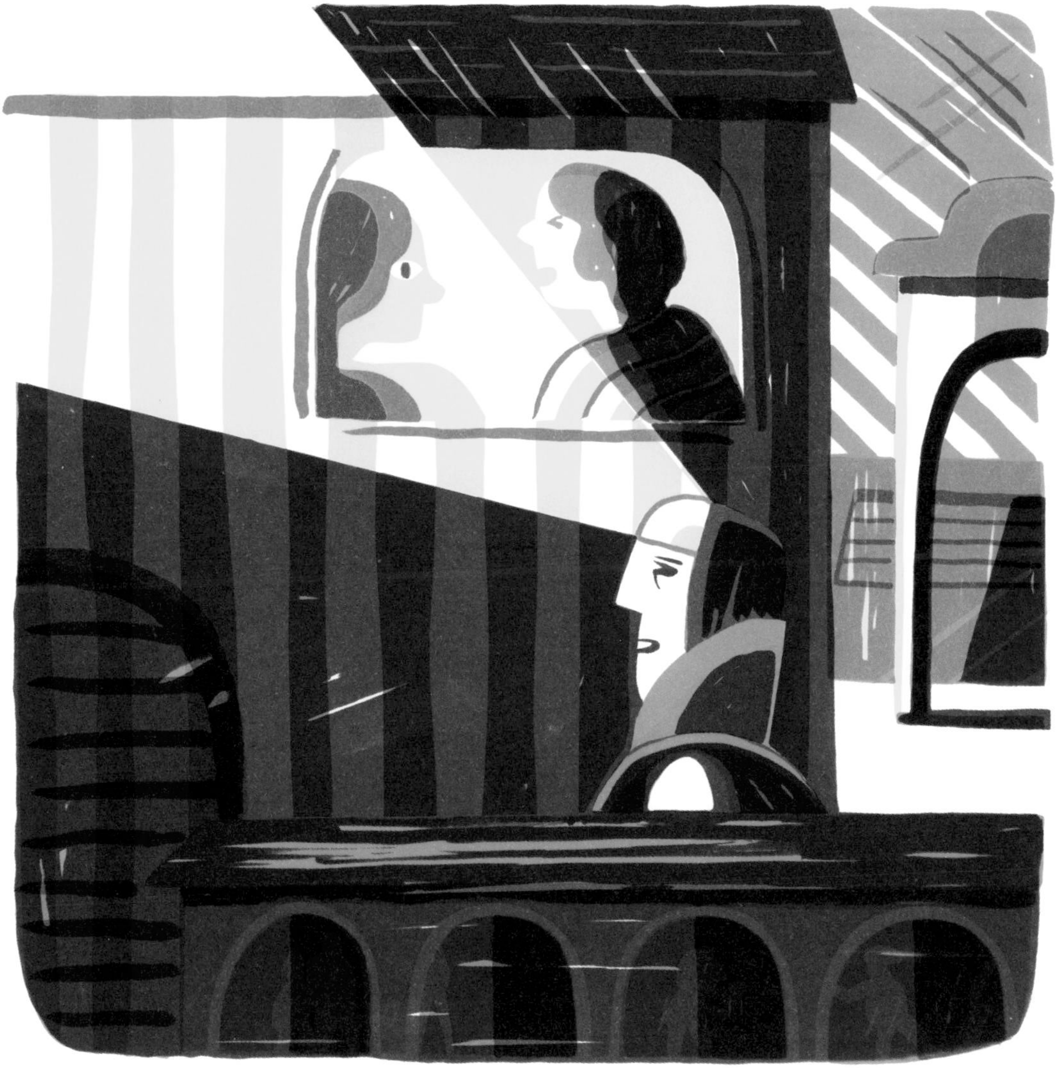

I am the guardian of all this, throughout the night.
That is my role. Nothing must hold back the flow
of the hours, and nothing must disturb the darkness.
No one else is allowed out.

My helpers: a thousand pairs of eyes scattered
round the city. The rats with their pointed ears know
all about the subterranean sighs. The dogs guard
the winding streets, and there is no scent that their
noses cannot follow. The piercing eyes of the buzzards
survey the tiled dunes of the roofs.

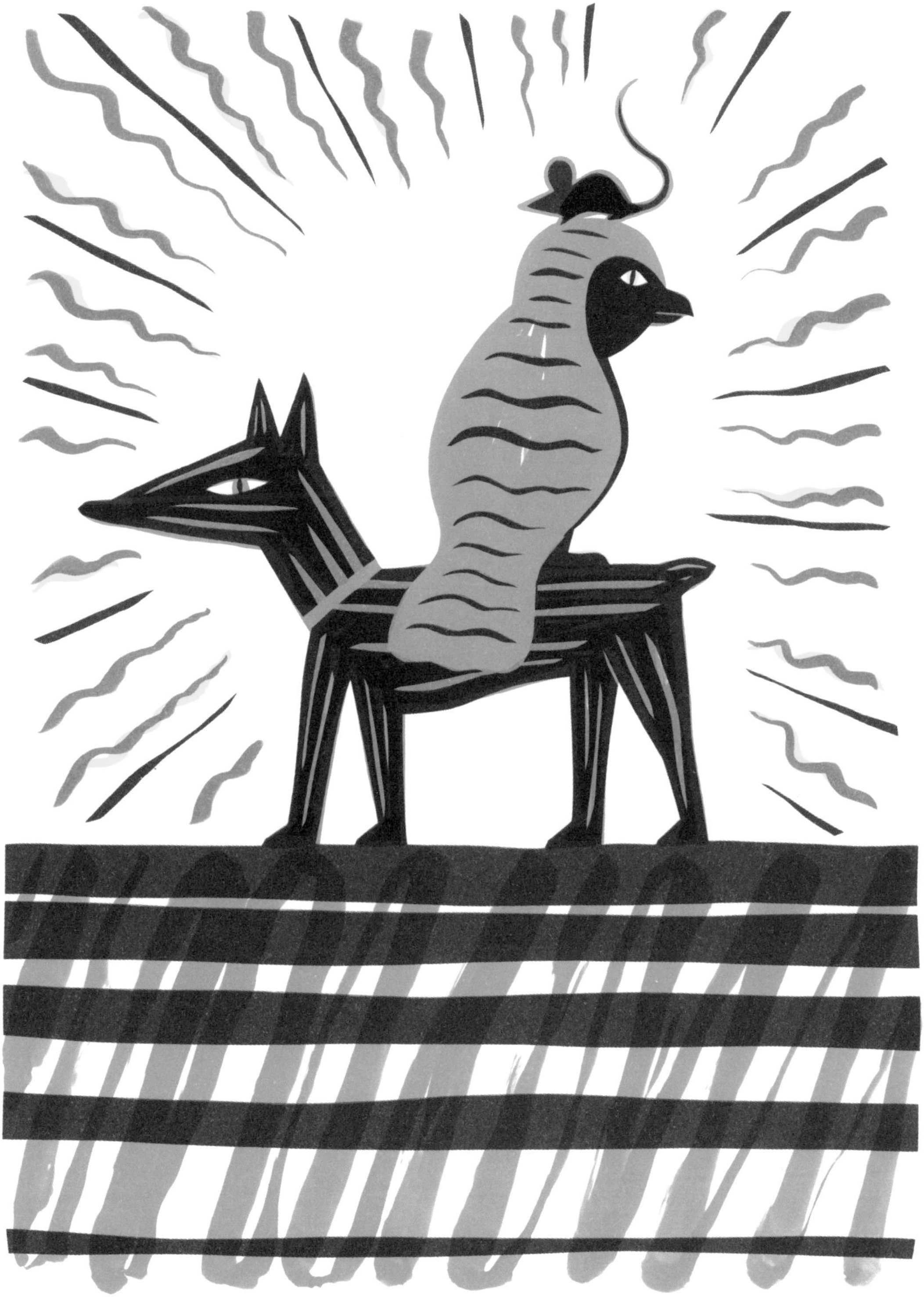

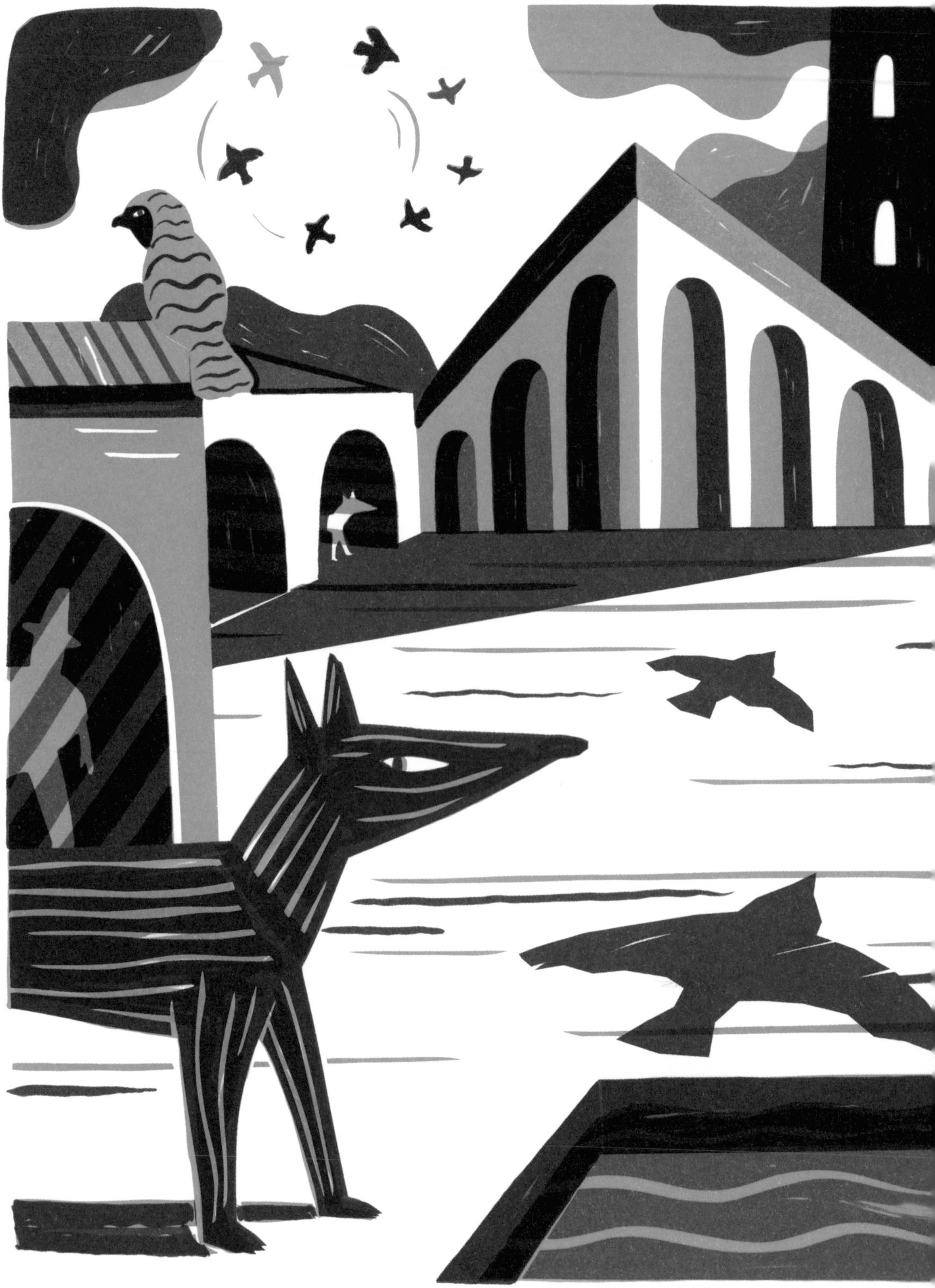

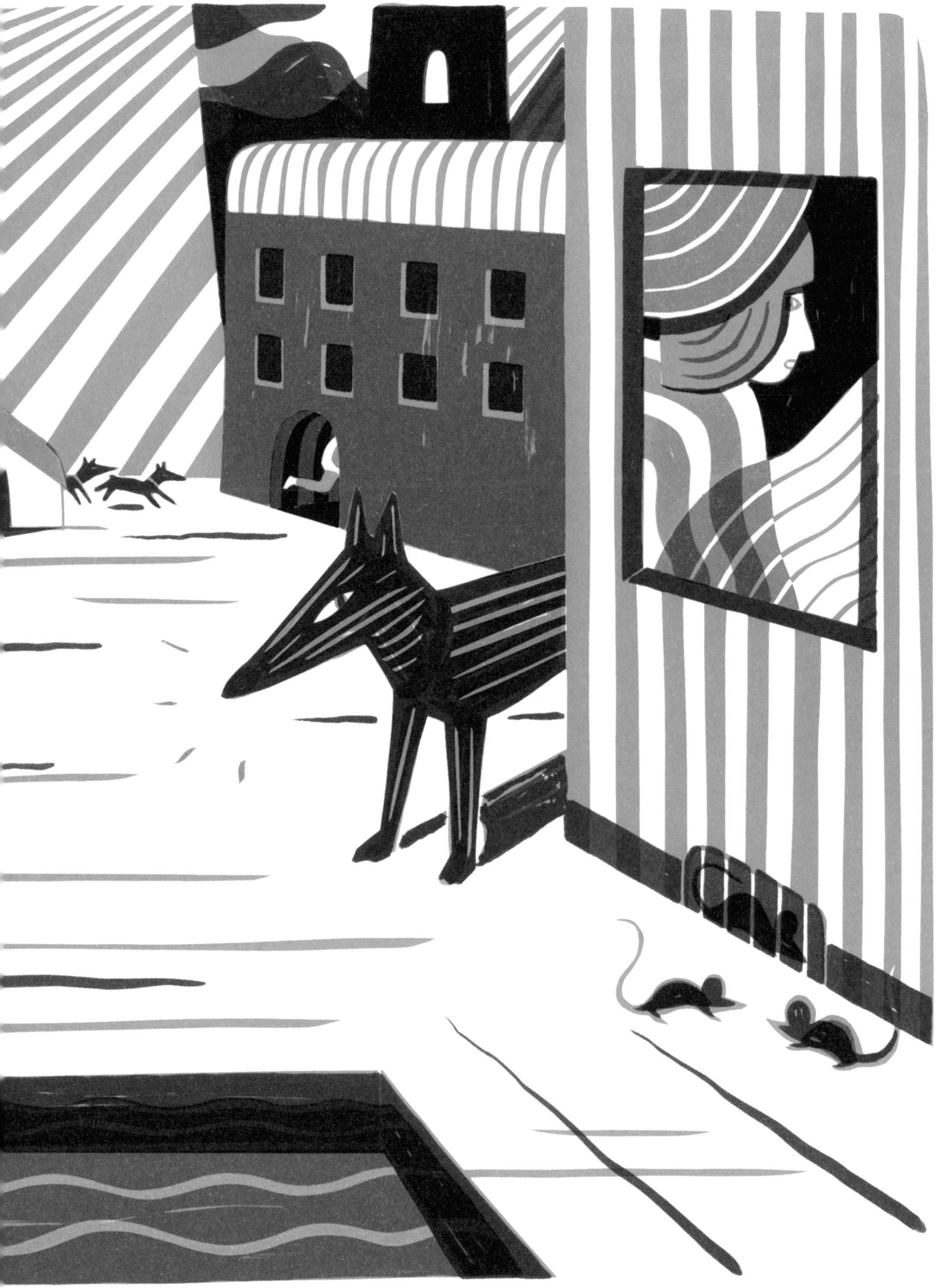

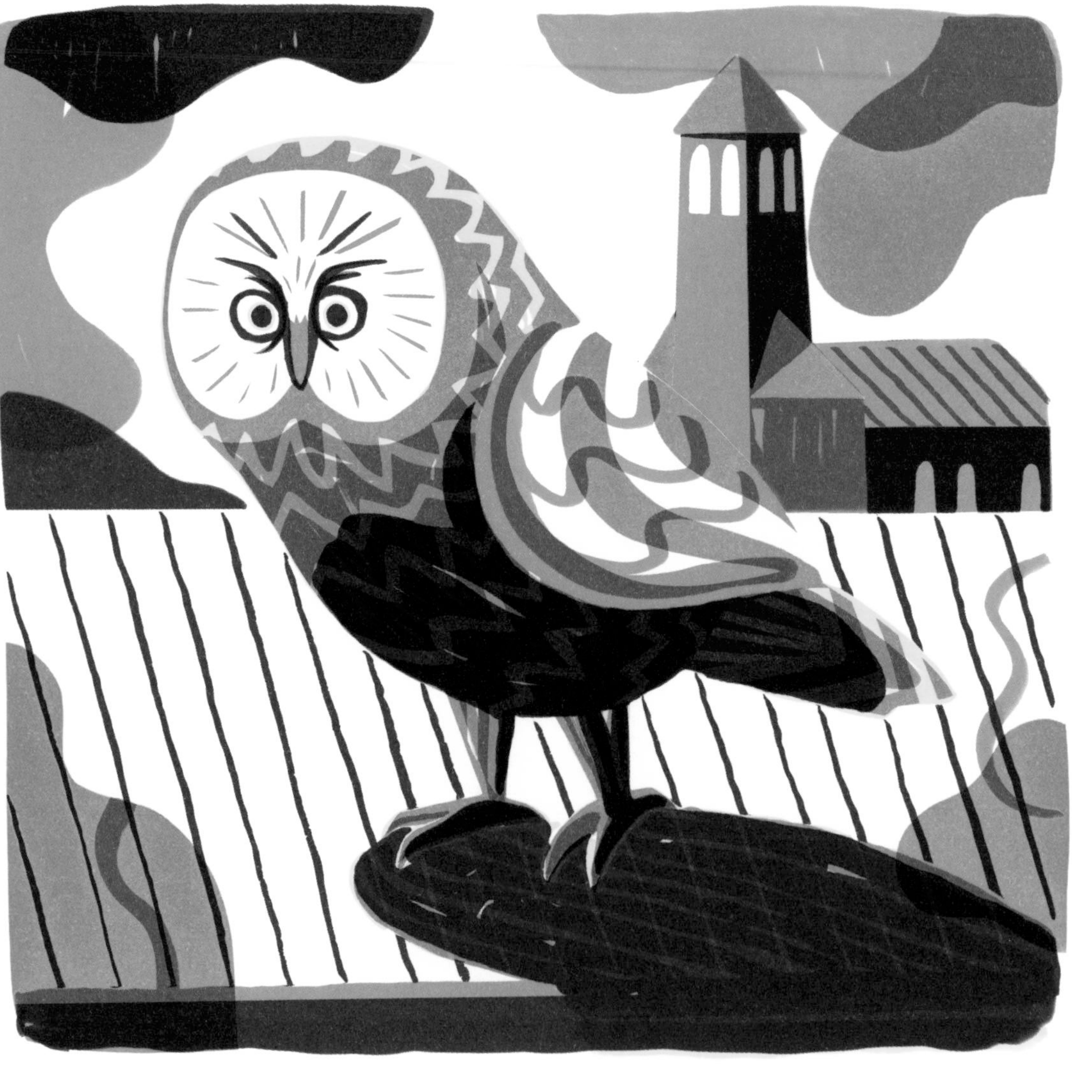

The owl in the old bell-tower has never spoken
a word to me. She has always been there. She watches in silence,
the last living witness of Olden Times, that distant age,
gone forever, when the shadows triumphed.

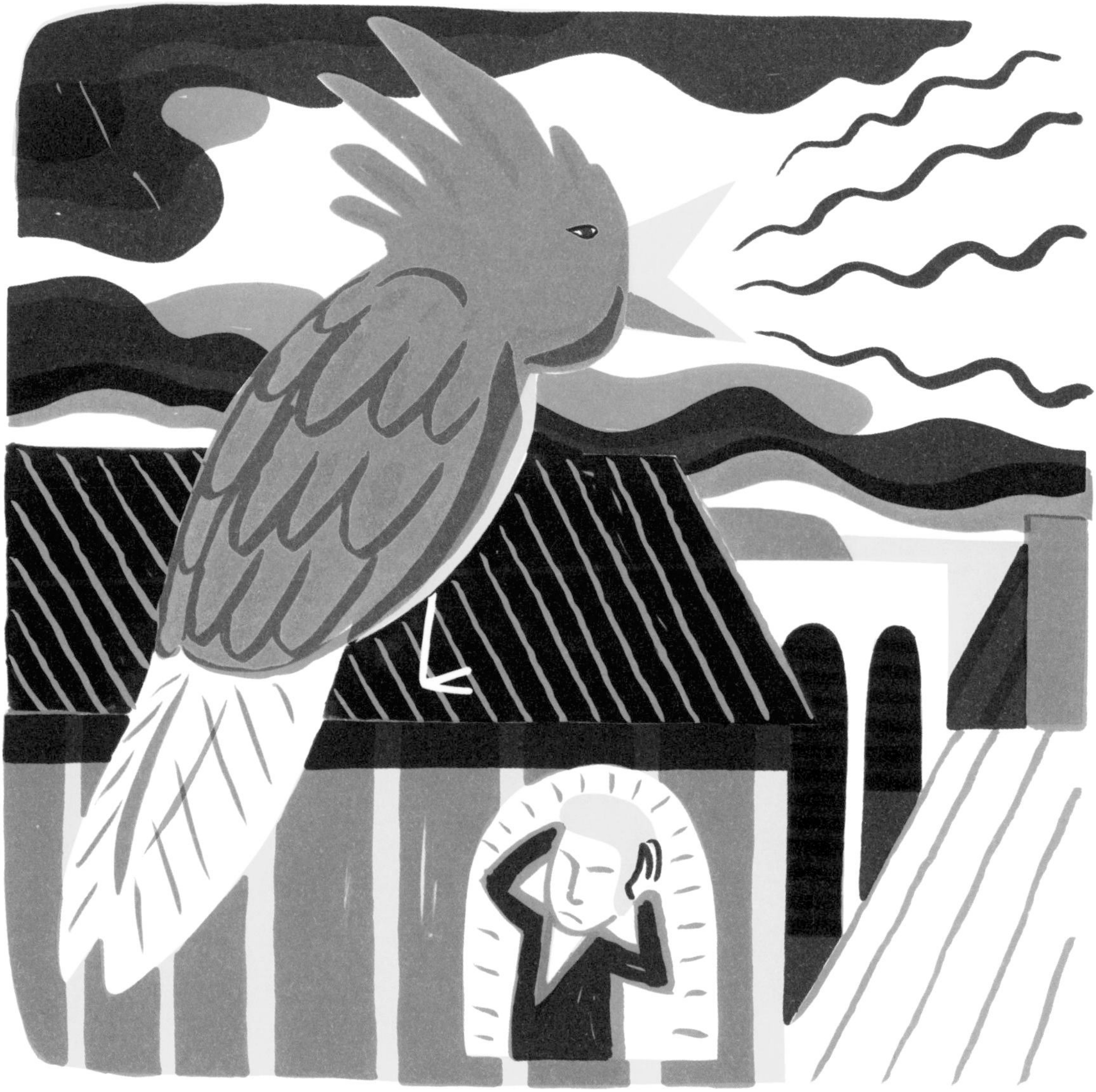

I finish my rounds.

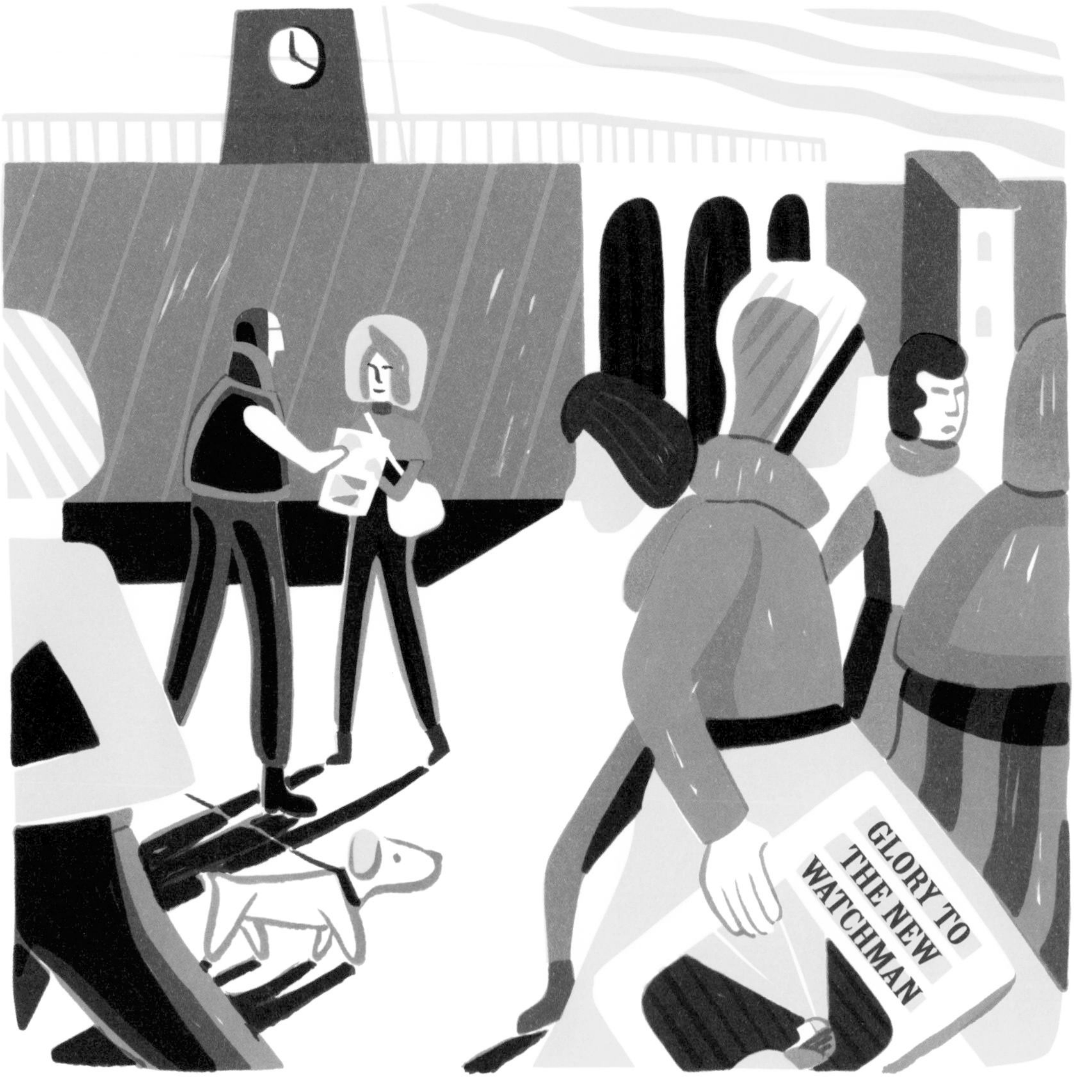
GLORY TO
THE NEW
WATCHMAN

The city awakens. The din of the morning is my lullaby,
and the sunshine frames my sleep...
until it's night again.

Second Night

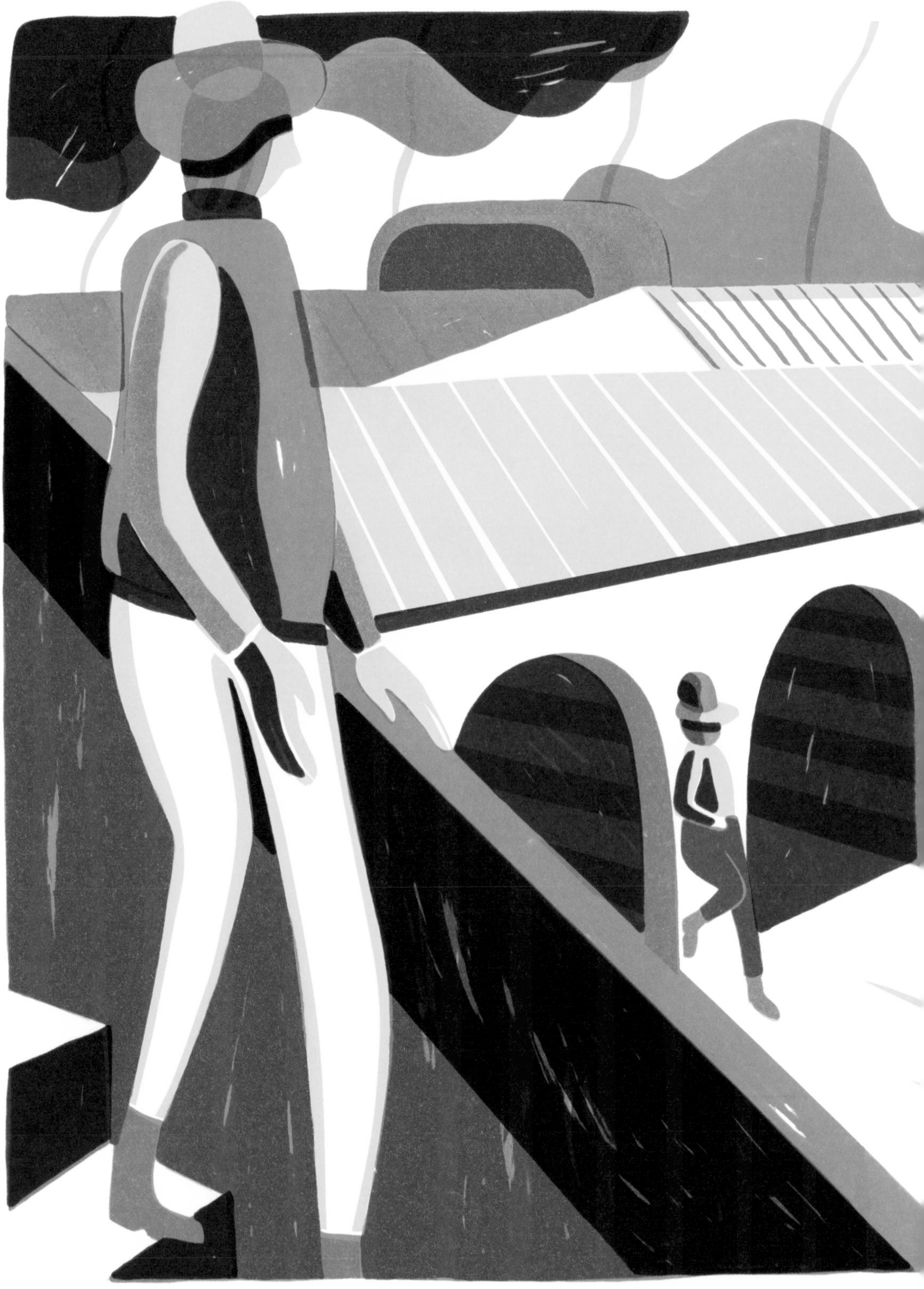

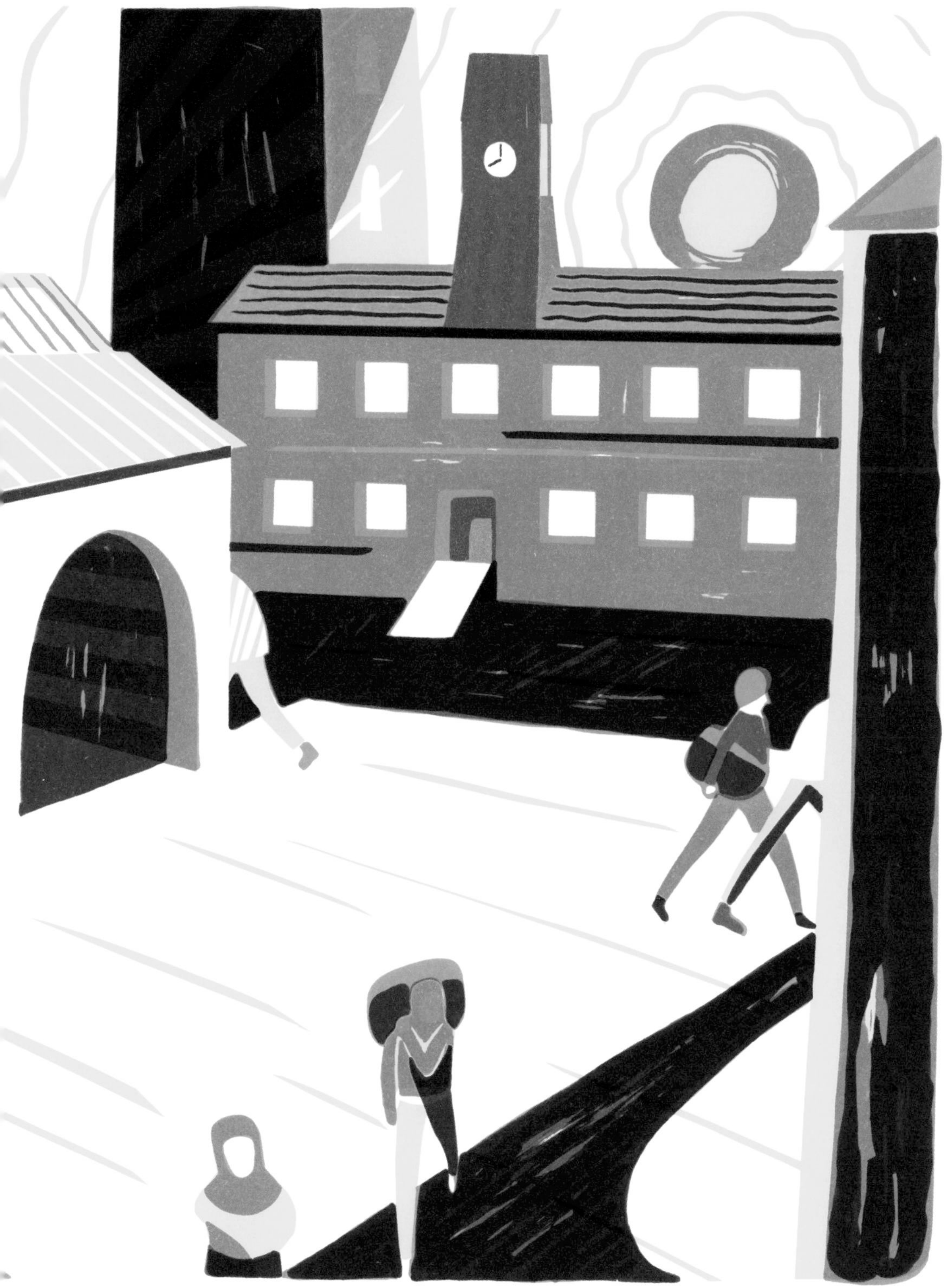

It's an evening like so many others.

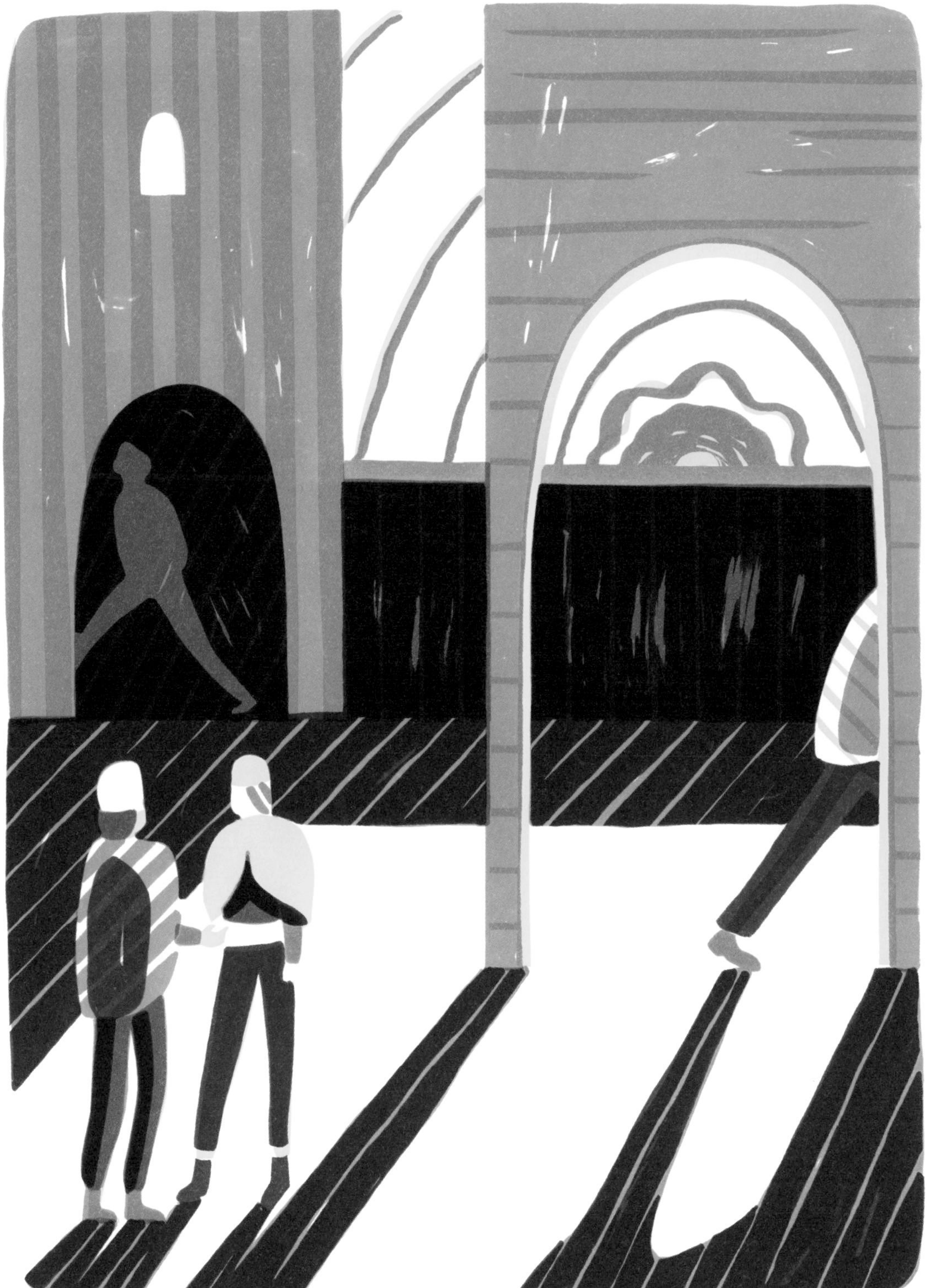

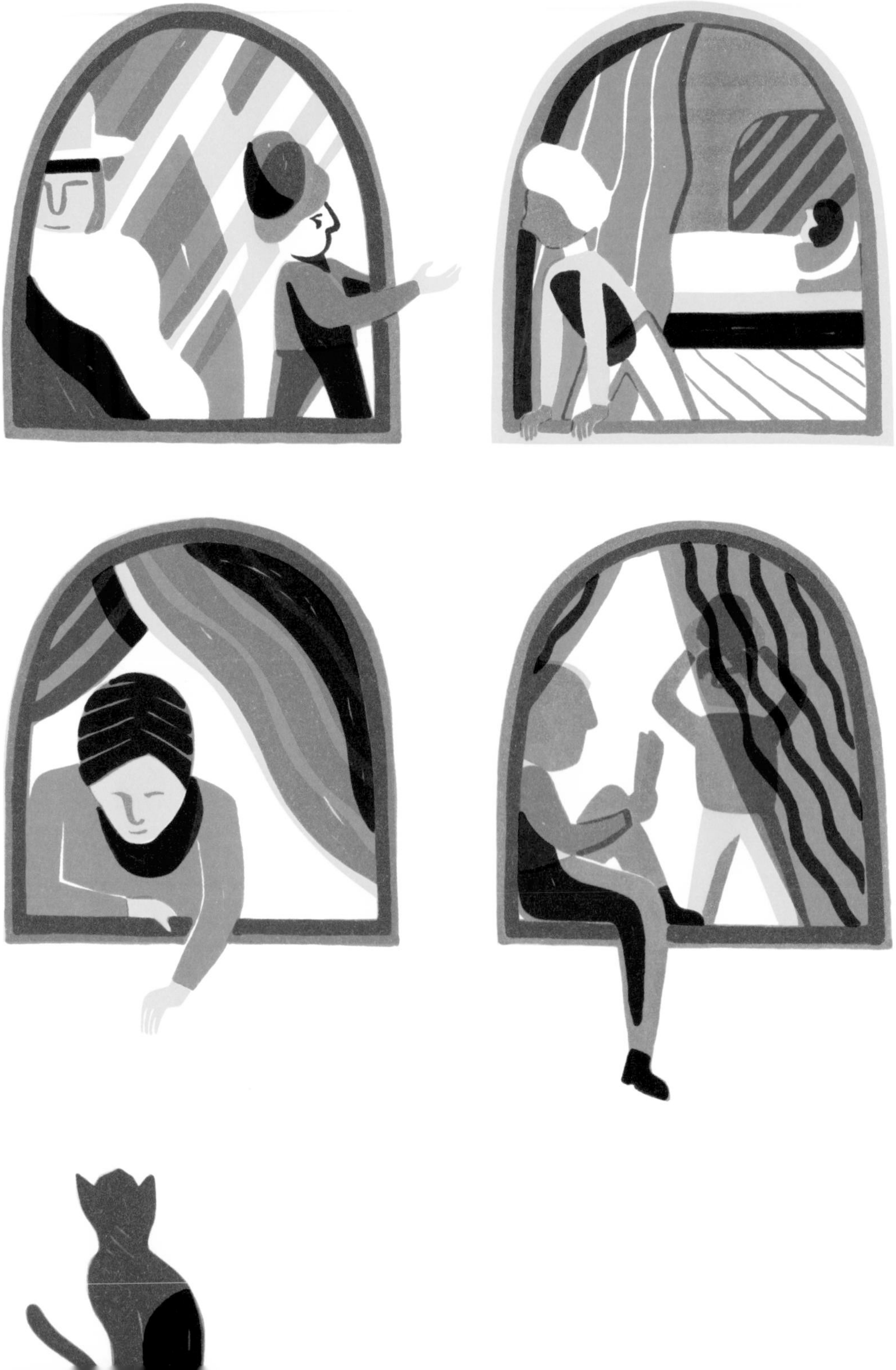

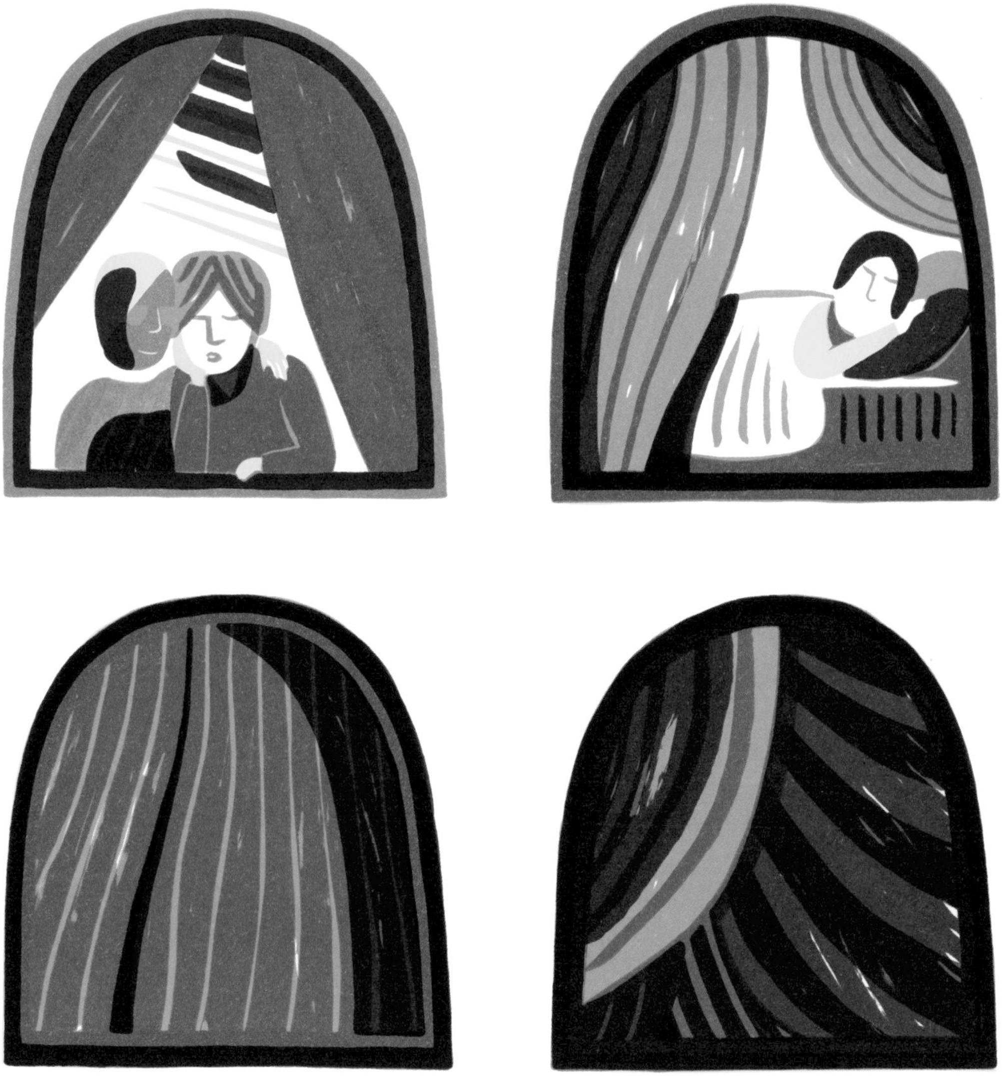

The city goes to sleep.
The silent roofs give shelter to the murmuring of dreams.
Night moves serenely on. Nothing disturbs it.
The regular rhythm of my footsteps on the black cobblestones
echoes the gentle snores of the sleepers.
*"Midnight, and all's well."*

We are easing our way into a new today.
But something draws my attention.
Something has gone quiet. A tiny
irregularity, like a heart that misses a beat.
I explore every lane, every cul-de-sac,
and the further I go in search of its cause,
the more the silence seems to deepen.

Soon I can hear nothing besides this strange, infinitesimal hush filling the hollows in the long wake of the night. It is everywhere, and yet whenever I think I'm about to locate it, away it goes again, ungraspable.

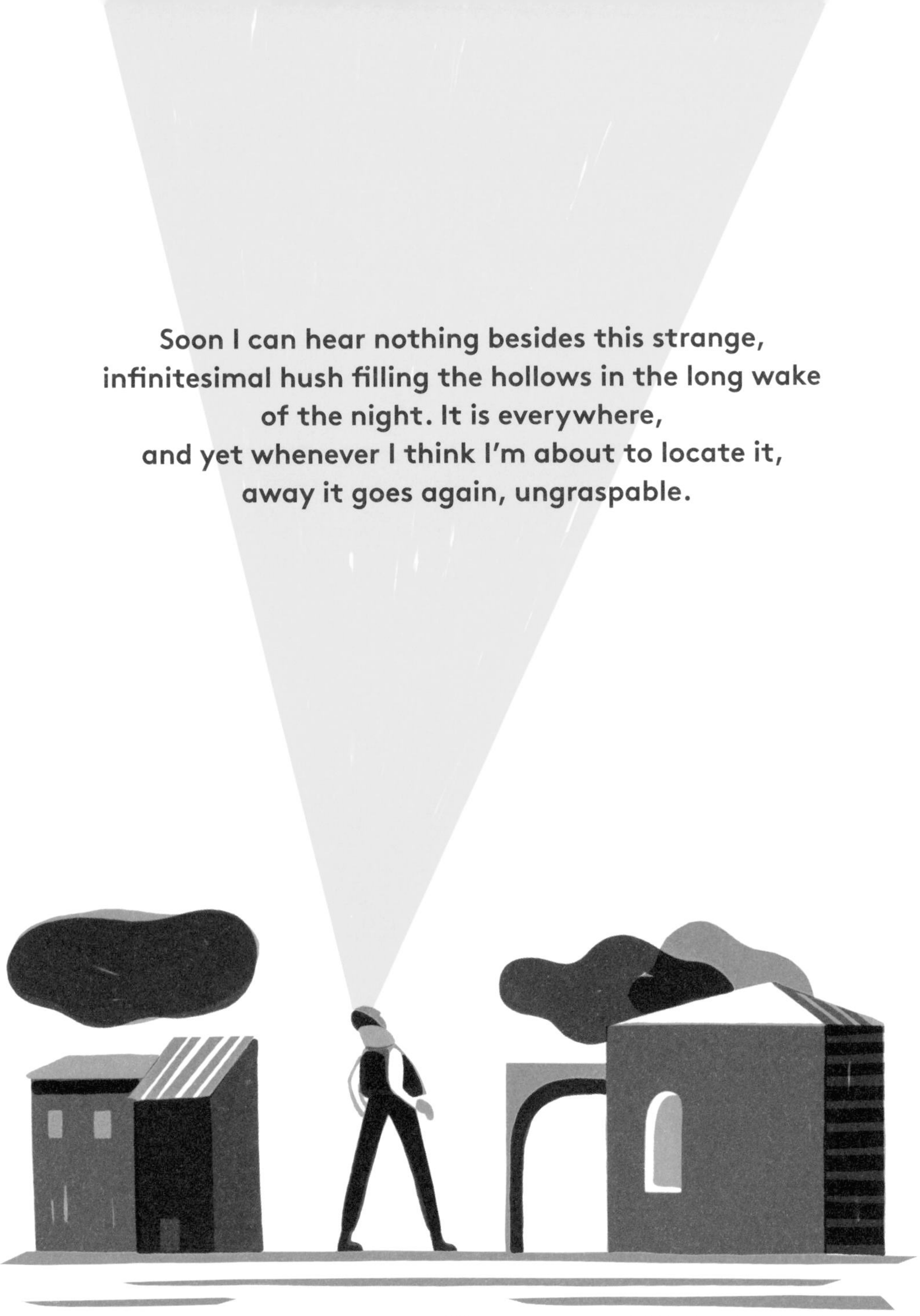

Finally, my lamp illuminates
the great silhouette of the Eastern Clock Tower,
and at last I understand. The dial of the clock has
been broken. Its hands have run their course.

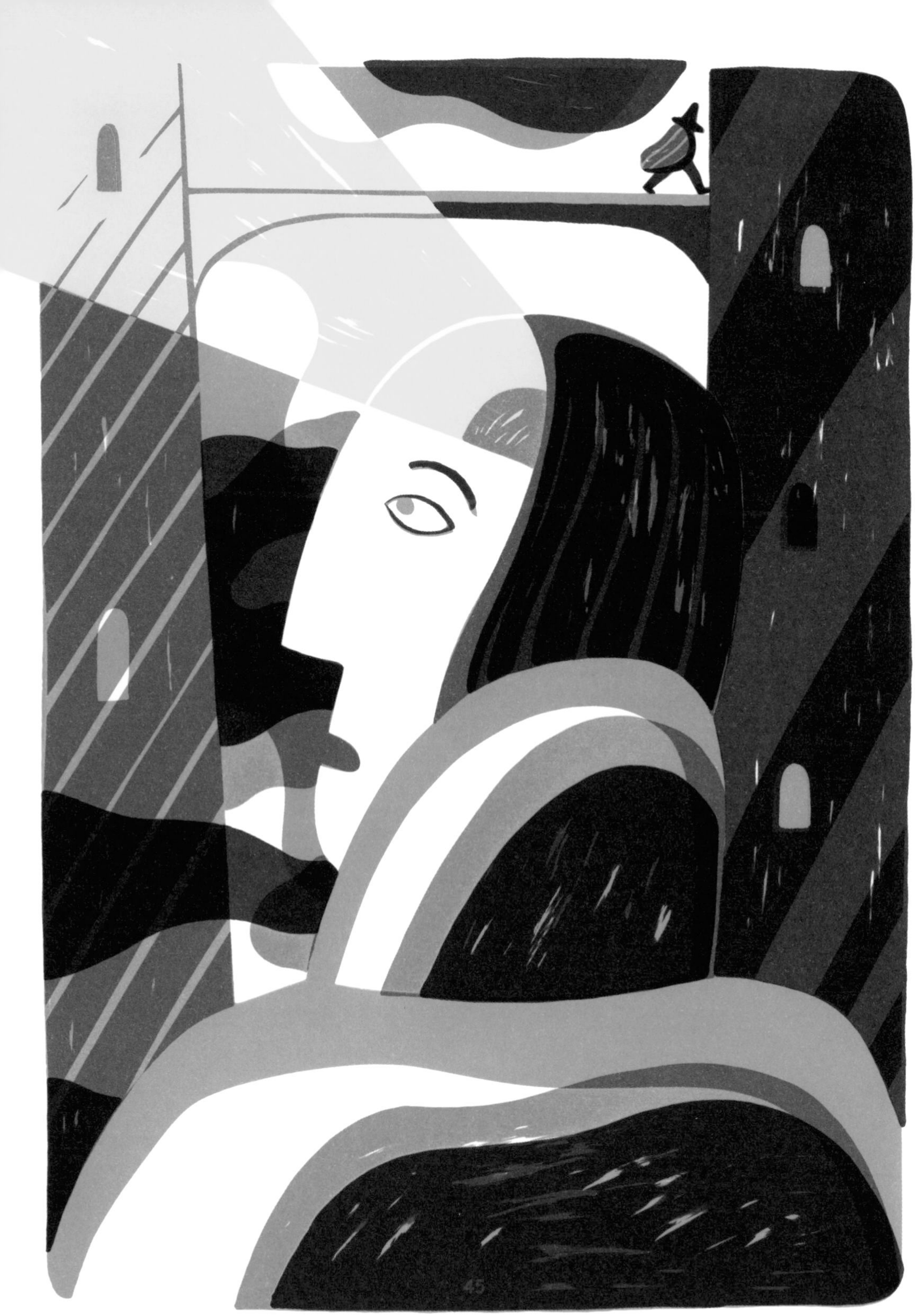

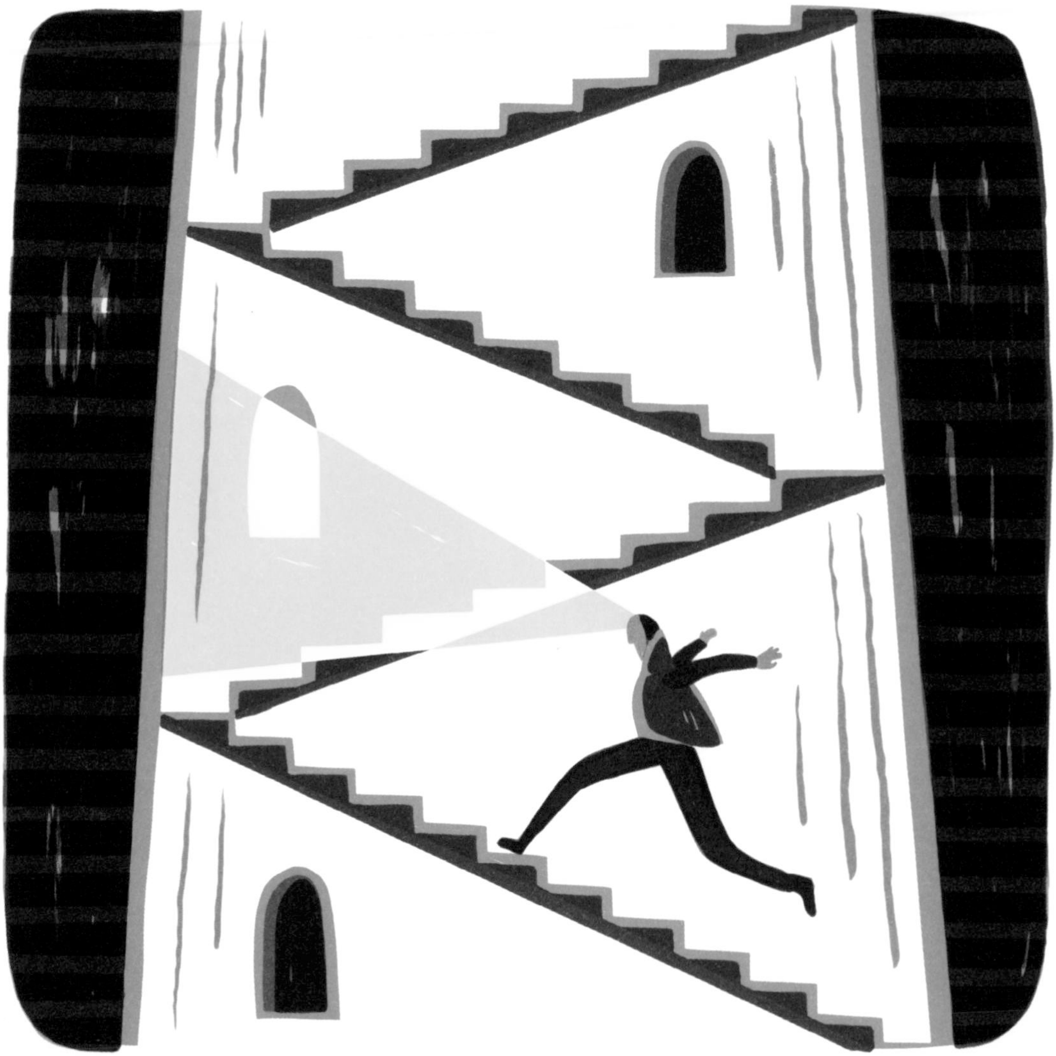

That is the cause of the silence. Time has lost its voice.
Someone has ended its gentle onward flow.

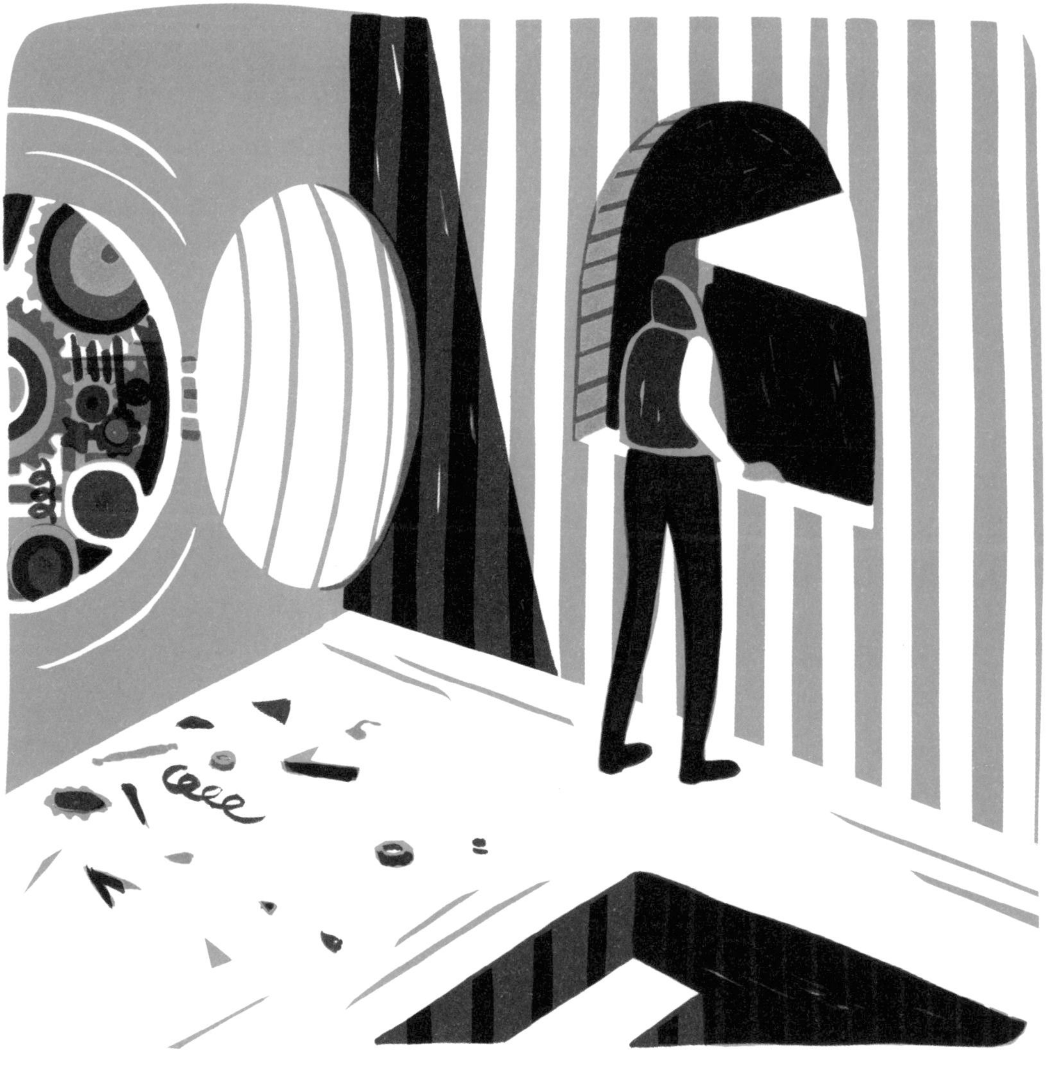

There is carnage ... Its gears have been dislocated, its pulleys ripped apart, its axles smashed. The clock has been slaughtered, and its entrails scattered. There could not be a more terrible crime. The clocks are the compasses that guide us through the night. I shall soon find the culprit.

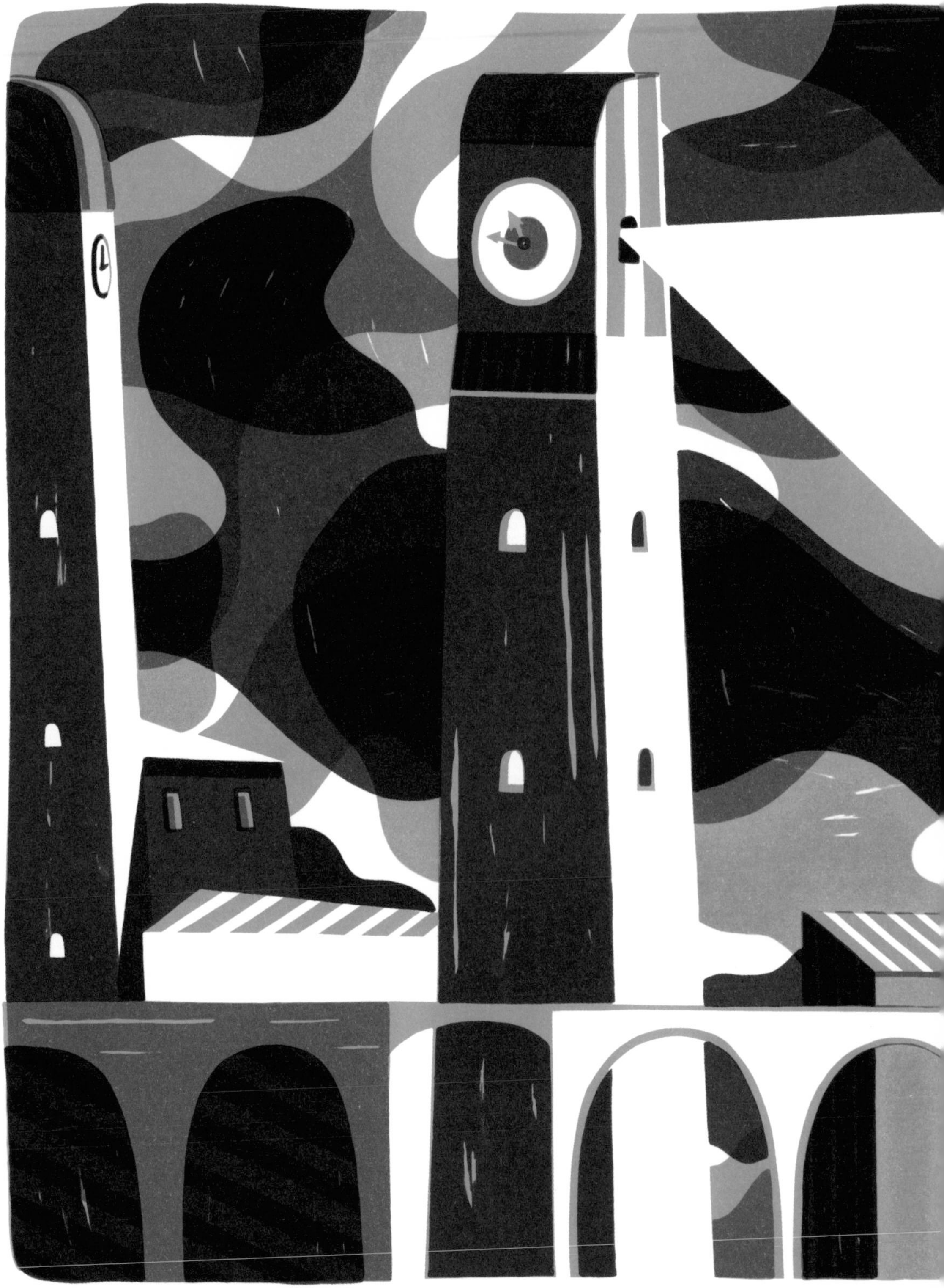

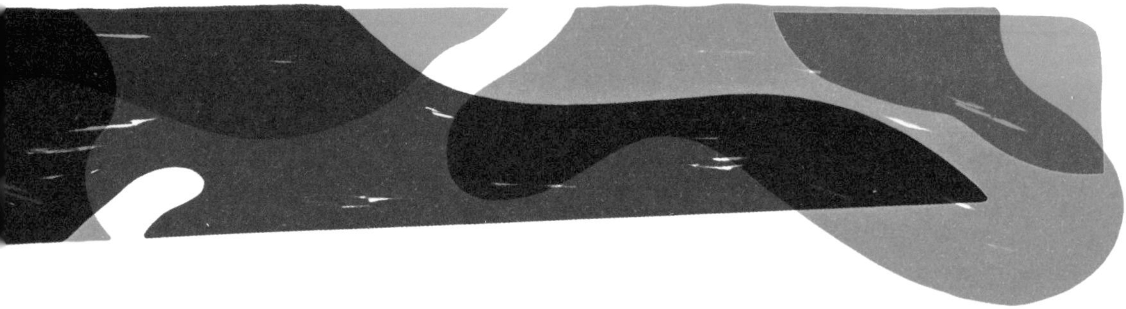

Whoever has disrupted the course of our dreams
shall be remorselessly pursued. No matter how swiftly he flees,
no matter where he hides, I shall hunt him down,
and light will reveal his face.

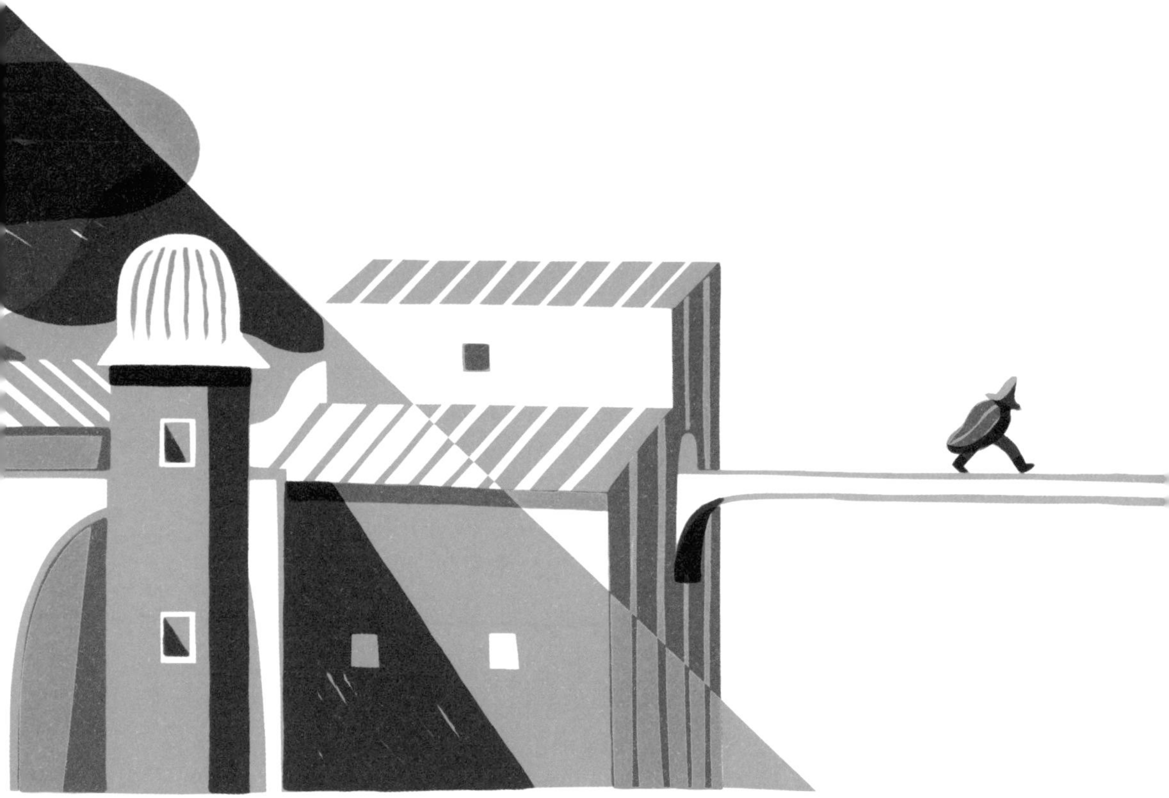

I descend again, and walk round the building searching for clues. I stumble. On the ground, clouds of little springs twinkle in the dark. They form streaks of light illuminating the labyrinth of the city.

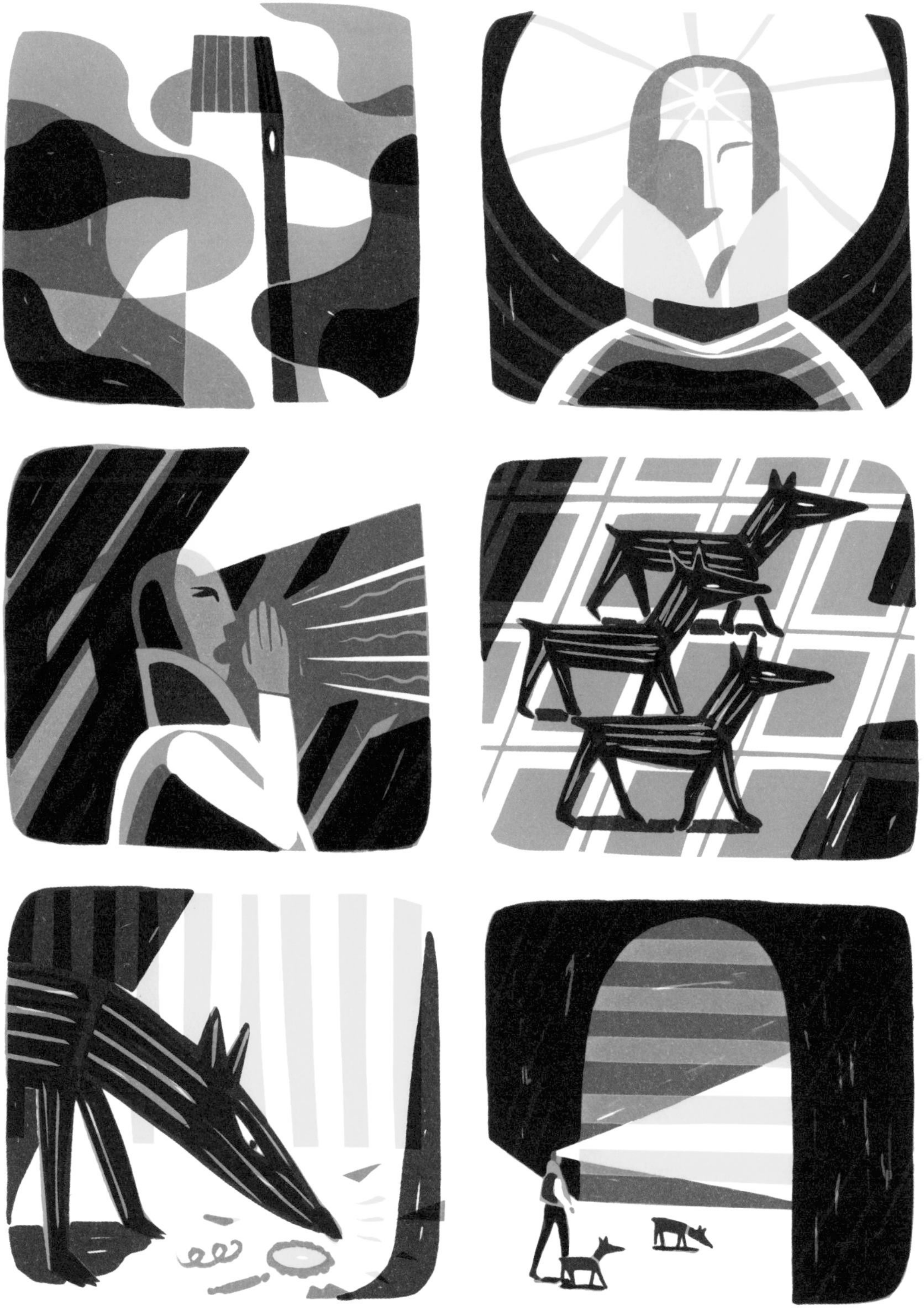

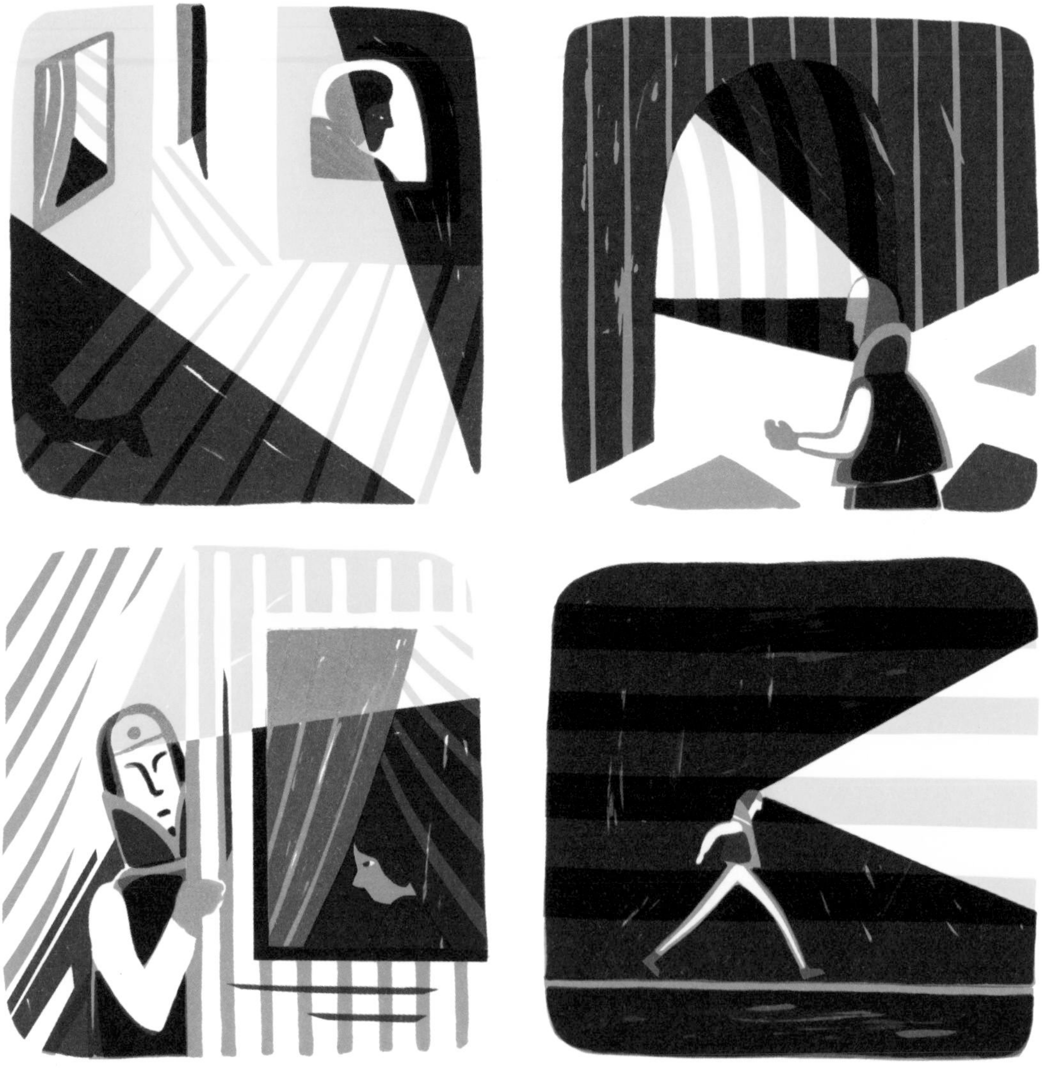

Feverishly I race along the shining trail
which splits into a thousand alleyways. Every crossroad,
every side street, every fork promises to deliver
my prey to his just deserts.

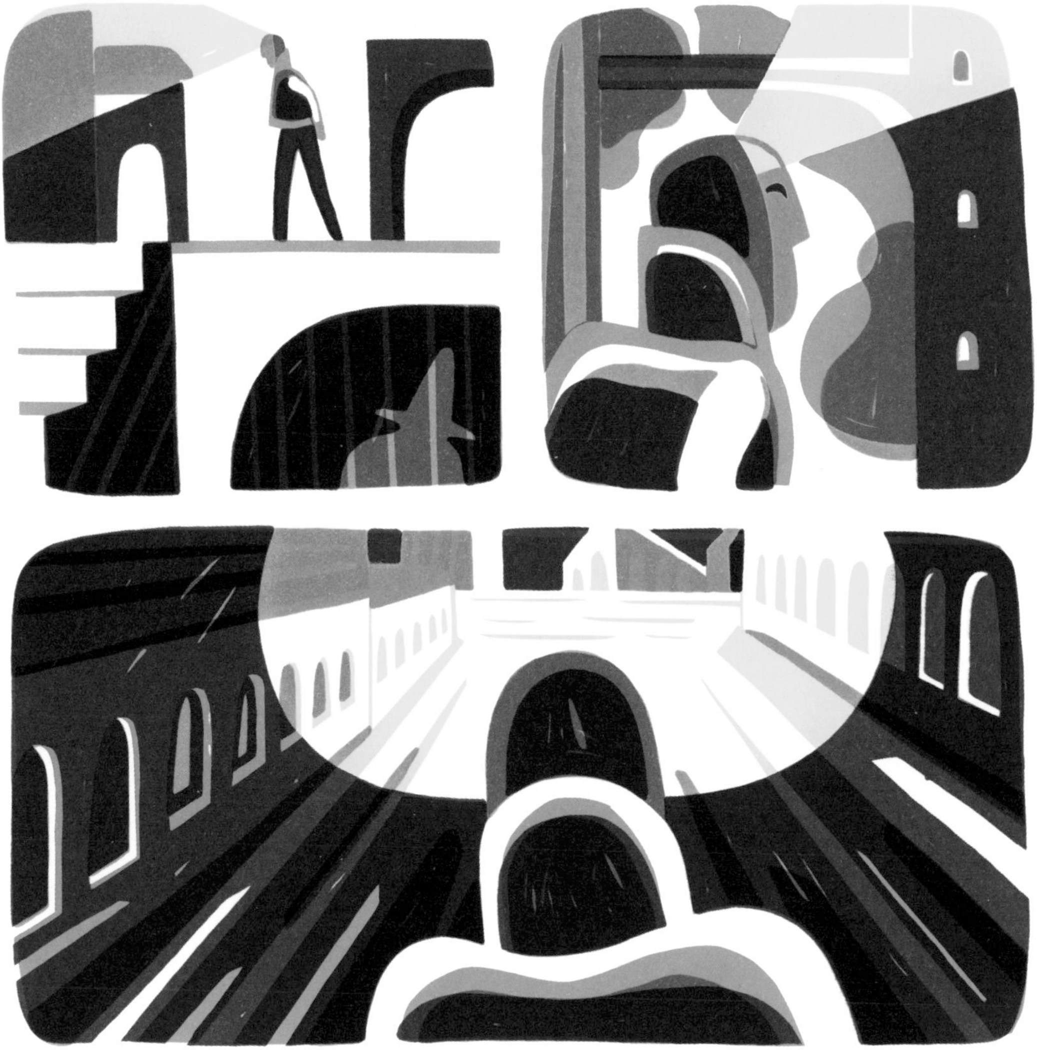

At last I think I can see something moving
in the half-light at the end of an alleyway.

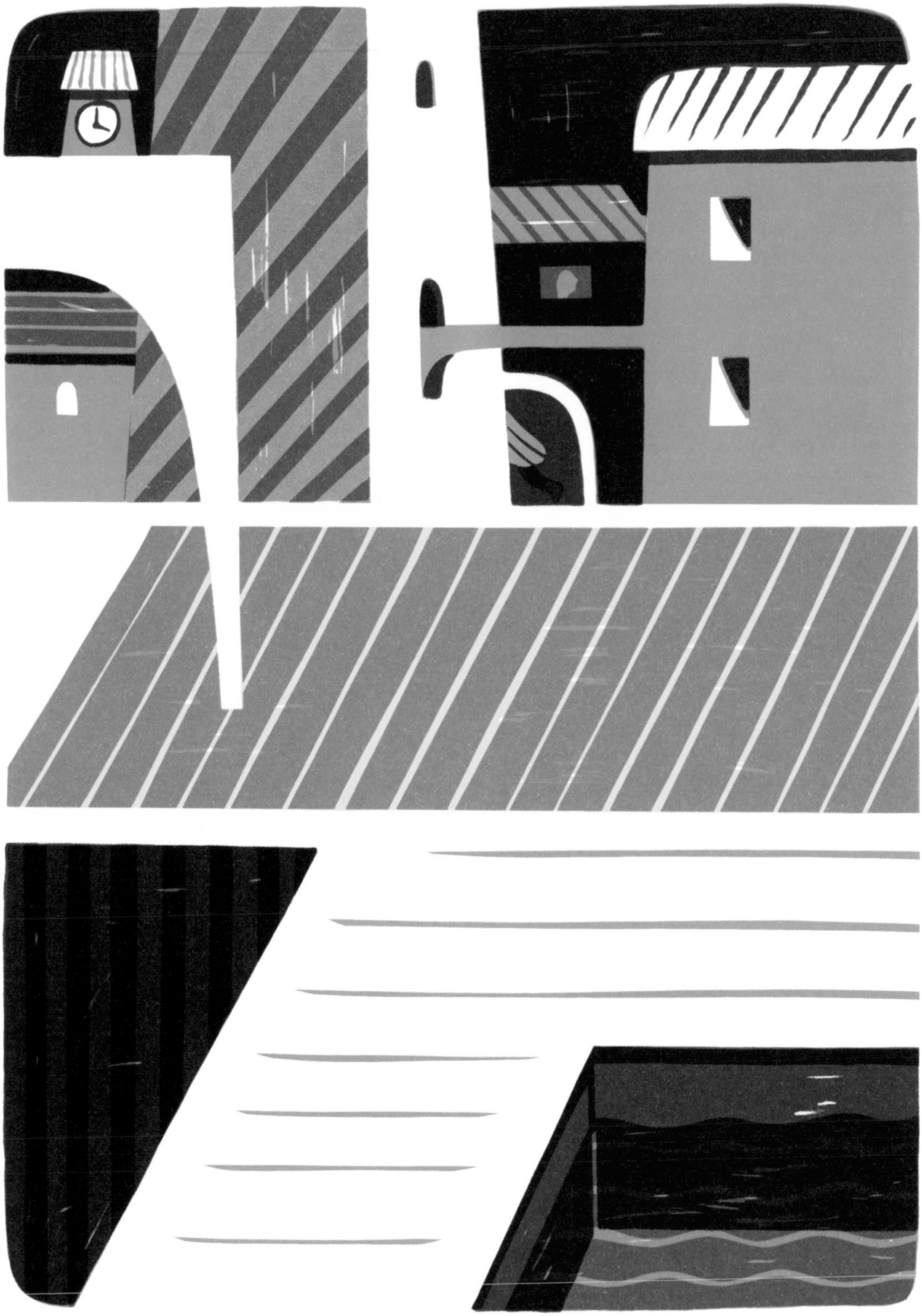

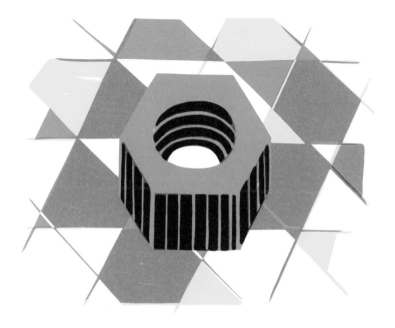

I emerge into a large square. Everything is still and peaceful. No tracks on the ground. The trail stops here. Then suddenly, in the vast silence of the night, comes a clear, light tinkling sound—a nut bouncing on the cobblestones. The metal shines out from across the square. I approach, bend down, and pick it up. It is a piece from the clock. Behind me, once more, the same metallic sound.

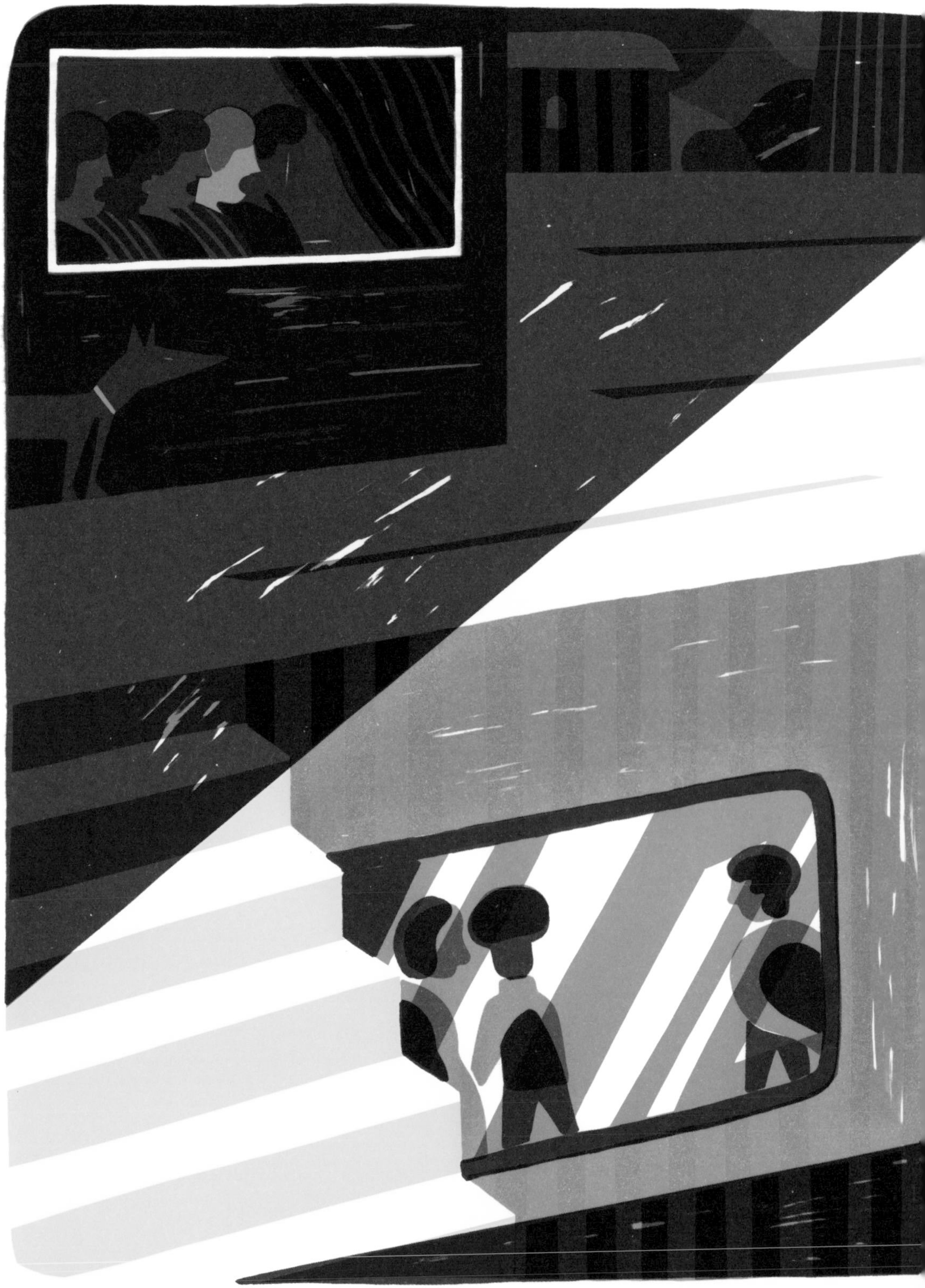

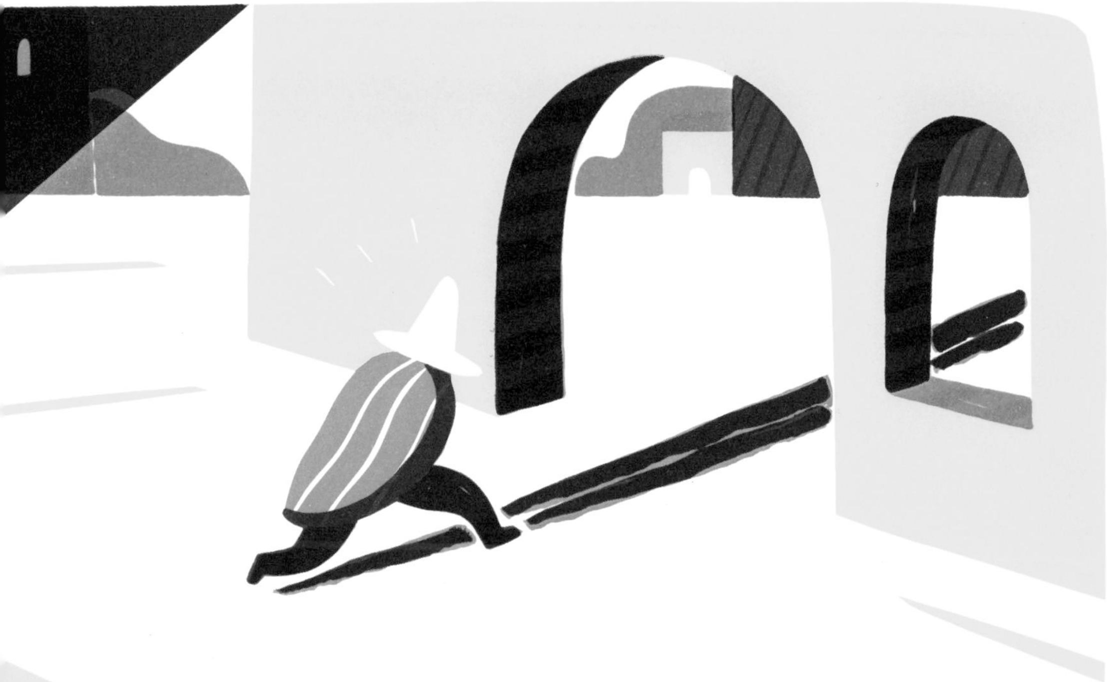

*"Stop! You are under arrest!"*

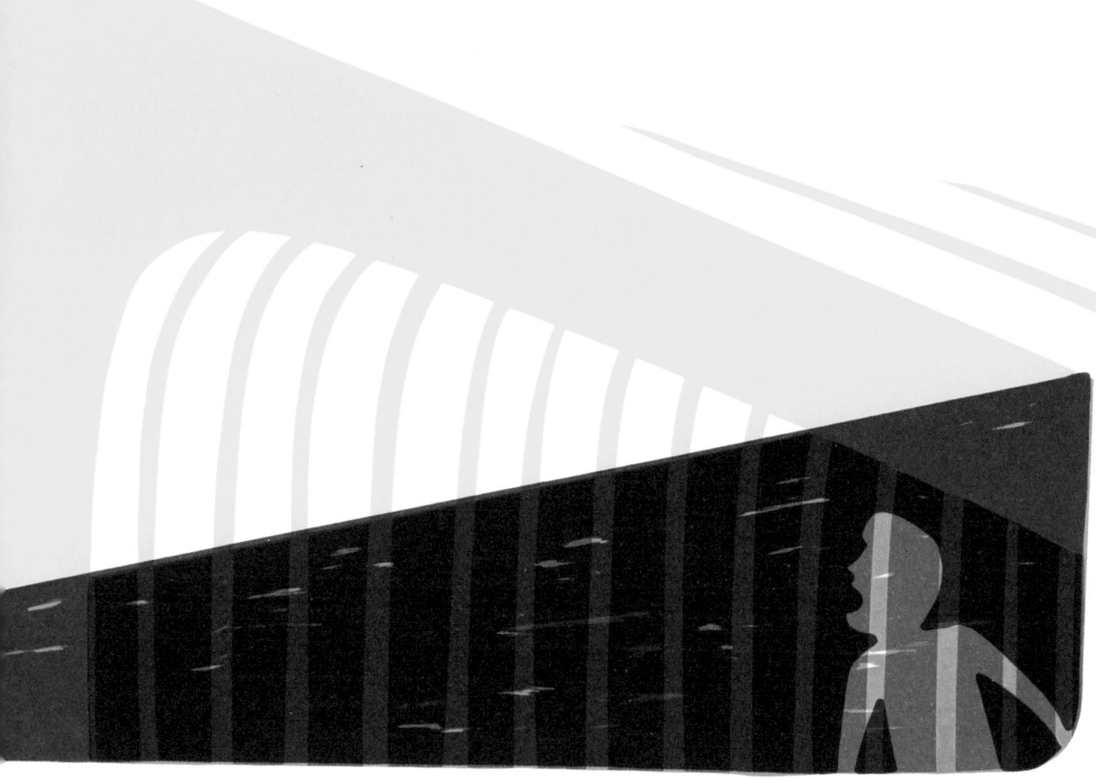

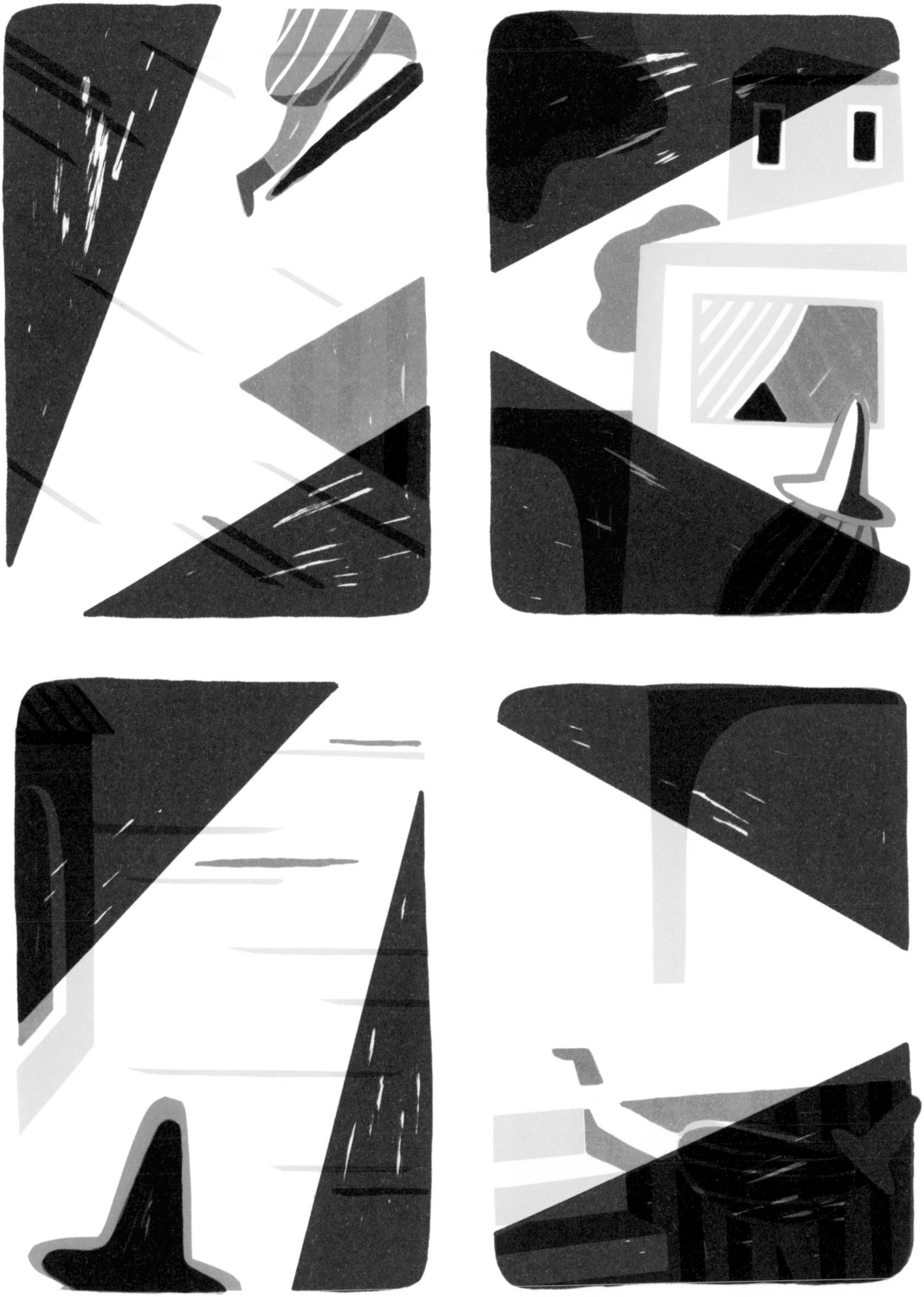

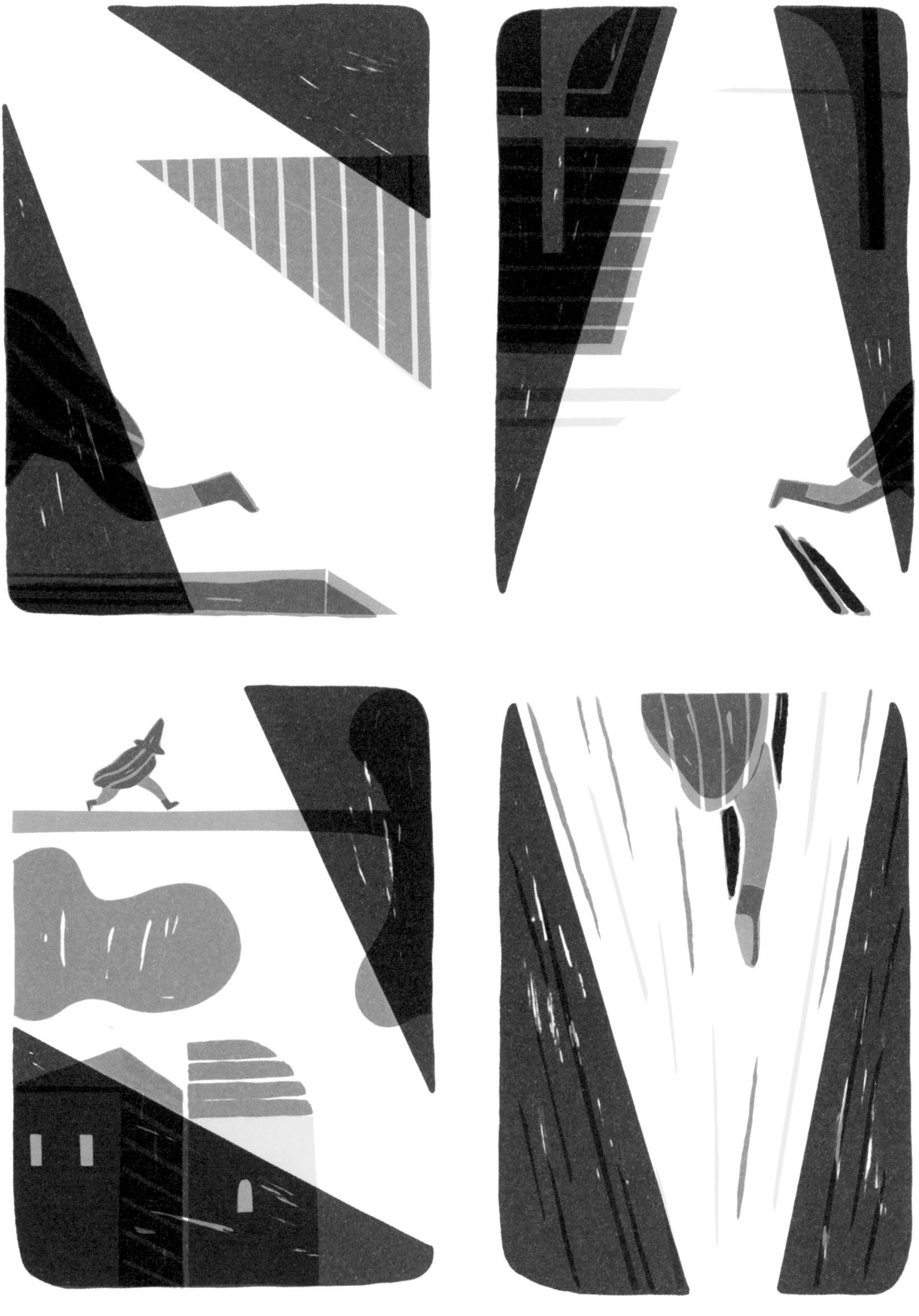

He hurries onto the bridge.
He is limping, and behind him
he scatters a trail of tiny wheels
that tinkle as they fall.

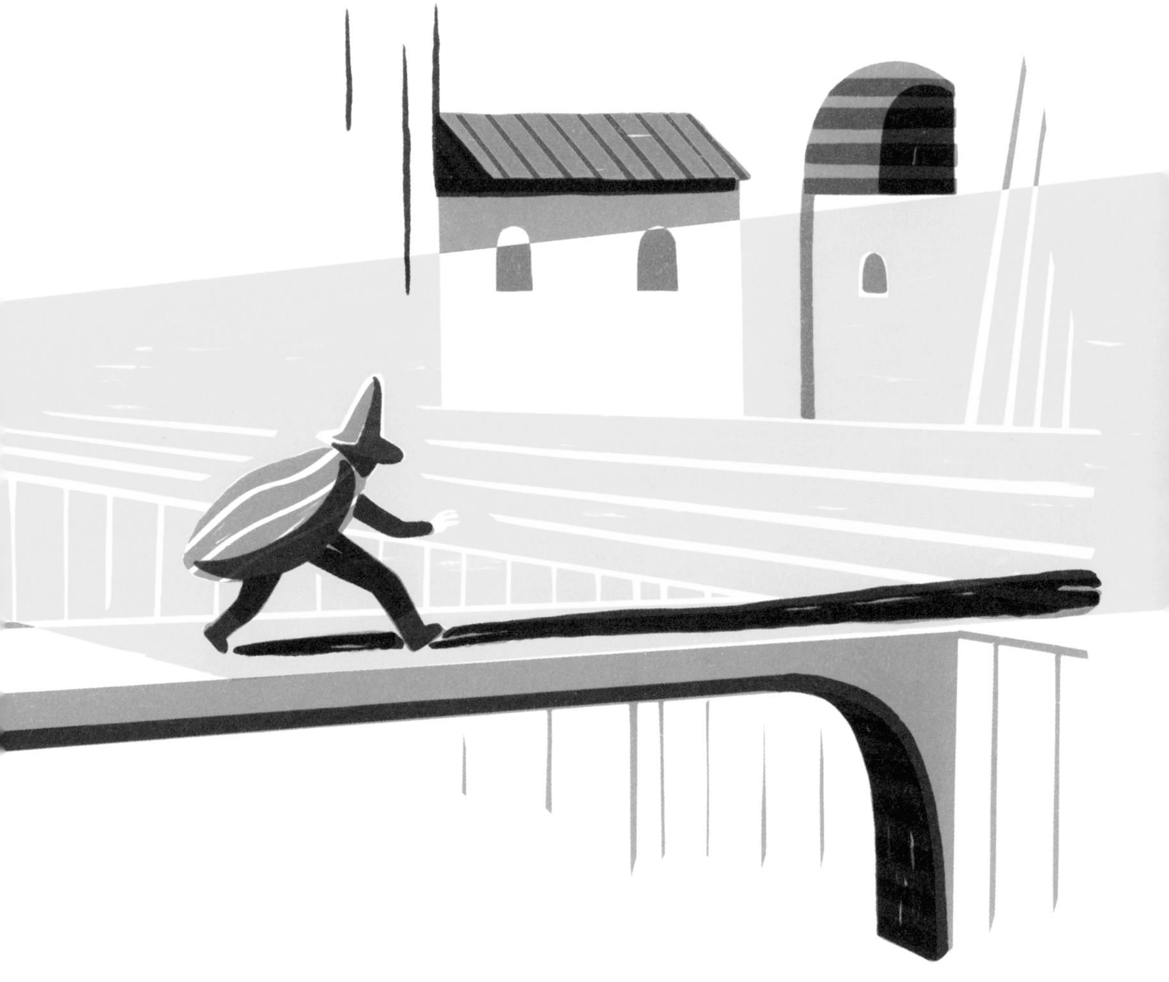

I seize hold of him.
He cannot escape.
I am on him.

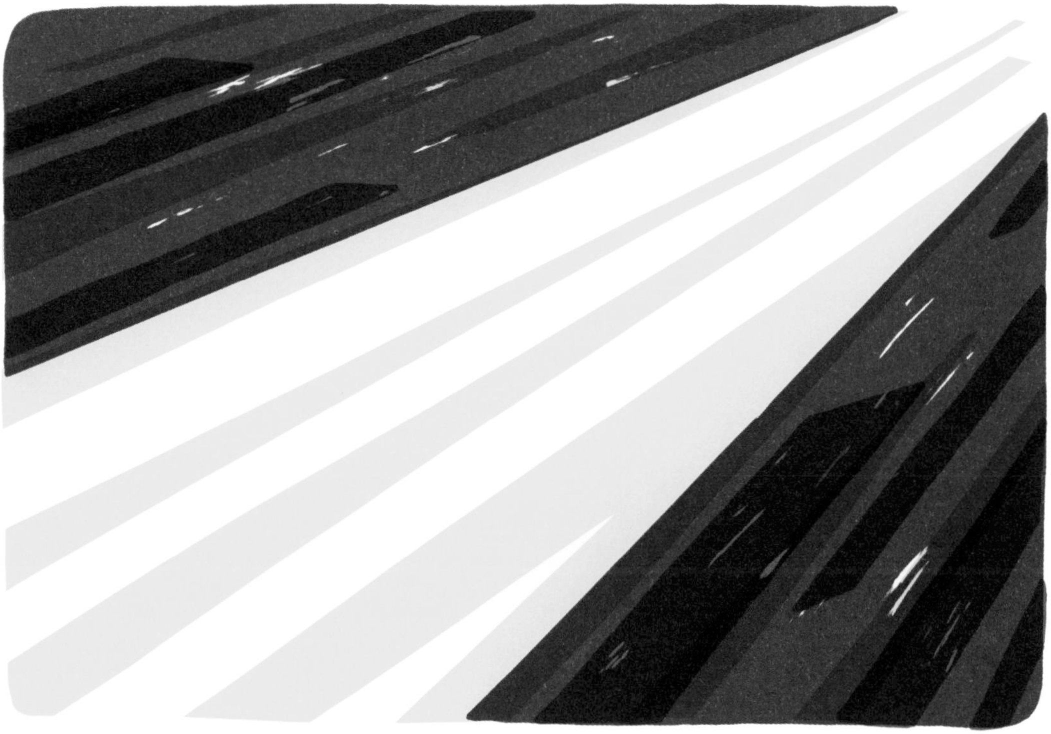
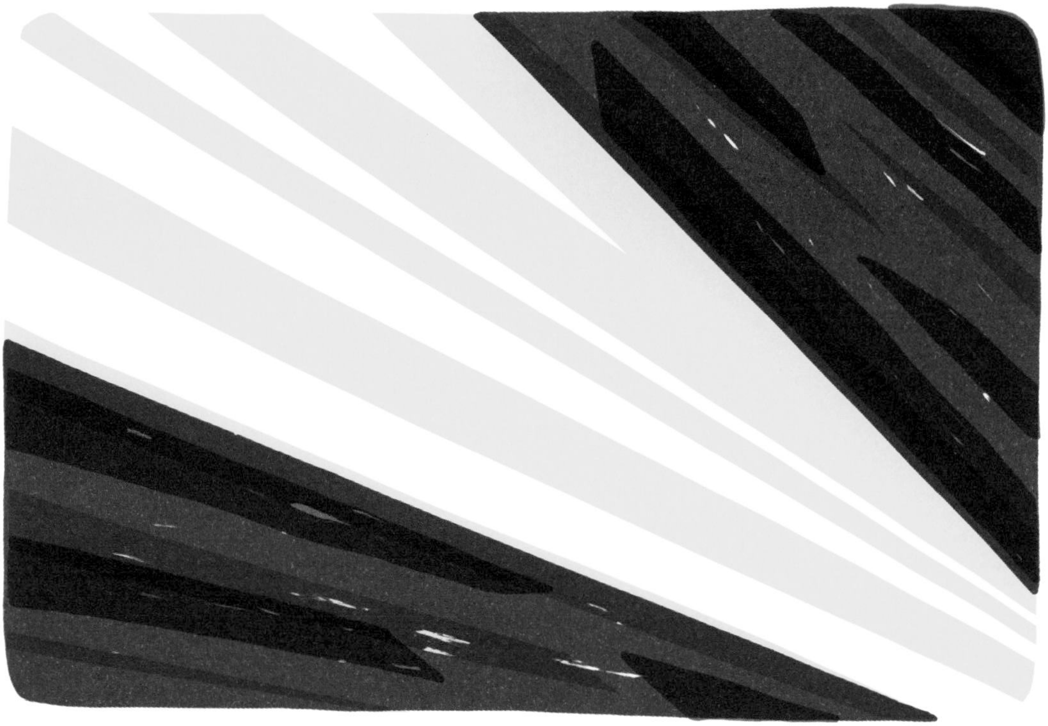

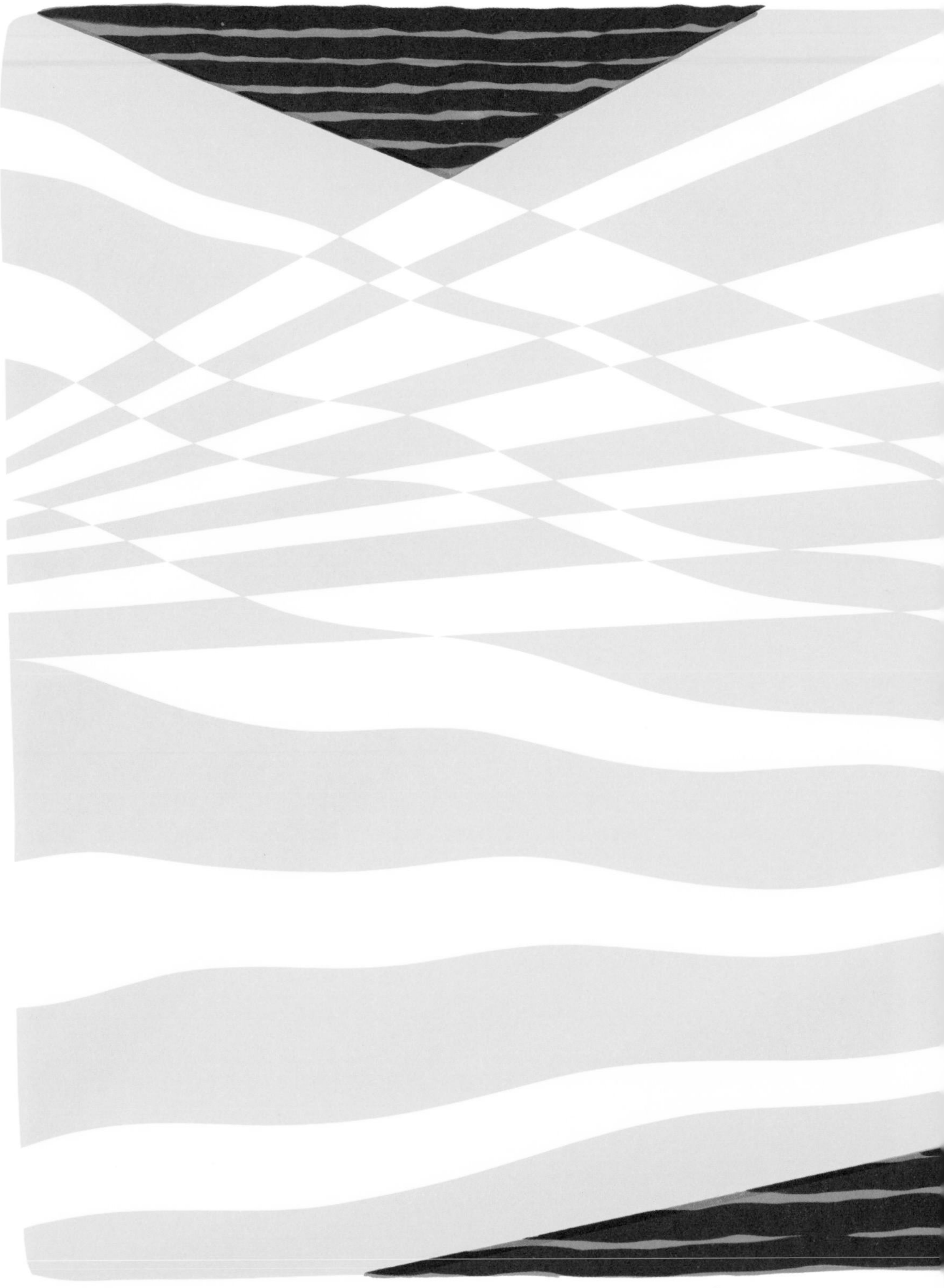

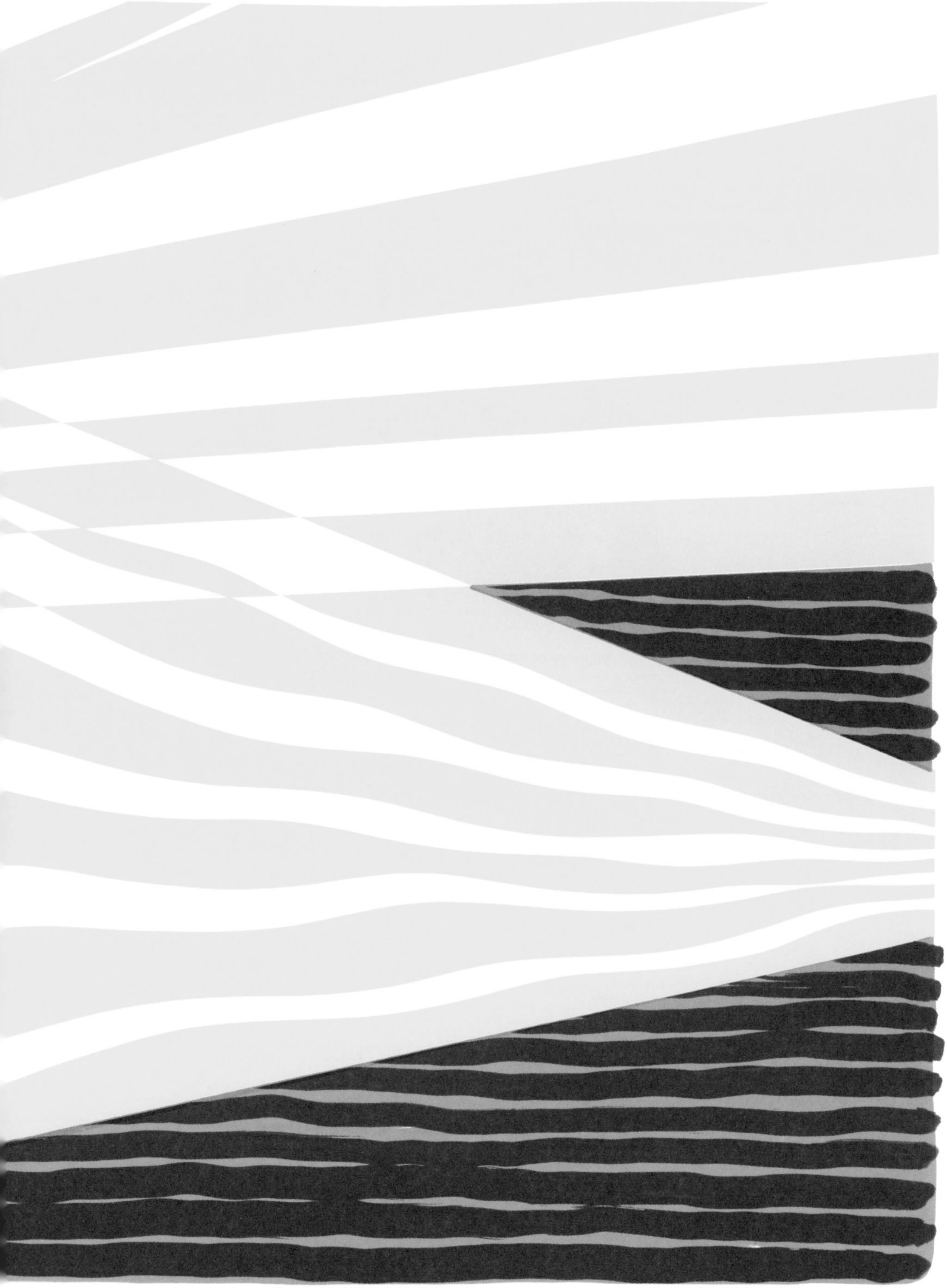

I fell. I can hear the noise of his footsteps in flight. They grow fainter. He is getting away. I am losing him. What happened? I had hold of him, gripping his shoulder in the vice of my hand; I was about to uncover his face, but then ...a dazzling beam of light blinded me. By the time I am able to make out the shapes of the buildings again, the Vagabond has disappeared. On the ground there is nothing to be seen—no springs, no nuts and bolts, no wheels.

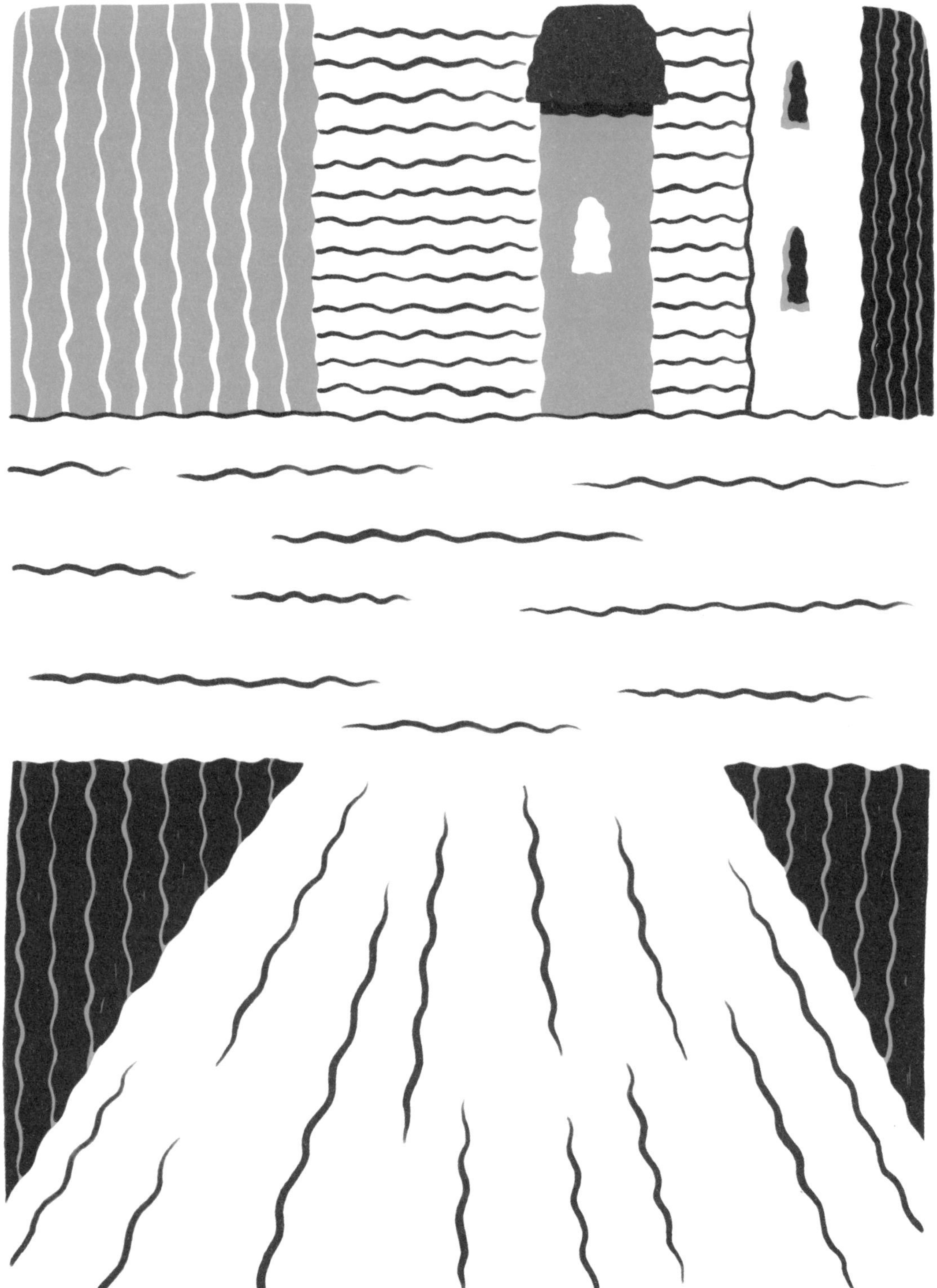

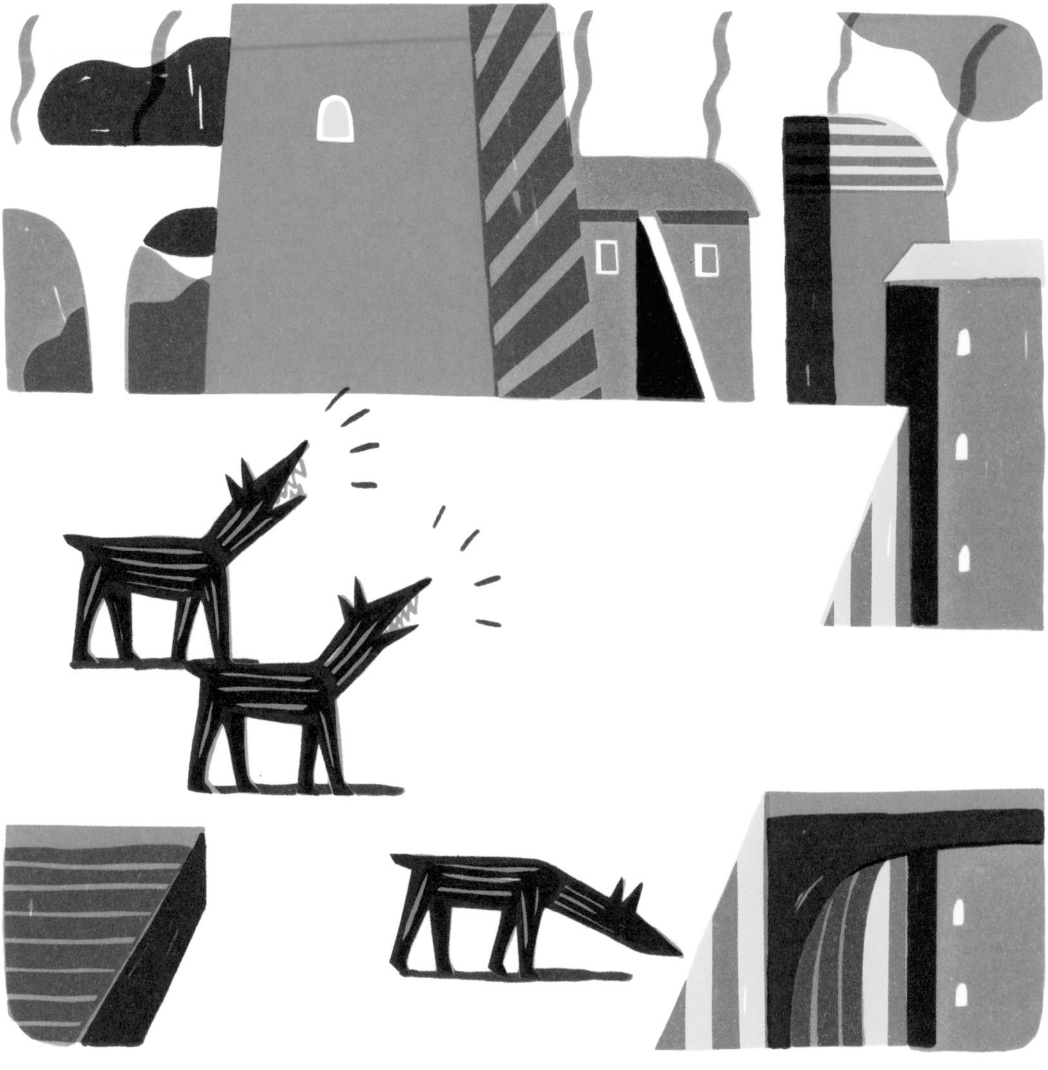

I have allowed my quarry to escape.
It's no use trying to pursue the fading echoes of his flight. There are no tracks for me to follow.
The winding lanes have swallowed him up. He has vanished into the night and left not a trace.

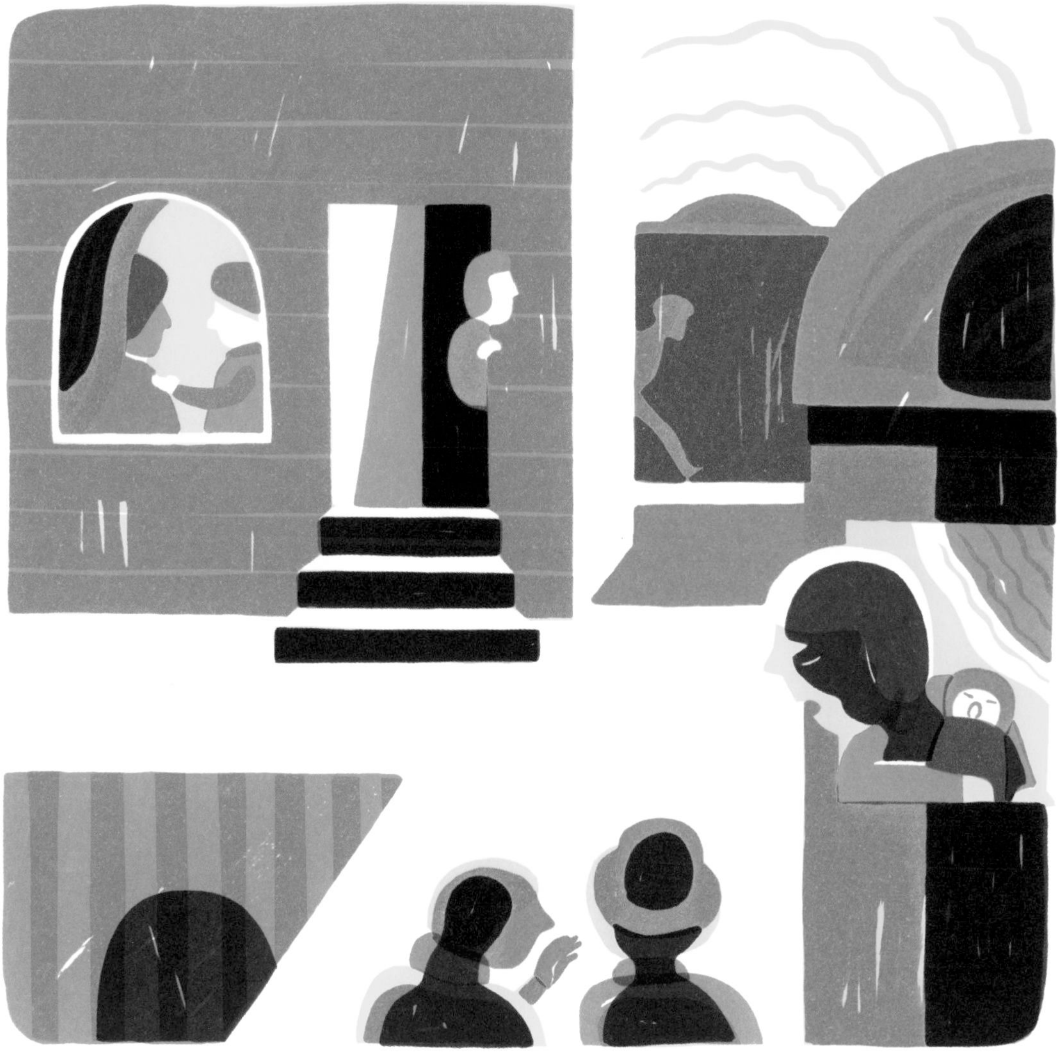

The shadows are lightening. Dawn approaches. Already I can hear the agitated murmurings of the city. I shall wait to take my revenge, tomorrow night.

It is time to go home. The morning light
spreads across the sky. The day has come,
accompanied by its star.

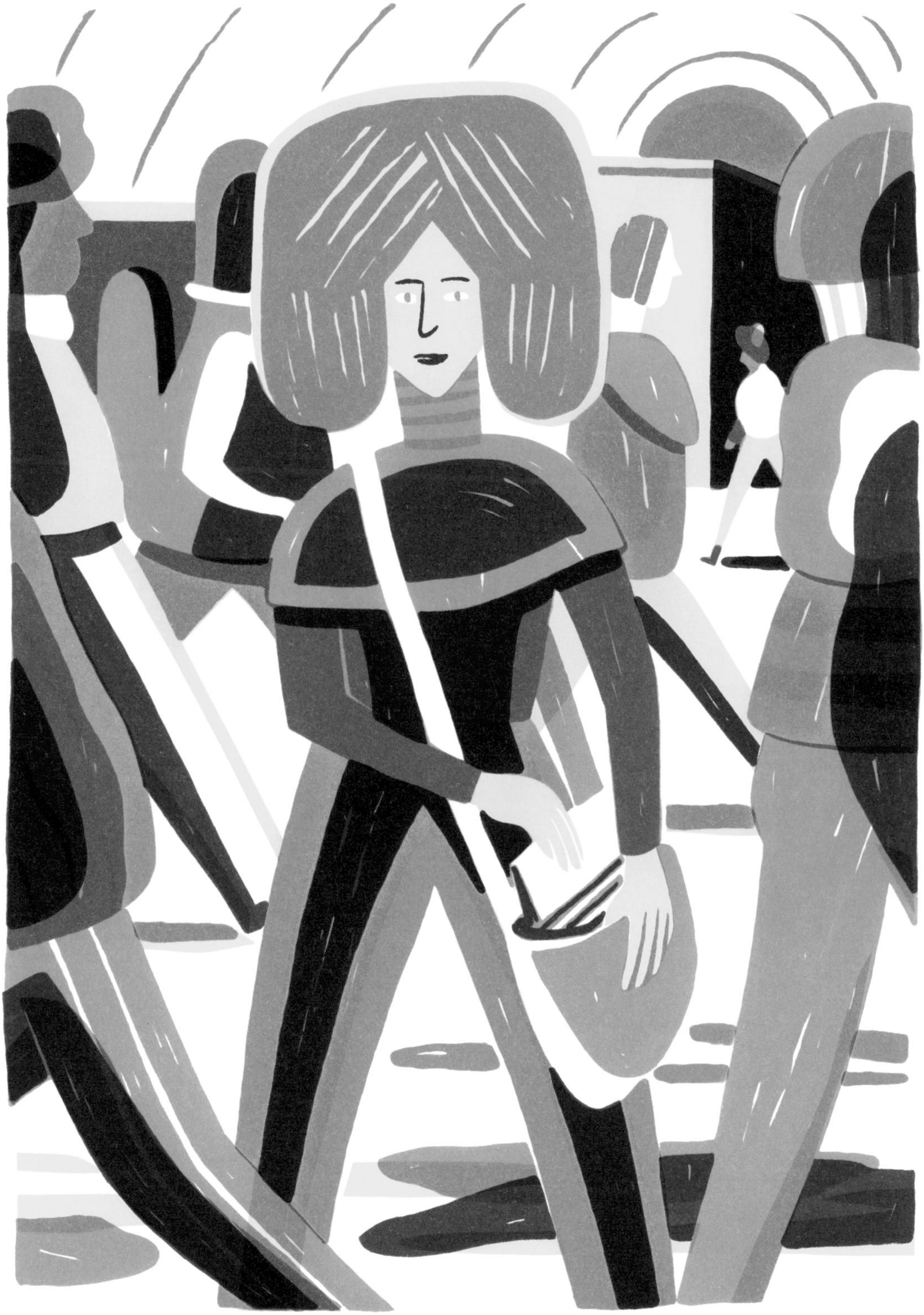

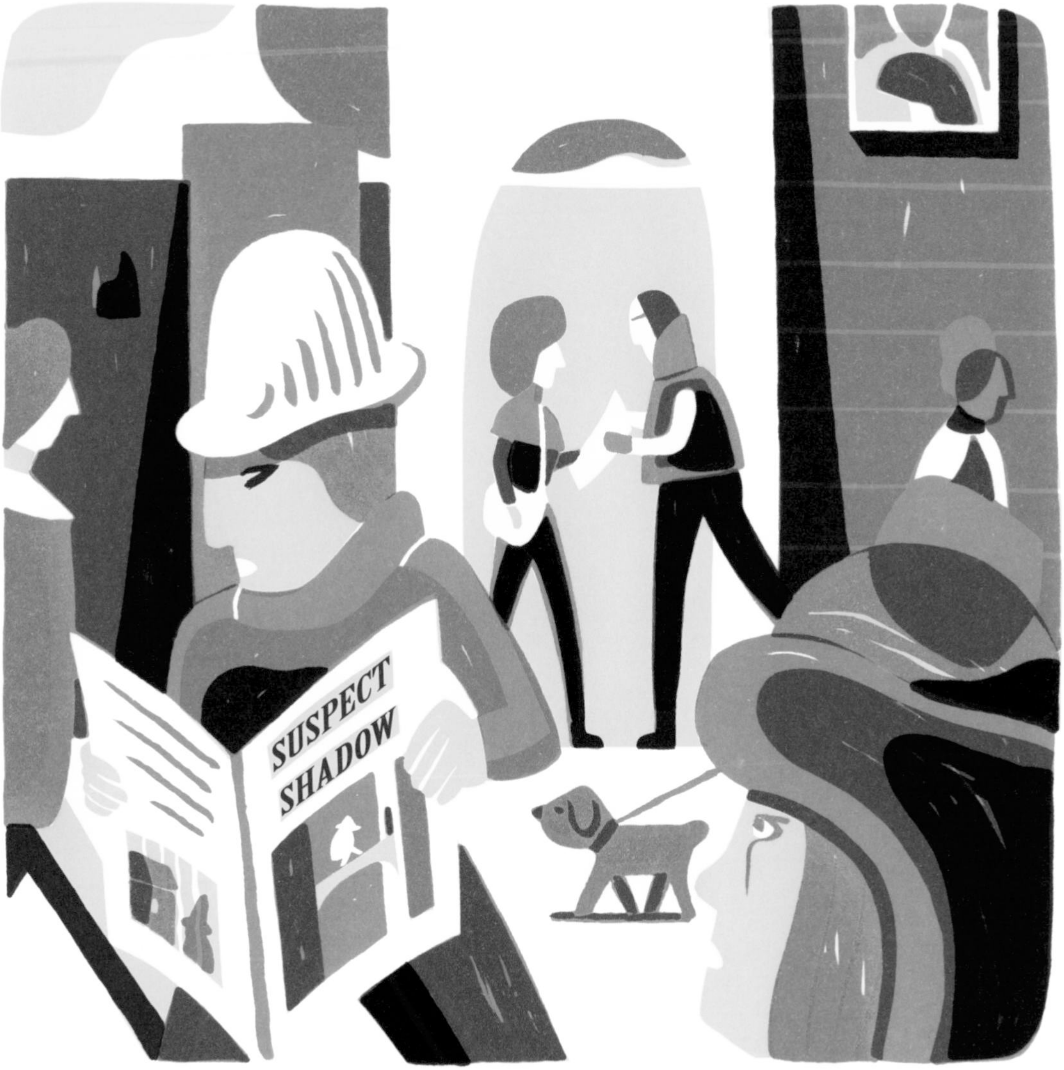
SUSPECT
SHADOW

I buy my newspaper, as I do every morning, from the beautiful Vendor. She has always been there, in the middle of this square. I venture to look into her eyes for the very first time. They shine on me with an enchanting glow. I take some of their warmth with me, to stop at source the churnings of my nightmares.

Third Night

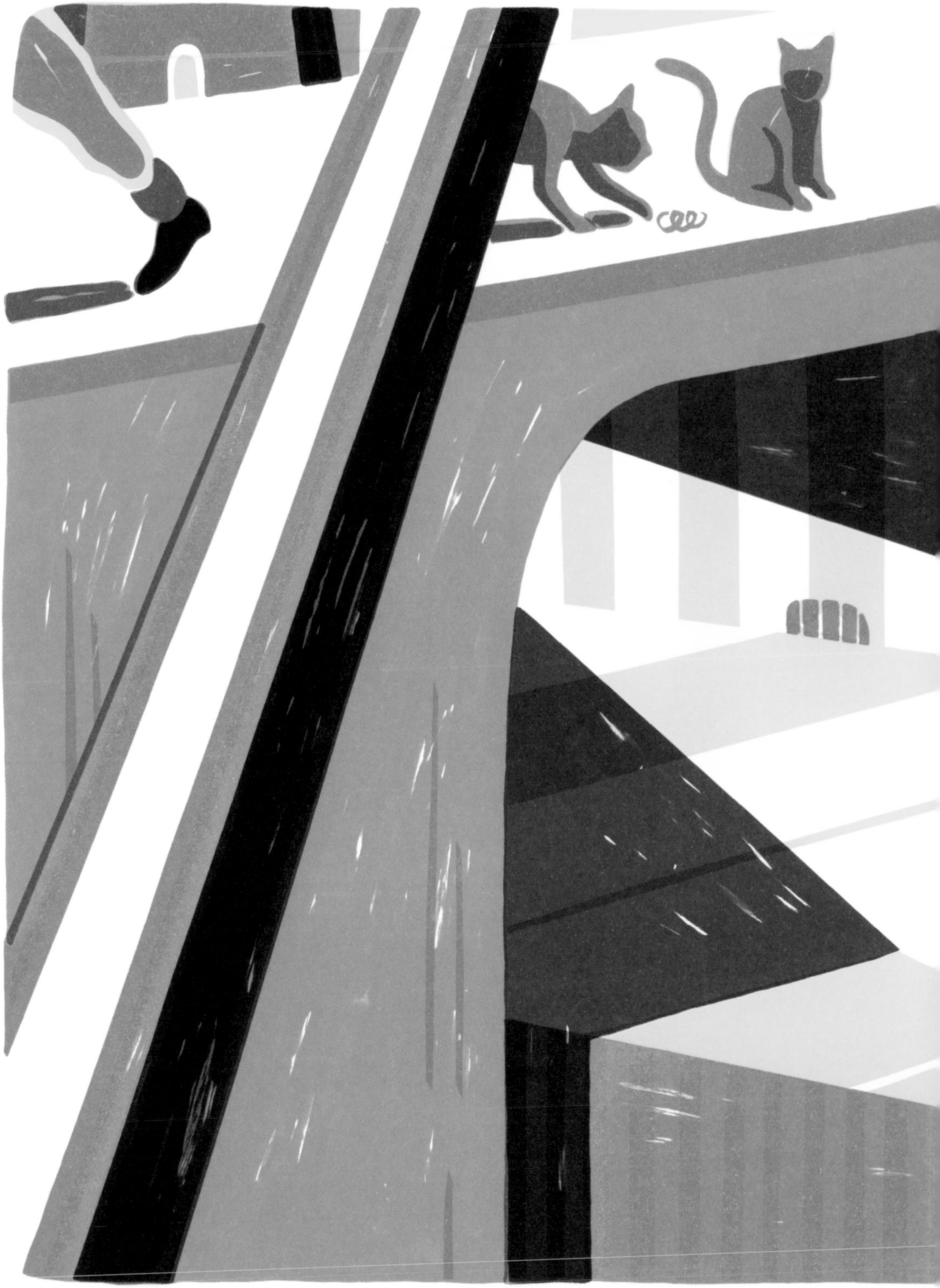

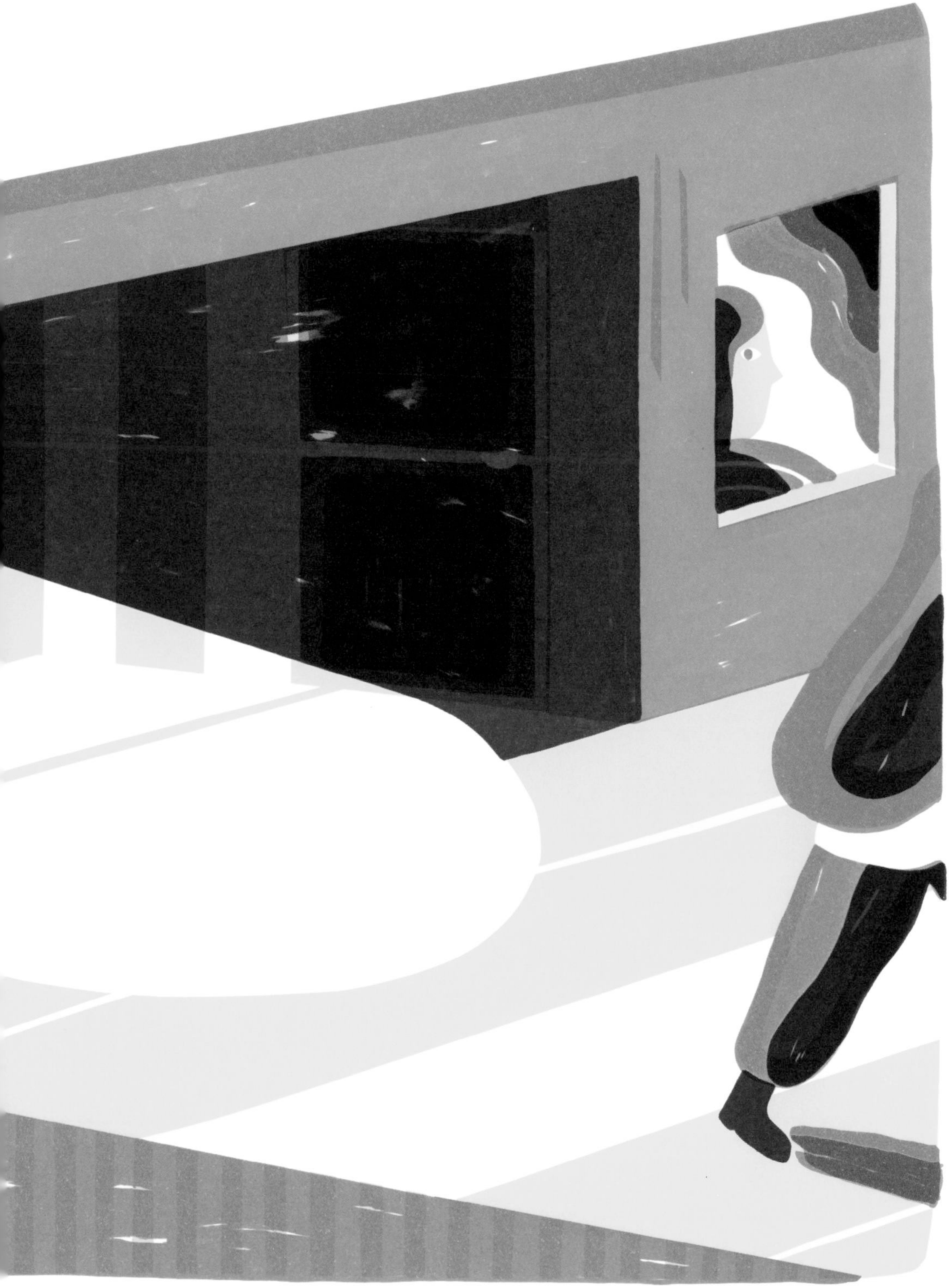

I have been on the lookout since nightfall.

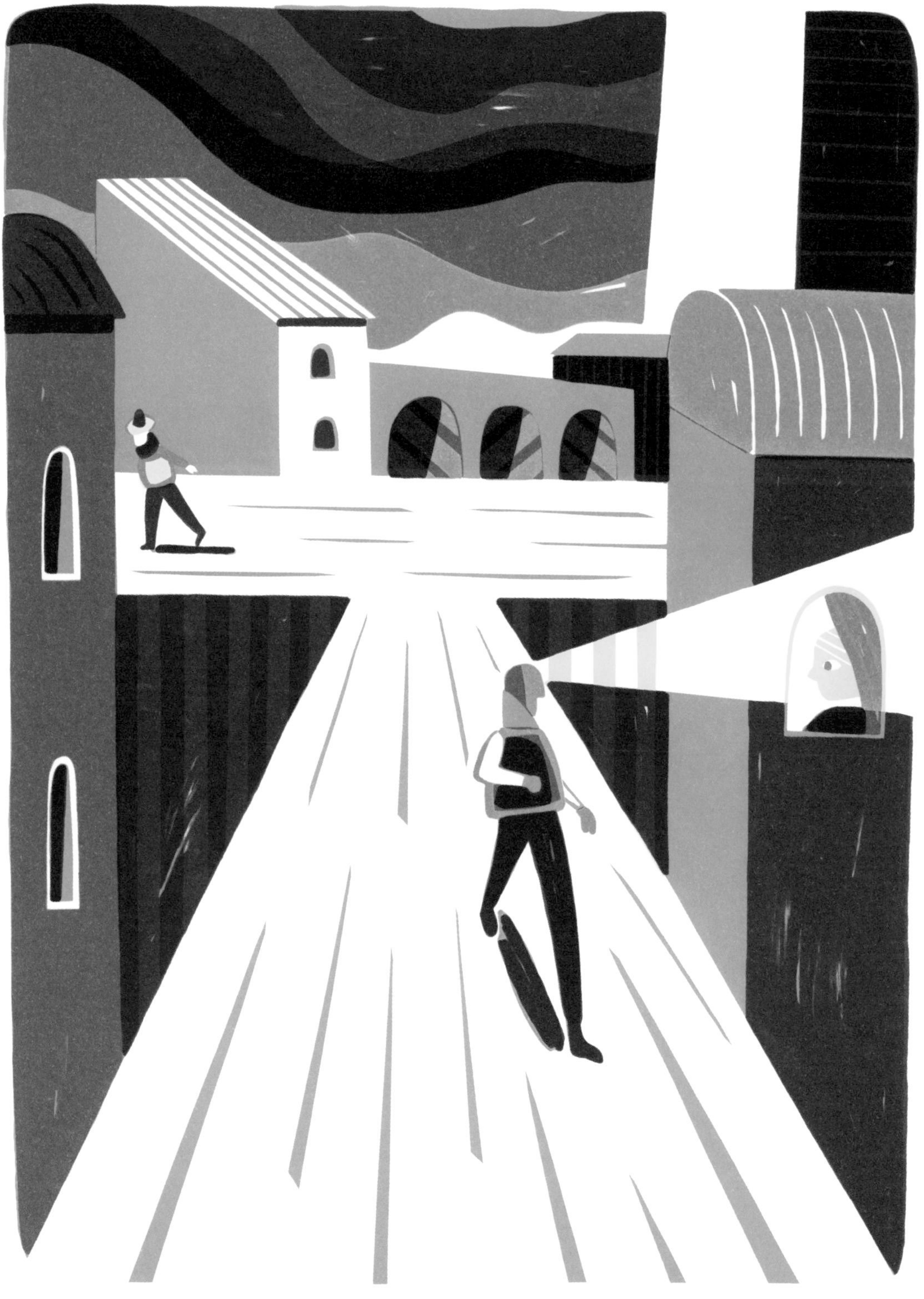

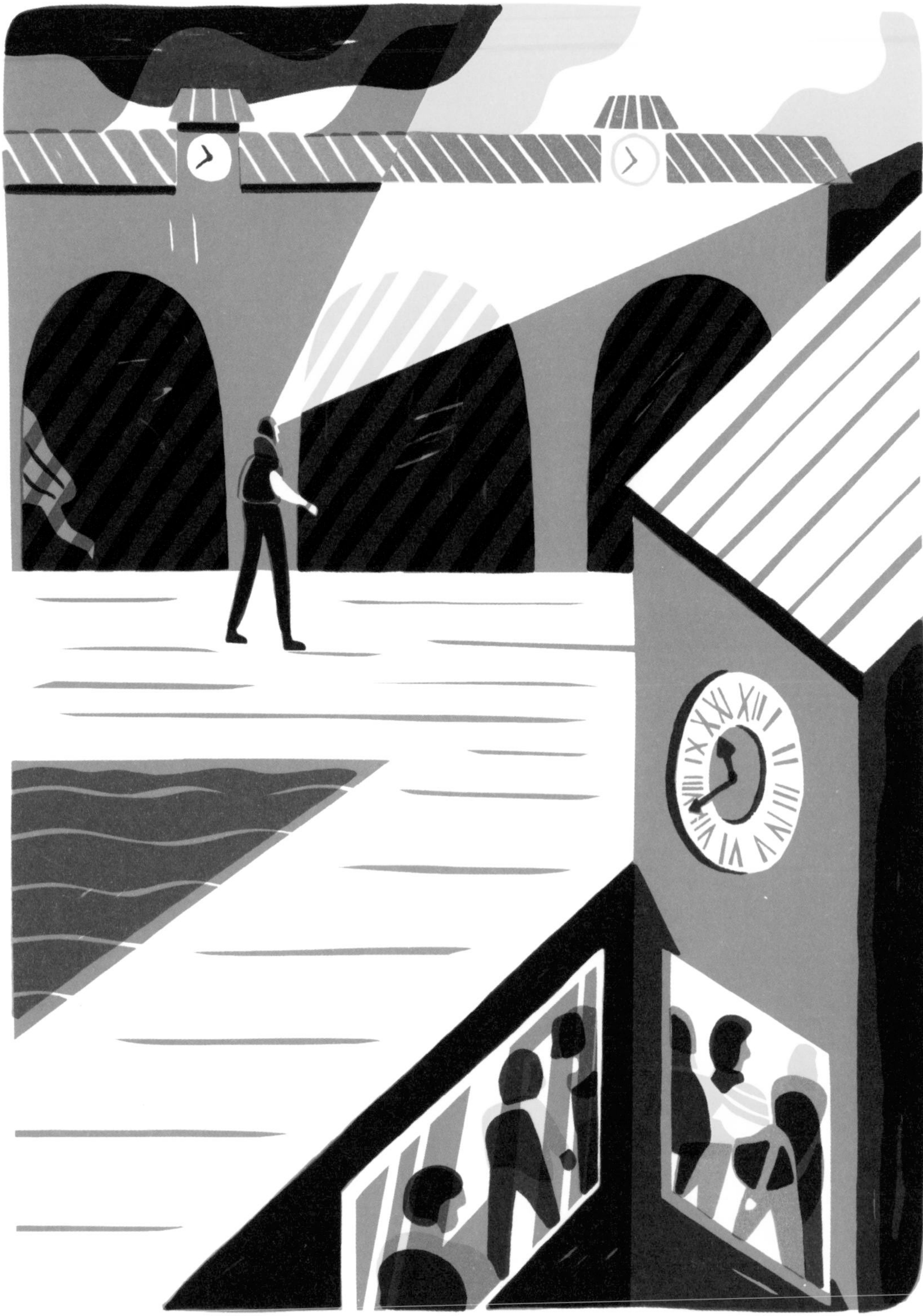

I observe the slightest hesitation,
the slightest ripple in the incessant
surge of the city.

At last, the deafening silence.
The ever onward movement of the wheels
has been stopped.

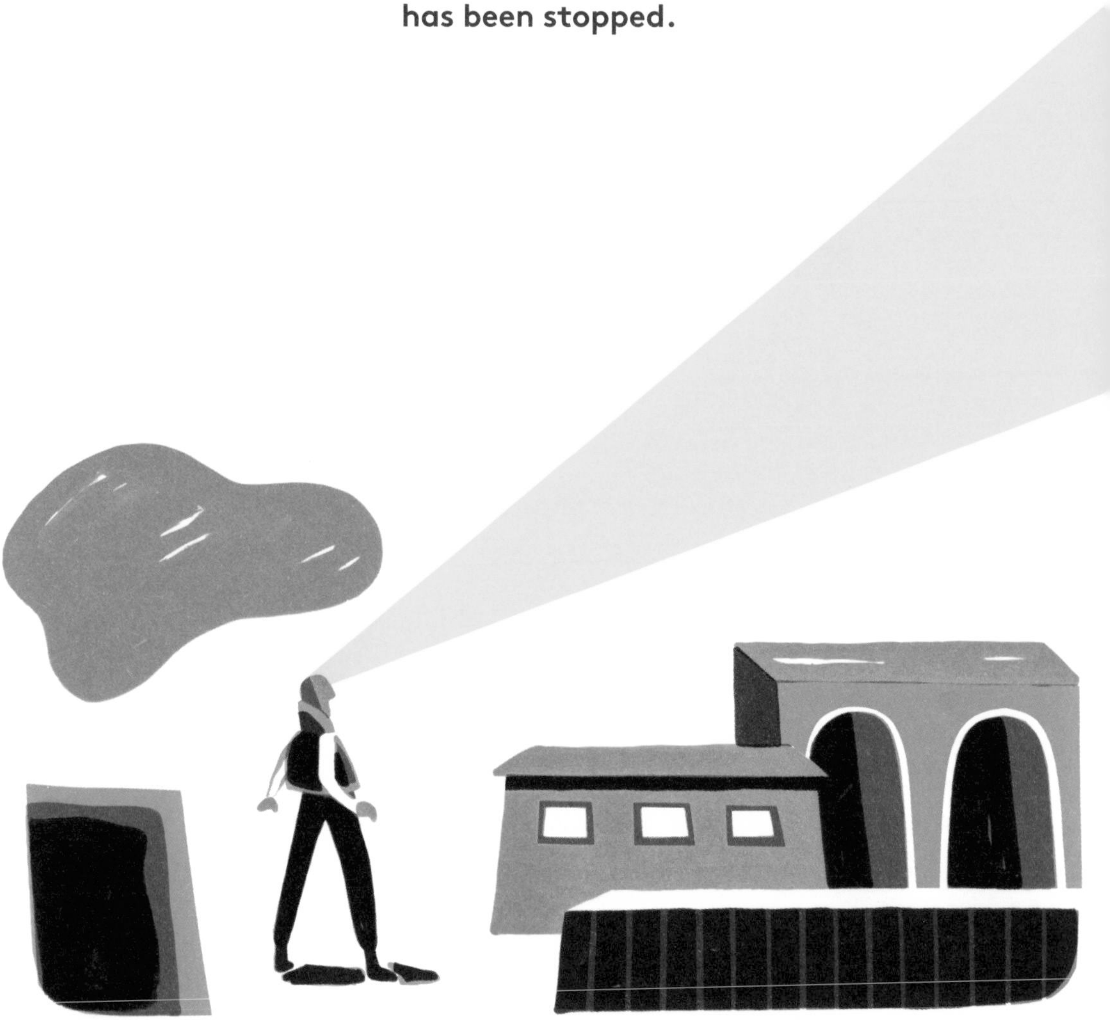

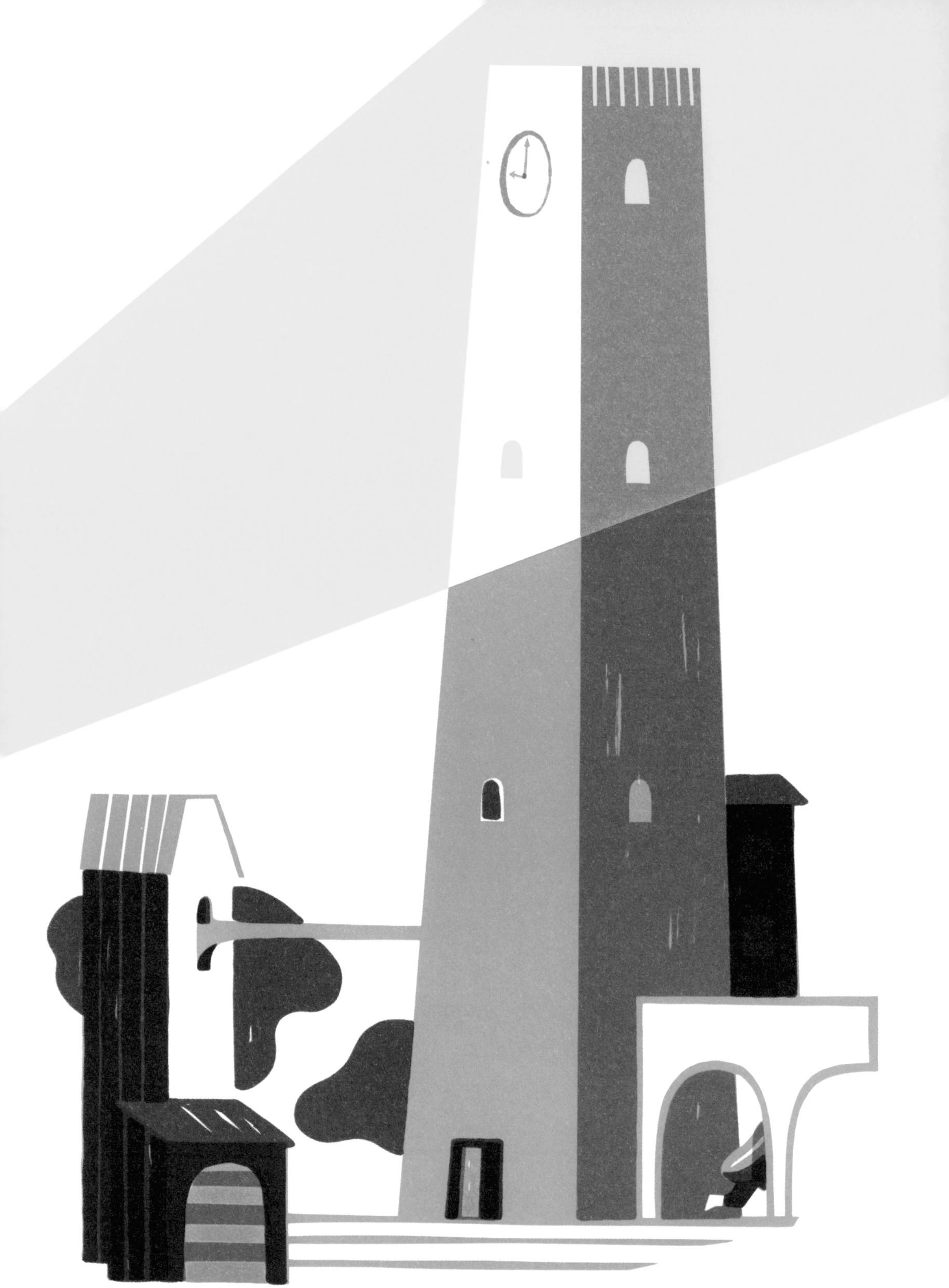

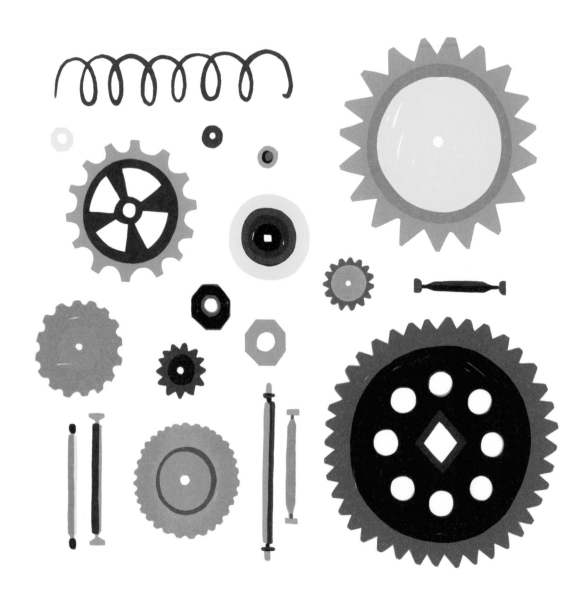

I approach, dipping my lamp.
The Western Clock Tower has been sabotaged,
just like its twin yesterday. The Vagabond has passed
this way, once more spreading behind him
a cloud of sparkling scrap metal.

I turn off my lamp. Under cover of night
I shall be a shadow among shadows.
He will not see me coming.

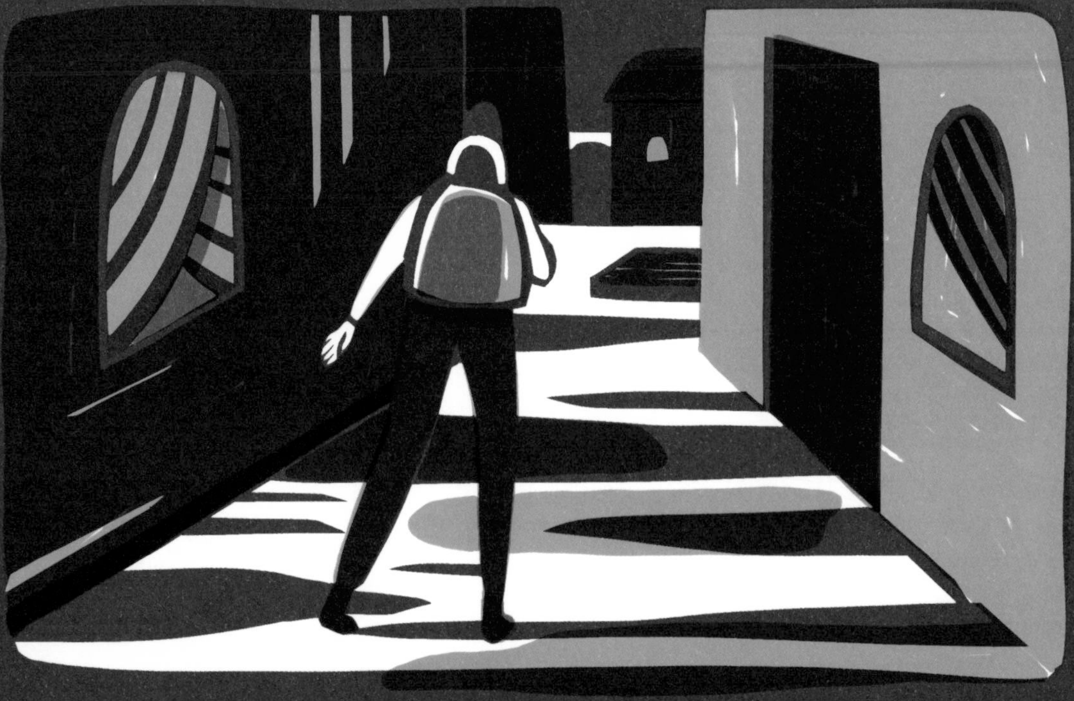

I set out on the chase. Noiselessly I glide from alley to alley, following the path he has traced towards his own destruction.

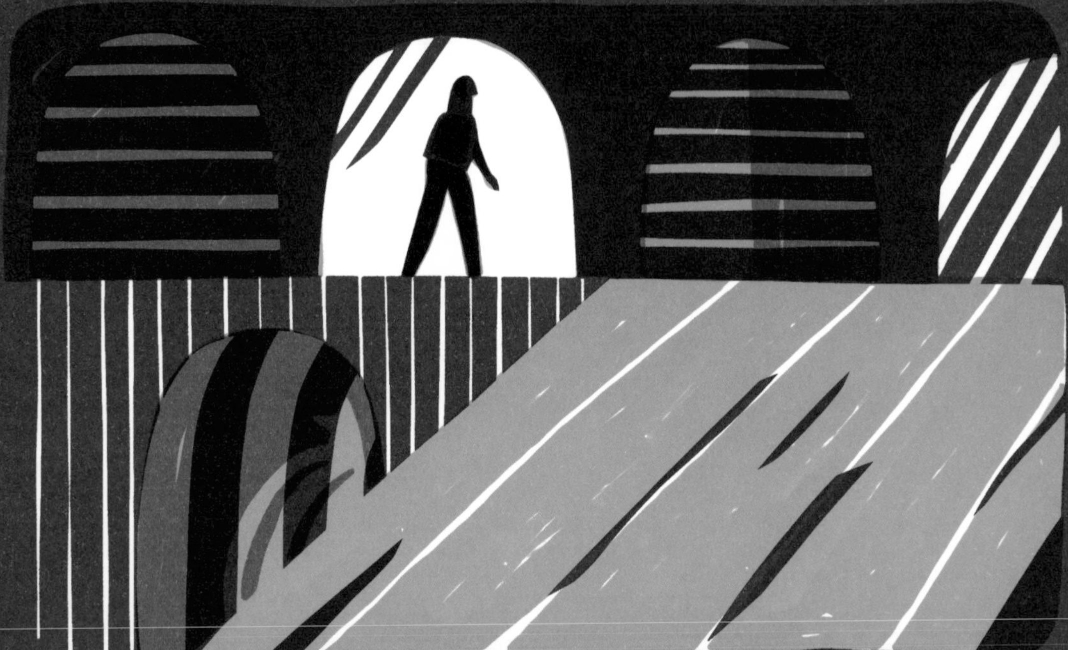

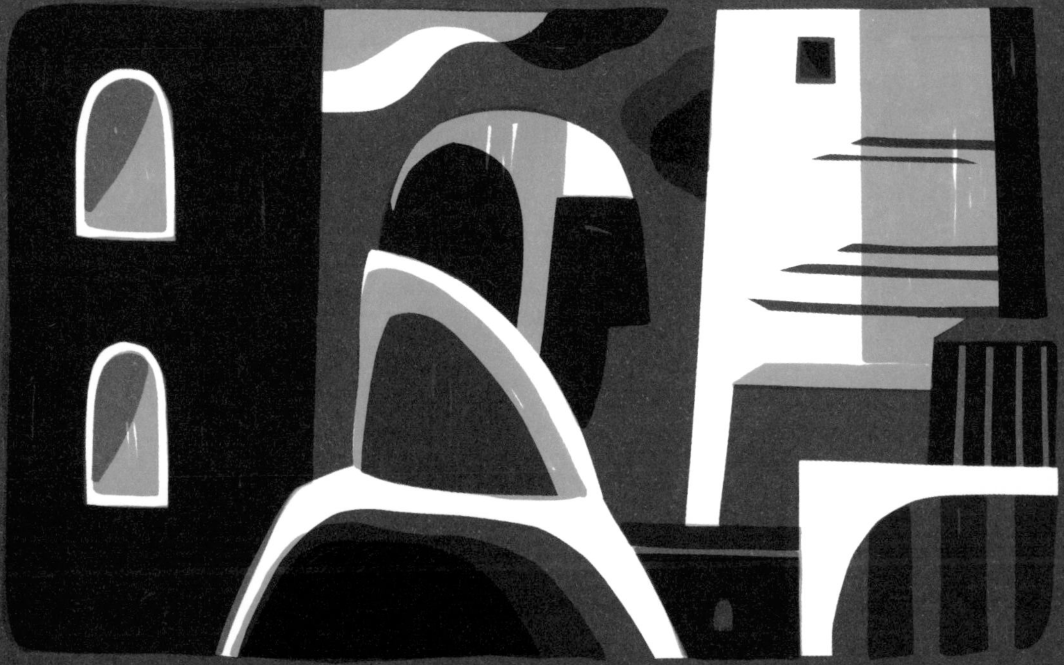

Already I can hear the sound of his panting. He must be very close, enjoying the fruits of his crime, hiding in the darkness.

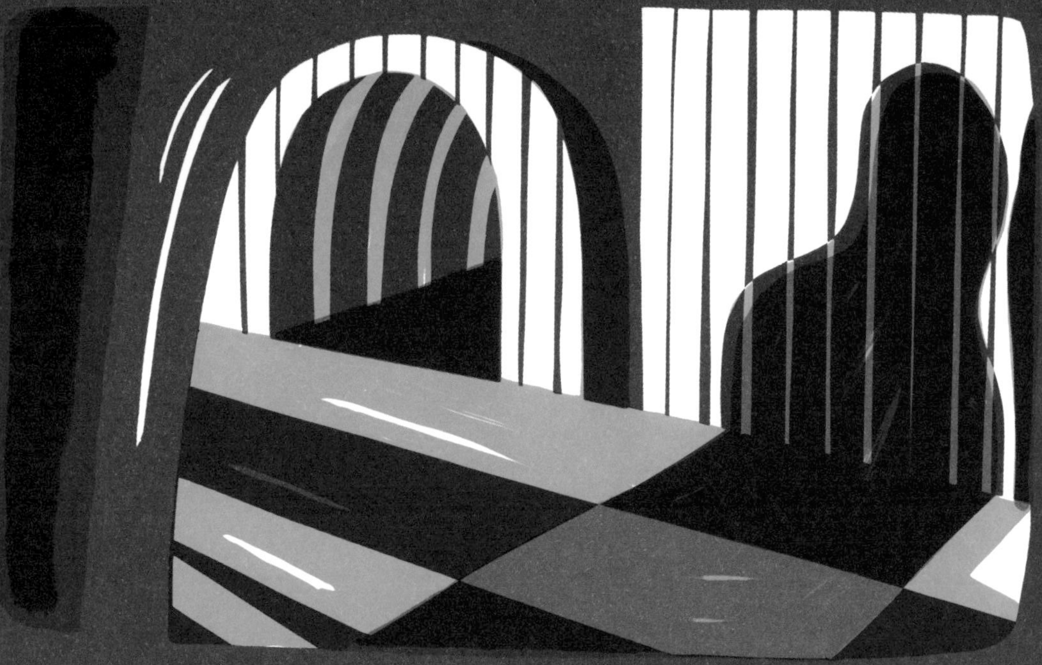

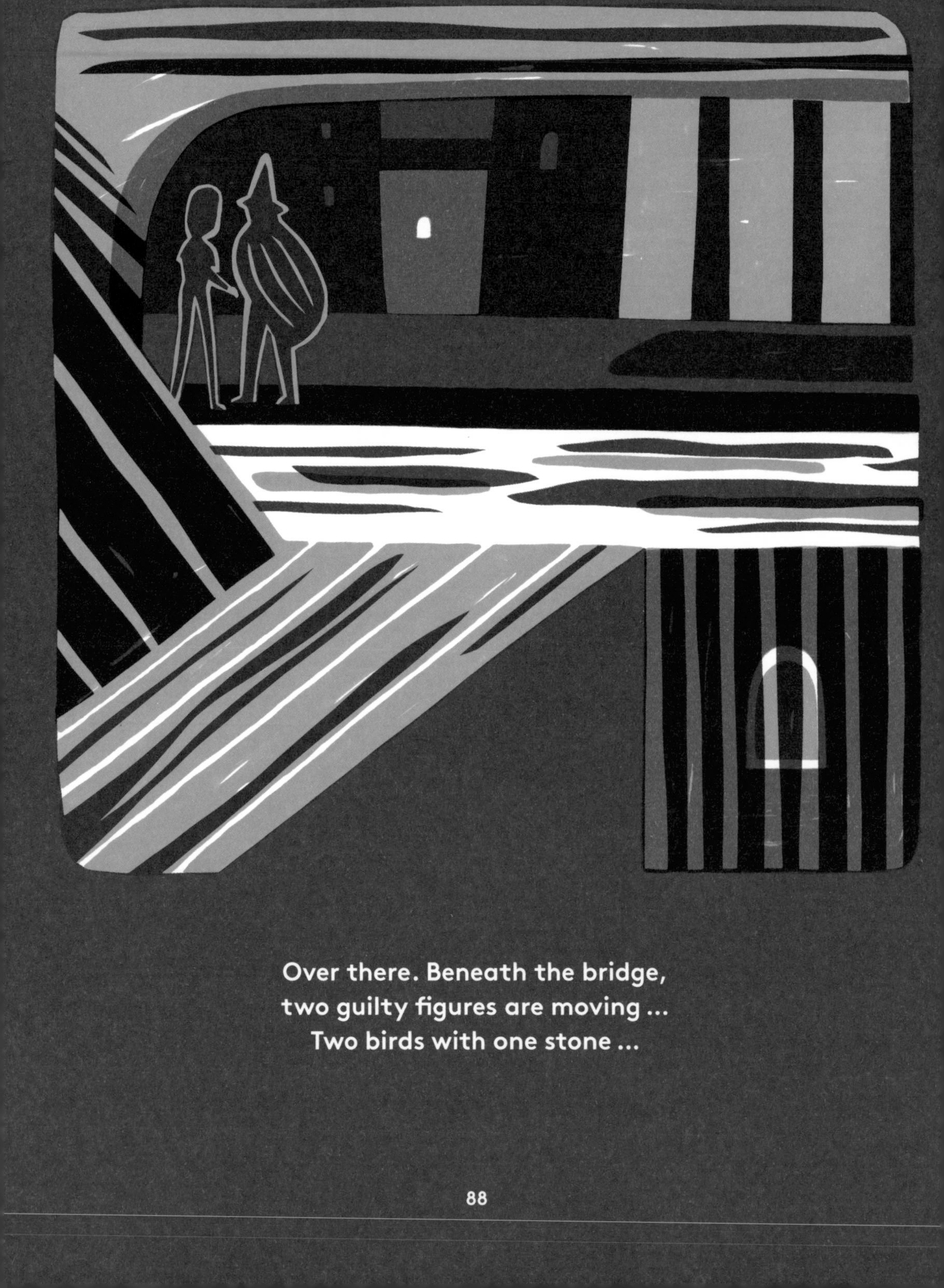

Over there. Beneath the bridge,
two guilty figures are moving ...
Two birds with one stone ...

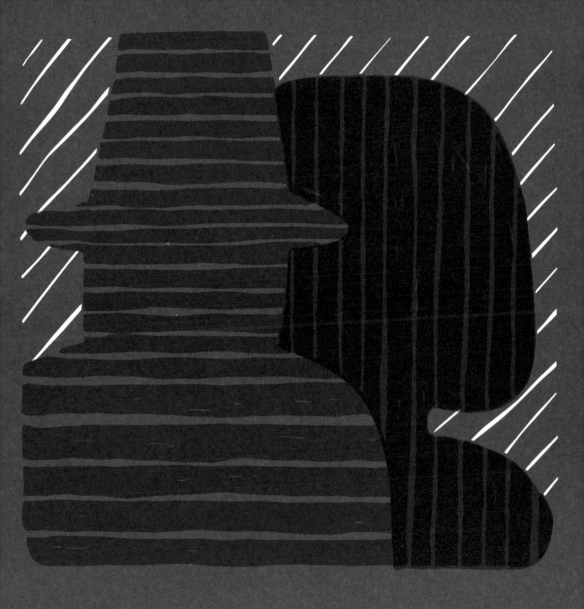

"You are both under arrest!"

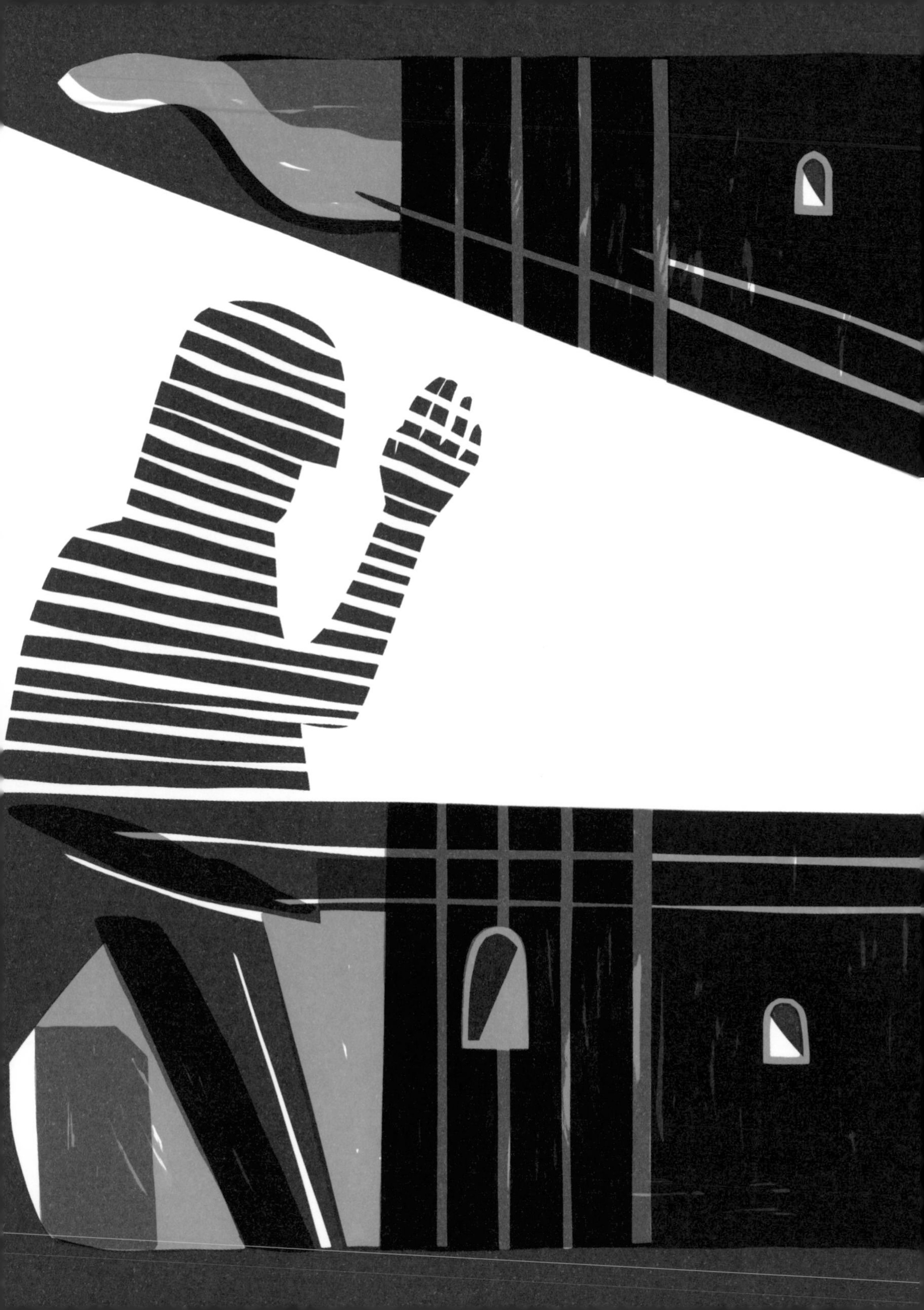

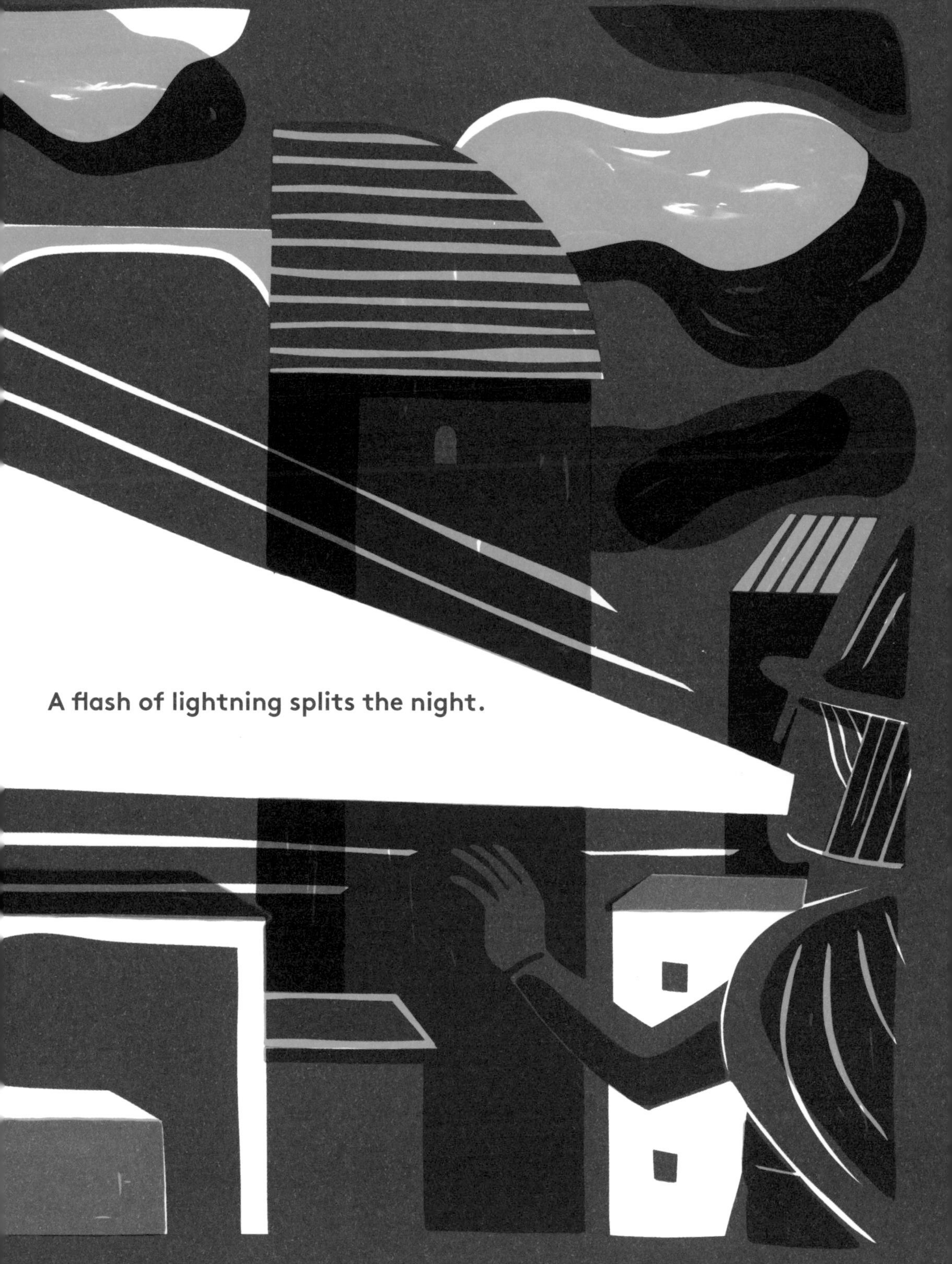

A flash of lightning splits the night.

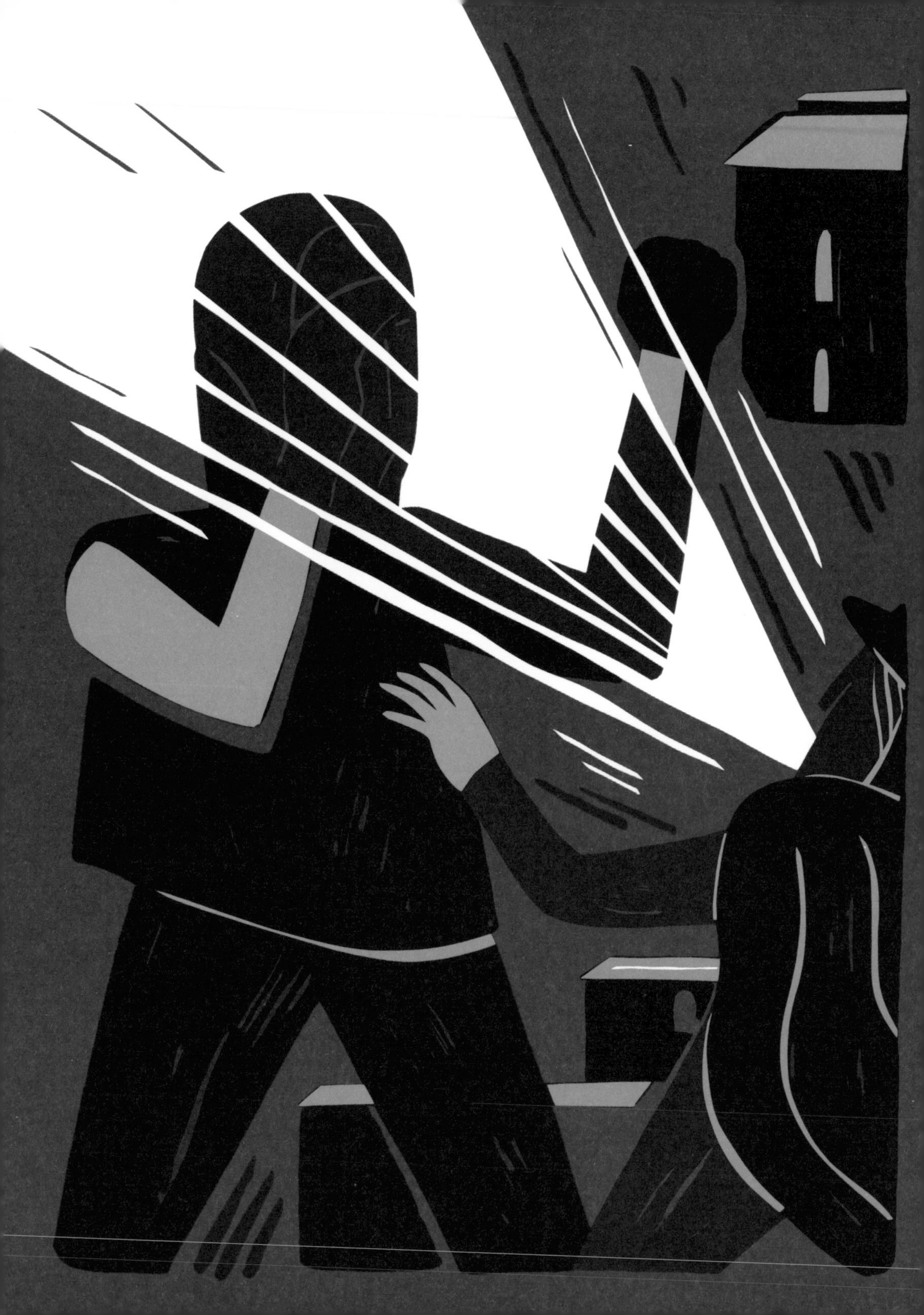

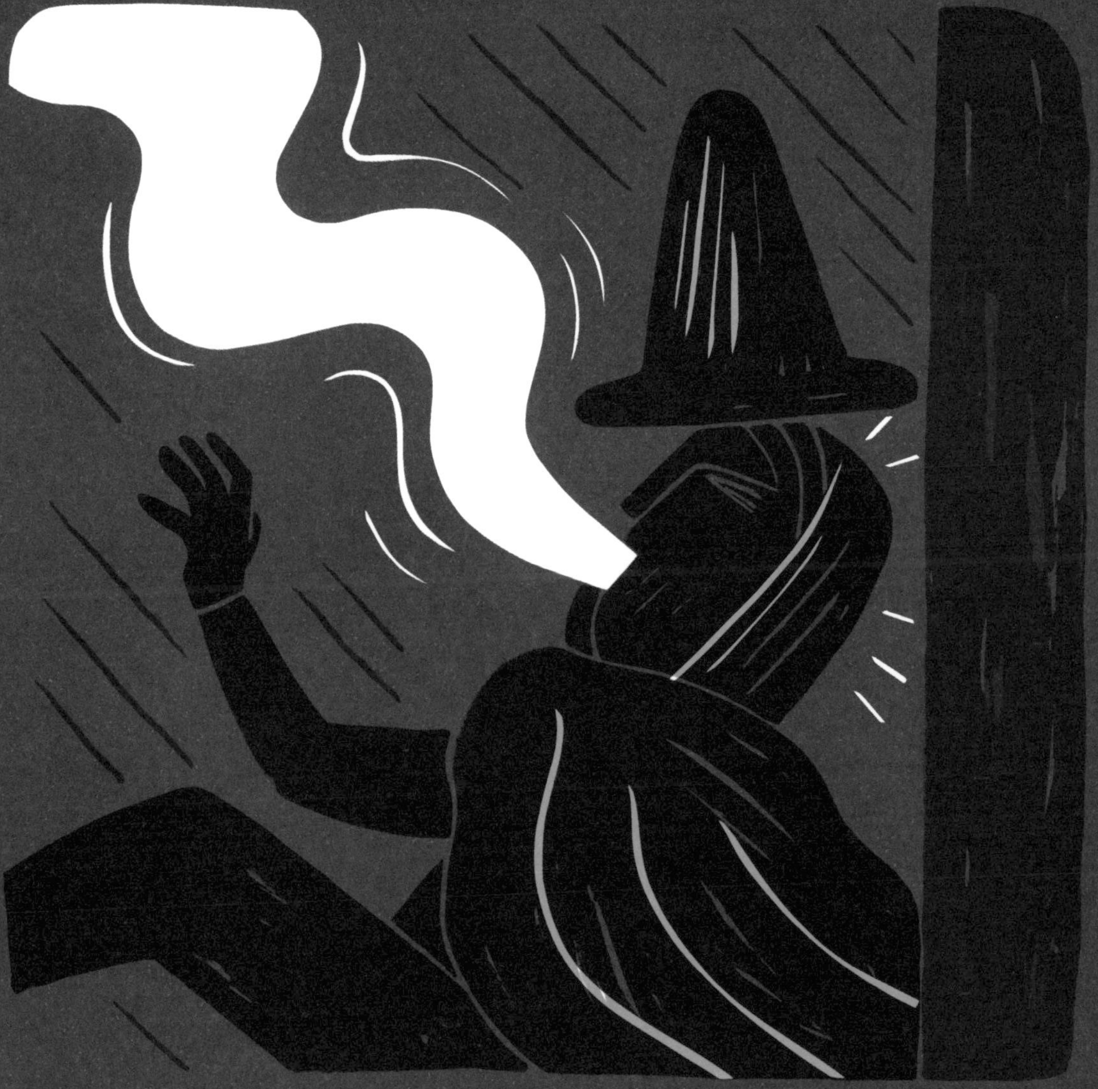

But this time I am ready.
With one hand shielding my eyes,
I blindly strike the shadows with the other.
The dull sound of a head striking the stone.

The light trembles, then goes out. I have won.
I can hear nothing but the panic-stricken breath of
my quarries. The body of the Vagabond, unconscious,
lies abandoned against the stone, head lowered onto
chest. The other, trembling with fear, turns away
from me. I think I recognize this quivering figure. I
turn on my lamp.

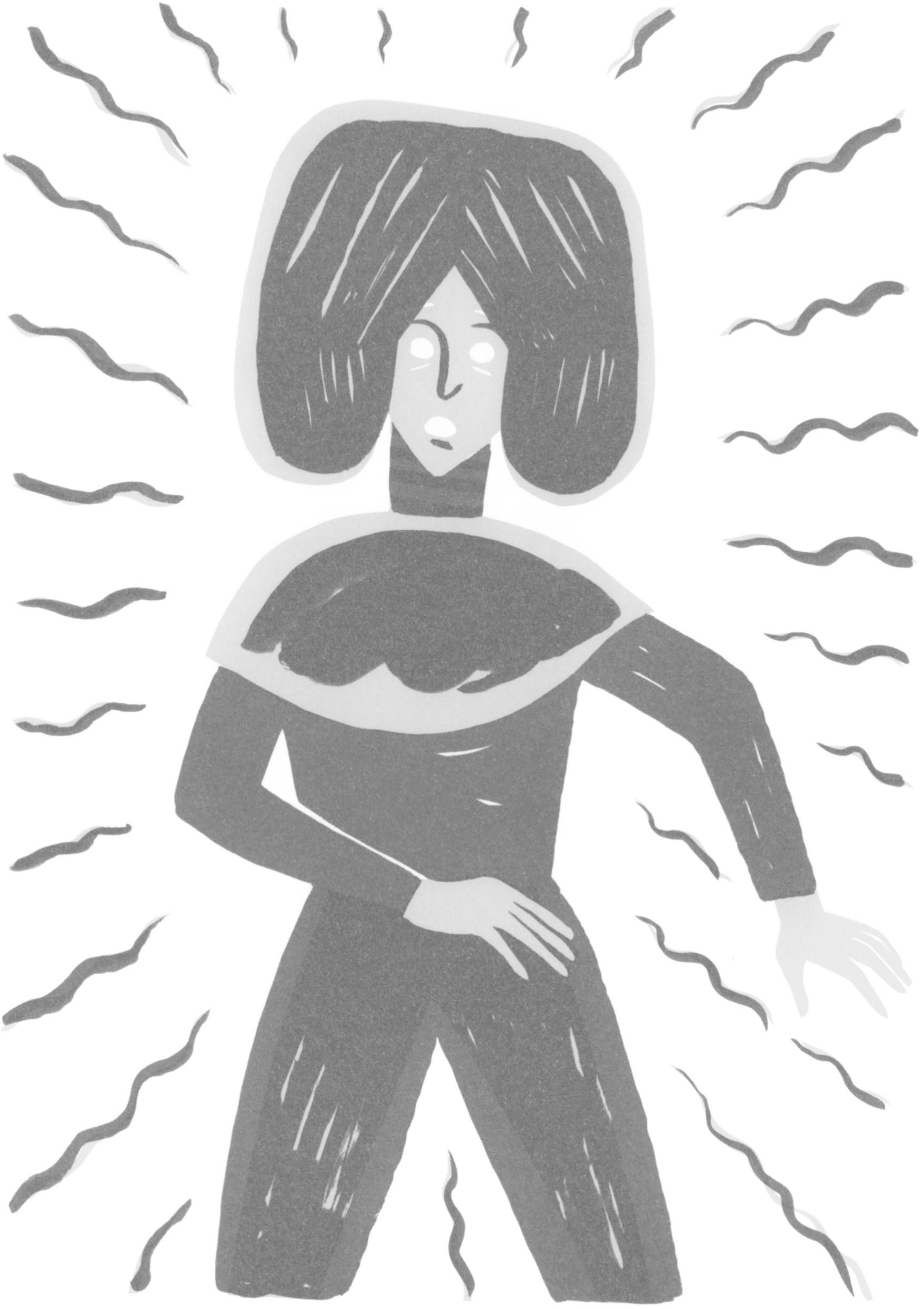

What is my newspaper Vendor doing with this criminal?

*"He's not a criminal!*
*They gave him no choice ...*
*Let me explain."*

But there is nothing to explain. It is too late.
They have wrecked the clock towers, at the
risk of reawakening the shades of Olden Times.
They have exposed the whole city to mortal danger.

*"You do not know about the city that you serve.*
*You apply its laws blindly. You speak of the Olden Times,*
*but you know nothing about them.*
*You know only what you have been told."*

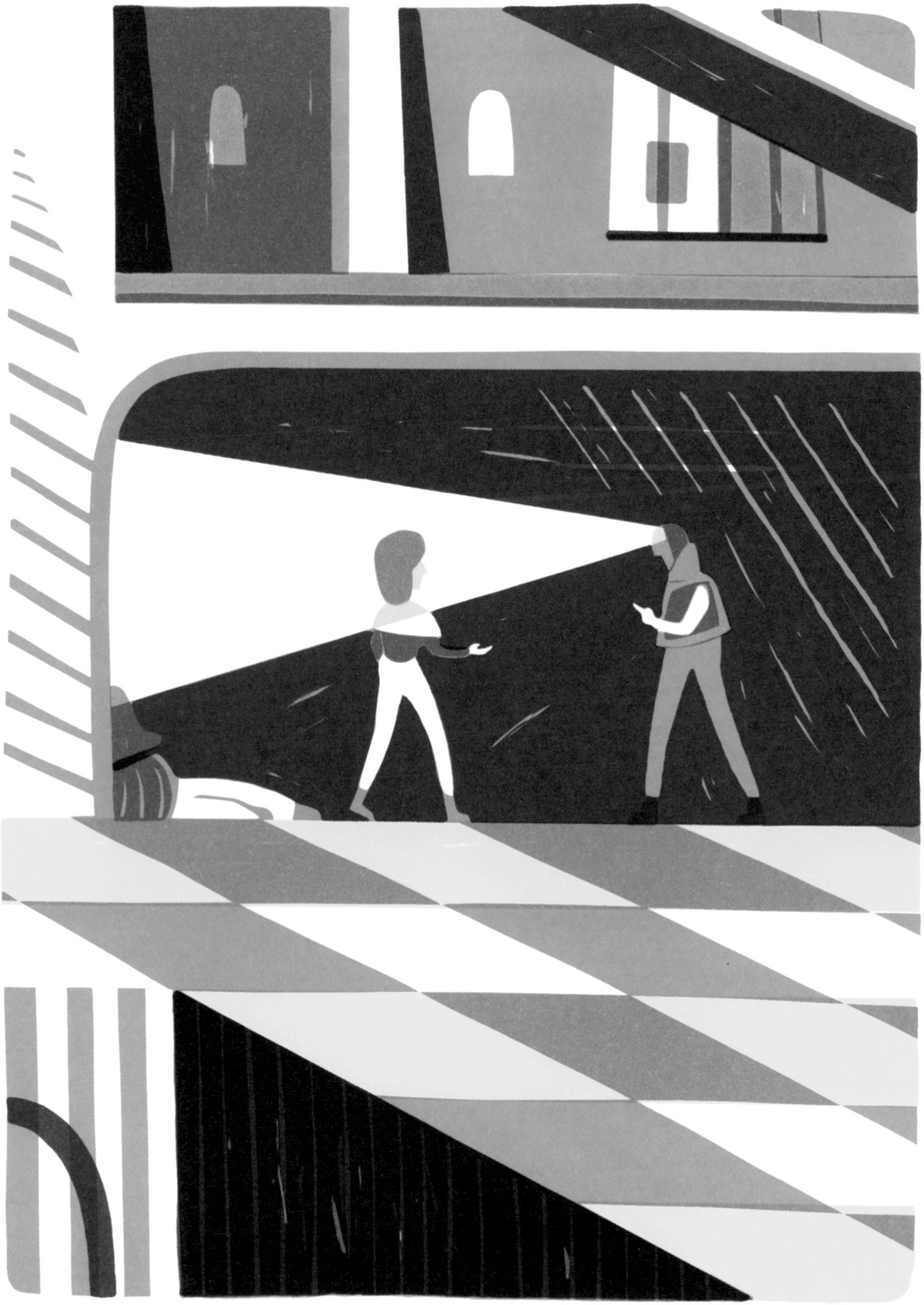

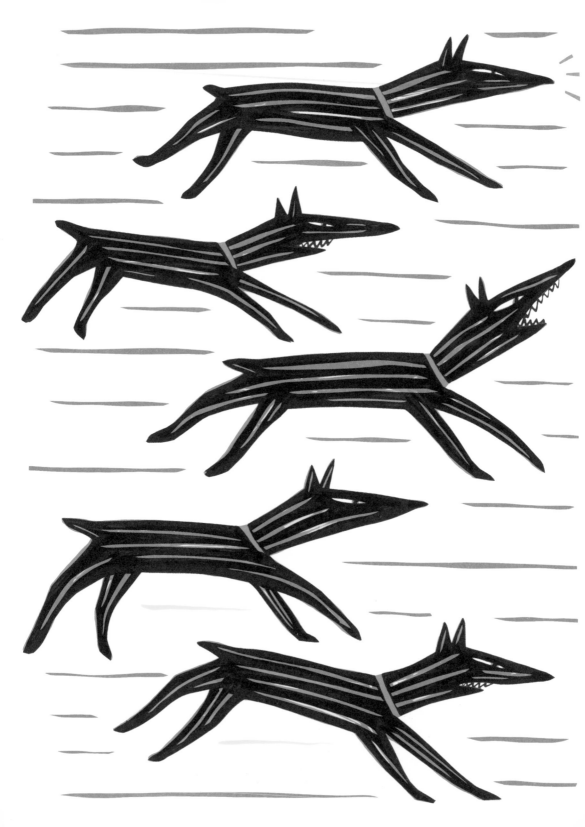

The night echoes with barking. The dogs have heard
us. They will be here at any moment, to help me
subdue the malefactors. I have to make a decision.
The eyes of the Vendor glow.
What buried secret is she guarding?

*"Follow me."*

I heave the still unconscious Vagabond over my
shoulder, and drag the Vendor across the city.
We make our way without a sound between the
sightless walls while the night shyly withdraws.

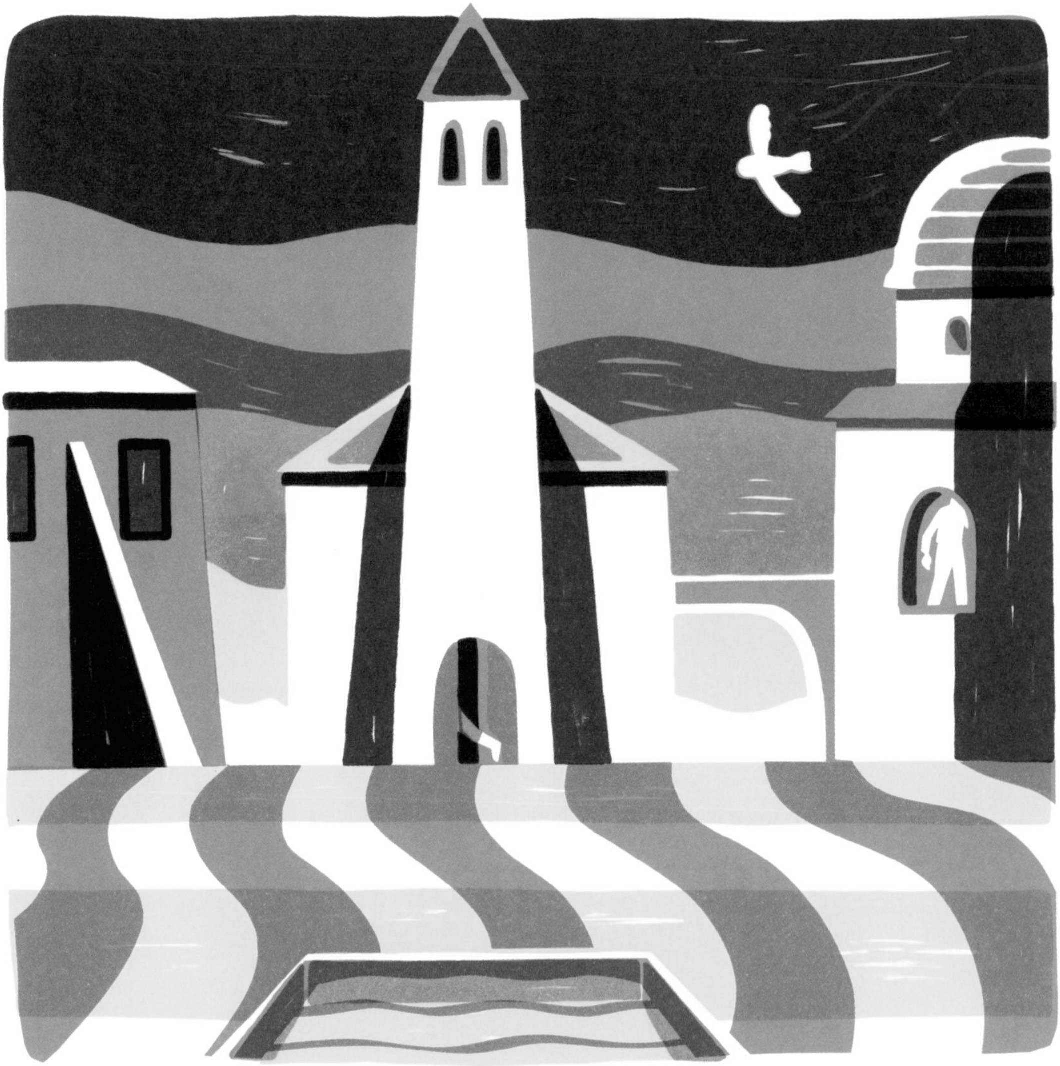

There is the old church. No one ever goes there now.
The only occupant, the owl in the bell-tower,
watches us in silence. We go in under her mute gaze.
We can still hear the yapping dogs in the distance,
but they fade away with the coming of the day.

I lay the Vagabond down on the flagstones.
He will be safe till tomorrow night. The Vendor smiles,
and the first rays of the sun shine
through the windows to caress her face.

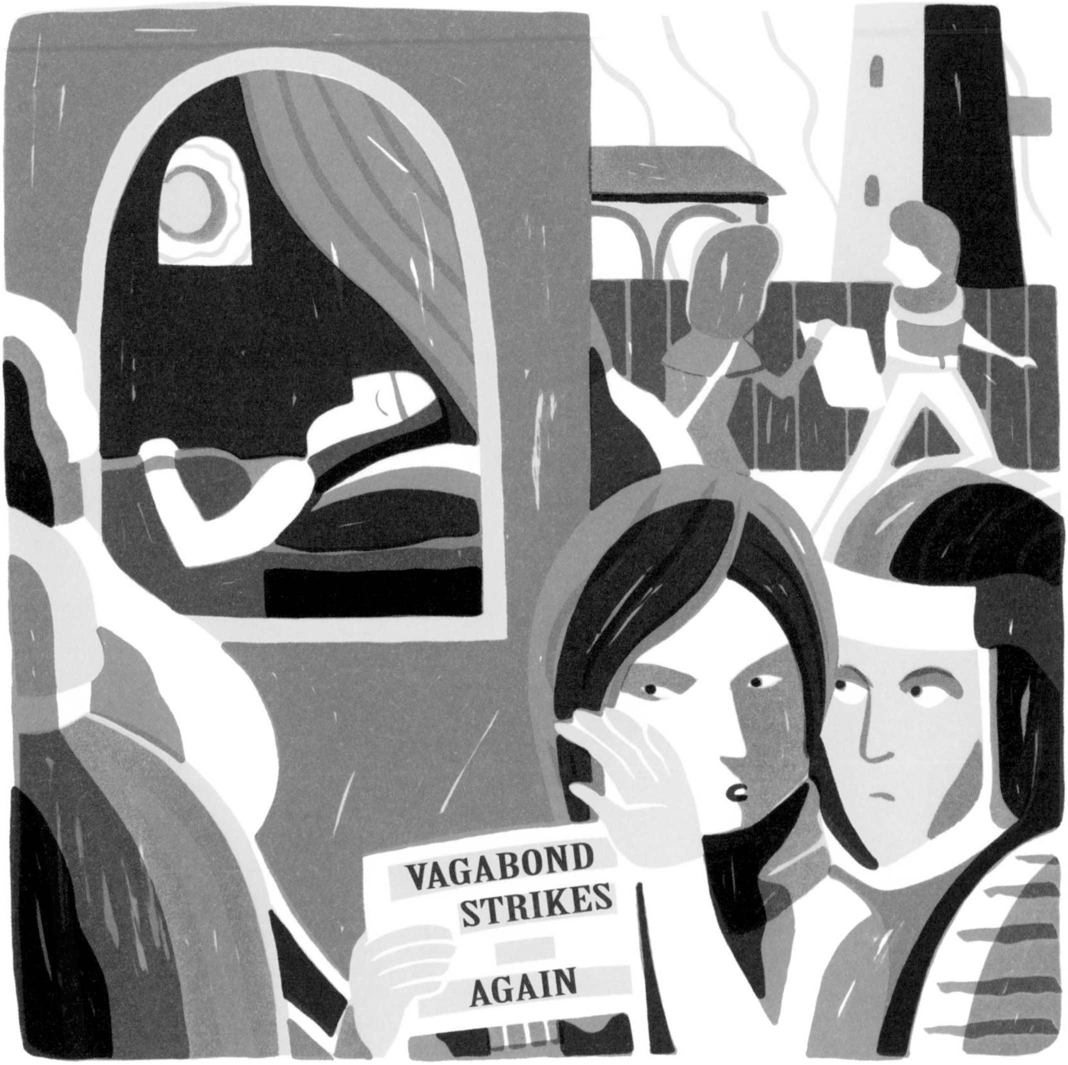
VAGABOND
STRIKES
AGAIN

The two of us leave the church and walk to the square together. The piles of newspapers are waiting on the cobbles. The sun has risen. The city begins to hum.

*"Let's meet at the church tonight."*

She agrees, and begins to call out to the first passers-by. I go home. Her voice lulls me to the threshold of restless sleep.

Fourth Night

Throughout the day I have teetered
on the borders of the dream,
ravaged by uncertainty. What am I going to learn?
What am I going to do?

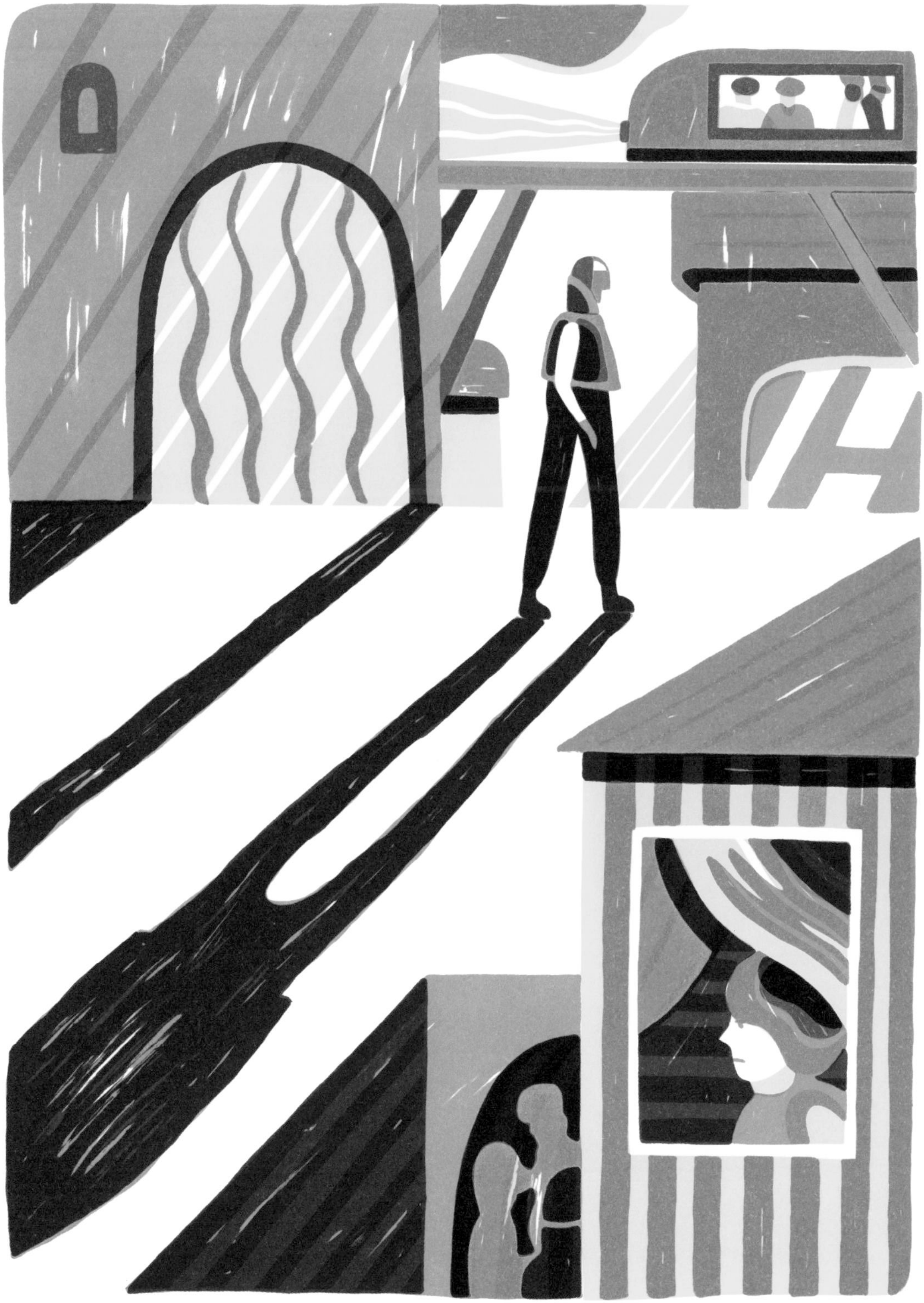

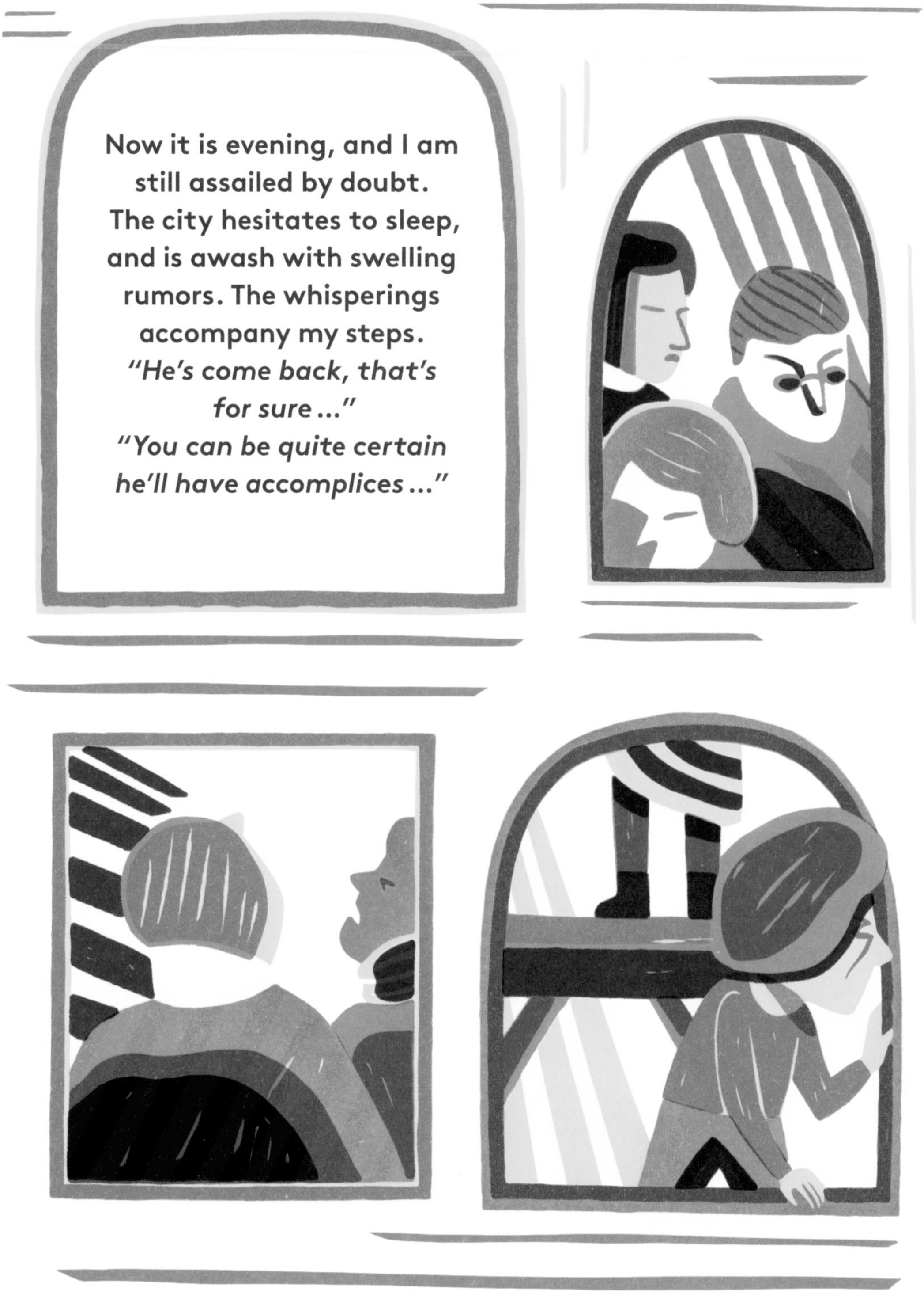
Now it is evening, and I am still assailed by doubt. The city hesitates to sleep, and is awash with swelling rumors. The whisperings accompany my steps.
"He's come back, that's for sure ..."
"You can be quite certain he'll have accomplices ..."

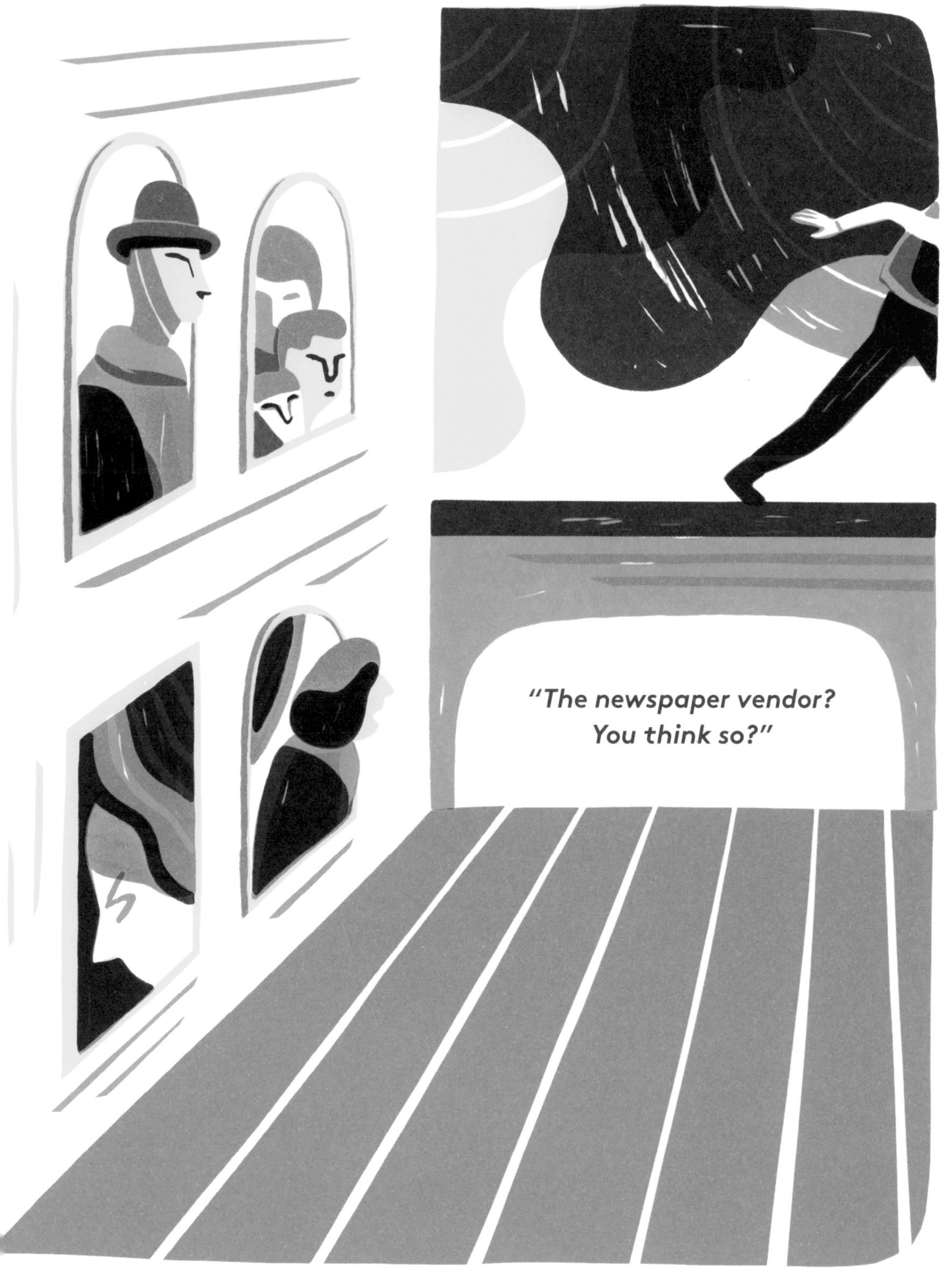
"The newspaper vendor?
You think so?"

Warily I enter the church. No one has seen me go in. The Vendor is already there. She is facing the Vagabond, and seems to be listening to him. I can hear nothing except a mechanical clicking. I approach and sit down with them. It is not words that are coming out of the Vagabond's mouth but an ever changing light that spreads over the uneven walls. Little by little the light forms images. Then, as the images pass over the walls, the Vendor tells me the story of the Vagabond:

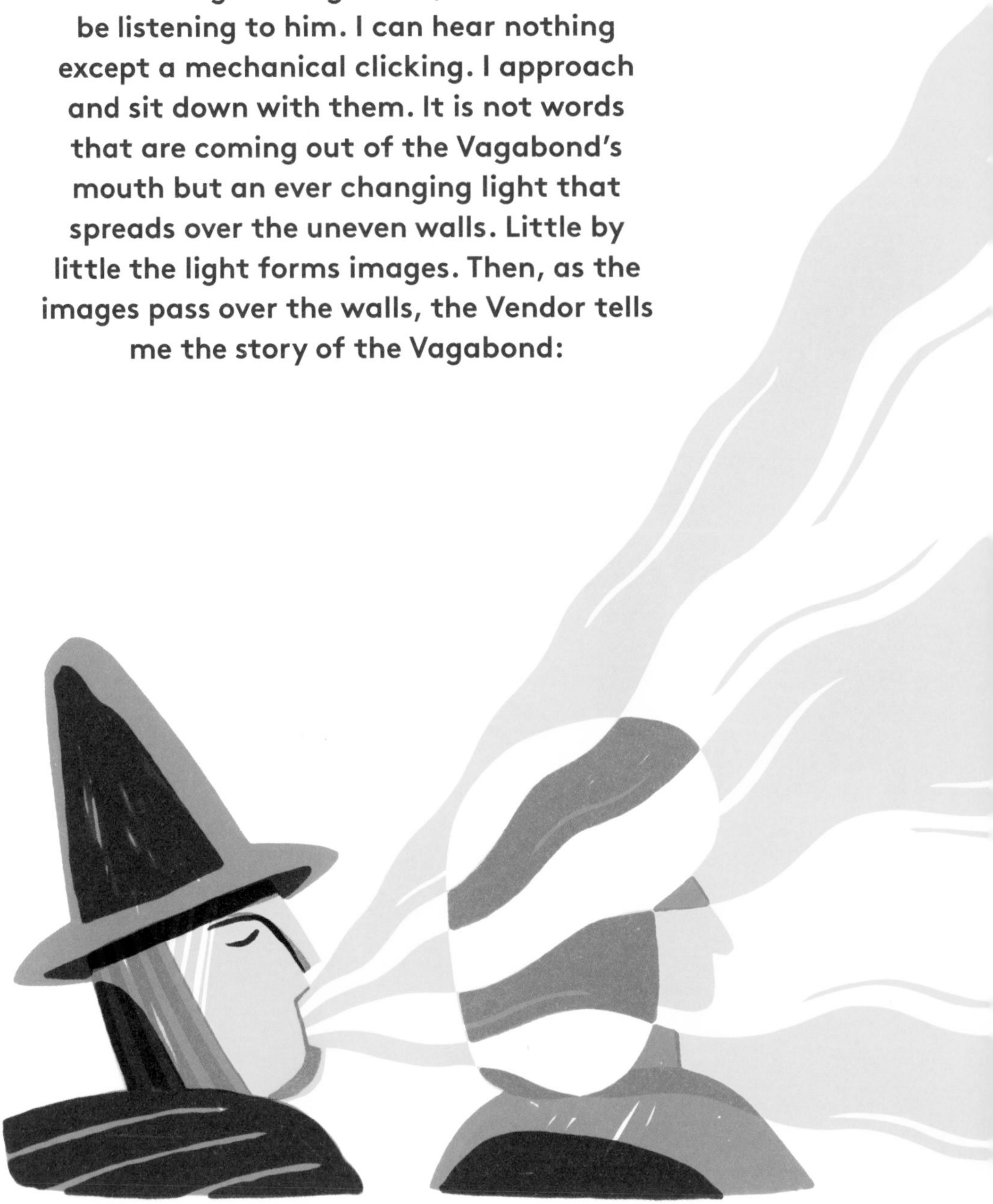

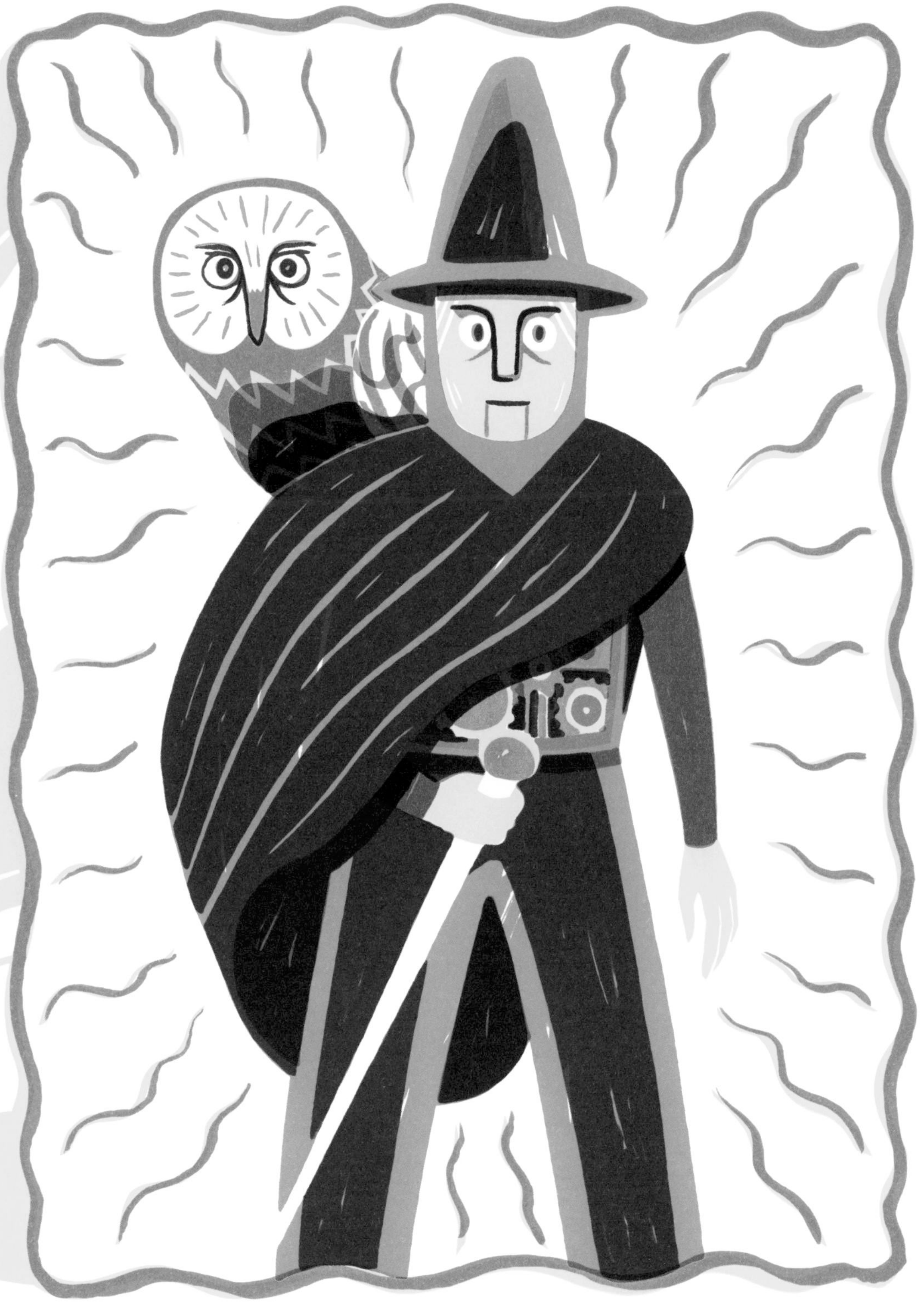

"A long time ago, the city was just a village. Every morning, our grateful hearts welcomed the day with overflowing joy, because our sleep was filled with nightmares. The night belonged to the crocodiles. Every evening, as the sky fearfully hatched the stars, one could look out through the barricaded windows and see the hideous, bulbous balls of their eyes as they slithered through the dust. And people prayed, surrounded by the moist crunching of scales on cobblestones.

Until one night, a long drawn out hoot-
ing sound drowned the slow-moving melody
of the reptiles. The scaly shadows stood still.
It was an owl, sitting on the bell-tower. The
crocodiles looked at her, anxiously, this bird
that was singing a death knell, and then a bolt
of light suddenly shattered the darkness. A
burning ray like a sunbeam descended on the
monsters, forcing them to retreat, to turn,
to flee, driving them down into the sewers,
where every single one of them disappeared.
At last all was silent again. The day dawned
and revealed the face of our savior.

The whole village was in a state of euphoria. Thanks to the lamp-man, night and day were reconciled. At last the scales of our lives were perfectly balanced.

We entered a new era: the day was witness to our labors, and soon the city was filled with huge building sites; we erected giant structures, and the Three Clock Towers began to rise up into the sky. When the sun dipped below the horizon, the lamp-man began his rounds and watched over us as we slept. That is why we called him the Watchman. He was the star of the night.

Time took its course, imperturbably. Nothing now disturbed our dreams. We worked, full of confidence, absorbed in constructing the great mechanisms of the Three Clock Towers. But one day the Watchman fell ill. His gear wheels became unsynchronized and the light that came from his mouth trembled and faded.

No one heard his moans. With so much work to do, no one had time. He'd caught a chill, nothing serious, it would soon pass.

And so he continued to keep watch at night. The owl warned of imminent dangers, and the Watchman's luminous cough was sufficient to dissuade the darkness from seeking to recapture its rights. But the Watchman's sickness did not pass. It became worse, and in the end it extinguished the very last flicker of light in him.

Then one night, a crocodile came up out of the sewers. The Watchman, now blind, was unable to stop it, and the beast wrought havoc in the city. In the morning, when the people finally managed to kill the reptile, in their fury they went in search of the lamp-man. They hurled insults at him, beat him mercilessly, and cold-bloodedly threw him out onto the street.

The Watchman now lived a life of con-cealment, hiding away beneath the bridges, forced to search through the refuse in the hope of finding scraps of metal to keep him alive. He had become the Vagabond.

Time passed. The Three Clock Towers were completed under the silent supervision of the owl. She had found refuge in the bell-tower, and people passed before her without even remembering the existence of her master. The Vagabond had vanished into oblivion. I alone kept him in my memory: every night I brought him nuts and bolts and springs that I gleaned from here and there. I gave him words of comfort. I alone in this proud city continued to care for him.

Since he had been driven away, no one kept watch over the night. The city slept on unconcerned. But slowly the servants of the shadows began to re-emerge. When night fell, locusts invaded the sky, snakes slithered between the joints of the walls. Soon the sound of woodlice seething in the gutters could be heard again every morning. The city returned to its state of fear.

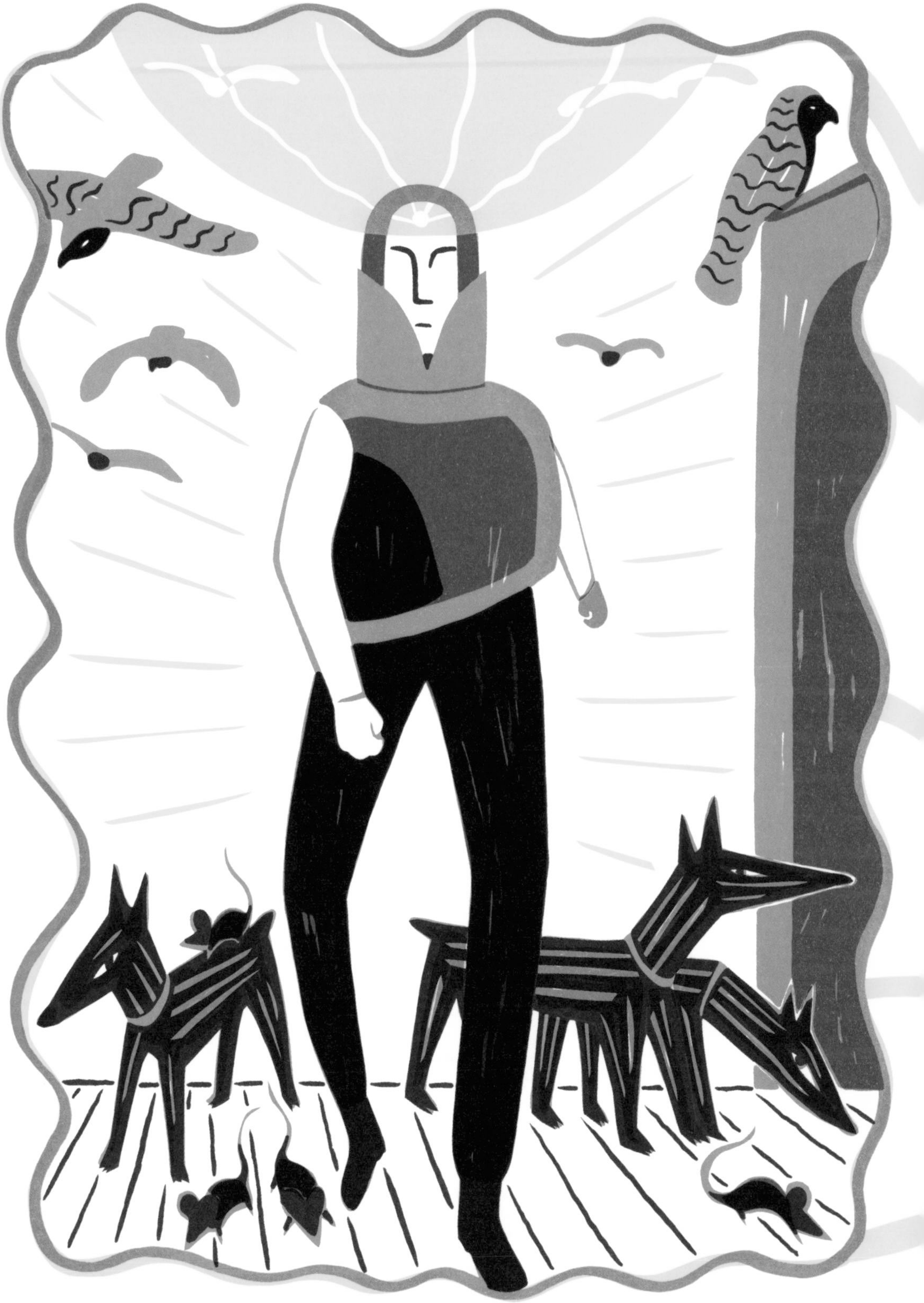

That was when you arrived, with your buzzards, dogs, and rats. You drove away the vermin that disturbed our nights. You restored perfect order, and the city, now reassured, had found a new hero. But in the face of your great deeds, the metallic heart of the Vagabond was filled with bitterness and envy. I tried to dissuade him, but he decided to wreck the Three Clock Towers, to steal the mechanisms he needed to bring himself back to life. He succeeded, and yesterday, when you took us by surprise, the Vagabond was preparing to reappear in public in order to take his place again."

121

The light coming out of the Vagabond's mouth crackles. He spits a metallic cough. He lies down. The light illuminates the ceiling for a moment, and then dies.

The Vendor looks at me, panic-stricken. She searches my eyes for help. There is nothing I can do. This man is sick, but he must pay for his crimes.

The Vendor's cheeks are burning, and her mouth shrivels. Tears gather at the edges of her eyelids.

What does she expect of me?
To help a criminal?

*"Don't you understand? What would you have done in his place? And what do you think they will do to you when the night escapes from you? You will not be able to hold back the shuddering of the shadows forever. And the city always finds out in the end."*

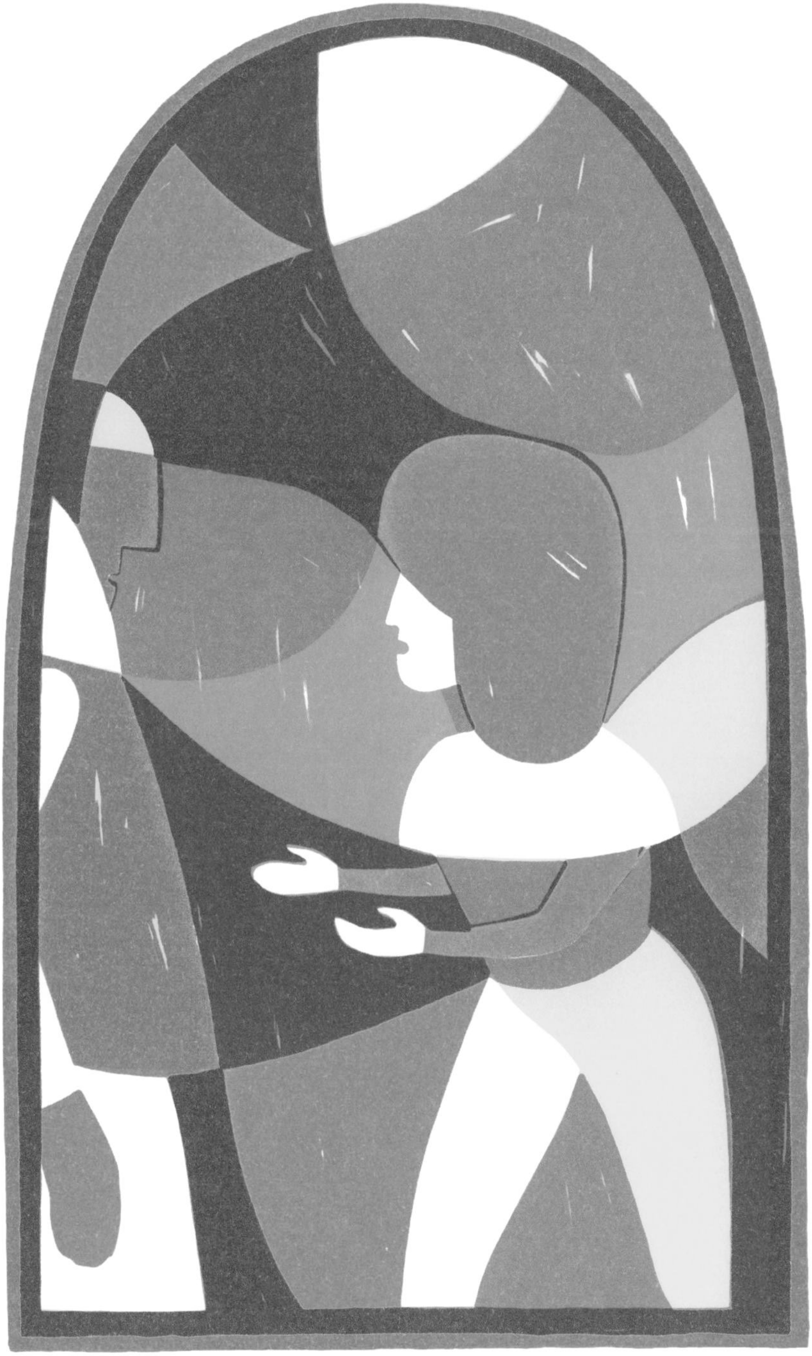

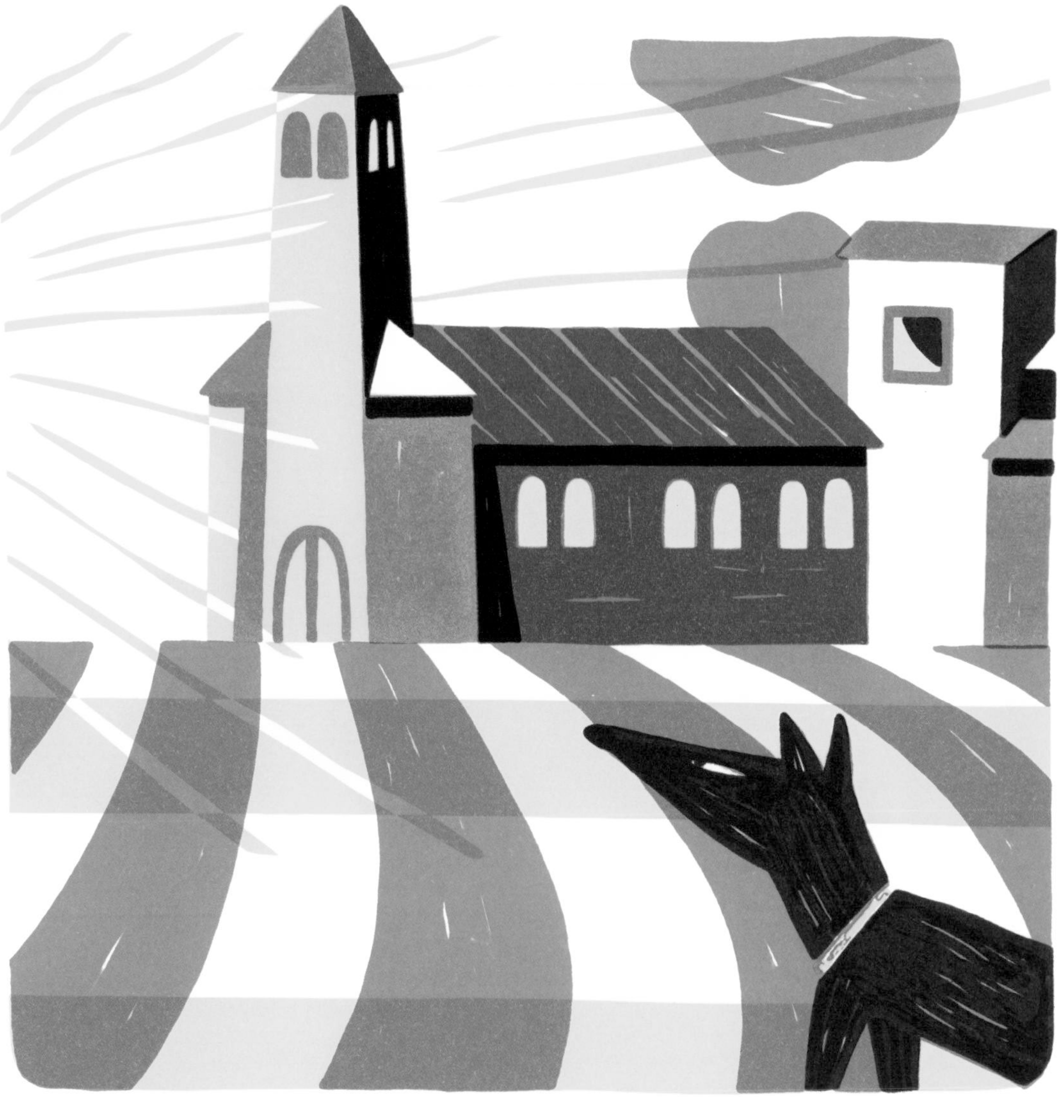

Outside, the night is already retreating.
I am the guardian of peaceful dawns.
The city depends on me.
The only thing I can try to do is help
the Vagabond escape from it.
Forever. He must never return.

The Vendor dries her eyes. She thanks me,
and her smile gives me more warmth
than the fires of day could ever do.

*"If you trust me, avoid the eyes of the people.
The city suspects you."*
*"And my work? Who will sell the newspapers?"*
*"It doesn't matter. Stay in hiding here until order
has been restored."*
*"But..."*
*"I'll come back for the Vagabond
when I think it's safe."*

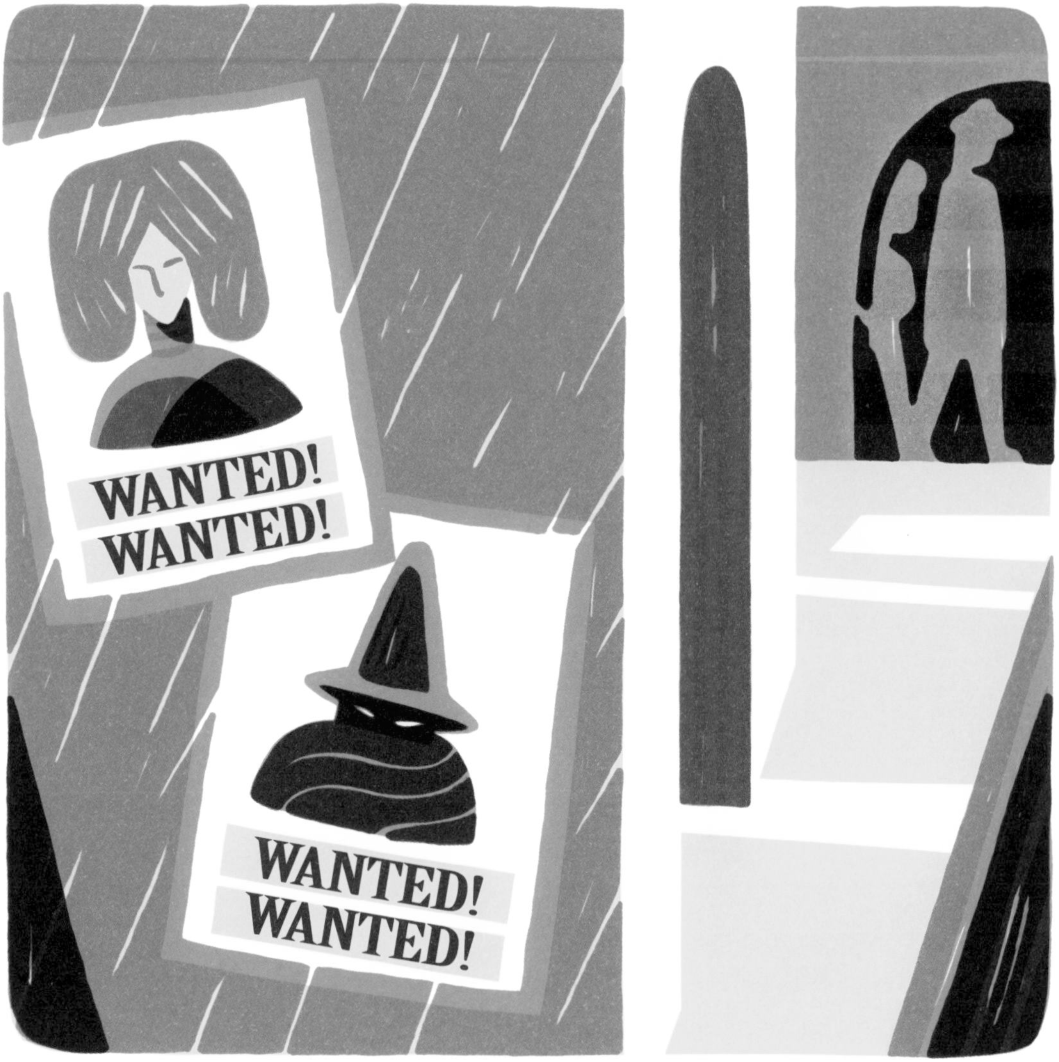
WANTED!
WANTED!
WANTED!
WANTED!

I leave the church. The still hesitant
sun sheds a crimson light on the square. The city seems empty.
This morning the endless litany of the Vendor
is not to be heard. Only the piles of newspapers
await the hands of the passers-by. Slowly the silence
is filled with suspicious whisperings.

**Fifth Night**

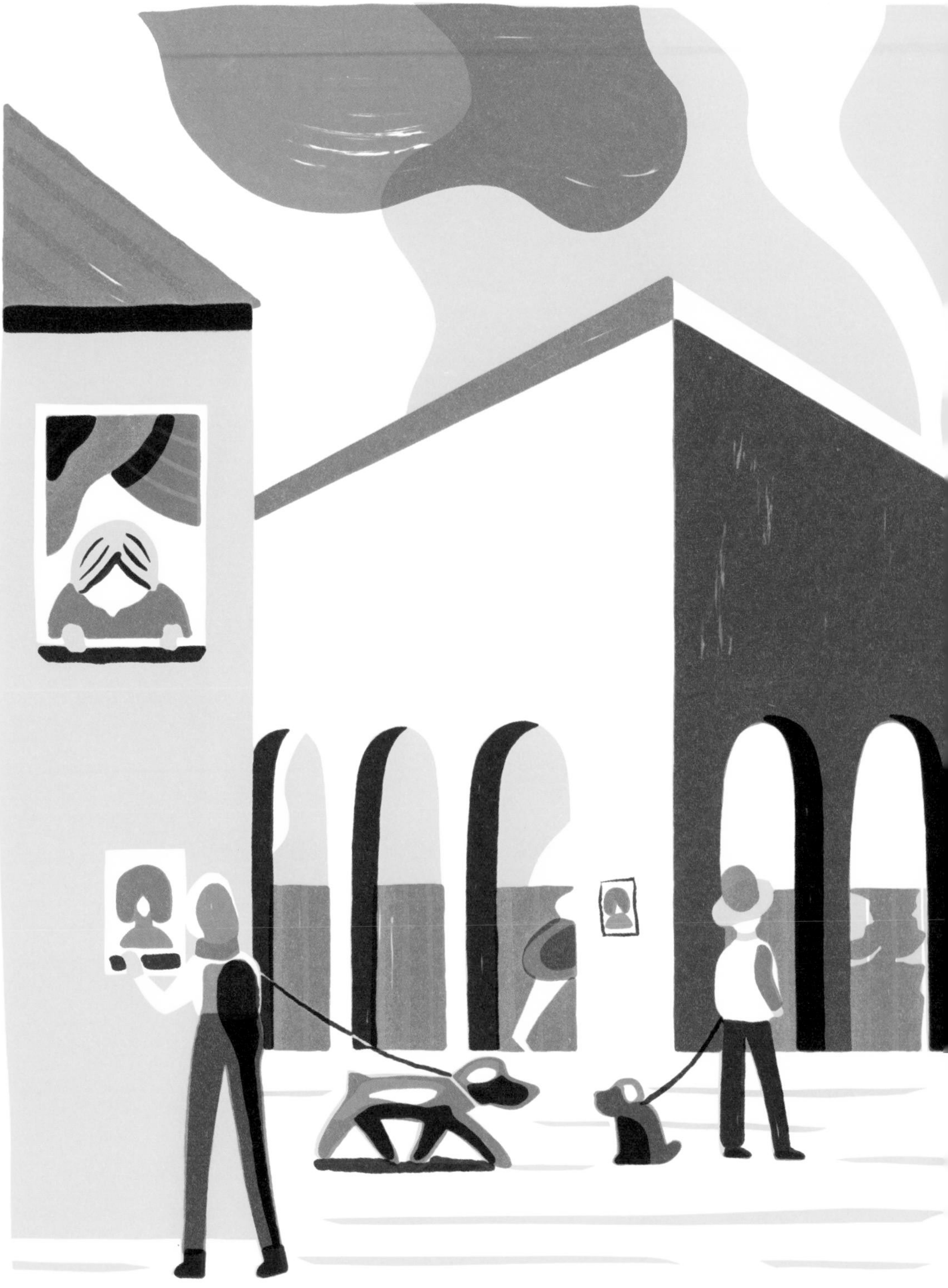

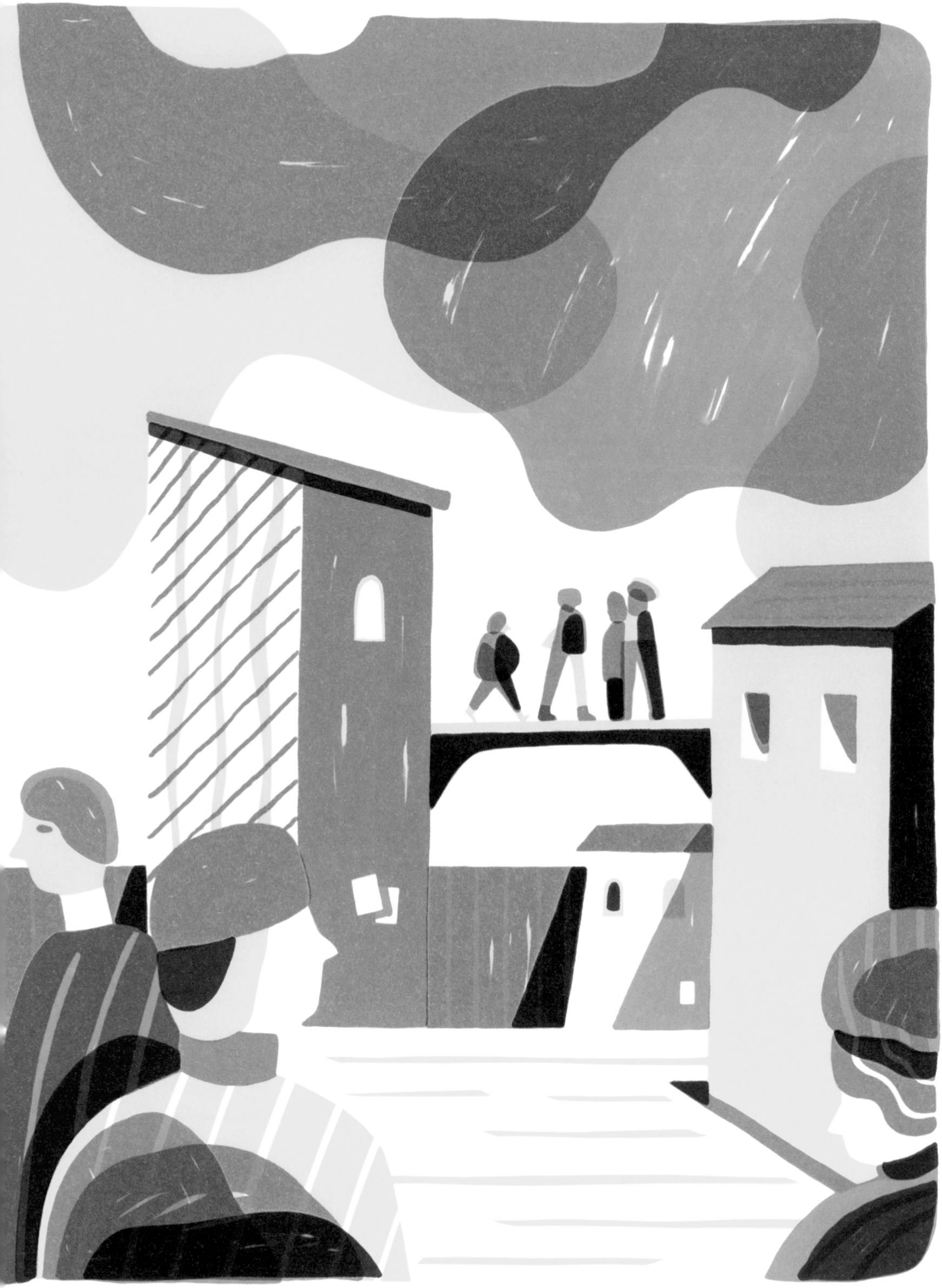

It is my time.

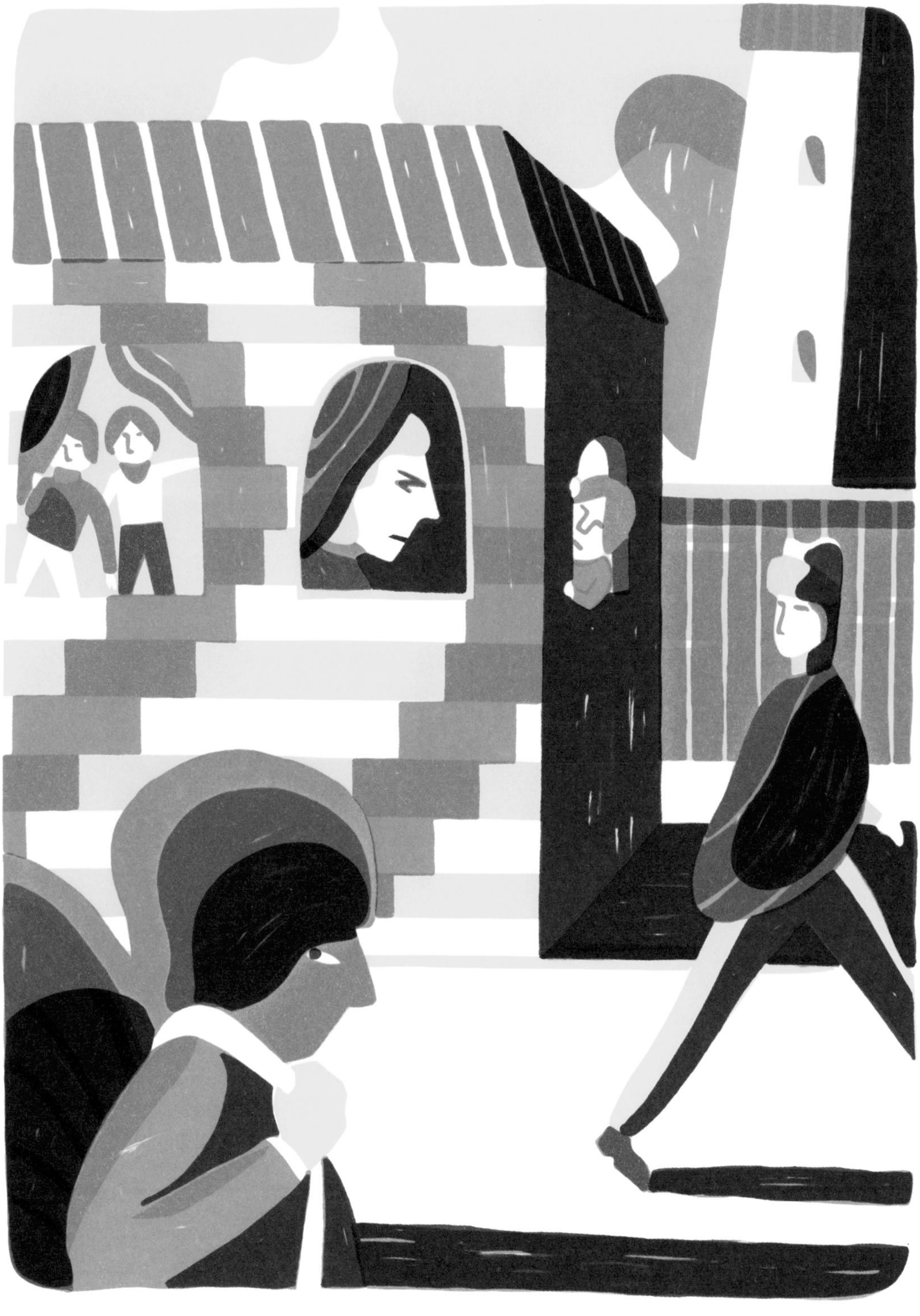

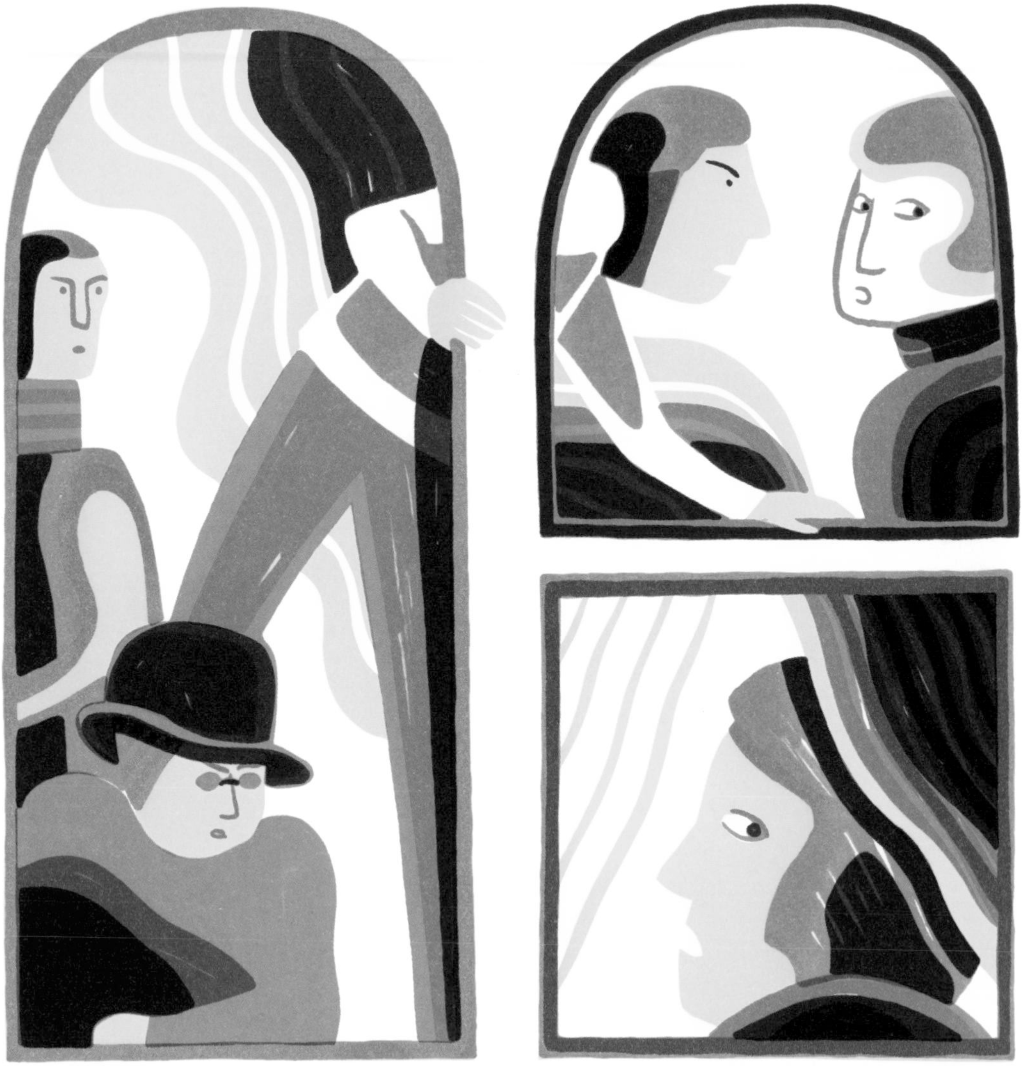

People greet me. They know they can sleep
in peace so long as I am here. I walk by,
wearing my smile like a mask
turned towards the trusting faces.

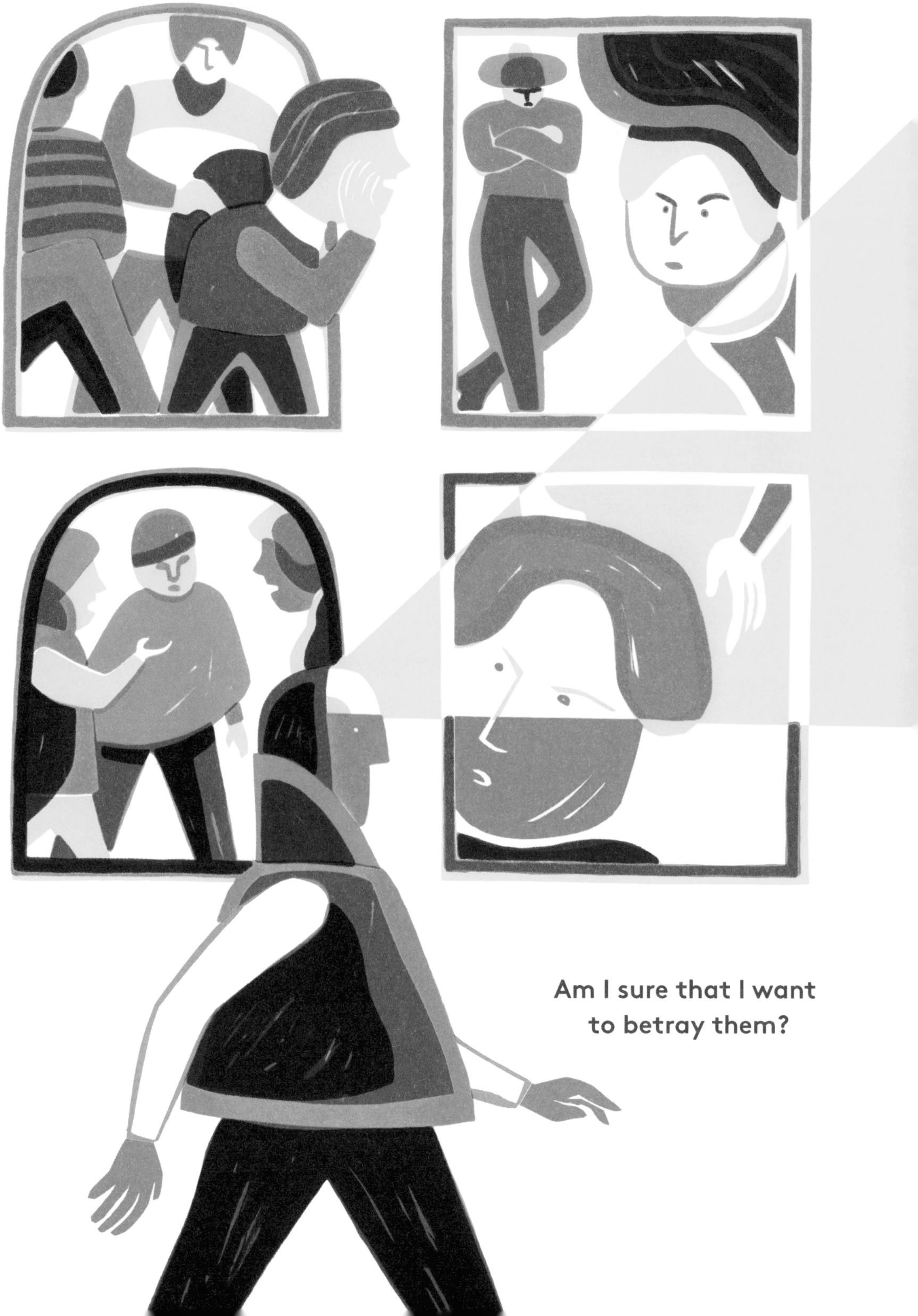
Am I sure that I want
to betray them?

Supposing they suspected something? But how would they know? The Vagabond will secretly disappear, and once more the city will cast him into oblivion. All this will have been nothing but a murmur. Time will resume its course, just as it has always done. And I shall return to my walls, my patrols, my night.

I have scarcely slept. I spent the whole day perfecting my plan. The city is inviolable. The wind that whistles between the walls is my breath. When in a storm the rain streaks the stone, it is I who shiver. In order to flee I know there is only one escape route, but first I must clear the way. Evening approaches, and I have made my decision.

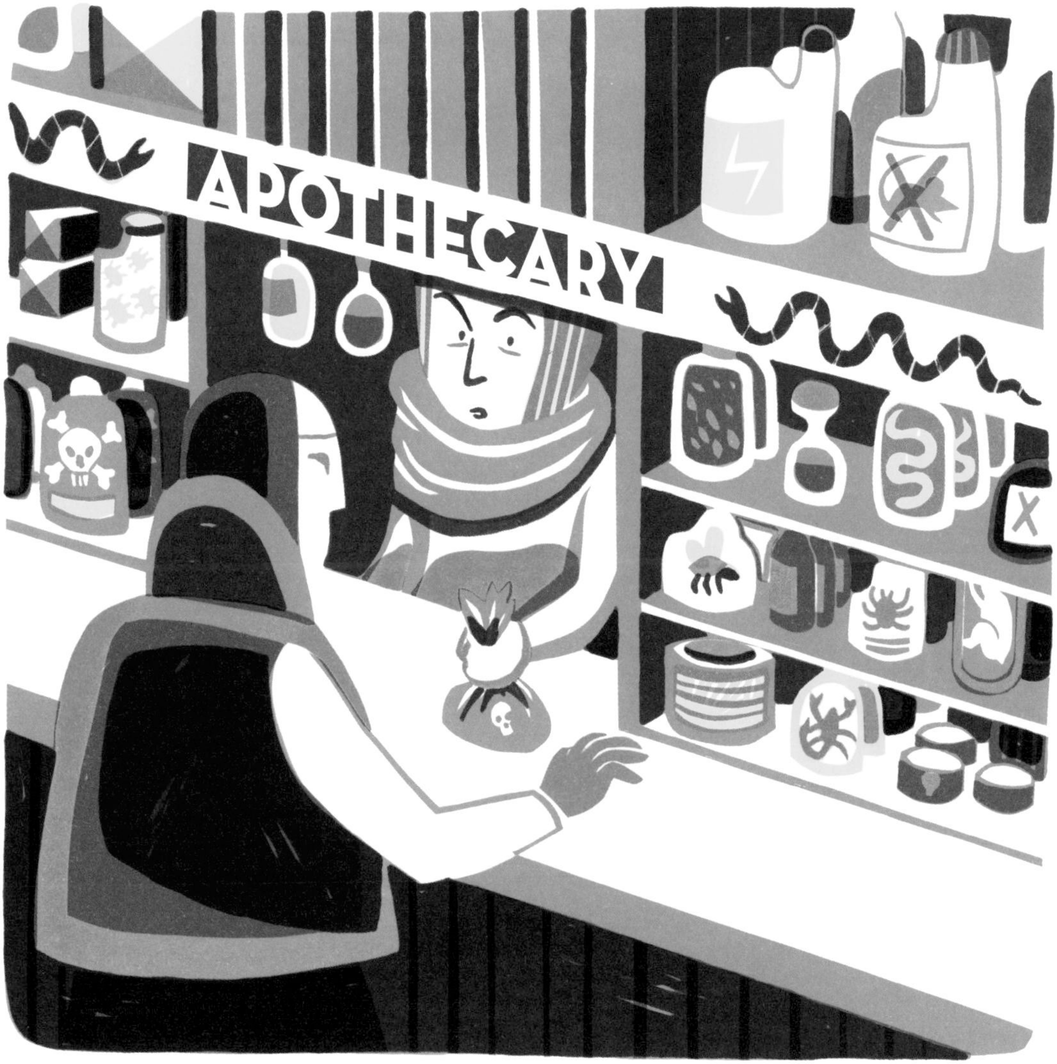
APOTHECARY

From a booth that is about to close for the night
I buy the three things I need for my plan:
a phial of mist, a bottle of perfume,
and a bag of seeds.

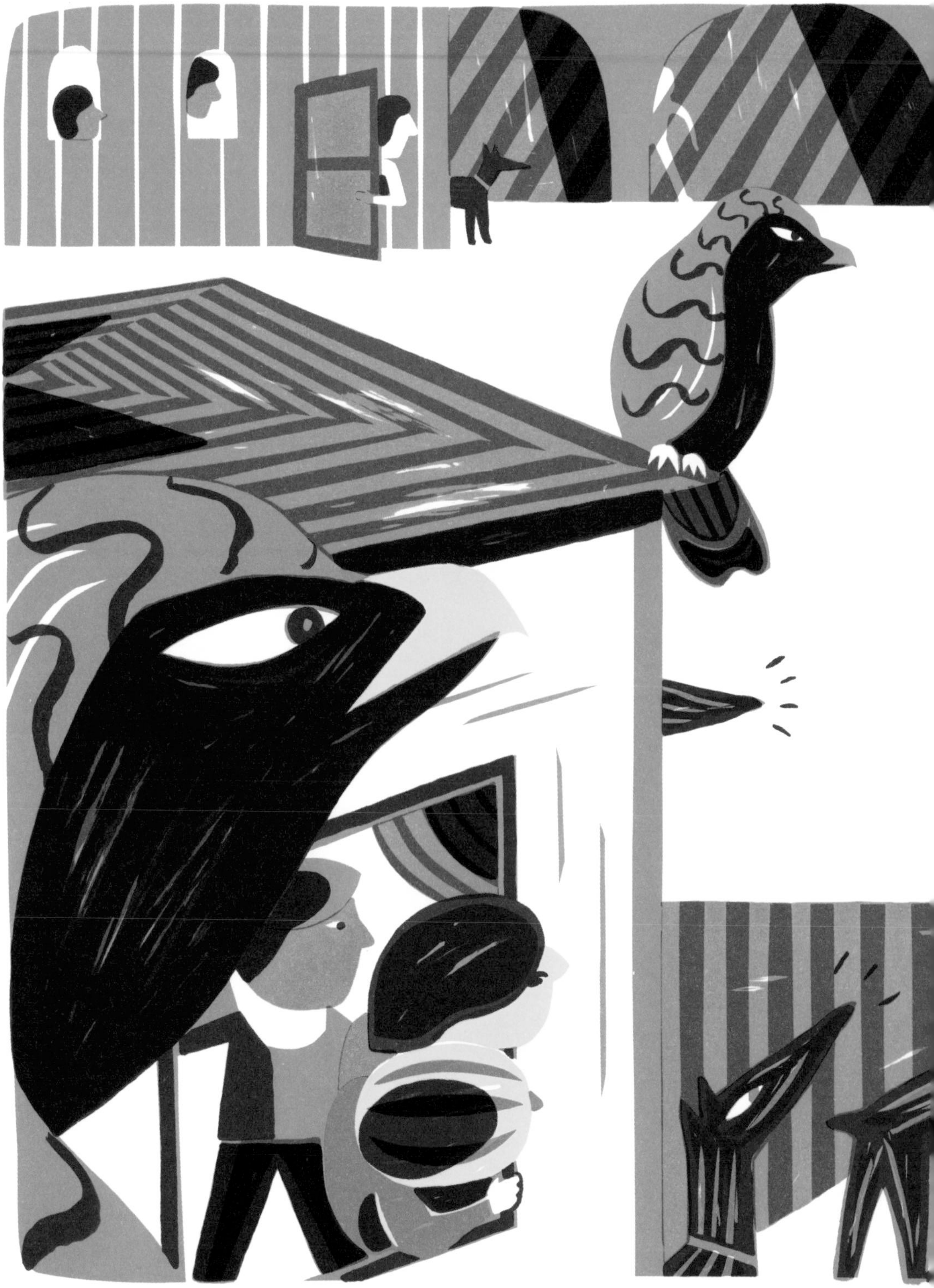

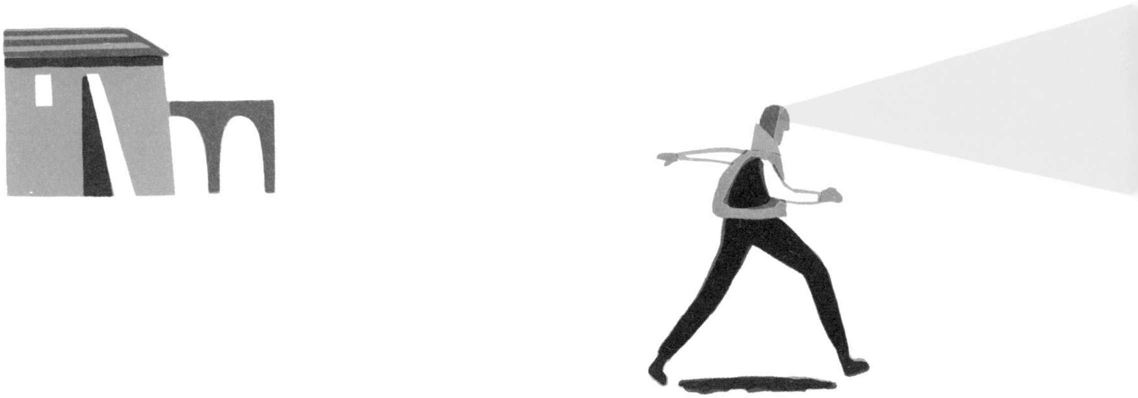

Night finishes casting its hood over the city.
The gentle movement of the stars lulls the last eyelids to close. Silence deals its hand, and it is my turn to play. Now I shall have to deceive my long-time helpers.

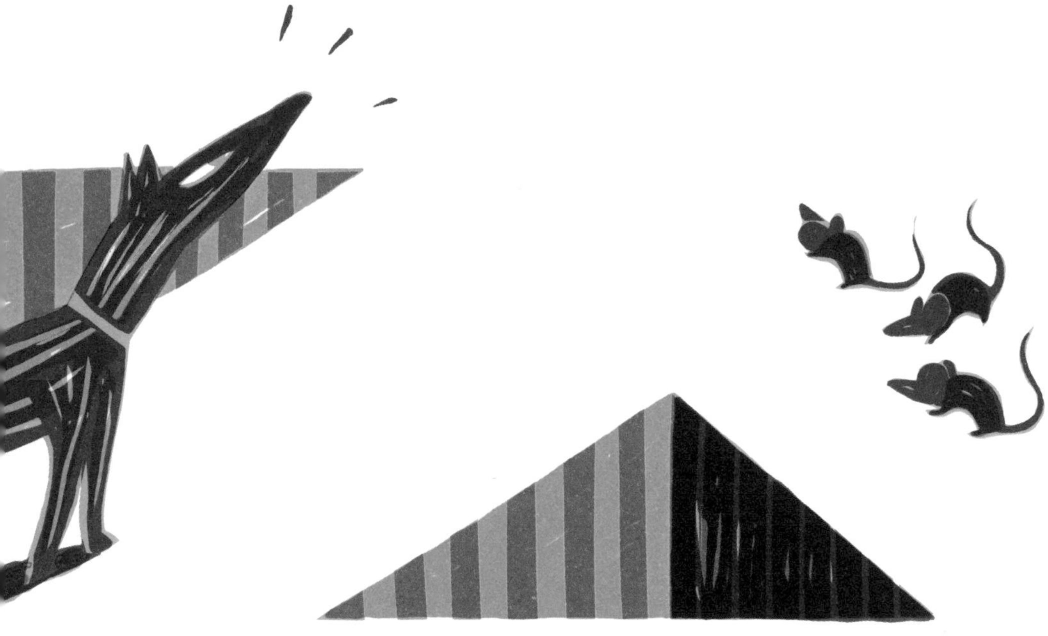

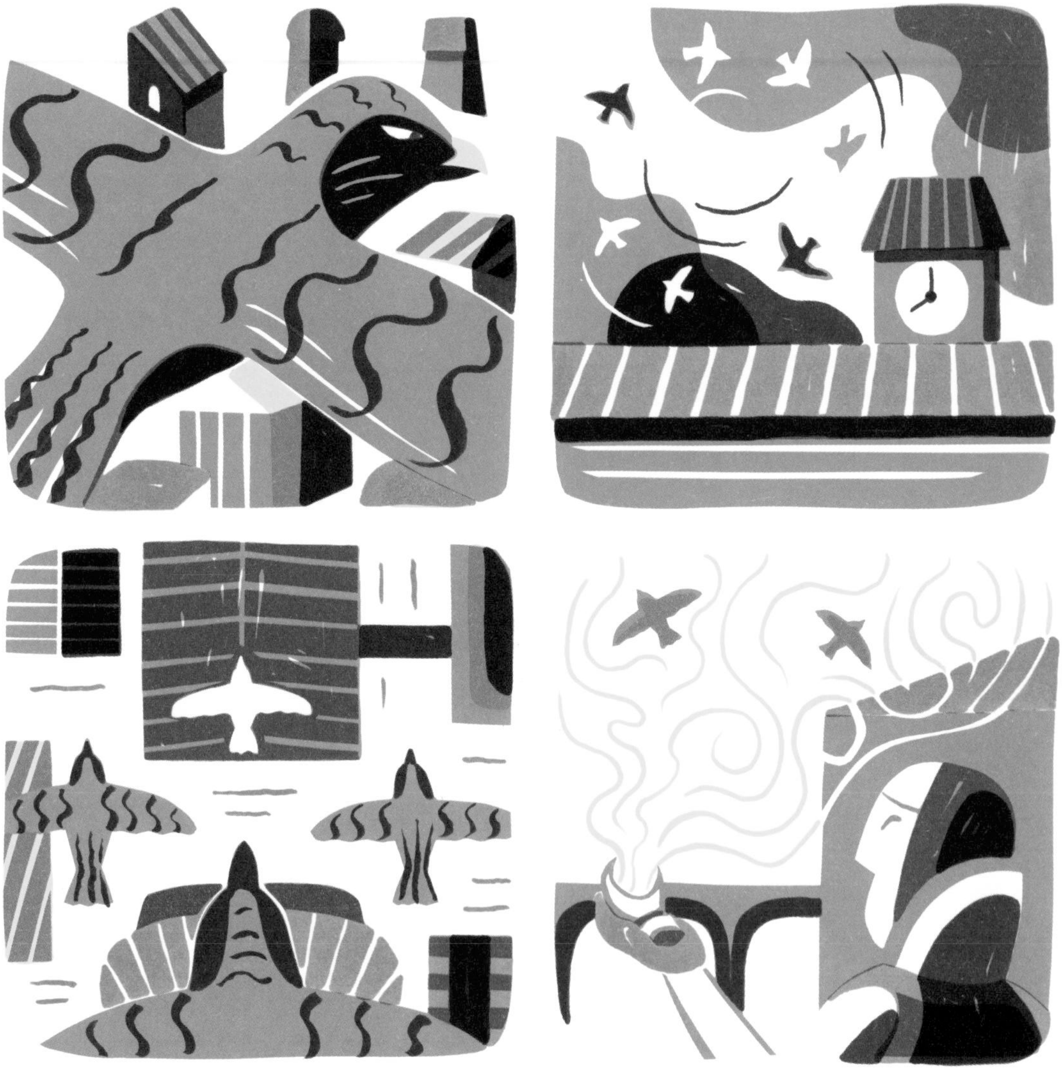

The buzzards are my eyes. Their silhouettes stretch out over the roofs. Wherever I am, I see myself through them, tiny, making my way through the traceries of the streets. Impossible to escape from them. I throw the phial of mist behind me, and so hide myself from the eyes of the hunters.

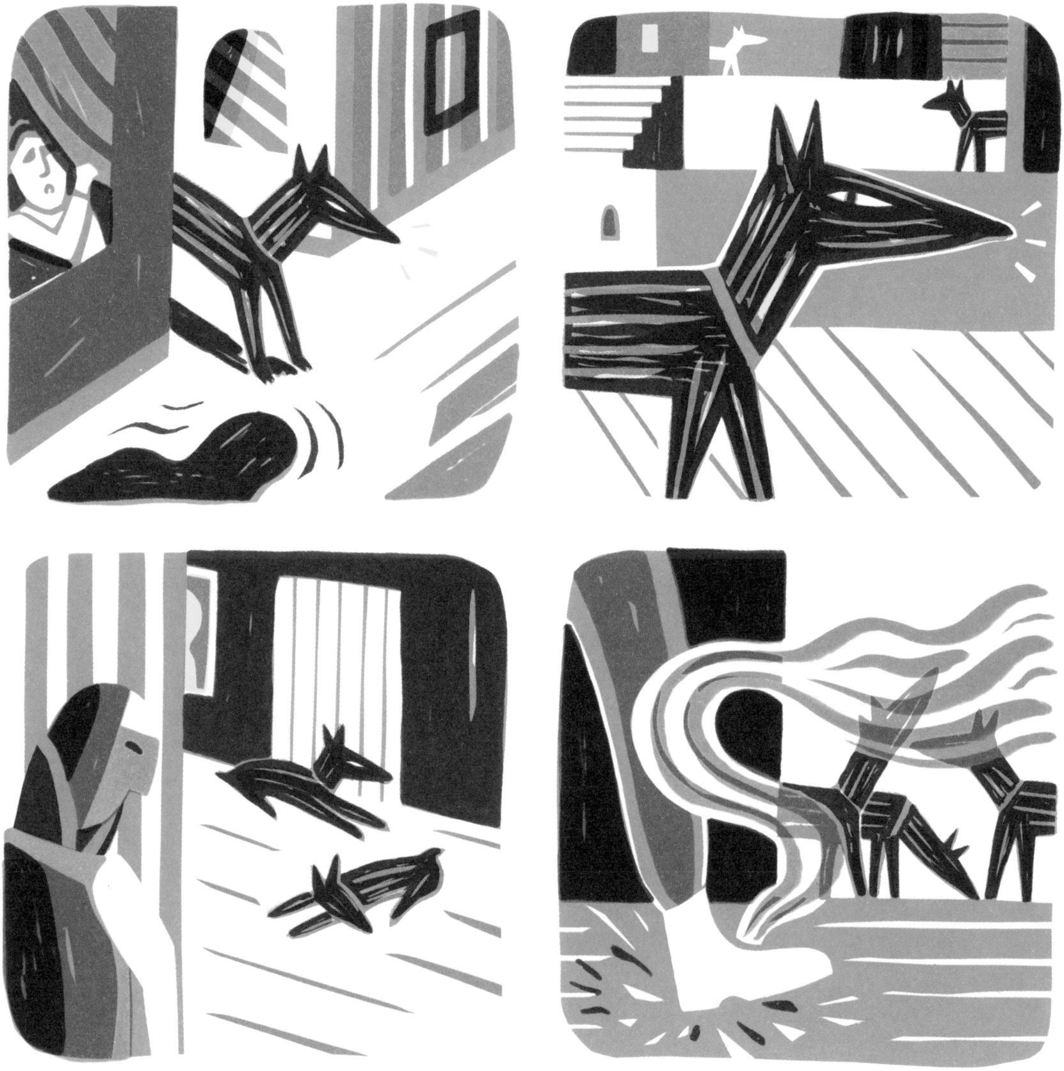

The dogs sniff out for me the odors that permeate the labyrinth of the night. Smell knows no lies. Their noses will scent the breath of my treason. They cannot be deceived. With my foot I crush the bottle of perfume, and escape from their olfactory powers.

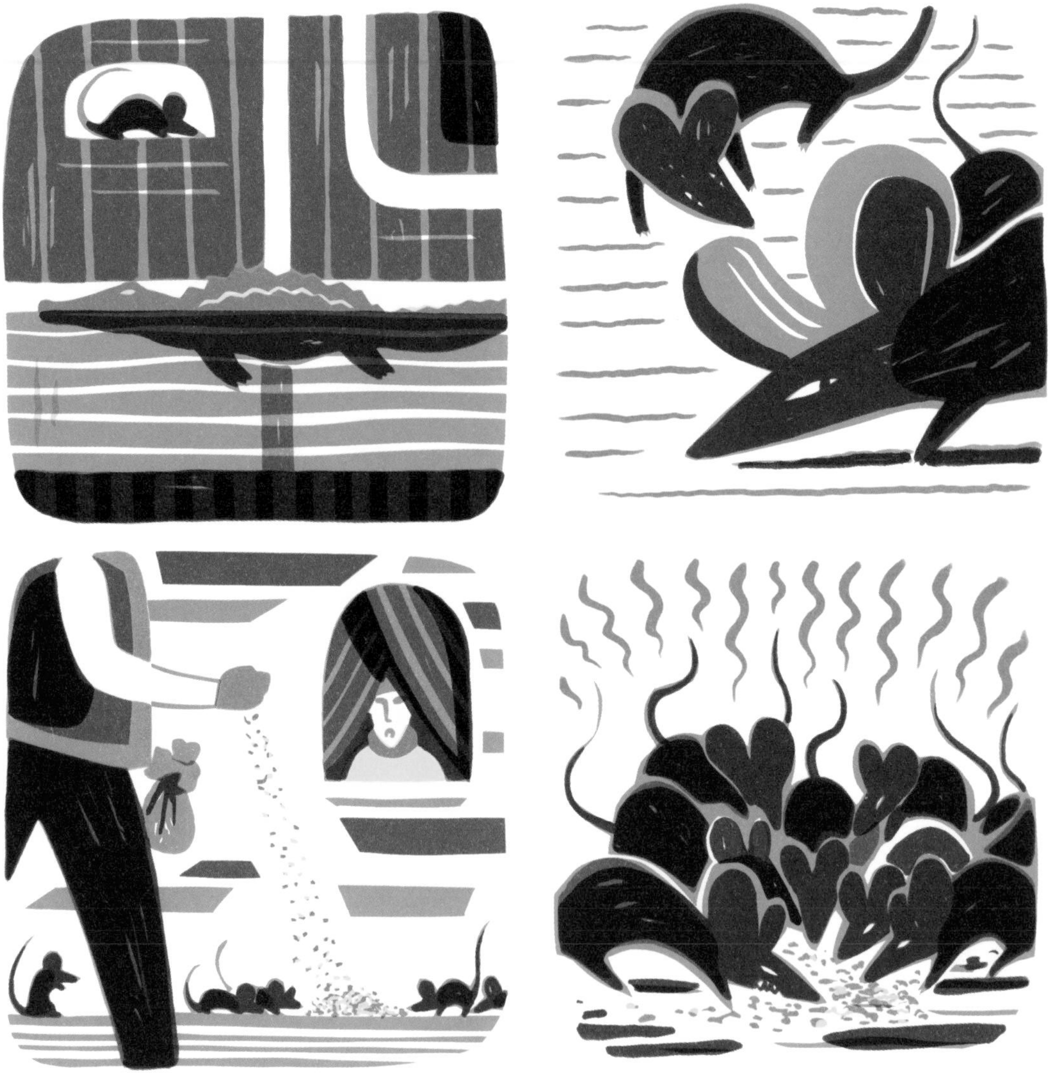

As for the rats ...the rats are my ears. They guard the subterranean depths. They will hear any catch in my breath, any break in the rhythm of my heart, but ... a hungry belly has no ears. I offer them the poison.

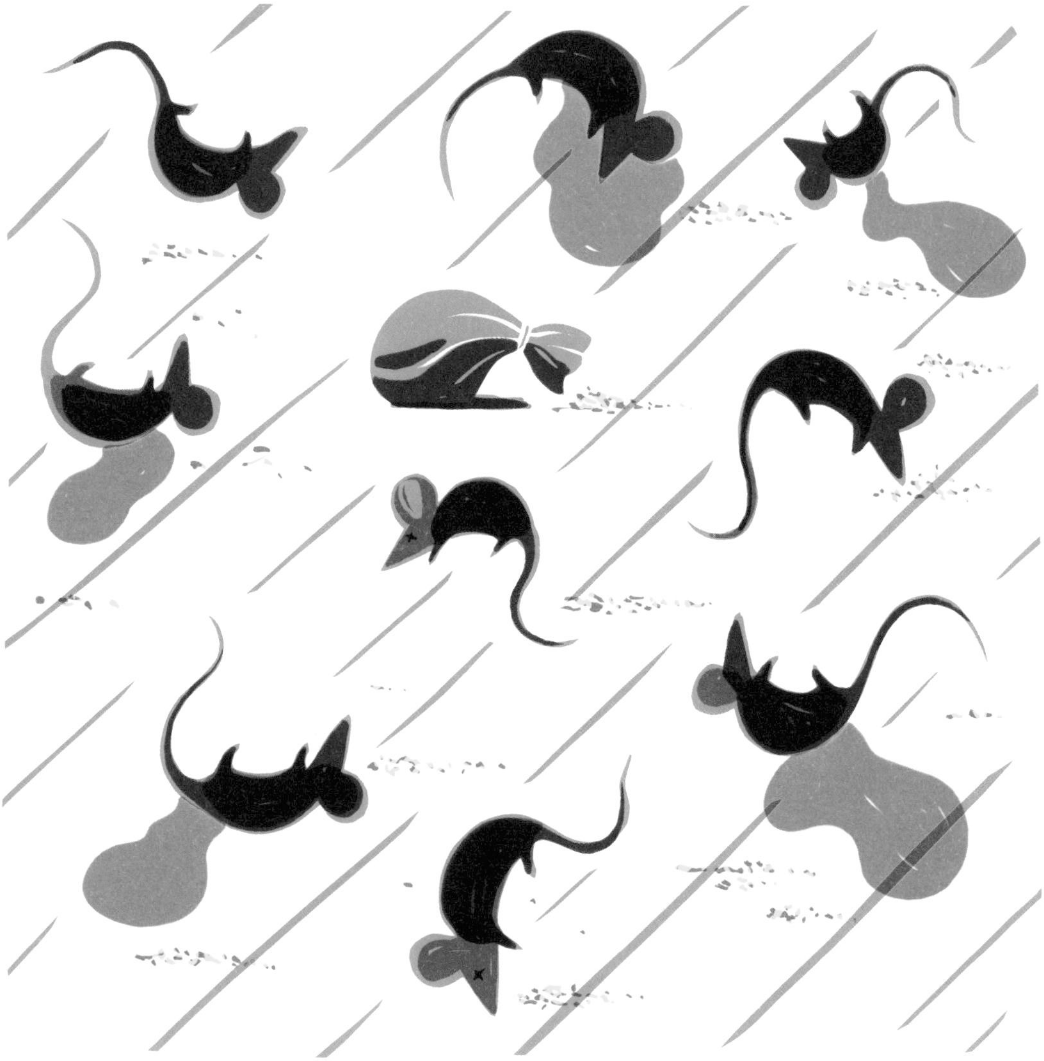

They squeal with greed.
And soon there is silence.

The coast is clear.

The sky turns blue, but everyone is still asleep.
The city belongs to me. I move around it as if it were
my own body. Its streets are my veins, its roofs the
convolutions of my brain. But for the first time,
I walk my body as if it were that of a stranger.
The sun crowns the horizon. It brushes the roofs and
makes them shimmer with the touch of its caress.

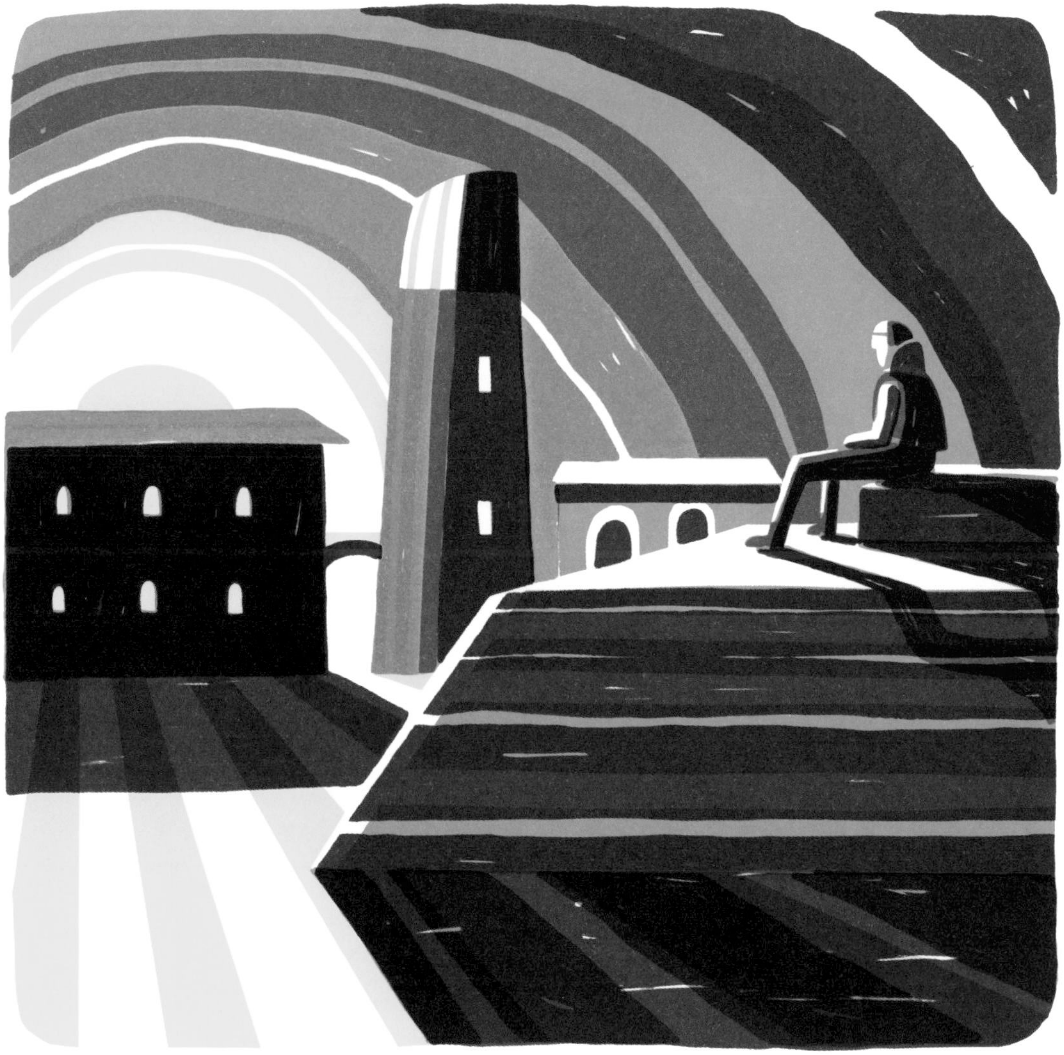

The city stretches, yawns, awakens.
This night will have been nothing but a bad dream.
A strange unease will accompany the day,
but from tomorrow the disquiet will have gone and all
will be forgotten. I must hasten to fetch
the Vagabond.

Piercing cries reach my ears. The square ends in the red sunrise, as if entering an open wound. Such turmoil ... Can the morning papers bring this much disquiet to the new dawn?

It is the Vendor. She has not taken my advice. She has committed the folly of leaving her hiding place, and now there she is, in the center of the square, visible to all, her voice loud and shrill in the brightening daylight, and echoing from the crowd that surrounds her. They accuse her, and in turn she defends herself, but faces harden, bodies tense, and the crowd tightens its grip.

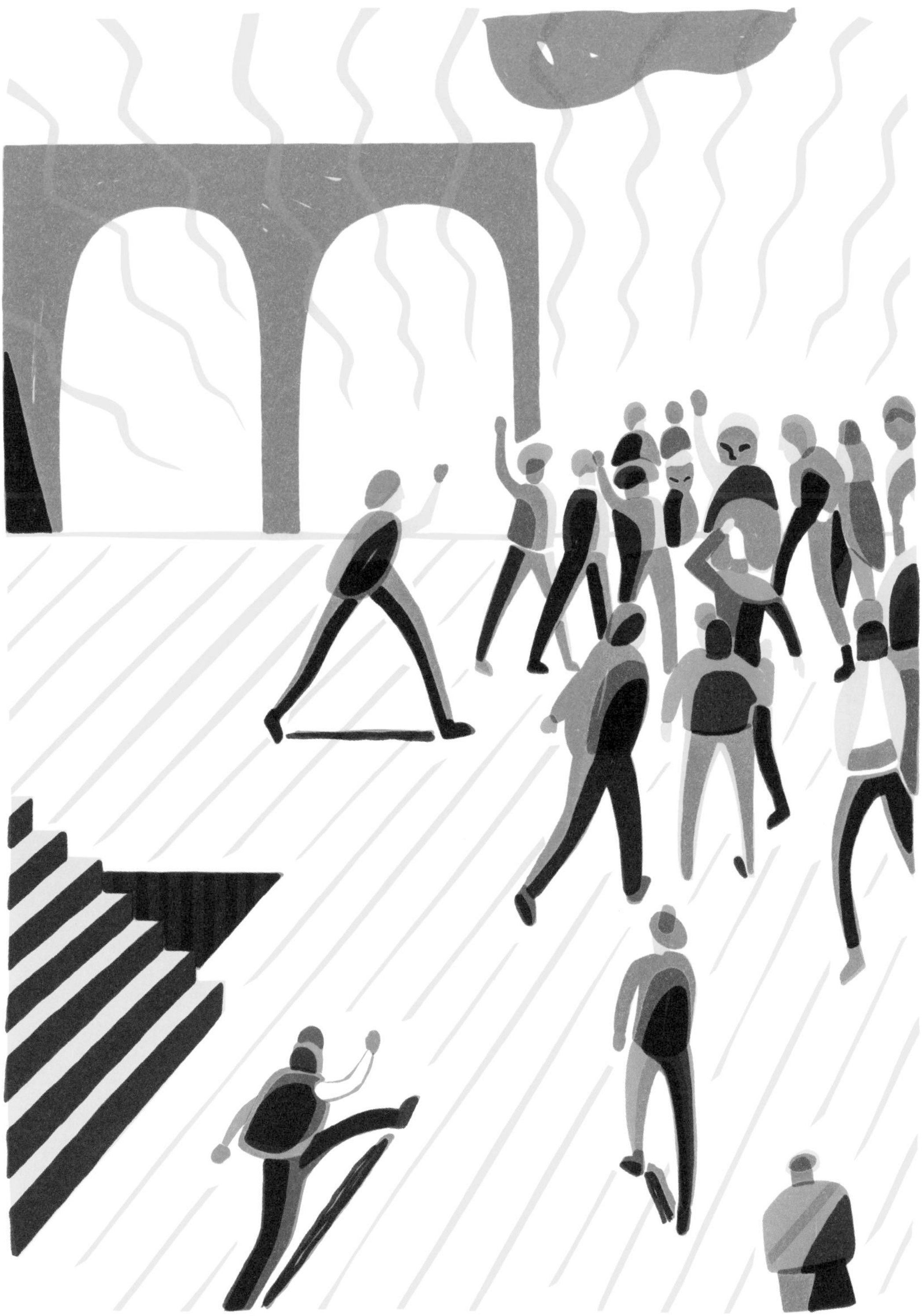

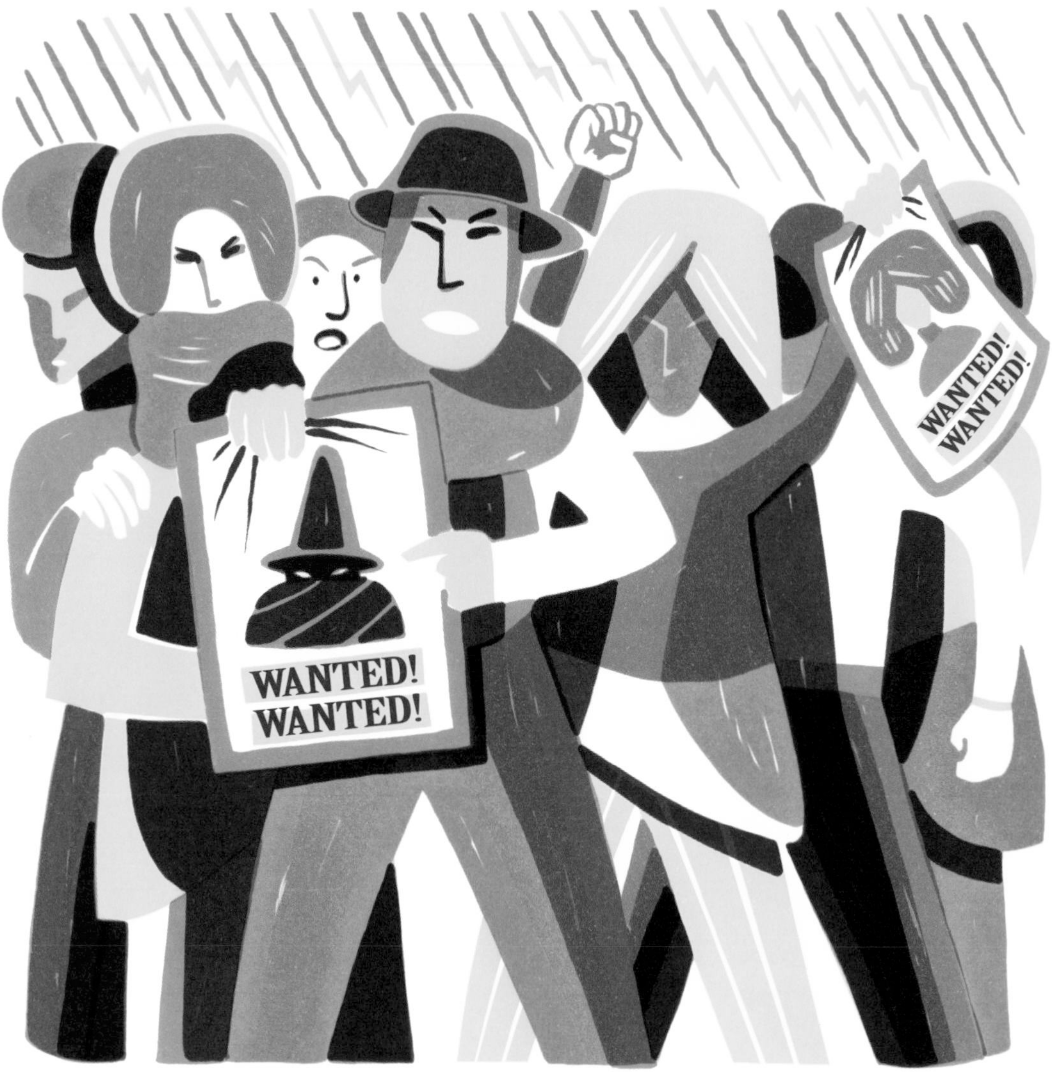

WANTED!
WANTED!
WANTED!
WANTED!


*"Tell us where he's hiding! Give us your accomplice!*
*Give us the man who has destroyed our clocks!*
*Give us the man who is ruining our nights!*
*Give us the Vagabond!"*

I snatch the Vendor from the spitting mob around her.
The eyes of the city are filled with hatred.
Threats pursue us. We flee to our refuge from the
insults, and secretly enter the church. No one has seen
us. The Vagabond is there, sitting in a corner, sleeping
peacefully. We shall have to wait till nightfall before
we can leave. By then the city will be calmer.
I look sadly at the Vendor. We both know that she too
will have to leave. The city has unmasked her.
There will be no forgiveness.

*"Come with us. With me."*

She kisses me. Her breath fills my body
with a new warmth. Supposing I put out my lamp
forever, and let this new fire burn in me?

It is impossible. I am the Night Watchman.
I cannot leave.

*"Be ready to depart. I shall come for you at nightfall."*

**Sixth Night**

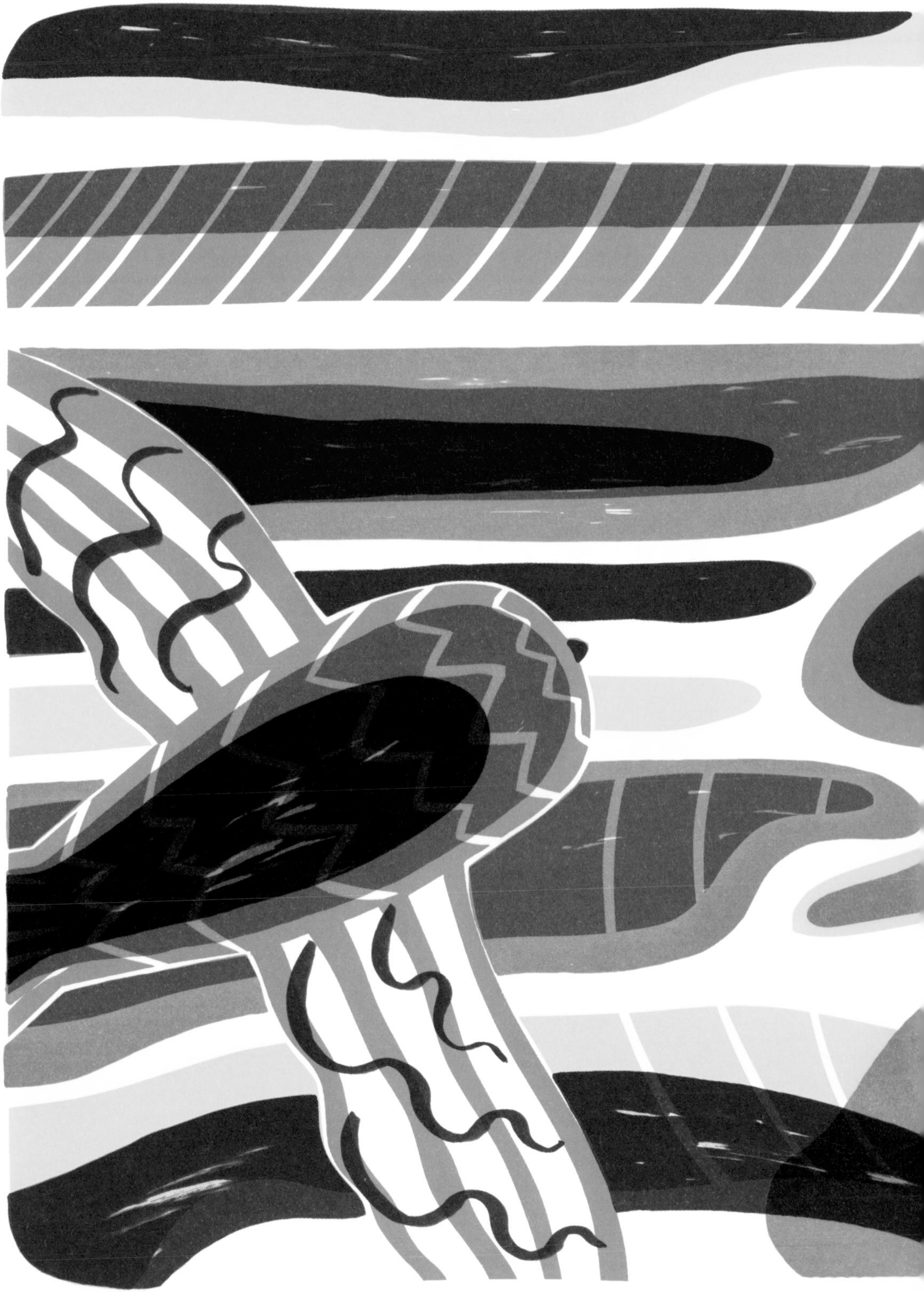

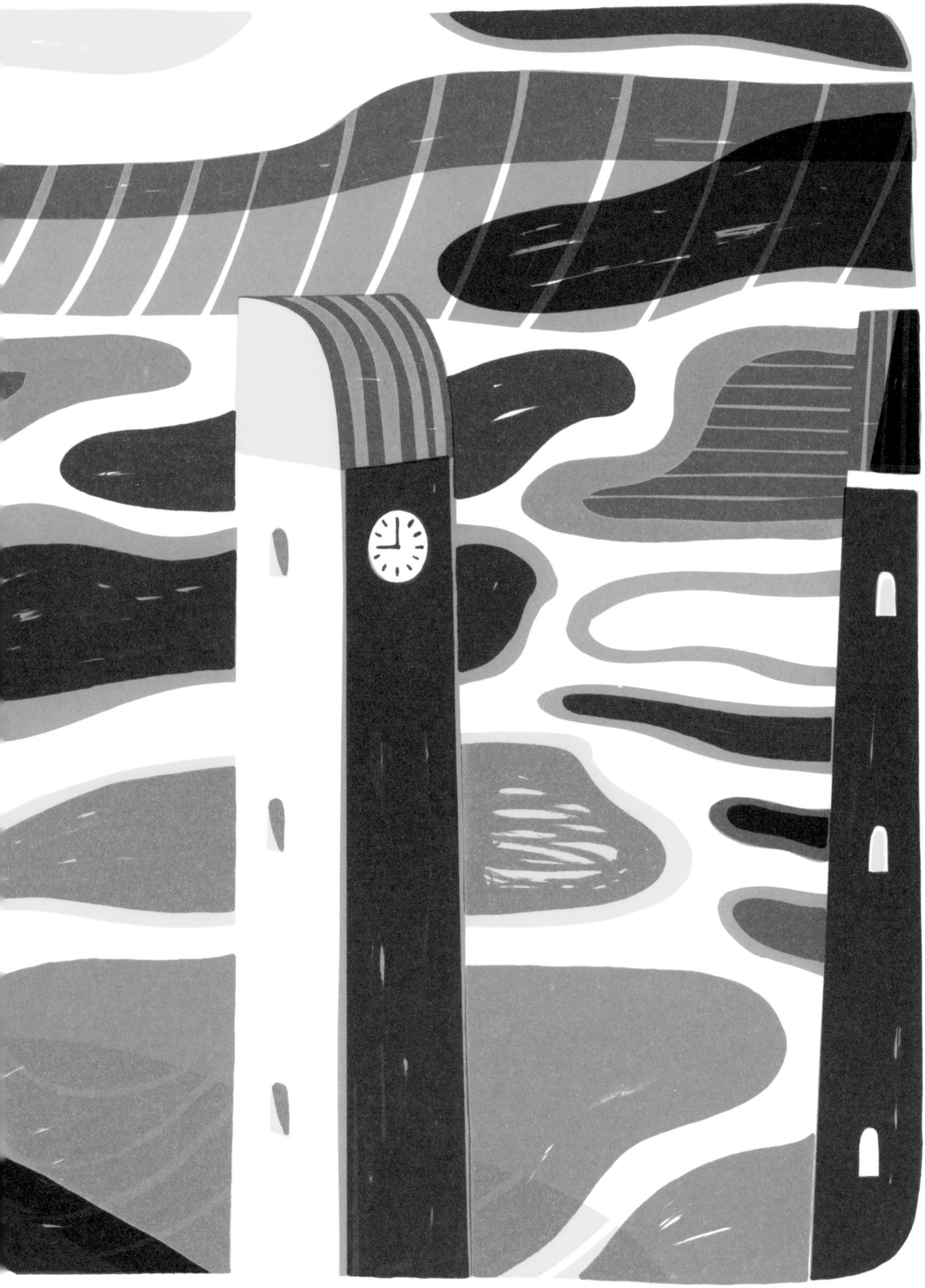

The day leaves a feverish
twilight in its wake.

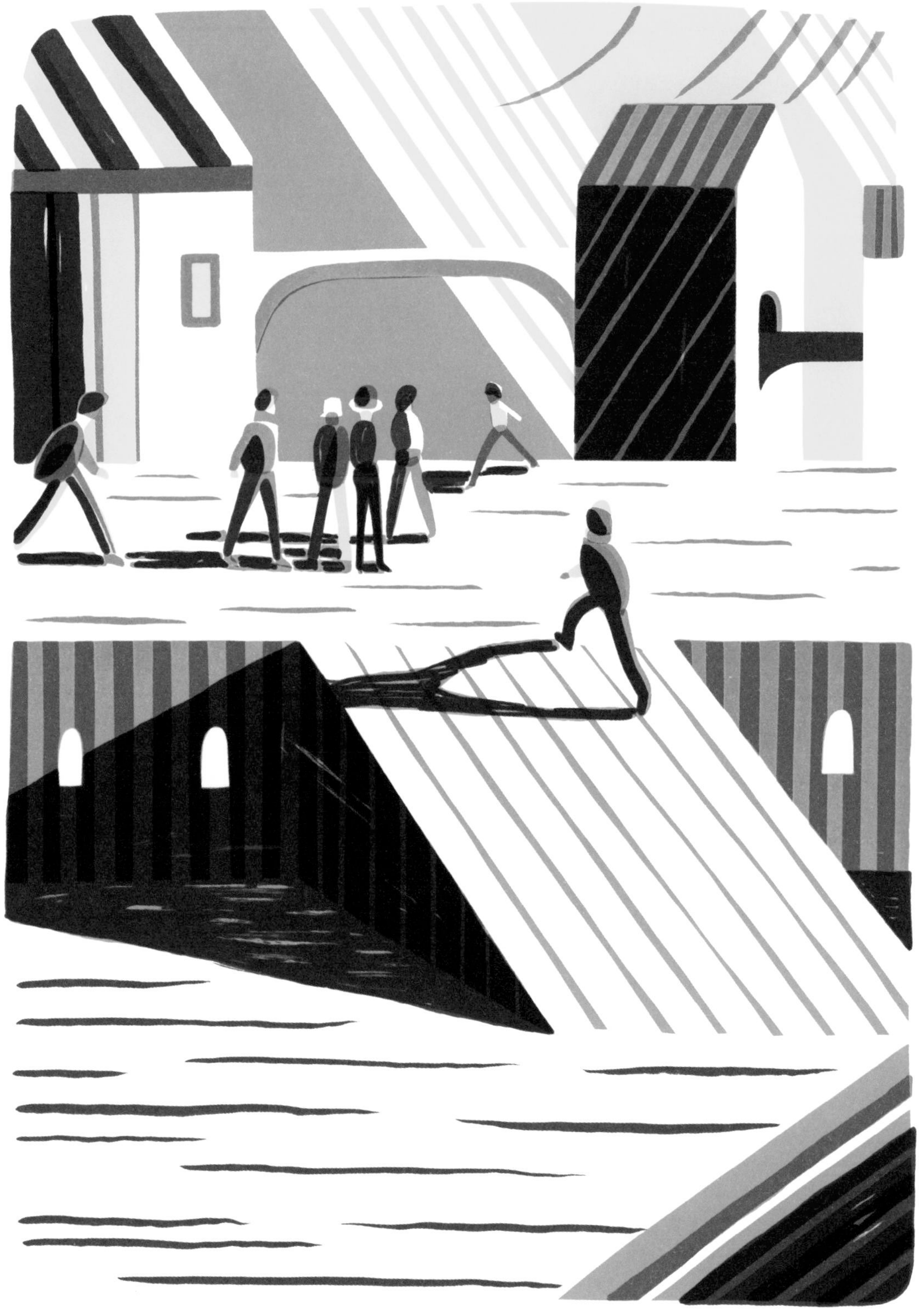

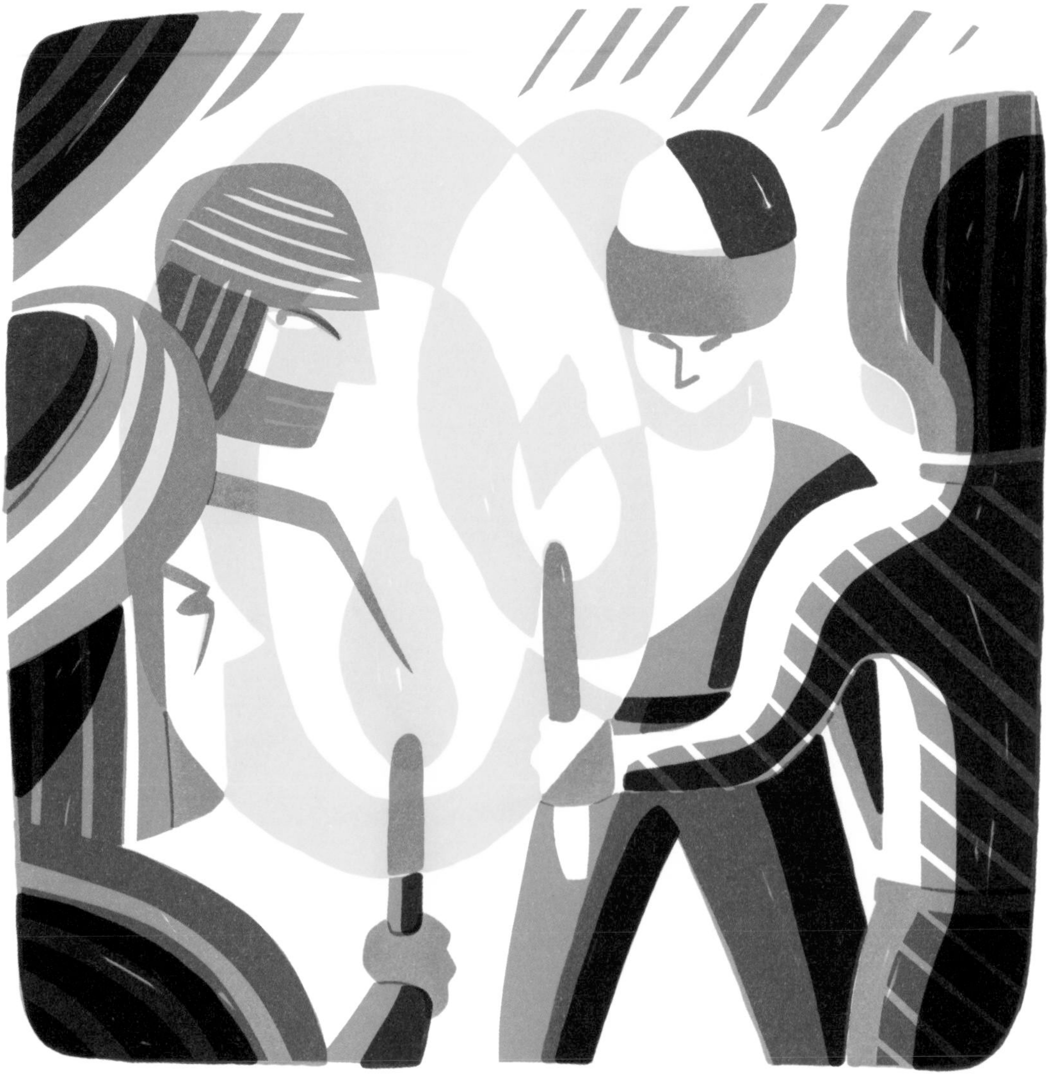

It fades, and people light their torches.
The shadows break up, intermingle,
and endlessly multiply.

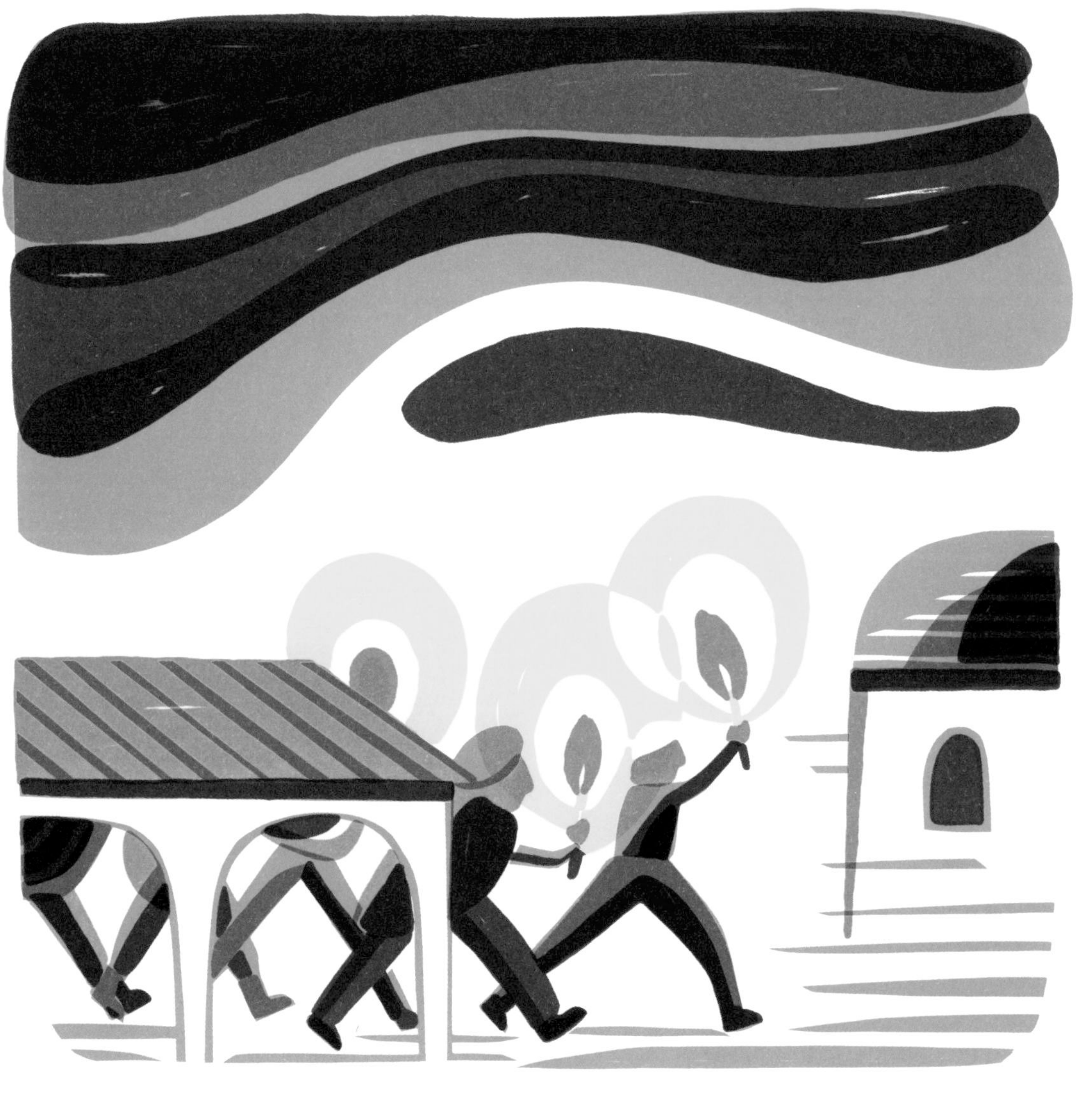

In the square, there is a hubbub of rumors. The crowd surges in waves, like the swell before the storm. Tonight the city will have no rest.

I cross the square, and people gaze at me, undecided. Anxious eyes seek in all directions, and mouths murmur a hundred different prophecies. But no one makes a move. Nothing is certain. For them, I am still making my rounds. Faces turn aside and I am allowed to go on my way.

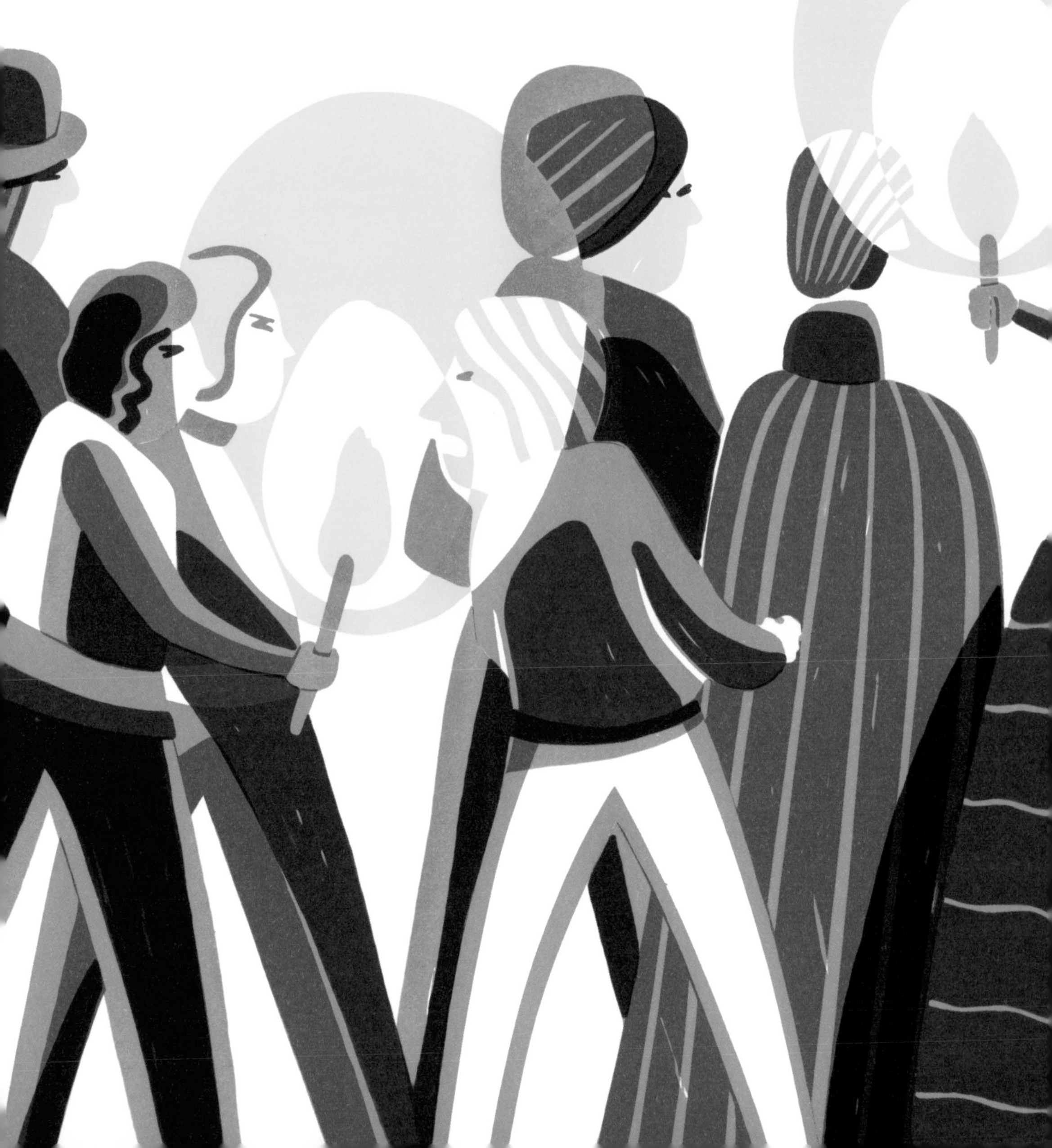

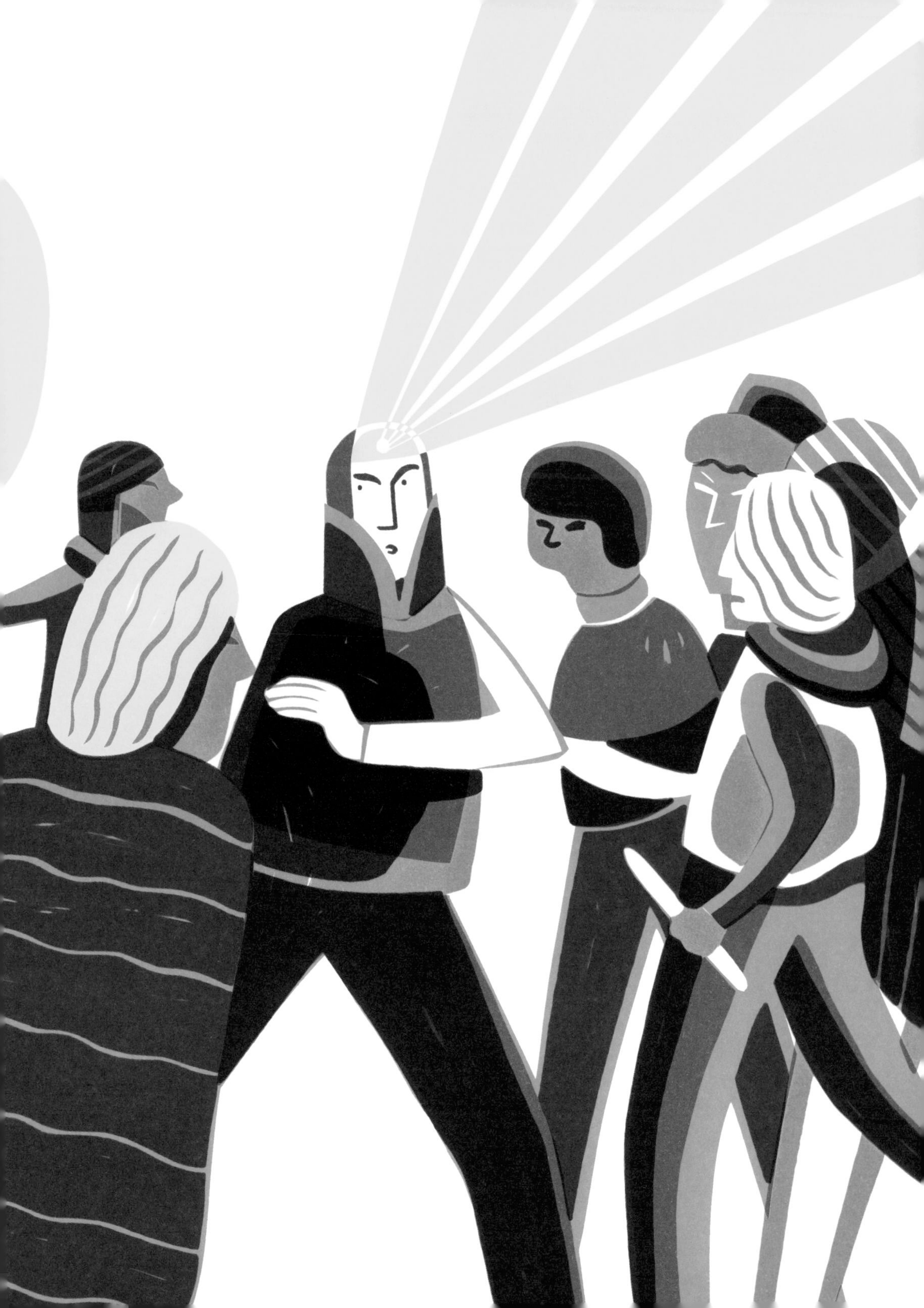

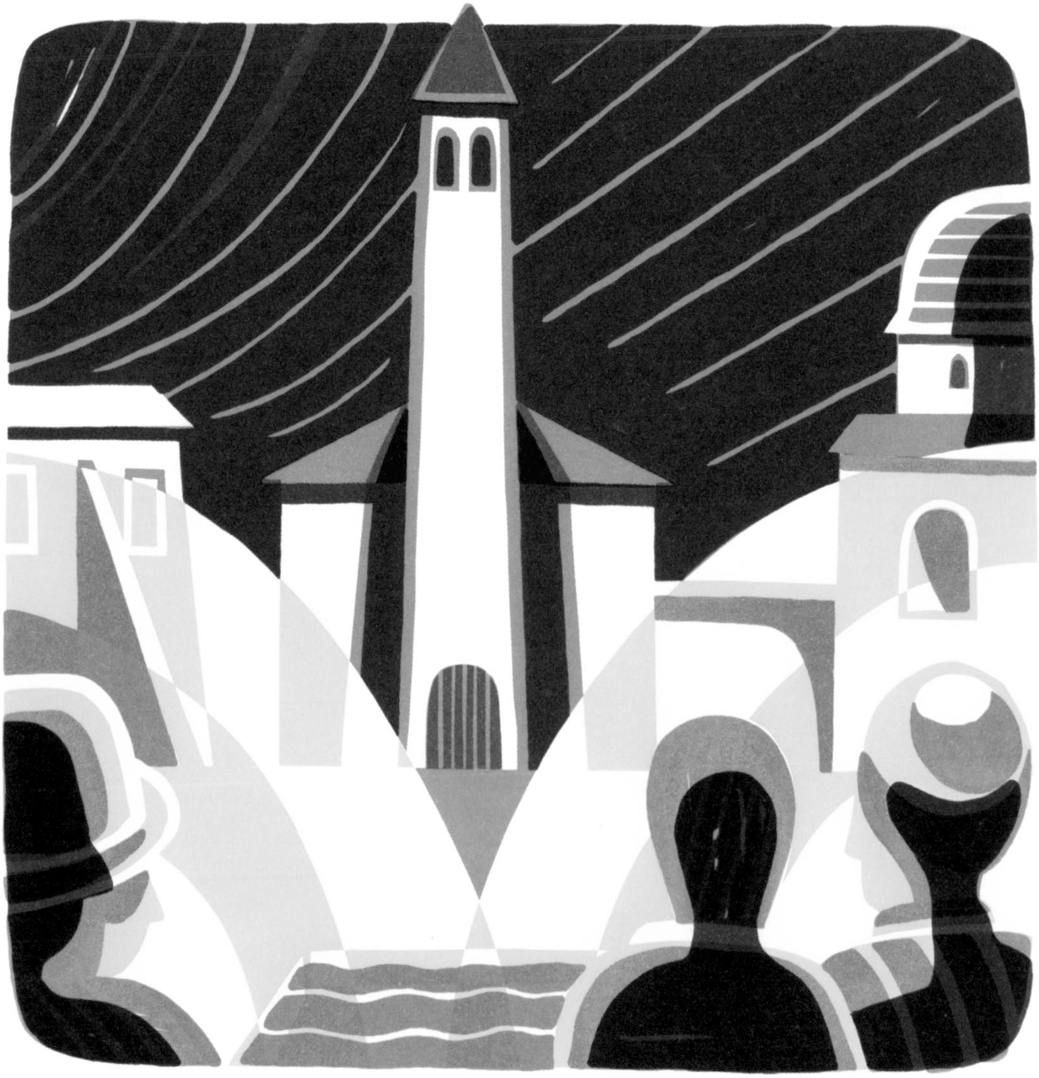

I reach the church. The light from the stained glass windows sends will-o'-the-wisps dancing nervously over the archways. The owl flies away.

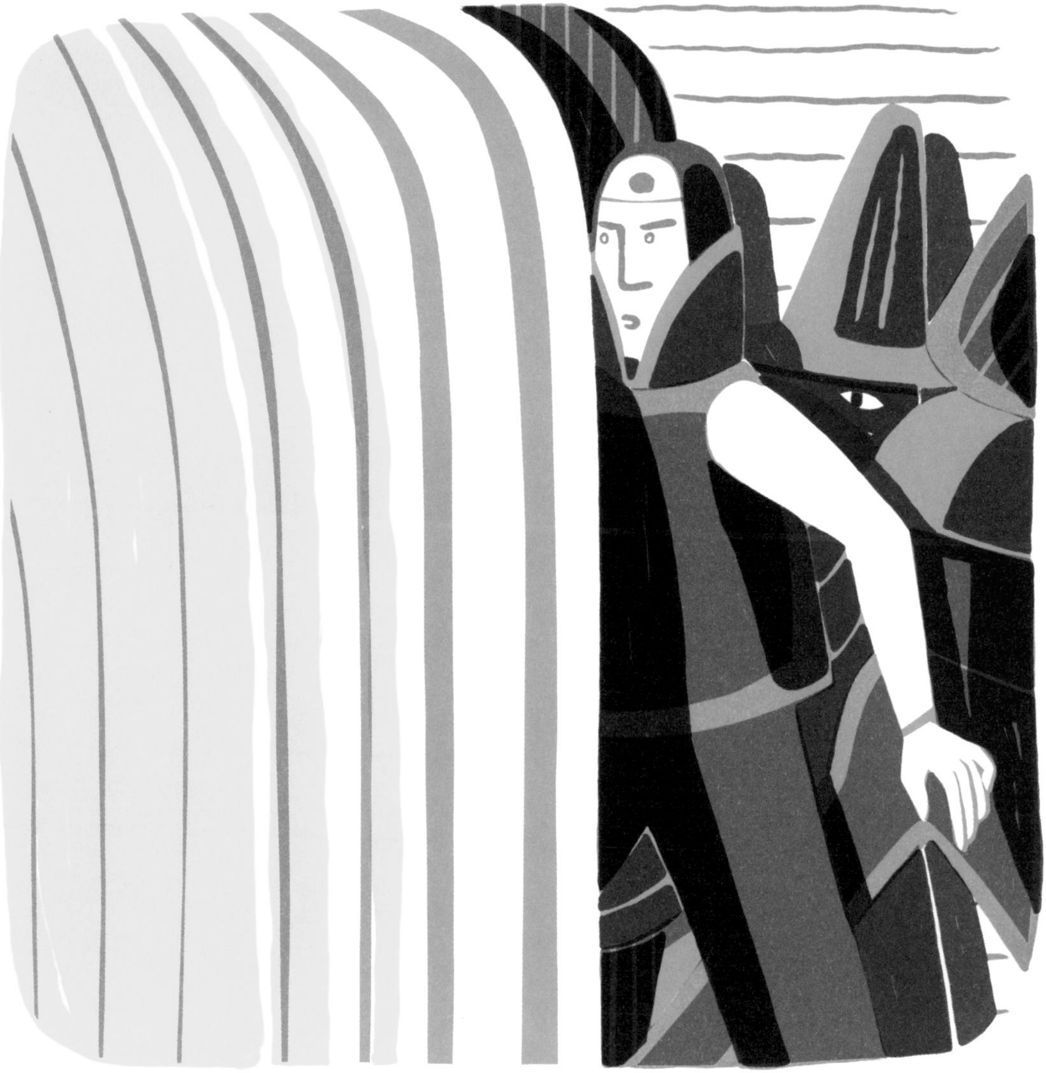

We must leave before it's too late—make our way through the alleyways without being seen.

*"Stay close behind me and you will have nothing to fear."*

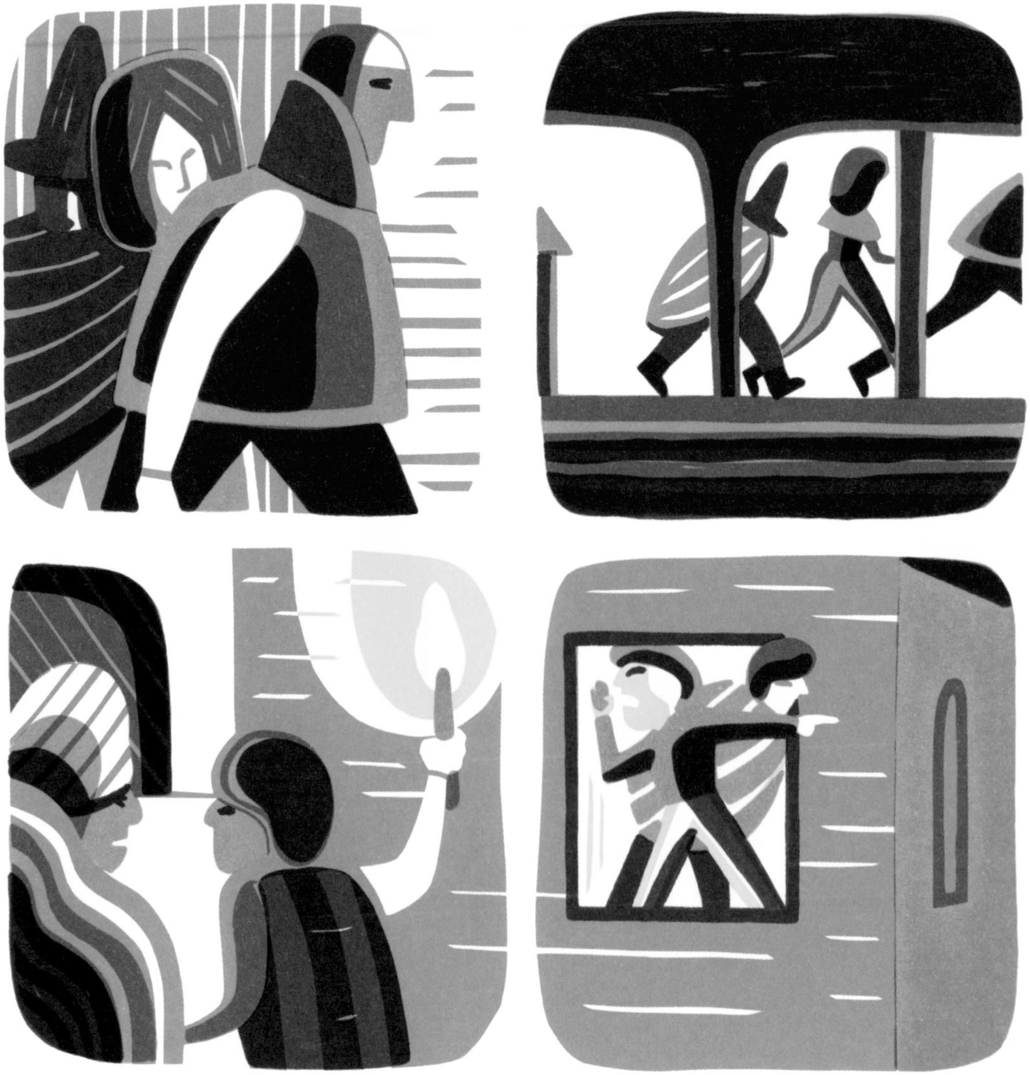

The city brushes past us.
We hold our breath.

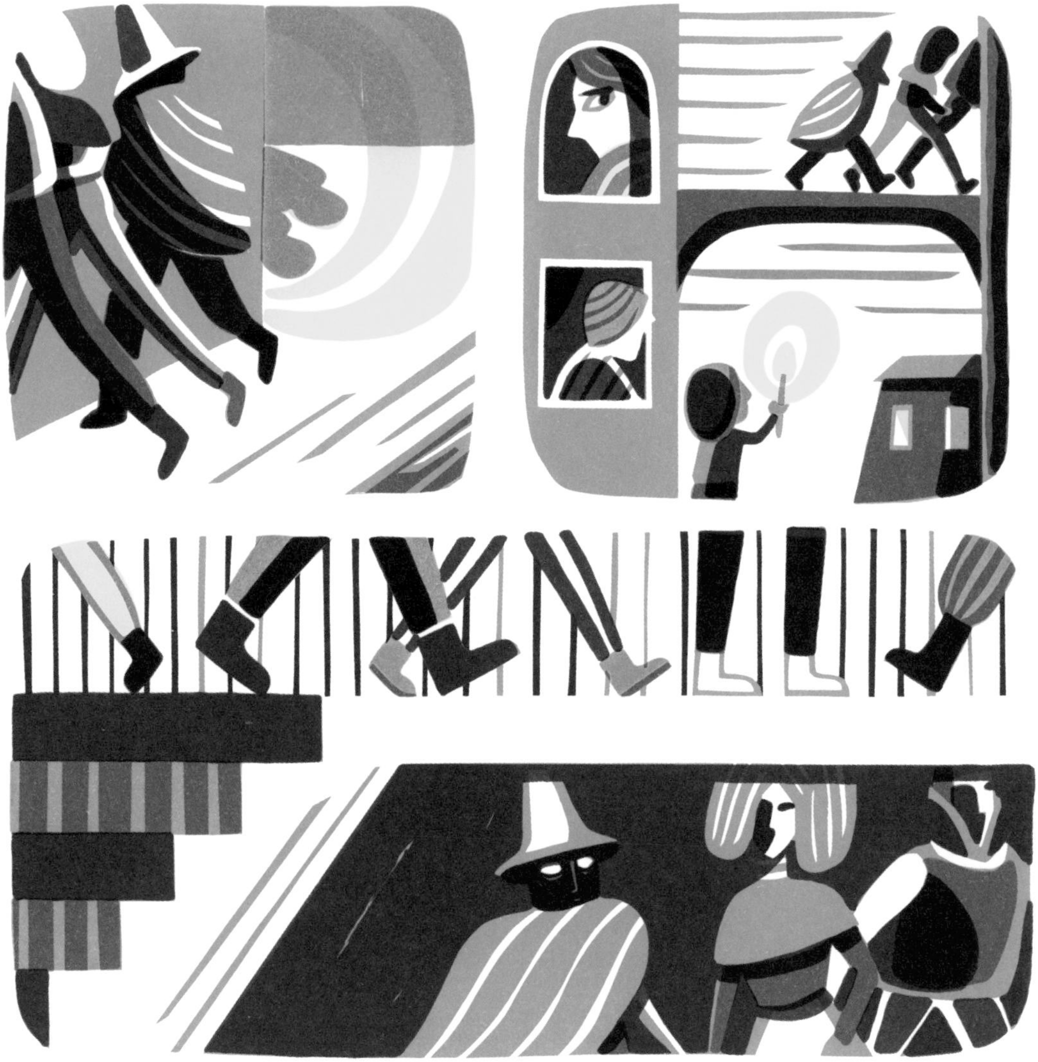

It smells us, scents us, senses us, loses us. We move on again, and once more the crowd gathers, jostling us, entwining us, seeing our silhouettes and groaning in the night which catches fire.

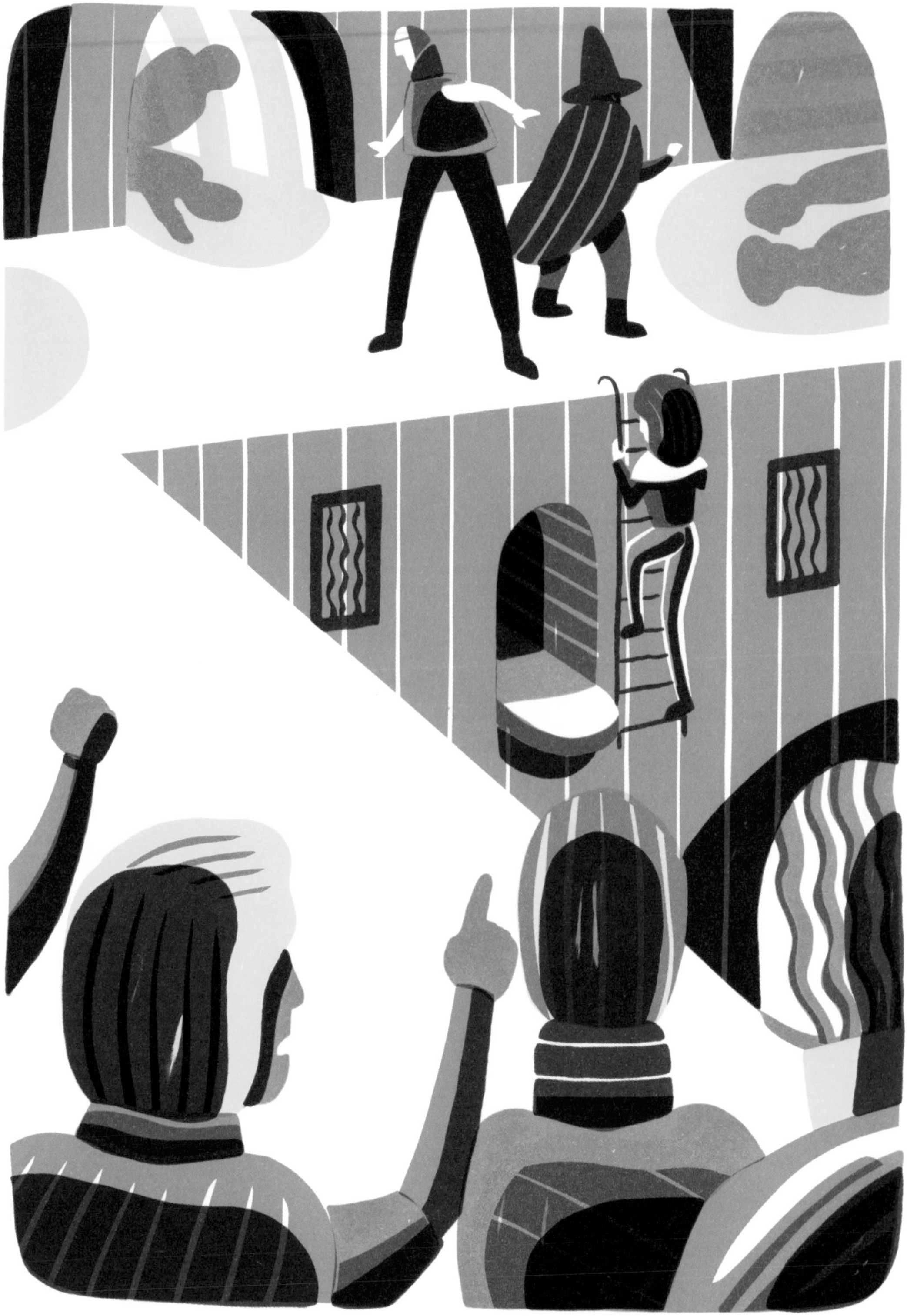

We make a detour, but they have seen our shadows appearing and disappearing in the crevices of the walls, and the noise of their pursuit drowns the echoes of our footsteps. At last, beneath our feet, there is the escape route.

*"Quick, into the sewers!"*

The Vendor has slipped through, but for the two of us it is now too late. The noose has tightened. The city swoops down on us. Voices thunder, overwhelming us. But then, suddenly, there is a backward movement, voices stick in throats, the torches go out. The darkness deepens.

It's them.

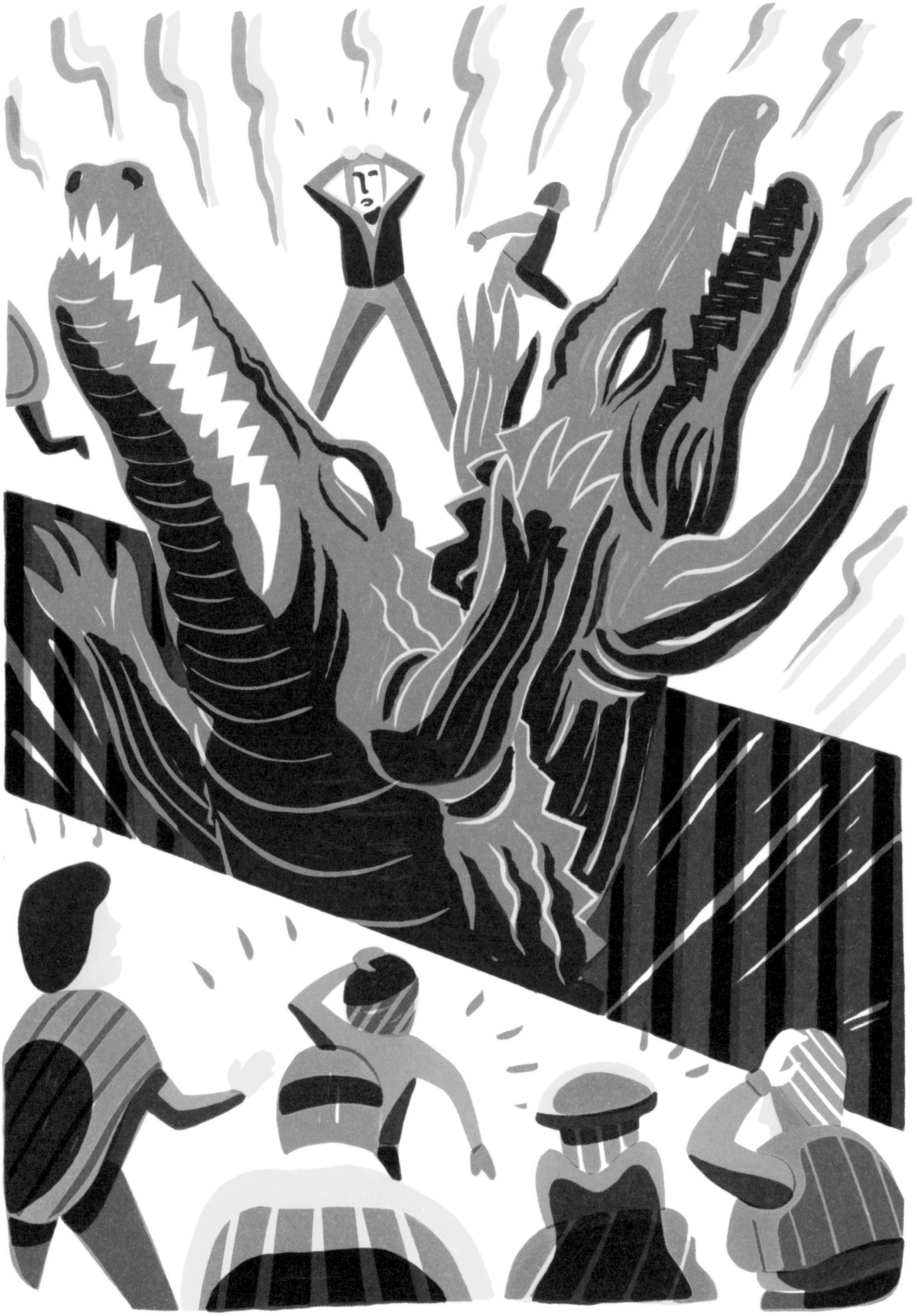

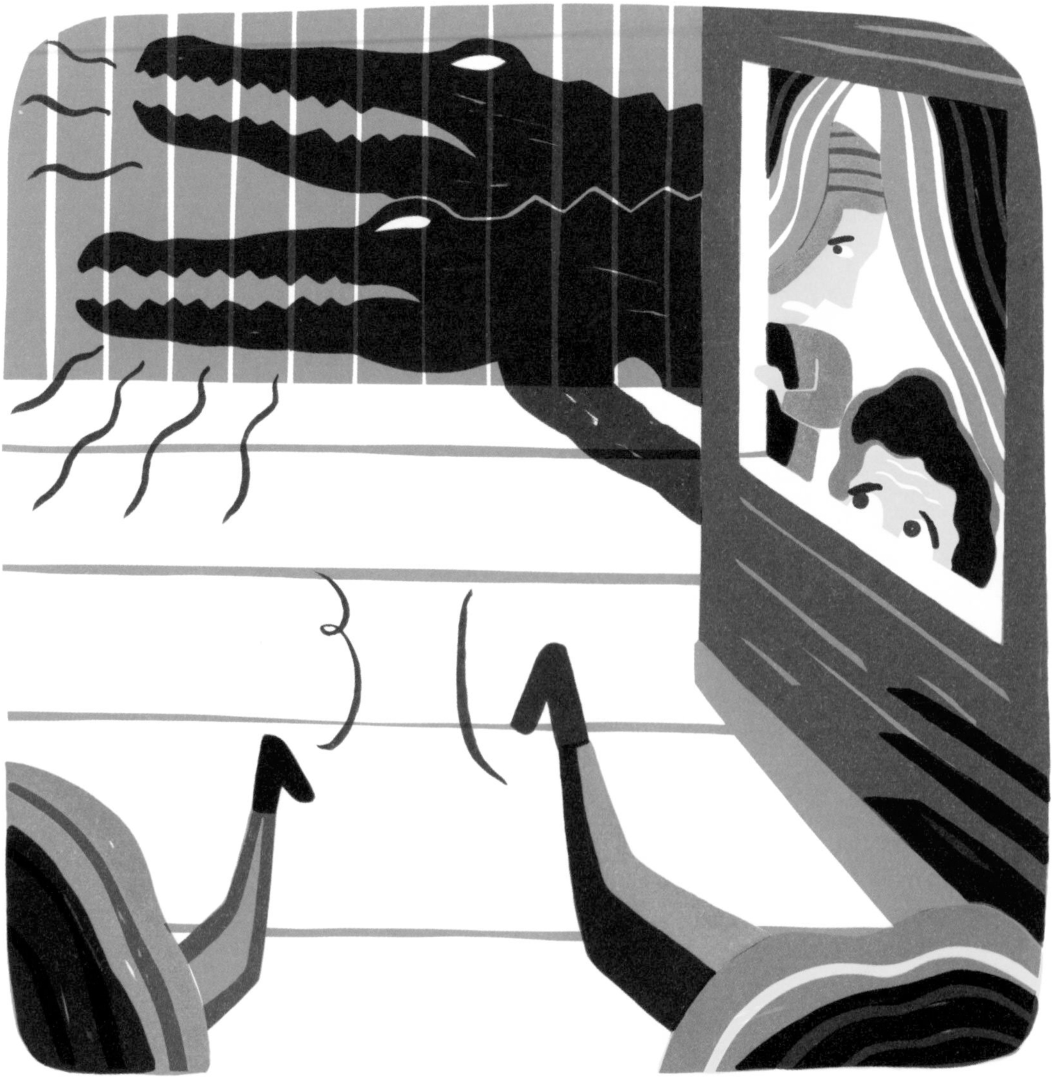

They have returned to haunt the night, disgorging themselves into the streets through the suppurating wound of the sewers. The cesspool regurgitates them, and they spread out all over the city.

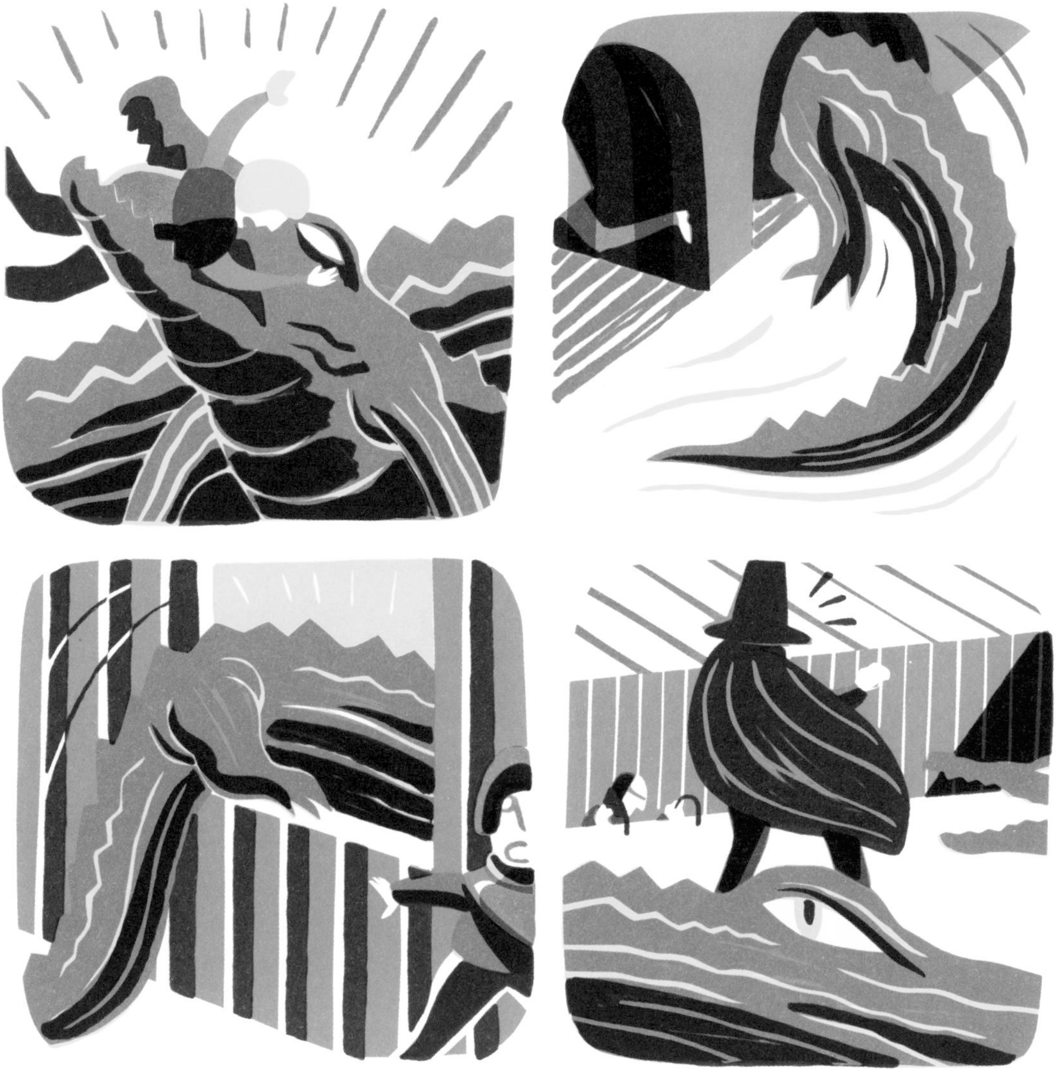

Two jaws rip the darkness to pieces. I have no choice.
I too must flee.

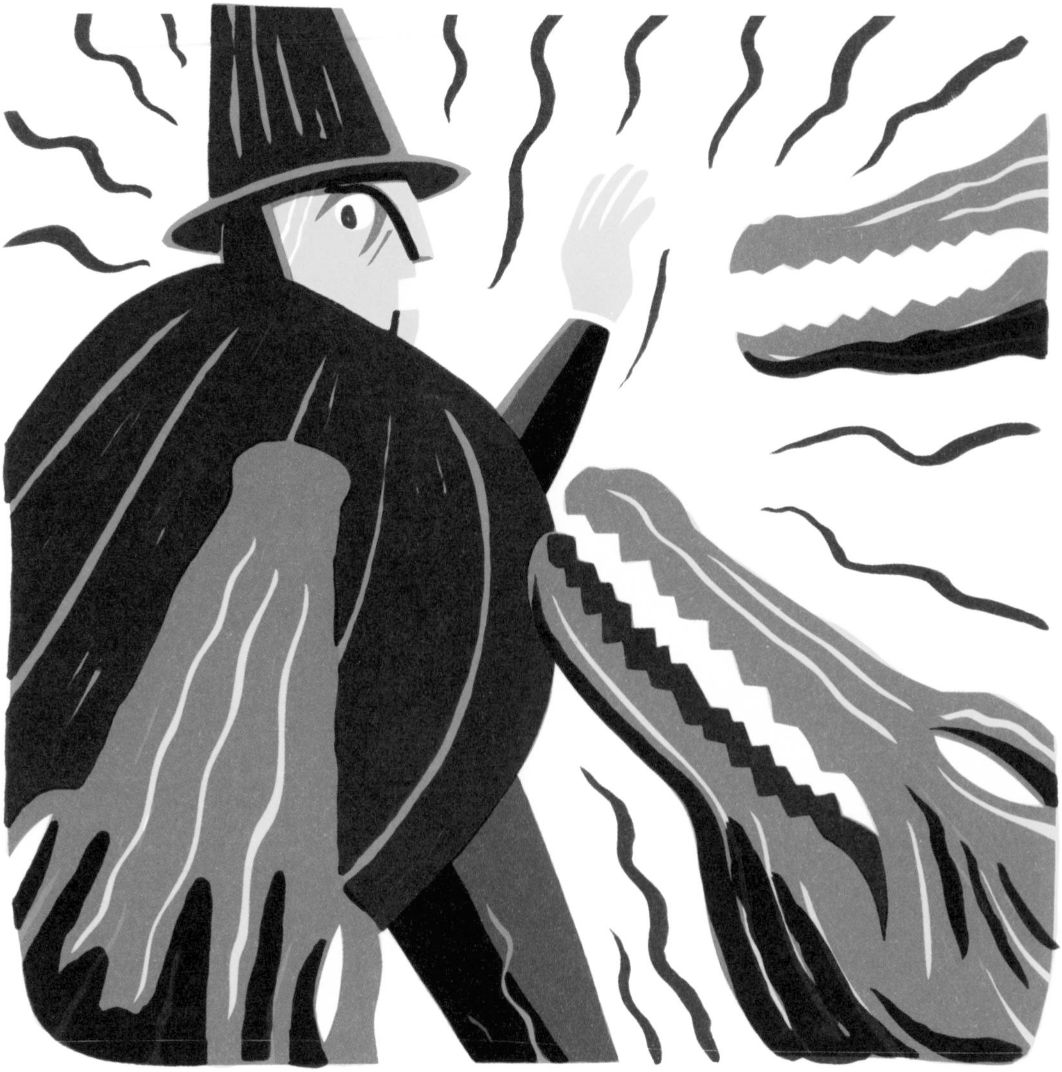

I have already entered the sewer. But the Vagabond is still fighting. He did not follow me. The jaws are gaining ground...they have surrounded him. I cannot help him now.

Behind us, the cracking jaws smash the night to splinters. The sewers swallow us up.

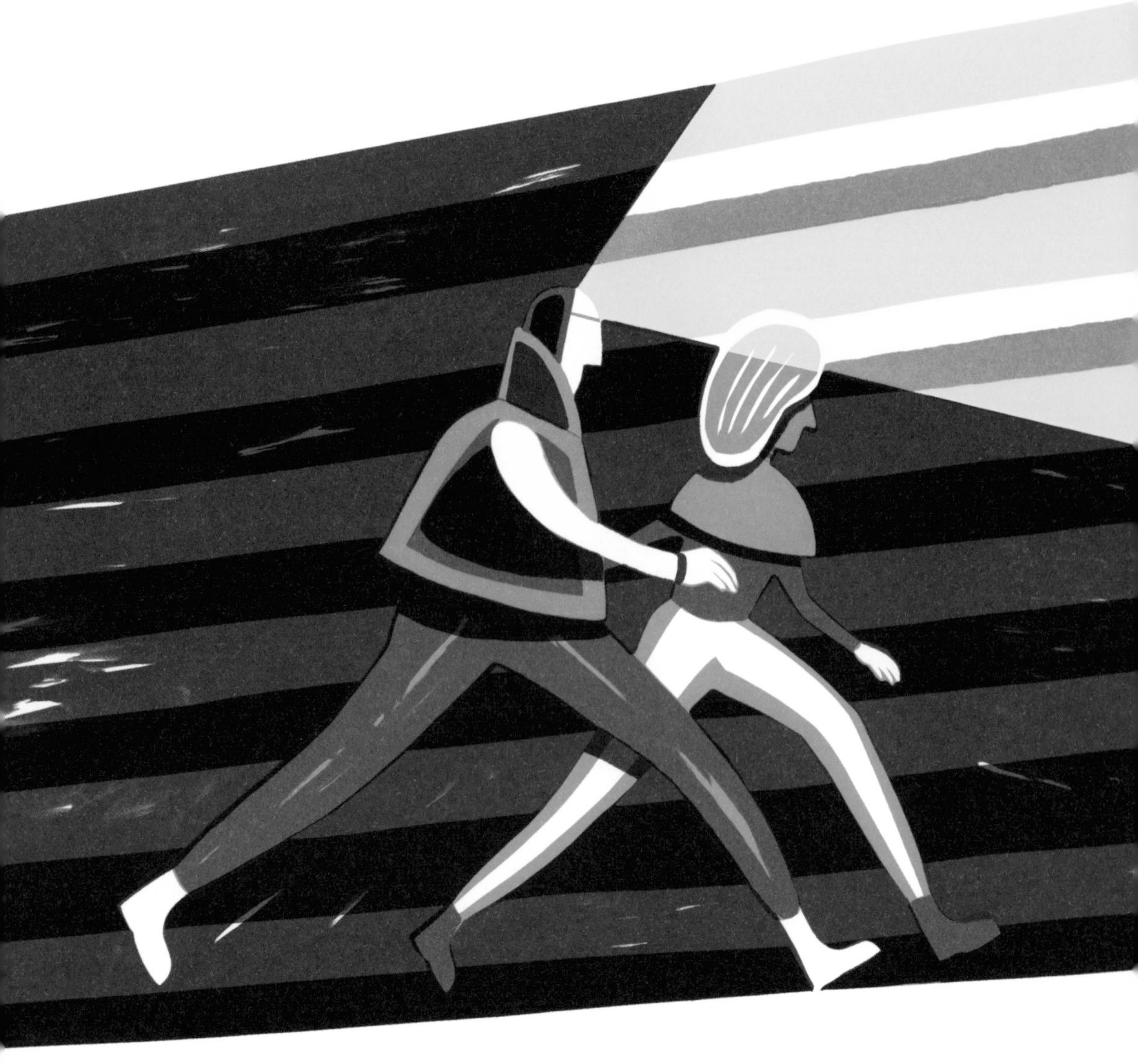

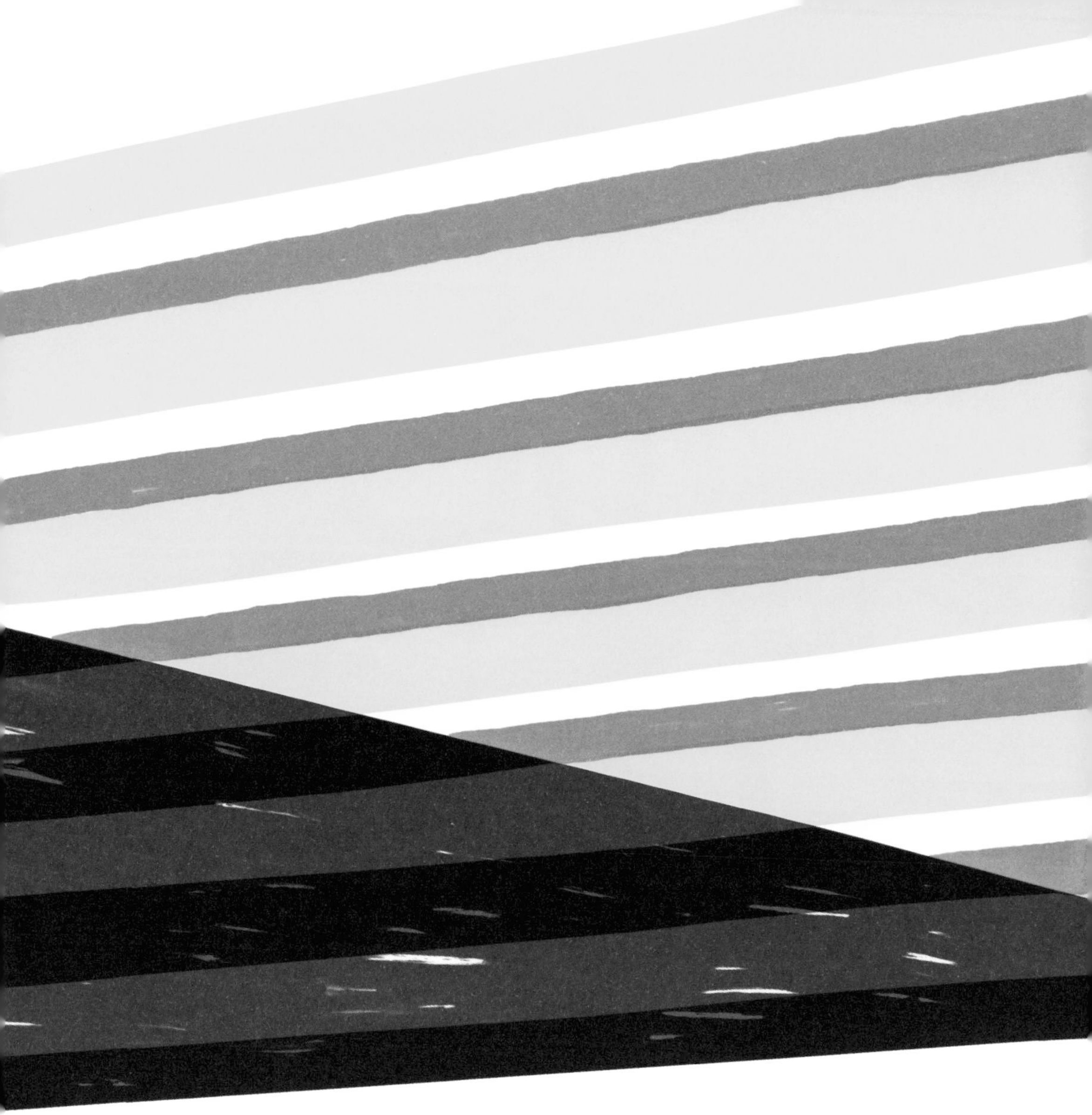

For hours we slither like snakes along the tunnels that wind their way through the underside of the city. We drift endlessly through the foul mists where night reigns supreme, and we do not know if outside the day will finally come.

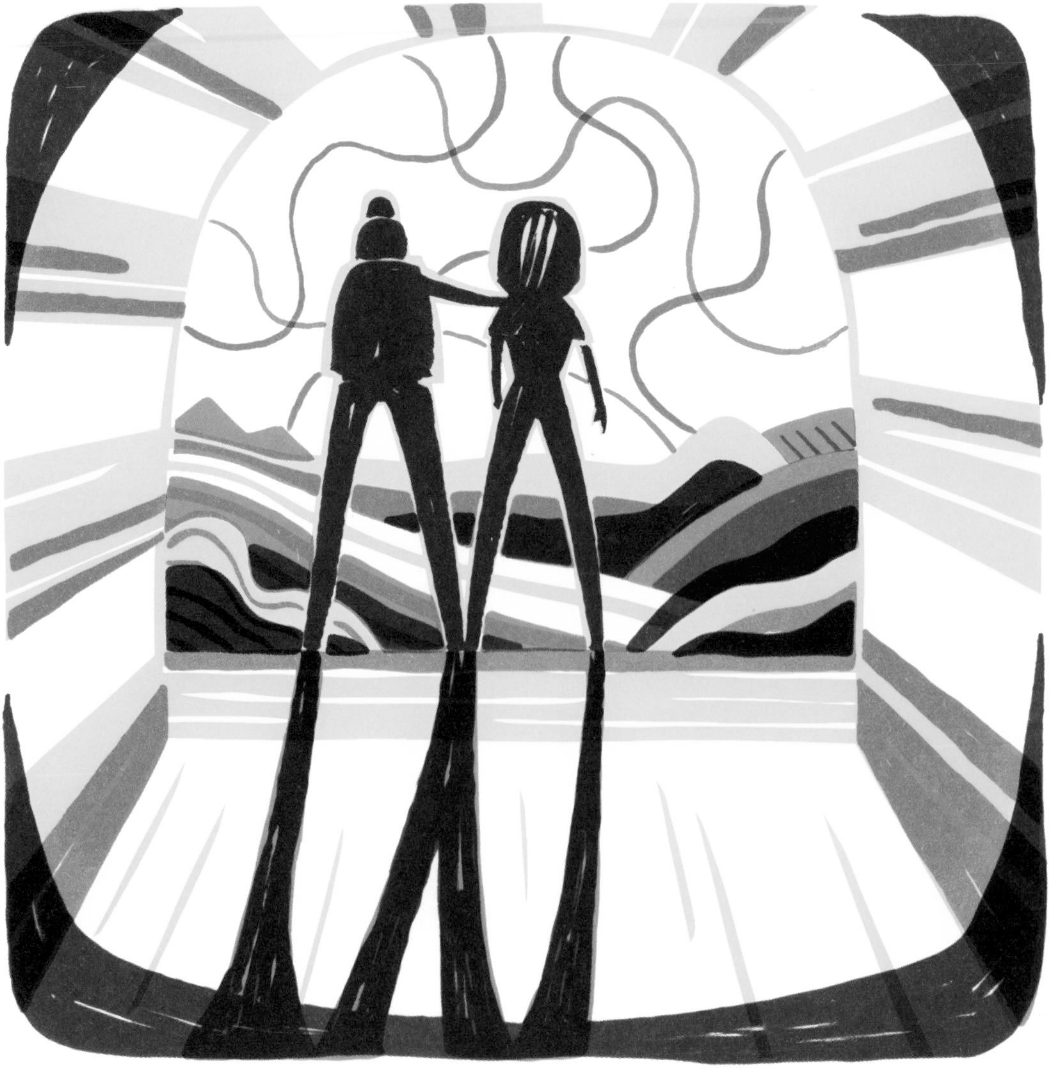

At last, however, I extinguish my lamp, for in the distance is the eye of dawn. The city has digested us. The wind envelops us and still brings us the faint crunching sounds of battle. But we are far away now.

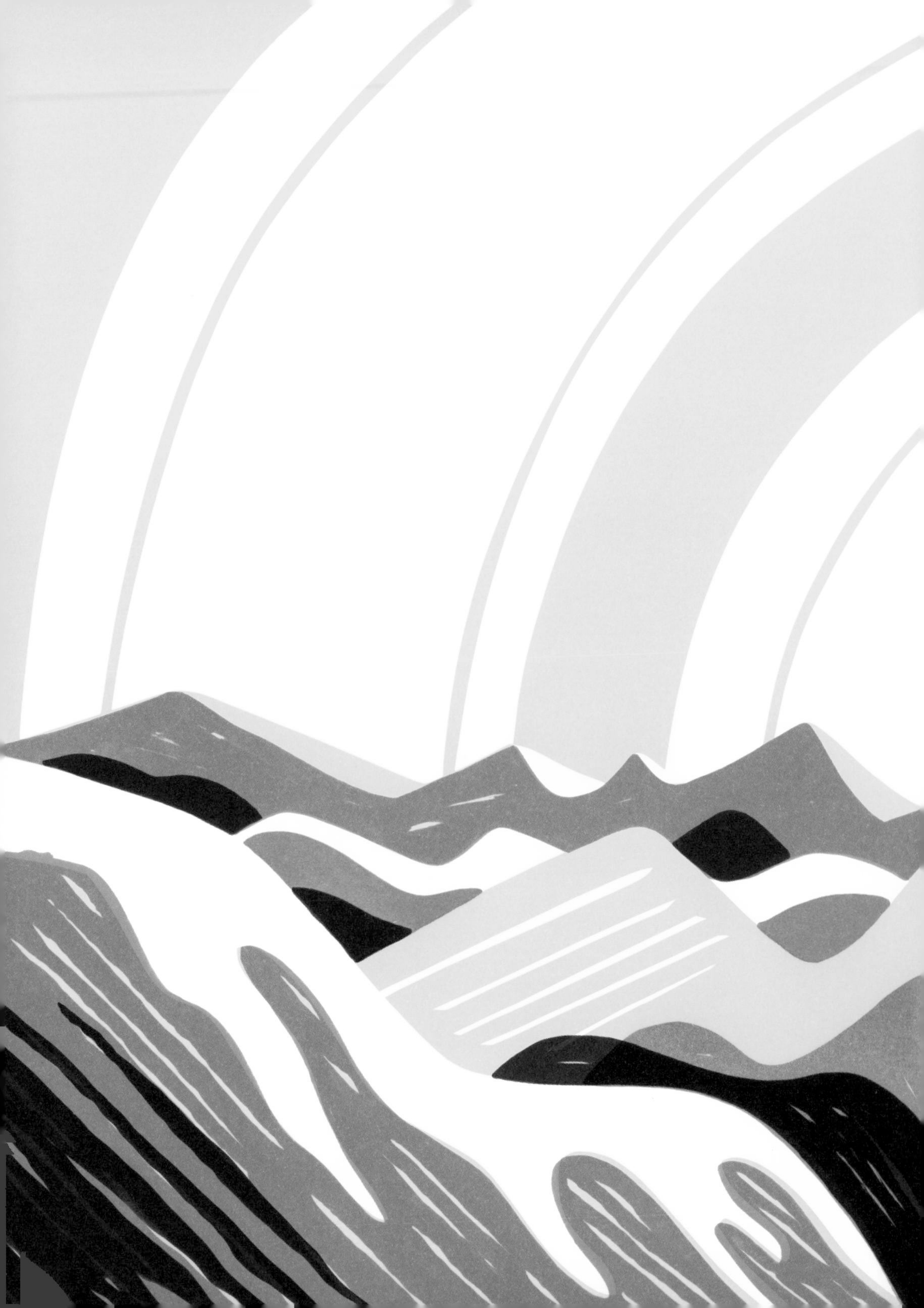

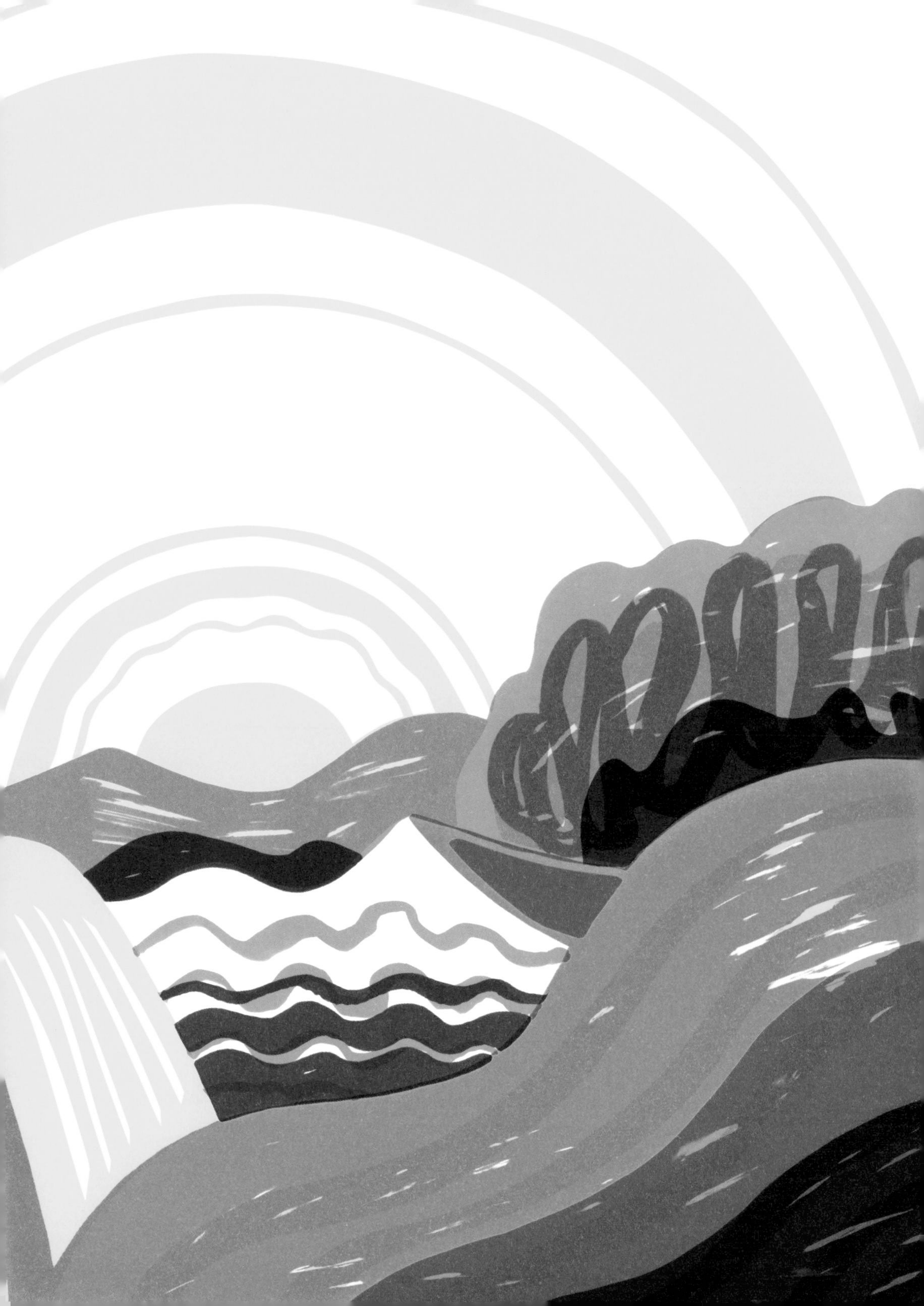

This morning the earth steams. The fresh water of its slumber evaporates; it hoists the sun onto the canopy of the sky. Soon the flowers will open their petals, the forests will languidly exhale their moisture, filling the azure with delicate clouds as pink as fresh wounds. The horizon will broaden, and it will be day.

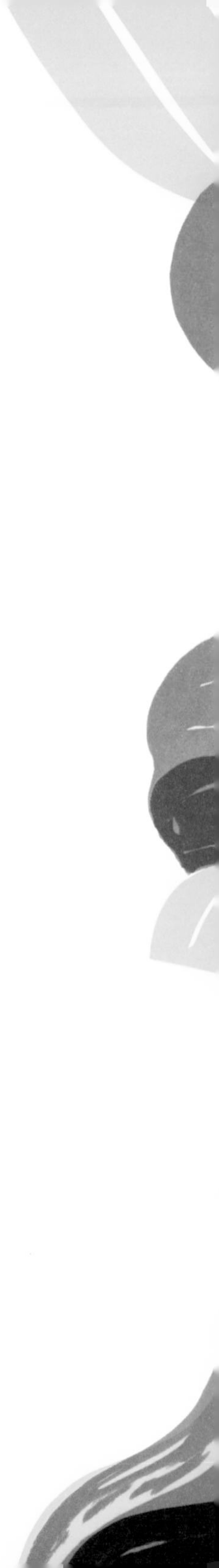

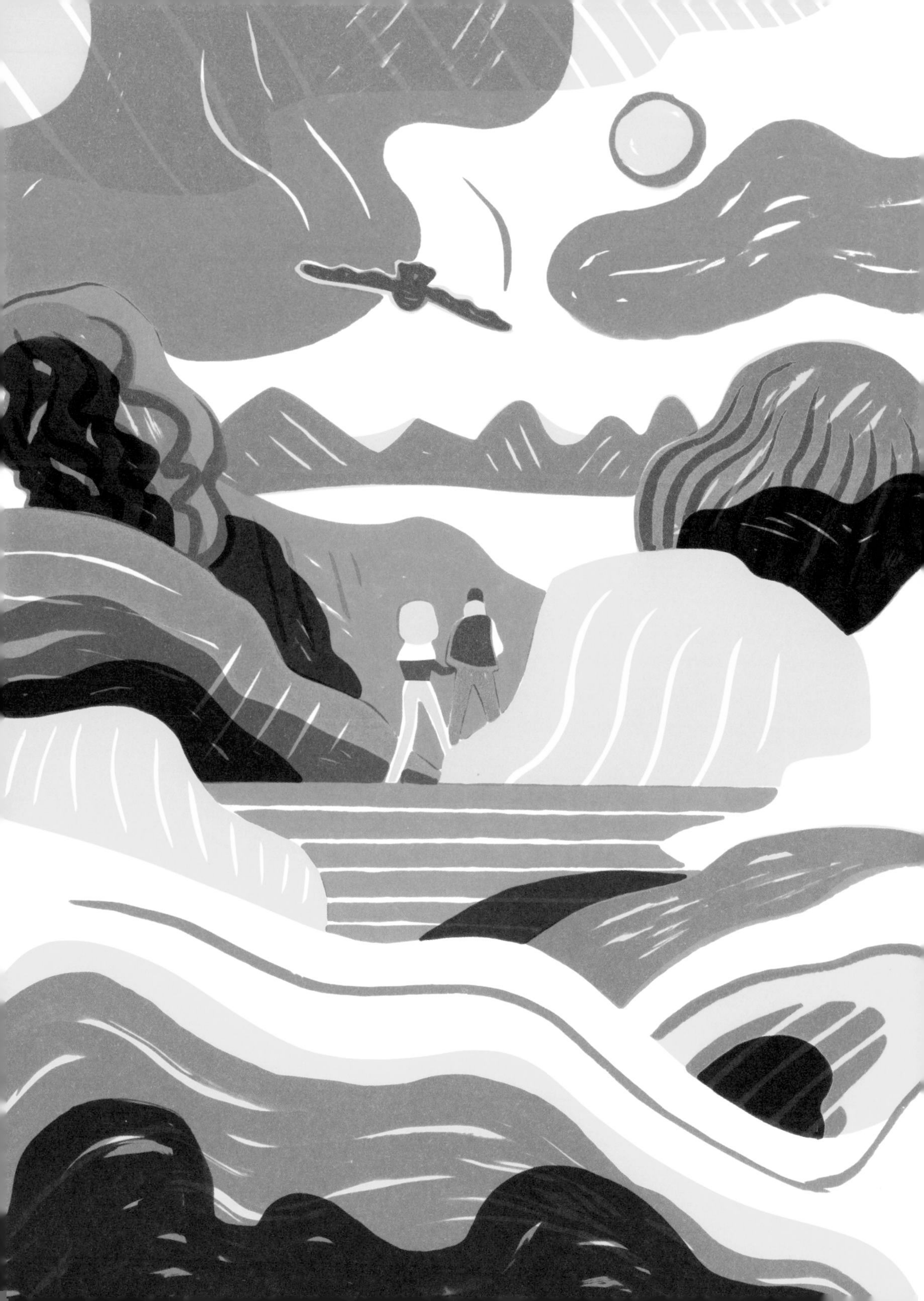

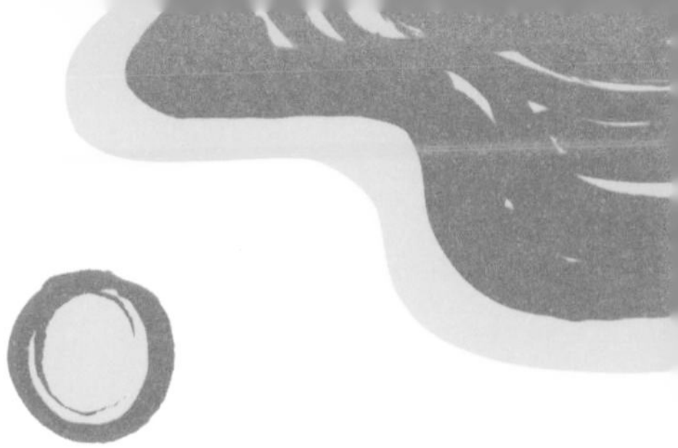

We shall live in the day. We shall fill it with our memories.

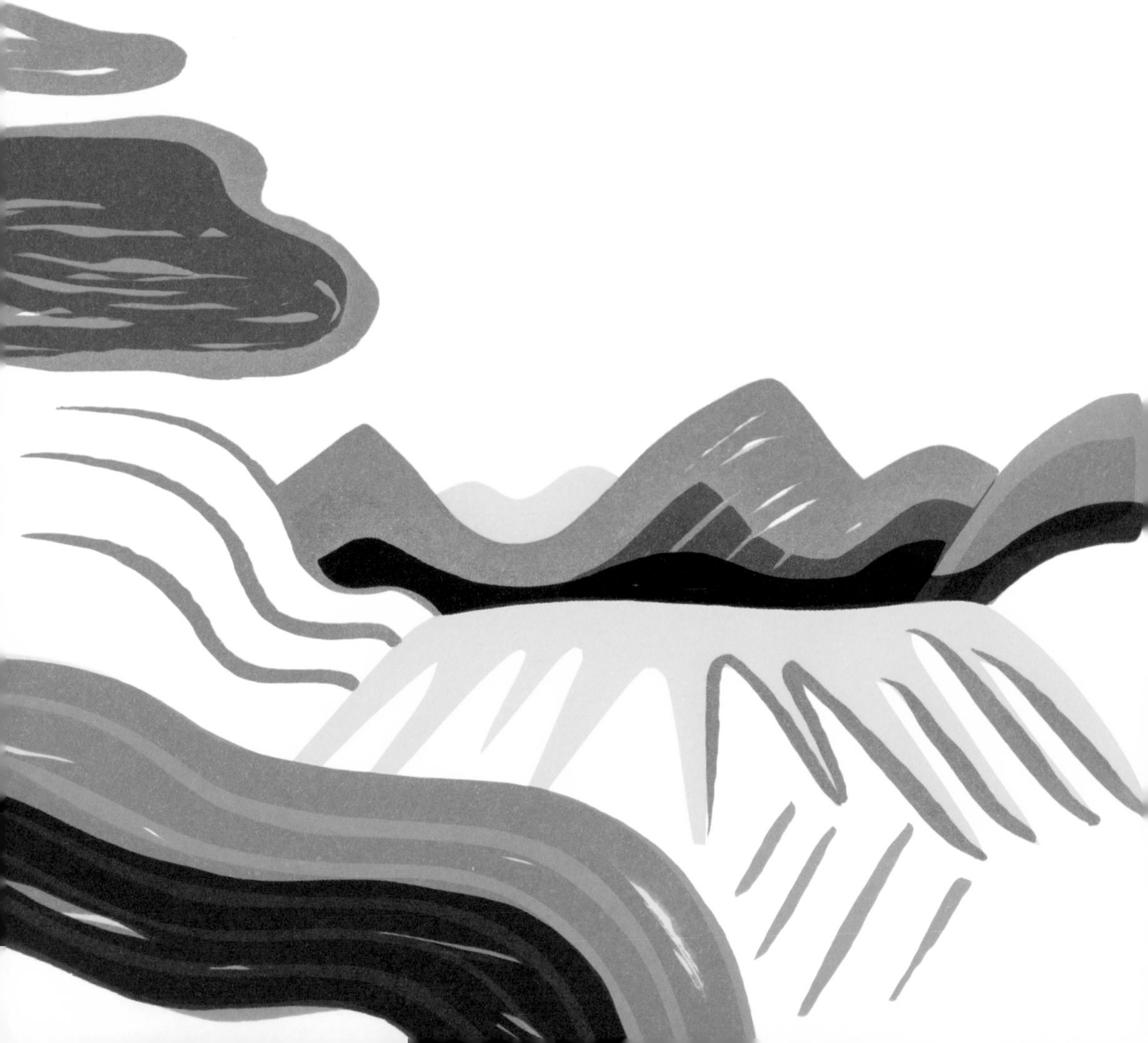

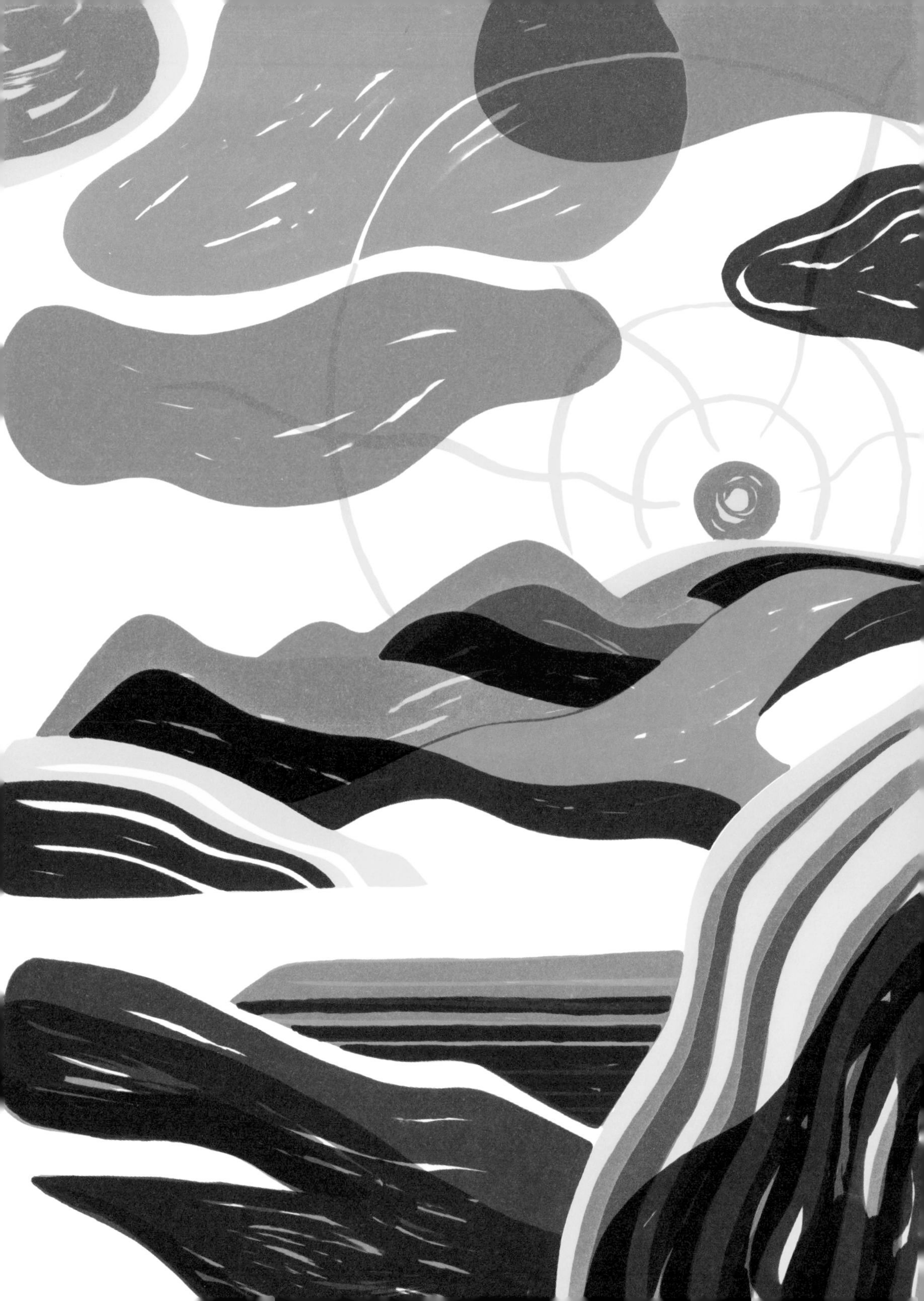

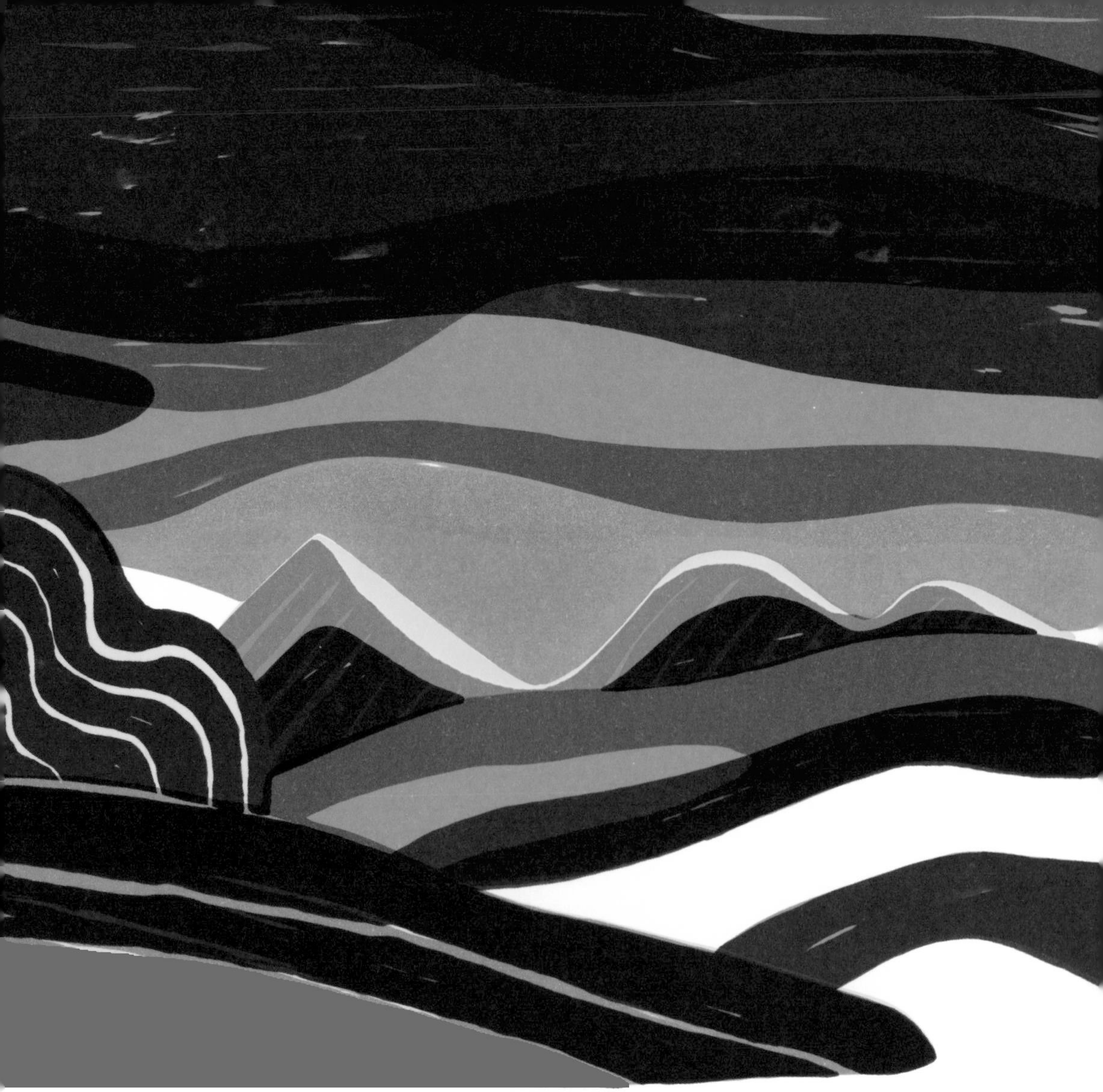

And then night will come again.
Once, I was its guardian. I encompassed it entirely, and erased all the terrors that fear projected onto it. Night was my servant.

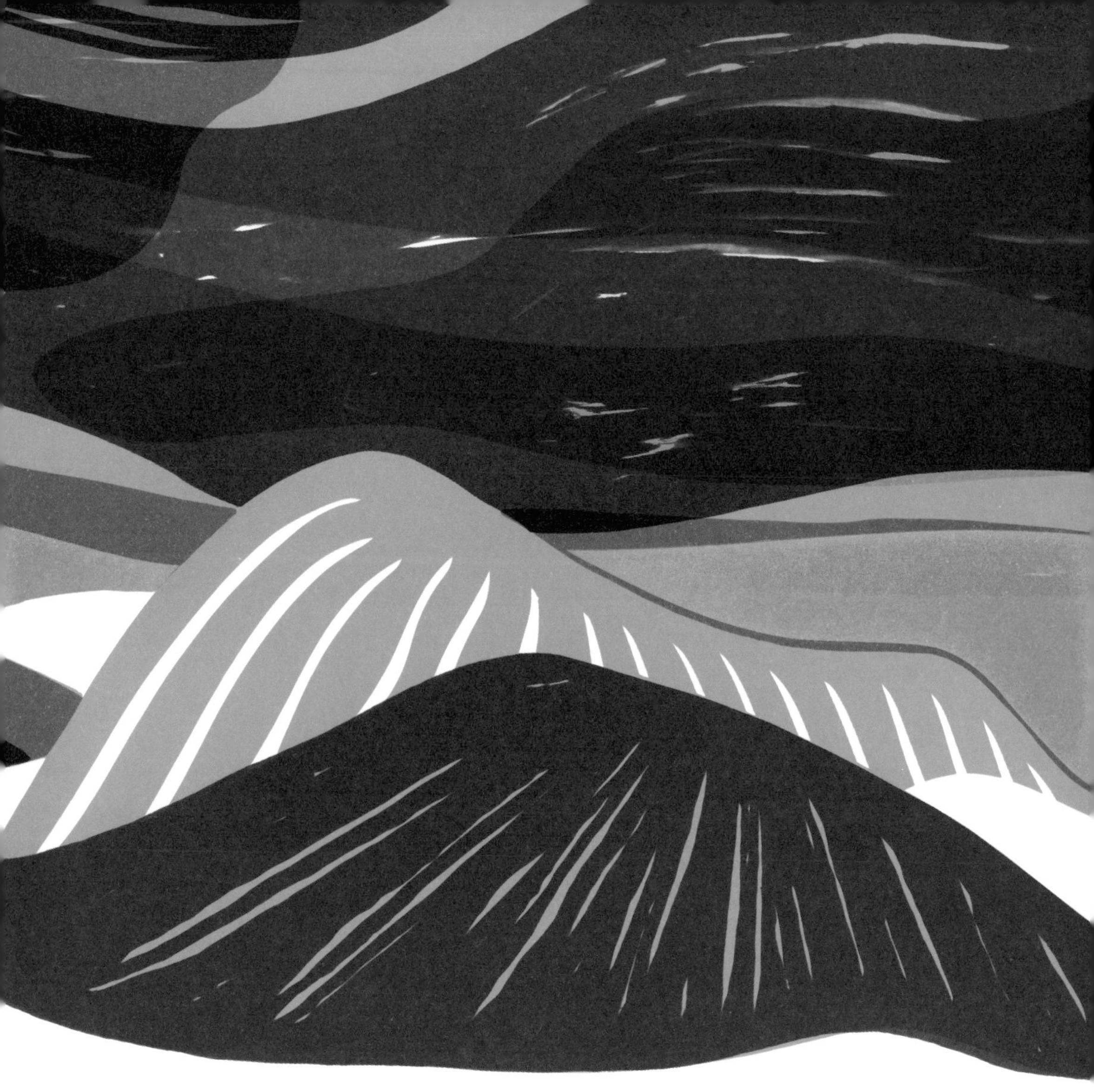

But the darkness always has the last word.
I shall not light my lamp again.

We shall let the night come. Confidently, we shall relax
our bodies and entrust them to its safekeeping.
And its heavy quilt will cover our dreams.

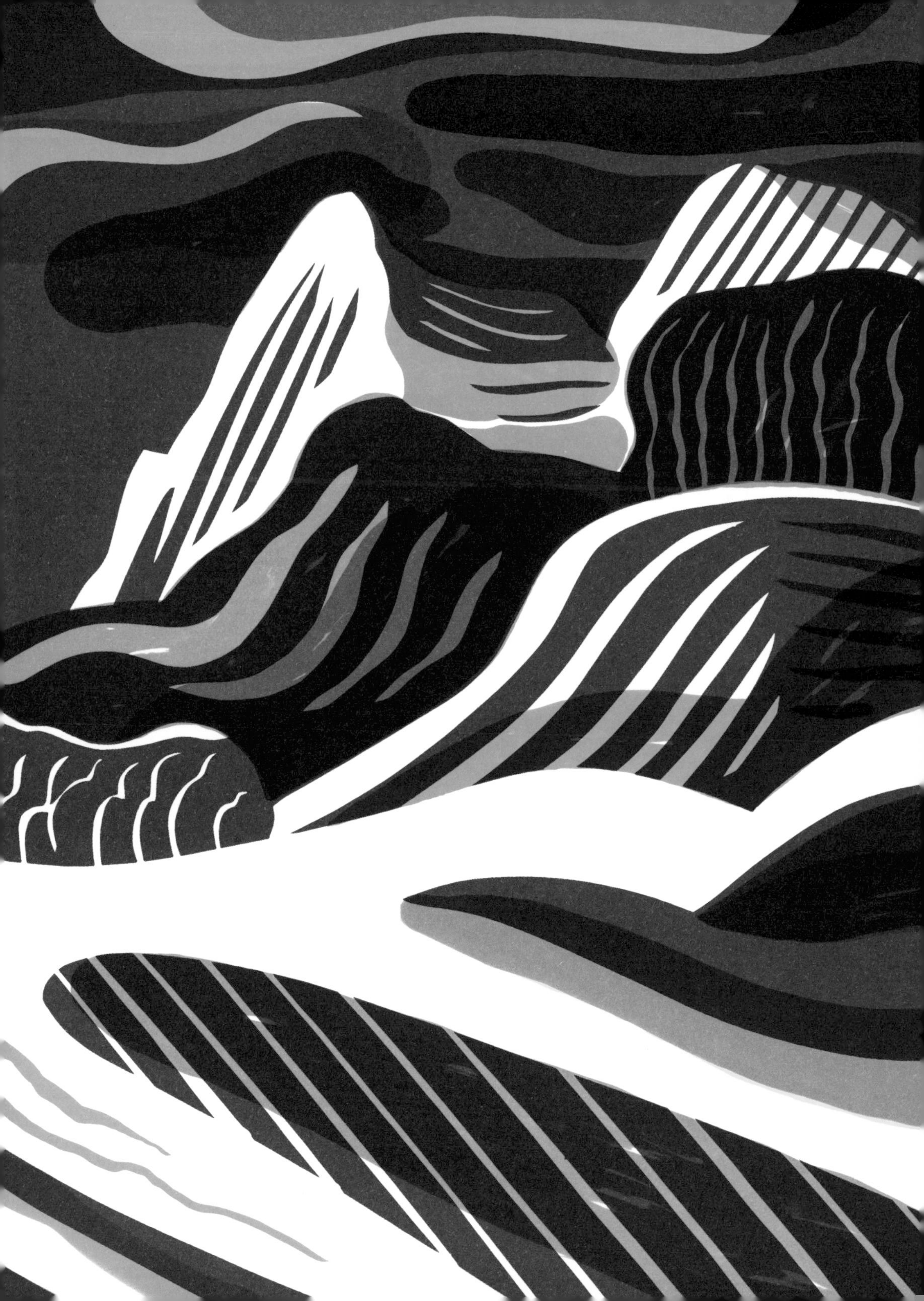

**For Marine**

**For Esther and Charlotte**

The Night Watchman
by Jérémie Fischer (Illustrations) and Jean-Baptiste Labrune (Text)
The French original edition *Le Veilleur de Nuit* was published
by Éditions Magnani.

Translated from the French by David Henry Wilson
Copy-edited by Noelia Hobeika

Published by Little Gestalten, Berlin 2015
ISBN: 978-3-89955-749-7

Typeface: BrownPro by Aurèle Sack

Printed by Livonia Print, Riga
Made in Europe



For more information, please visit little.gestalten.com.

Bibliographic information published by the Deutsche Nationalbibliothek:
The Deutsche Nationalbibliothek lists this publication in the Deutsche Nationalbibliografie; detailed bibliographic data are available online at http://dnb.d-nb.de.

This book was printed on paper certified according to the standards of the FSC®.

FSC
www.fsc.org
MIX
Paper from responsible sources
FSC® C002795

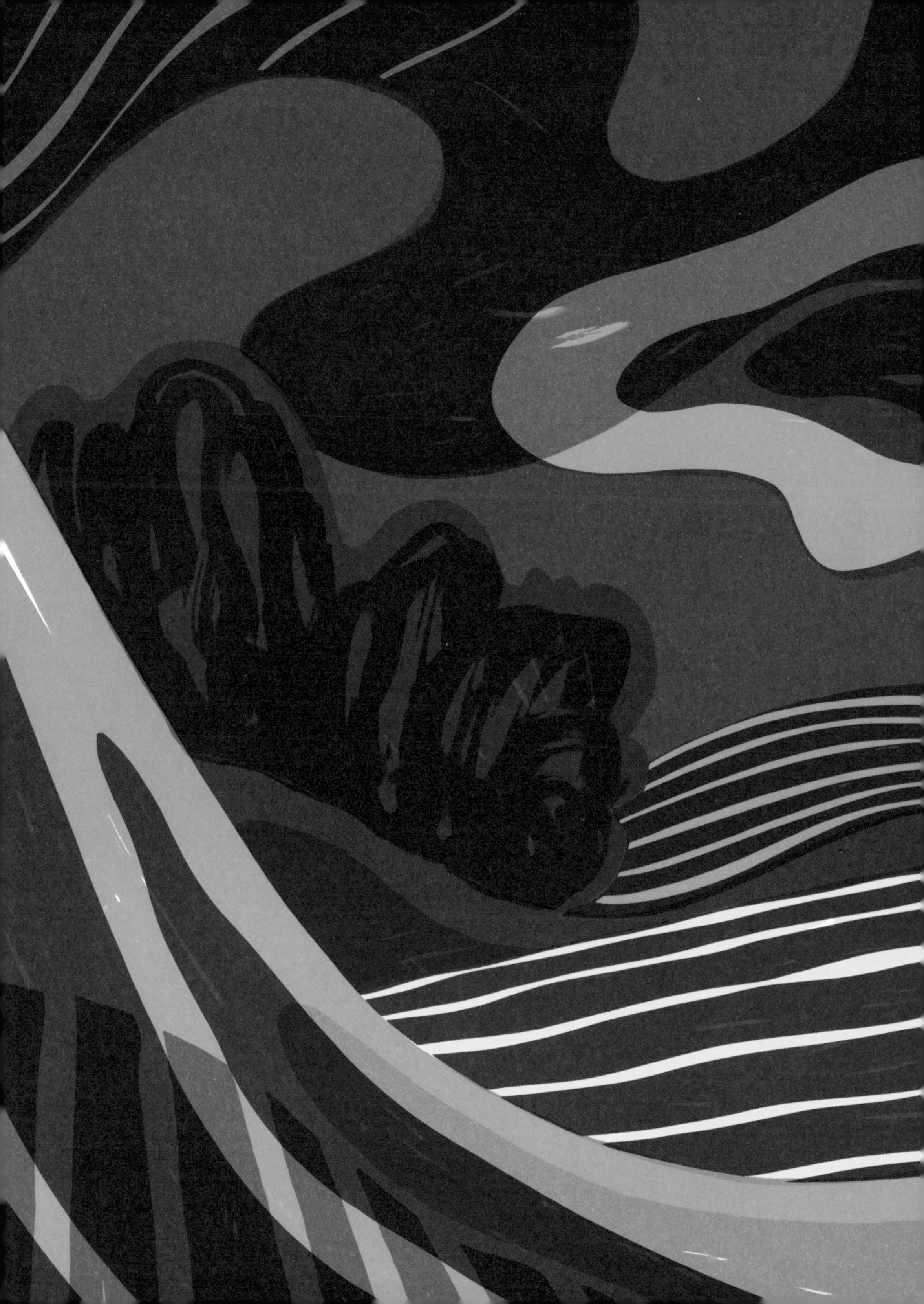

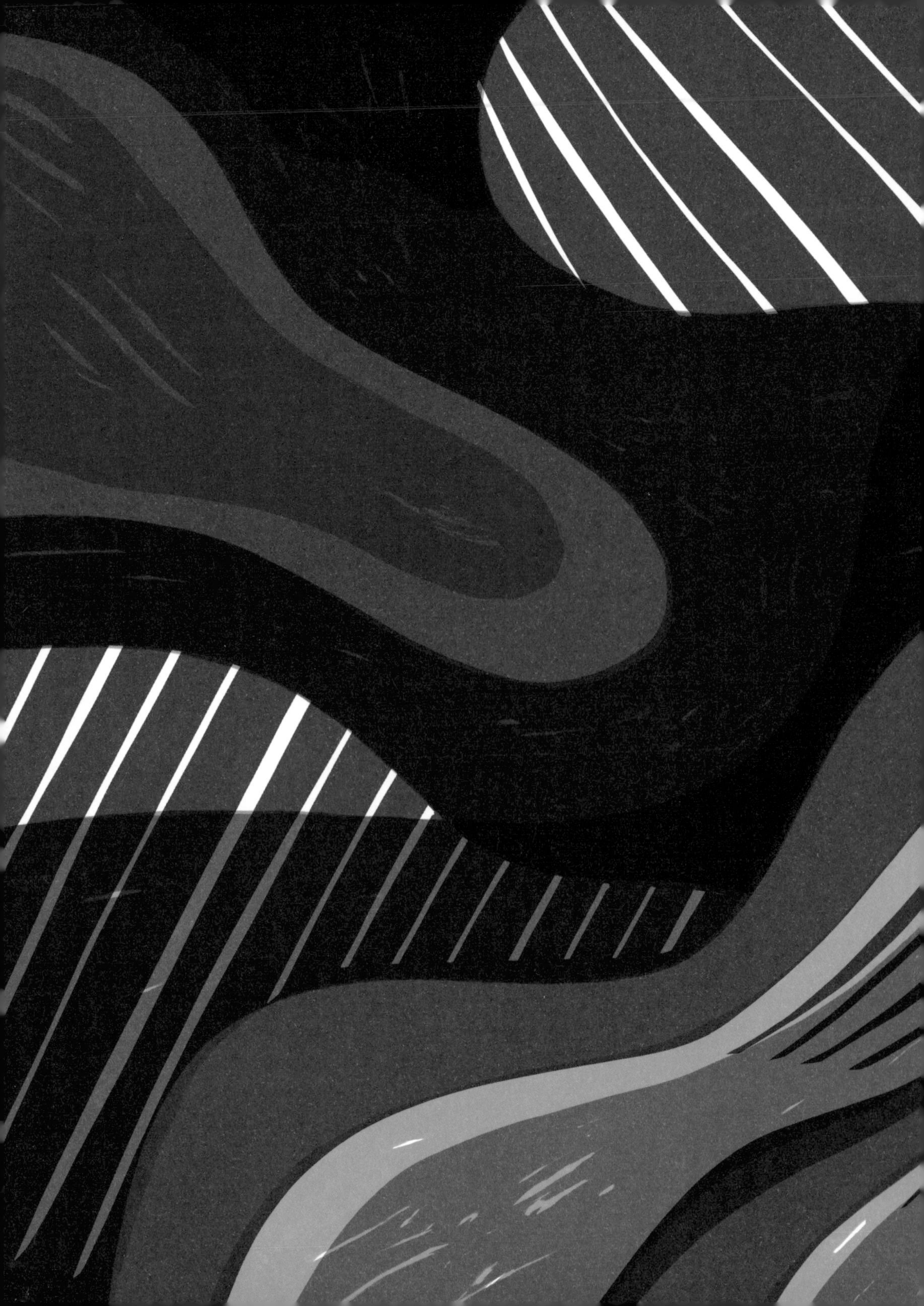